# LINDY CAMERON

# GOLDEN RELIC

CLAN
DESTINE
PRESS

This edition published by: Clan Destine Press in 2017

PO Box 121, Bittern

Victoria 3918 Australia

First published by HarperCollins Australia 1998

Copyright © Lindy Cameron 1997

National Library of Australia Cataloguing-In-Publication data:

Cameron, Lindy

Golden Relic

ISBN: 978-0-9954394-9-8 (paperback)

ISBN: 978-0-9924925-2-6 (eBook)

Cover Design © Willsin Rowe

Design & Typesetting: Clan Destine Press

Clan Destine Press

www.clandestinepress.com.au

FOR CHELE

ALWAYS AND FOREVER

# Chapter One

THE HANDS TORE AT LLOYD MARSDEN'S FLESH WITH A SURPRISING savagery. It was hardly fair, he thought, that in his last moments of life he was being tormented by a gathering of avenging gods.

He stared, unblinking, at the carved stone feet of Toltac, noticing for the first time how disproportionate the toenails were. They were all he could see from where he was sprawled on his workroom floor; the feet, surrounded by little dust balls that rolled slightly with each laboured breath he took.

He was going to die, a relic among relics. The fingers of monsters scraped at his throat while the Furies flapped and screeched in the darkness at the edge of his life. It occurred to Lloyd, however, that at least one of the hands striking at him had been human. Was this the price for refusing to accept that things must change; the punishment for not going quietly into the future?

No, this was history. This was 'punishment for *all* the desecrations' – that's what the chanting, spiteful voices were saying. Anubis, curling his jackal-lips into a snarl, poked at Lloyd's chest; the three-jawed hound of hell drooled and clawed at his paralysed feet; and Quetzalcoatl, crouching behind, removed Lloyd's spine with his fingernails.

When the 'destroyer' in his necklace of skulls hovered above him, Lloyd recognised the poisonous hallucinations for what they were – this Hindu apparition was proof of that. "I've never even been to India!" his mind screamed. Shiva vanished, to be replaced by the Sun God who smiled sadly down on Professor Lloyd Marsden, waved his tormentors away, then melted into the dark and dust.

Desecrations indeed. How ridiculous. He made a curse of his own – on a dead old friend and *his* bloody curse and visions. Lloyd still had the pen in his hand but couldn't remember whether he'd written the words, or whether he cared anymore.

Charon stood over him, offering his hand.

That's more like it. An experienced guide to the next world was what he needed right now. In his mind he fumbled for a coin, hoping Muu-Muu would take care of things here for him.

## Paris, Wednesday September 16, 1998

Pablo Escobar was seething. It was making him sweat and causing a severe irritation in his left armpit that he could not attend to in this polite company. Polite? He glanced around the negotiating table. Nobody had been listening to him; nobody *ever* listened to him. Hell, half the time nobody even noticed him. He could swing from the light fitting and these people wouldn't even acknowledge that he'd moved from his chair. Still, he didn't scratch; that would have been bad manners. He banged on the table instead.

'Excuse me, but I am losing my patience over this issue.'

'Dr Escobar,' said the dragon lady on his left, 'I think if you were to consult a dictionary for the precise definition of that word you would find that you can't lose what you've never been known to have.'

Escobar stared at the so-called mediator for a moment, while he replayed her statement in his mind to make sure it had in fact been an insult, before he insulted her in return.

'Dr Tremaine,' he stated softly, 'the only reason you are here is because the right *man* for the job is sadly no longer with us.'

'Dr Escobar, the *only* reason I am here is because I'm being paid, and not nearly enough as it turns out, to help you, Professor Jorge and your respective museums sort this mess out once and for all. And we all know that had Dr Mercier been alive to deal with this situation, he wouldn't put up with your nonsense any more than I plan to. And would you please stop scratching. It's very hard to hold a serious conversation with someone who can't sit still.'

Escobar, mortified, sat on his hands and didn't say a word for ten minutes.

Dr Maggie Tremaine glared at Pierre Dessalines, the man who had talked her into this job, and silently swore that she would never again allow money to influence her better judgement; she should have stayed at home.

Professor Benjamin Jorge, Director of the Archaeological Museum in Santiago, Chile, sat forward eagerly and made the most of Escobar's silence to reiterate his position and that of his institution, and indeed his government, on the rightful ownership of the famous Tahuantinsuyu Bracelet.

'Would you agree,' Maggie interrupted him, 'that it is only famous because of the dispute between your governments?'

'I don't follow,' Jorge stated.

Escobar snorted.

'The artefact in dispute is a bracelet, quite beautiful and valuable in its own right, but just a bracelet,' Maggie said. 'Melt down the gold and sell the gems, you might be able to put a down-payment on a new car. As a cultural artefact, however, it *is* priceless. But famous? I don't think so. Everybody knows about it because of your dispute, but even you, and I'm talking to both of you now, cannot agree on when or where or even why it was made. The only thing you do agree on is that it *is* genuine Inca jewellery. But it is still *just* a bracelet.' Maggie gave a palms-up shrug as she looked from one man to the other. 'It has no other significance, does it?' she added.

Jorge and Escobar exchanged guarded glances before returning their puzzled attention to Maggie.

'If it has no significance, *why* are we here?' Maggie asked.

'We are here, Dr Tremaine, because that Peruvian weasel over there,' Jorge said, waving dismissively at Escobar, 'thinks he can use against us our generosity in lending the Tahuantinsuyu Bracelet to the exhibition of Monsieur Dessalines here at the Paris Museum. Escobar believes that because *our* bracelet is about to go on display in neutral territory that he can make a case in this international arena to steal it from us – with your blessing. When it sits at home in its glass case in Santiago he can deal with no one but me, my institution and my government. In Paris he thinks he has the chance to create an incident.'

'Create an incident?' Maggie repeated. 'Don't you mean open a debate?'

Professor Jorge ran his fingers through his moustache thoughtfully. 'It depends on where you are sitting.'

'Would you like to comment on this, Dr Escobar?' Maggie asked.

Escobar cleared his throat. He would like to have used his hands for emphasis but he was still sitting on them. 'The one fact that my esteemed colleague continues to ignore, is that this is an Inca relic. It belongs to Peru. It is part of our cultural heritage.'

'It is as much our heritage as yours, Escobar,' Jorge stated. 'The border that has divided us for the last 70 years is not even the same one which separated us 120 years ago, and further back when

Tahuantinsuyu, the Inca Empire, was at its height there was *no* Chile or Peru. The northern reaches of what is *now* my country were part of that Empire, and therefore we share that heritage.'

'So the borders have changed,' Escobar shrugged. 'They can change again.'

Jorge gave Maggie an I-told-you-so look. 'Would you call a not-so-veiled threat to our borders a debate or an incident?'

Maggie closed her eyes for a moment and then said, 'I think I would call a ten minute recess.'

Jorge and Escobar left the room together in silence, but as soon as the door closed behind them Maggie could tell that their heated conversation in Spanish had a lot more to do with animal husbandry than any kind of professional discourse or attempt at diplomacy.

Maggie put her head down on the table and took a breath before sitting up and shaking her head at Pierre Dessalines. 'This is intolerable,' she said. 'I realise the need for a mediator to stop Escobar and Jorge from throttling each other and causing some kind of international incident, but quite honestly I'm going to need a Valium or a whisky or I might just strangle Escobar myself.' Maggie smiled. 'With my own bare hands and a great deal of enjoyment.'

'I am sorry, Maggie,' Pierre said. 'I have on three occasions stopped myself from throwing Dr Escobar in the Seine. Even Professor Jorge is becoming a little tiresome. That is why I asked you to come. I thought you would be the best person to handle this.'

Maggie waved her hands at nothing in particular. 'I probably am, Pierre. It's just that, apart from the fact that Escobar is so irritating, I can't understand why the Director of his Museum in Cuzco has delegated this job to him. If the Peruvians really are serious about claiming this relic as their own, why isn't Emilio himself here arguing this rather dubious case, rather than entrusting it to his most inept assistant?'

'It is Escobar's grail. To him it is personal.'

'But he has no case. And when the personal becomes political it also becomes dangerous. We have to convince him of that. Or more sensibly we have to inform Emilio of the danger, so that he will recall Escobar and end this nonsense.'

When the two rivals returned to the conference room Escobar took up his argument at almost the same point, as if there had been no recess or verbal fracas in the hallway outside.

'I return to Professor Jorge's own statement, with which I cannot help but agree,' he said, 'that the northern reaches of what is now Chile *did* form part of Tahuantinsuyu. However, as the relic in question was unearthed in Punta Arenas, so far away from any part of the Empire that it couldn't have gone any further south without crossing the ocean and turning up in Antarctica, one can only assume that it was stolen. It therefore belongs to Peru.'

Maggie felt a tension headache crawling across the top of her head and pressing on her eyebrows. Pierre excused himself from the table, with obvious relief, to attend to his assistant who had entered the room.

'I'm sorry, but I don't follow your logic, Dr Escobar,' Maggie said, as politely as possible. 'Who do you think stole it?'

Escobar flung out his hands. 'Who knows? Probably a conquistador four centuries ago, but *maybe* it was the German tourist caught trying to smuggle it out of Chile 10 years ago. He *claims* he stole it from a little museum in Punta Arenas; but he was a thief, which makes it likely he was a also liar. He could just as easily have taken it from a house in Cuzco, Lima or anywhere else in Peru.'

'Or Santiago in Chile, or Sydney, Australia for that matter,' Maggie stated, quite baffled at what passed for sound argument in Escobar's little corner of the universe. 'I can't imagine why the thief would lie about where he found the bracelet unless... oh, of course, he was trying to sabotage your claim to ownership.'

Maggie hesitated long enough for Escobar to take a breath before continuing. 'Unless you have proof, which you have yet to present, there is no reason *not* to believe that the German tourist found the bracelet, just as he said, in Punta Arenas – which is in Chile, is it not Dr Escobar?'

'Yes, but–'

'There are no buts. You have defeated your own argument. It matters not where it was found when you cannot prove where it came from in the first place.'

Escobar began rifling through the notes in front of him looking for another stand to take, while Jorge grinned triumphantly at Maggie who tried to ignore them both.

Maggie pondered instead, the consummate skill of professional mediators whom, she assumed, managed to remain objective while dealing with opposing points of view. She concluded, however, that they probably only ever dealt with valid disputes between evenly-matched sides with justifiable though differing opinions presented by sane people with well-researched arguments. Dr Pablo Escobar would not be found within spitting distance of a negotiation of that kind and, well, she was an archaeologist not a mediator, professional or otherwise, and objectivity was not a concept she normally associated with fools or foolish notions.

Pierre, his expression a mixture of disbelief and trepidation, returned to the table. 'We have a problem,' he stated quietly.

'Another one?' Maggie asked.

'The van transporting some of the exhibits for the *Pre-Columbian Treasures of the Americas* exhibition has been hijacked en route from the airport.'

Pierre's statement was met with stony silence. He cleared his throat. 'The thieves have acquired an Aztec dagger, a gold Sicán ceremonial mask, three Toltec figurines and the, em, Tahuantinsuyu Bracelet.'

Paris, Thursday September 17, 1998

It was 6.30 am, but even so the airport bar was crowded with passengers, well-wishing families and friends, and a bizarre variety of yet-to-be checked-in luggage, including a unicycle, a surfboard, and what looked to Maggie like a suitcase-sized stealth bomber wrapped in brown paper.

Pierre struggled through the throng and handed Maggie a cup of coffee before taking his seat. 'What do you suppose an American is doing in Paris with a surfboard?' he asked.

'Perhaps he thinks he's in Texas,' Maggie suggested.

'I don't think there is surfing in that Paris either,' Pierre stated.

Maggie shrugged, 'Maybe he's taking my flight to Sydney. Do you really care?'

'No, but I am trying to–'

'I am going home, Pierre.' Maggie put her hand affectionately on his arm. 'There is nothing you could say or offer to make me stay, so you may as well say goodbye now.'

'But, we see each other so rarely these days. And I do so enjoy your company.' Pierre placed his hand on hers.

Maggie nearly choked on her coffee. 'This tactic is beneath even you, Pierre,' she laughed. 'Are you saying that you wish me to stay here and share the flack from this hijacking, help you face the criticism regarding the safety and feasibility of eclectic exhibitions like yours, and deal with the international fallout in general because you enjoy my company?'

Pierre shrugged and smiled. 'What can I say, Maggie? I–'

'You can say "goodbye Maggie" that's what you can say.'

'This is a nightmare.'

'That is an understatement, my friend,' Maggie said. 'But you don't really think Jorge is right about Escobar being behind the hijacking?'

'I doubt it. That would mean his demand for a hearing of his case for rightful ownership was a complete charade. His claim on the bracelet, as you say, was dubious but if it was a sham to cover his part in a plot to steal the artefact in question, it didn't work because Escobar was the first person that Jorge accused.'

'I agree, but only because I find it impossible to imagine Dr Pablo Escobar as a criminal mastermind. I don't believe anyone could *pretend* to be that incompetent. Mind you, if the real brains behind this operation sent Escobar in as the court jester then he certainly succeeded in creating a diversion.'

'*Merde, merde, merde,*' Pierre swore uncharacteristically. He shrugged at Maggie's surprised look. 'I don't have energy for anything else at the moment.'

'There is one thing you haven't considered yet.' Maggie tried to sound positive. 'Maybe this has nothing to do with the Tahuantinsuyu Bracelet – specifically, I mean.'

'I don't understand,' Pierre said.

'Correct me if I'm wrong, but the Sicán ceremonial mask that was also hijacked was the one from the London collection.'

When Pierre nodded, Maggie continued. 'The same mask that Alistair Nash found near Batán Grande in the early 70s and agreed to lend to your exhibition just before he died last year?'

Pierre nodded again.

'What do you think it's worth?'

'I have no idea,' Pierre admitted.

'It's solid gold,' Maggie reminded him. 'It's worth twenty times what the Tahuantinsuyu Bracelet is worth – both for its intrinsic value and as a cultural artefact. At least there's no question about where it came from. So maybe that's what the thieves were after; or perhaps they were just after what they could get.'

Pierre looked miserable, so Maggie smiled and said, 'Of course the field of investigation is much narrower if we limit our – sorry, if you limit your suspicions to Escobar and the bracelet.'

'Oh Maggie, please stay,' Pierre pleaded. 'Your thoughts on this debacle are much clearer than mine.'

'That's because, unlike you, I am not accepting responsibility for it.'

Pierre ran his hand through his hair. 'It *is* my fault, isn't it.'

'No Pierre, it is not. But for a while to come it will feel like it is, and you *will* be the one that everyone blames – except Professor Jorge who will continue to accuse Escobar, even if it turns out the hijack was carried out by soccer hooligans who wanted the van and not its contents.'

# Chapter Two

'YOU DO REALISE YOU'RE GOING TO MISS THE WRITERS' FESTIVAL BECAUSE of this so-called red tape. Are you listening, Sam?'

'Yes Jacqui, I'm listening,' Sam lied, dragging her attention away from the acrobats performing a gravity-defying act on the Southbank promenade below, and back to her sister and the remains of their shared platter of anti pasto.

'I don't understand why you have to go to Canberra for six weeks to be reassigned to your new job which is here in Melbourne,' Jacqui continued, as she struggled back into her woollen coat. 'I take it this *is* a promotion?'

'Yes, it's a promotion.' Sam piled a piece of bread with prosciutto and eggplant.

'Yeah, well, given the nature of bureaucracies like yours, you probably won't even get a bigger desk, let alone a new office. But they'll drag you all the way to our nation's capital just to give you a new business card and say: "there's a good little Special Agent, now off you go back to your cubicle, next to the boring Detective Ben Muldoon, and we'll be in touch soon". They're *my* taxes at work flying you all over the country, you know.' Jacqui wagged her finger.

'They're my taxes too,' Sam reminded her. 'The ACB is a *Federal* organisation, that's why I have to go to Canberra to be briefed for this new position. And even though I'll still be based in Melbourne, I could be sent *anywhere*. At least my new boss, the Minister himself,' Sam straightened her back in mock respect, 'doesn't deem it necessary for me to actually *live* in Canberra in order to do my job.'

'God forbid!' Jacqui exclaimed.

'Having explained all that to you again, there's a couple of other things I'd like to clear up. I'm a detective not an agent. I hope you're not still telling your friends, and god knows who else, that I'm a spy.'

Jacqui rolled her eyes and looked everywhere but at Sam. 'Not since you became a 'Special' Detective.'

'That was only last week,' Sam said.

She ran her hands through her short, dark hair and gazed at the red-headed fruitloop opposite her, wondering for the umpteenth time which of them had been adopted, because they couldn't possibly have come from the same gene pool.

'I'm a cop, Jacqui. An ordinary, common or garden variety cop. I like what I do, you don't have to make it more glamorous for me.'

'I don't do it for you Sam, I do it for me. And I doubt your fellow Feds would appreciate being called common.'

'And another thing, Ben is not boring, he's preoccupied.'

'With tedium.' Jacqui shrugged off her coat again.

'What *I* don't understand,' Sam moved a wine glass out of the way of her sister's flailing arms, 'is why you insisted we eat outside when you're not dressed for this weather.'

'This weather?' Jacqui repeated. 'But it's Spring, it's glorious!'

'Yes, but it's Melbourne Spring, which means warm, bright

sunshine accompanied by a chilly wind straight off Bass Strait, followed by a serious hot flush and a cooling shower of rain – all in the space of one hour, with the likelihood of a hail storm later just for fun.'

'Ha, ha,' Jacqui said. 'Will you answer your phone before I relieve you of it and chuck it in the Yarra.'

Sam was already reaching into the pocket of her jacket for her mobile. 'Diamond,' she answered curtly.

'My name is Diamond. Sam Diamond.' Jacqui's attempt at Sean Connery sounded a lot more like Mae West.

'Oh, hi Ben,' Sam was saying. 'We were just talking about you. My sister thinks...'

Jacqui groaned and tried to hide behind her wine glass.

'...that your life could do with a bit of spicing up.' Sam listened, tried in vain not to smile, and said, 'Ben wants to know if you'd like to have dinner with him.'

'Yeah, sure, why not.' Jacqui waved her hands around. 'How about tonight?'

'She says she'd love to, Ben, but tonight's out because she has to take me to the airport.'

Sam's raised eyebrows and puzzled look, made Jacqui get quite antsy until it was obvious the half of the conversation she could hear had nothing to do with her, consisting mostly as it did of responses like: 'Really? Which boss? Why? Okay, put him on. Yes sir. Well I'm not really dressed for work. No, yes I am dressed, but I'm at a restaurant. Of course, sir. I'll be there in 15 minutes.' She hung up.

'Your plane doesn't leave until 8 pm. I could've gone to dinner tonight,' Jacqui said.

'With Ben. Who's suddenly not boring.'

Jacqui shurgged. 'He is quite the spunk though.'

'And you are quite the desperado. Anyway, I'm not going to Canberra now. At least not today.' Sam pulled her wallet out of the back pocket of her jeans. 'I have to go check out a body at the museum.'

'A body?' exclaimed Jacqui, a little too loud for Sam's liking. 'But you don't do that any more. You're with the Cultural Affairs Department now. Or have they changed their bloody minds again?'

'No, they haven't. Perhaps a dead body in the museum comes under the category of cultural murder. Whatever the reason, this *is* officially my first assignment for the CAD, so I have to love you and leave you. Here's my share of the bill.' Sam stood up and slipped 20 dollars under the salt shaker so it wouldn't be whisked into the river by the breeze that had just arrived from the Tropics by way of the Antarctic.

'Do you want a lift?' Jacqui offered, not in the least concerned that the rest of her day had just been casually unarranged by the person who'd arranged it in the first place.

'No thanks. I have to go to the office first, for a quick briefing, so I'll walk.' Sam bent down and gave Jacqui a peck on the cheek. 'See you at home later. Unless of course you ring that little cubicle of mine and arrange a date with the boring Ben Muldoon.'

'Hey,' Jacqui shrugged. 'I usually get my thrills vicariously by regaling my friends with lurid and fictitious accounts of your adventures as a secret agent. Even boring Ben has got to be better than that.'

An hour later Sam alighted from a Swanston Street tram in front of the sweeping steps of the green-domed State Library of Victoria. She was still trying to work out how a museum curator had been found murdered in a building that hadn't been a museum for over 12 months. But then, the rather disjointed briefing she'd been given by her new boss in Canberra *via* her old boss in Melbourne had been confusing on almost every level.

A man was dead, possibly murdered but probably not, in a building that no longer had anything to do with the museum, yet someone *from* the museum had bypassed the Victoria Police and the State Government completely and placed a call directly to the Federal Minister for Cultural Affairs, Sam's soon-to-be boss. And why? Because that *someone* was convinced the man's death was an "act of sabotage with international ramifications".

Good grief! Sam passed between the columns of the Library's imposing facade. She was often perplexed by how fast the paranoia virus was spreading through society as it rushed towards the new millennium, and sometimes worried that it might be contagious.

As if to confirm that, a woman – well-spoken, middle-aged, wearing a twin-set, pearls and a crisp tartan  skirt – stopped in front of her, nodded and said: 'The government will get you, you mark my words.'

Sam couldn't help herself. 'It's my job to get you,' she said.

Mrs-Middle-Class sidled away, swearing under her breath, and listing what sounded like the ingredients for a batch of lamingtons.

Sam muttered a few words to herself, like "dipstick" and "one too many diet pills", to reassure herself that all was hunkey-dorey in *her* world and then turned back to the task at hand. She calculated that it had been at least fifteen years since she'd set foot in this grand old building but she knew well the peace and quiet that lay beyond those unpretentious front doors. She'd spent several months at a desk under the impossibly high vaulted ceiling of the Library's Reading Room while she finished her Criminology thesis and wondered how they cleaned the windows.

Sam's memories fled in several horrified directions as she entered the foyer to find it packed with a noisy, ratty, pubescent horde in untidy uniforms. Her initial head count produced a tally of a thousand and three high school students; her second count was a more realistic thirty-three – and one poor demented teacher.

Sam made her way over to a uniformed police officer who was guarding against any incursions into the roped-off hallway behind him and, judging by the look on his face, was also responsible for scanning the crowd for terrorists. When she flashed her badge he smiled with relief and explained he was her escort.

'Can you fill me in?' Sam asked as they made their way into the section of the building that had, for nearly a century until the previous year, housed the various collections of the Museum of Victoria. Sam wondered where all those artefacts, those wondrous things she recalled from childhood visits, were being stored while the new Melbourne Museum was under construction.

> *British flintlock cavalry pistol, .590 calibre, recovered after the Indian Mutiny in 1857. Brought to Victoria by Viscount Canning, Governor General of India 1856-1862.*

Sam could picture the label for the handgun as clearly as if she was looking at it now. Then there was her favourite exhibit: stuffed, encased in glass and towering over her, Sam had been no less impressed by Australia's greatest racehorse than her grandfather who had actually watched Phar Lap win the 1930 Melbourne Cup.

'Where's Phar Lap?' Sam asked, interrupting Constable Rivers who had been telling her he couldn't tell her much, except that the deceased's body, lying by his work bench in one of the storage rooms, had been found by an assistant curator at nine that morning.

'I've no idea where he is,' Rivers said.

'Does the forensic pathologist know the cause of death?'

'Phar Lap's or the guy downstairs?' Rivers asked.

'Phar Lap was allegedly poisoned,' Sam said, as if this was a perfectly logical conversation. 'How about the guy downstairs?'

'I don't know about him,' Rivers shrugged and waited while a museum guard used a security card to open a door for them before continuing. 'The forensics team have only been here about half an hour and the pathologist arrived just before you did.'

Sam gave him a sideways glance and then looked at her watch. 'It's nearly 2.30.'

'Ah well, apparently,' Rivers explained, escorting Sam down a wide staircase to their left, 'the assistant curator, named Duncan Jones, found the body and informed the security boss, who came and had a look at it. He notified the Chief Librarian who also came and looked at it, and when she saw *who* it was she rang the Director of the Museum, who was in a whole other building in the city. After he too came and checked out the deceased, he called us. That was 11 am. We attended the scene and then called Homicide who arrived just before noon. The crime scene team only just got here because they were tied up on another job.'

'And the forensic pathologist?' Sam asked.

'He was doing lunch with the Commissioner, the Police Minister, the Premier and members of a citizen's group lobbying for – something,' Rivers said, running out of details.

'That's a pretty sound alibi, if he needs one,' Sam said dryly.

Rivers laughed. 'Yeah, but only for lunchtime. Where he was before that, is anyone's guess."

They passed through a door on the next landing and entered another hallway at the end of which Sam could see the obvious signs of a crime scene investigation in progress: police tape, police officers, police cameras and a familiar voice booming at everyone to get the hell out of the way.

'Am I allowed to know why you're here, Detective Diamond?' Rivers asked. 'I mean, what interest does the ACB have in all this?'

Sam grinned. 'Somewhere amongst all those phone calls this morning, someone also rang my boss – in Canberra – who rang me, at lunch on my day off, and said, "Get down there and have a look at that body". So here I am, at the end of a rather long queue of spectators by the sounds of it.'

"Is that Sam?" It was those familiar bellowing tones again, fast approaching the doorway Sam and Rivers were about to enter. 'It's about bloody time she got here.'

Detective-Sergeant Jack Rigby, all six-foot-five and three miles wide of him, came barrelling out of the room. Sam stepped aside; the Constable didn't stand a chance.

'Damn it Jack,' Sam said, helping Rivers up from the floor, 'this is not a football field.'

'The boy is half my size and age Sam, he should have better reflexes.' Rigby placed a hand on Rivers' shoulder. 'Isn't that right mate?"

'Yes sir. Whatever you say,' Rivers smiled.

'Good. Now step aside,' Rigby commanded and then wrapped Sam in a bear hug that left her breathless. 'Completely unprofessional, I know,' he said, letting her go. 'But it is so good to see you.'

'And it's reassuring to find you haven't changed a bit, Jack,' Sam said, giving him the once over. Jack Rigby's clear blue and ever-watchful eyes were the most noticeable things about him, apart from his height and despite the almost comical distortion of his ex-boxer's nose. His crew cut had turned quite grey since she'd last seen him but Sam felt sure that her mother, who'd met him briefly two years before, would still describe him as a fine and handsome man.

Despite Rigby's sheer bulk, which was all bone and muscle, not an ounce of fat, and his loud, irascible and at times downright stubborn personality, he was an agile and surprisingly gentle man. He'd probably seen the results of more terminally violent crime than anyone else in the city, yet away from work his relaxed demeanour and untroubled personality was more akin to someone who'd spent his life working in the Botanic Gardens.

'Now that the pleasantries are over, what the hell are you doing here?'

'It's just a guess, Jack, but I'd say it's probably the same thing you're doing,' Sam said.

Rigby cocked his head on the side and squinted down at her. 'Doc Baird says the guy probably had a stroke, so it looks like even we're not needed here,' he said. 'And if it does turn out to be murder then you can't get more local than a homicide in the heart of the city. This is barely State-related, let alone Federal. Therefore I'll rephrase my question: *why* are you here? What interest does the Australian Crime Bureau have in the demise of Professor Marsden in there?'

Sam shrugged. 'Jim Pilger called me at Walter's Wine Bar, where I *was* enjoying my day off, and told me to get down here and check things out.'

'Pilger? The Minister of... Whatever. That Pilger?' Rigby was baffled.

'Yes, Pilger the Minister for Cultural Affairs,' Sam agreed. 'He's my new boss, in that he is top of the tree when it comes to the Bureau's Cultural Affairs Department.'

Rigby looked blank, which was a rare occurrence.

'I've been transferred from Major Crimes to the ACB's CAD,' Sam explained. "I *was* going to Canberra this evening, for six weeks, to be briefed on my new job but instead I find myself here, still standing in the hallway, still lacking any real information about this situation, in fact, still without having laid eyes on the actual body – homicide victim or not.'

'Cultural Affairs? That explains the way you're dressed,' Rigby stated.

Sam looked down at her leather jacket, cotton shirt, jeans and runners. 'I did mention it was my day off, didn't I?'

'So, Pilger rang you. How did he find out about this? He's in Canberra for goodness sake!'

'Someone rang him, Jack,' Sam said.

'Who?'

'That would have been me,' came a soft-spoken voice from behind Sam.

'Ah,' Rigby said, as Sam turned around and found that after looking *up* at Rigby, she had to crick her neck to be able to look comfortably at someone slightly shorter than her own height of five-foot-six.

'This is the Director of the Museum, Mr...ah,' Rigby faltered.

'Daley Prescott,' the Director said. 'Assistant Director,' he amended.

'Special Detective Sam Diamond,' Sam said, shaking hands with the dapper bureaucrat. Prescott was neatness personified from his trim grey suit to his perfectly styled and perfectly white, collar-length hair.

'Can you tell me anything yet, Detective Diamond? I am simply dreading the ramifications of this should it turn out to be a case of murder,' Prescott said and then added, almost as an afterthought, 'not to mention what poor Lloyd must have gone through.'

Sam tried to keep her face expressionless as she glanced at Rigby and then back to Prescott. 'We'll discuss the possible ramifications after we ascertain the cause of death, Mr Prescott. I can't give you any details until Detective Rigby brings me up to speed on the investigation.'

'Well, we haven't done much yet,' Rigby admitted. 'We were told to wait for you.'

'Who told you that?' Sam asked in surprise.

'I'm afraid I did. Is that a problem?' Prescott asked. On seeing Sam's amusement and the annoyed look on Rigby's face, he continued hurriedly. 'Of course it is not official. I was simply advising you, Detective Rigby, of the imminent arrival of a representative from the ACB and mistakenly, so it seems, assumed her authority would supersede yours.'

'It's a *common* mistake, Mr Prescott,' Rigby said through clenched teeth. 'Now, if you could keep yourself available, or let Constable Rivers here know of your whereabouts, we'll get back to you when we have more information.' He turned to Sam and rolled his eyes. 'The body?' he suggested.

'The body,' she echoed.

The crime scene, for it would be treated as such until facts proved otherwise, was a long, narrow room lined with and divided by temporary shelving filled with labelled boxes and a variety of stone and wooden artefacts. At the far end Sam could see Doctor Ian Baird, the forensic pathologist, consulting with his team members, one of whom was busy taking photographs. Extra lights had obviously been brought in to illuminate what she guessed was normally a fairly dingy space.

'What's your best guess, Doc? Can we go home and let the family take over?' Rigby asked hopefully.

'Sorry, Jack. Definitely suspicious circumstances here. Foul play is evident,' Baird replied, his Scottish accent, even after twenty years in the country, still unconsciously fighting any Australian influences. 'Hello Sam, long time no see,' he added.

'Ian, it's good to see you,' Sam acknowledged, stepping forward to take a look at the body and the evidence of foul play.

Professor Lloyd Marsden lay almost in a foetal position on his left side, although his body had rolled slightly so that his chest and right arm were also touching the floor. He was holding a pen in his right hand, his right shoulder obscured the lower part of his face and the weight of his body was squashing his nose against the dusty floorboards.

To the right of the body, about two metres from the head, was a gruesome-looking stone statue of a squatting figure with very large toenails. It was much too heavy to be wielded by even the most determined assailant. To the left, about one metre away, was an overturned chair, a cluttered work bench and a drafting table. There was no likely-looking weapon, no blood and no signs of violence. It looked to Sam like the least suspicious of circumstances.

'It's looks pretty innocent to me,' Rigby said.

'That's because you haven't been down on the floor with me, lookin' at the poor man's face. Someone's dealt him a couple of good punches. Help me roll him over please, Steve.'

Steve obliged and between them they rolled the body onto its back.

There was still no blood but the late Professor Marsden had a black left eye and a large purple bruise on his right jaw.

'Injuries sustained during a fall following his stroke,' Rigby suggested hopefully.

Baird, who was still on his hands and knees, was inspecting the bruises with a magnifying glass. 'I don't think so, Jack. There's a wee puncture mark at the centre of both bruises,' he announced. 'I suspect the man was struck and poisoned.'

'Poisoned?' Sam and Rigby chorused, looking at each other and then back at Baird.

'I might be wrong,' Baird said doubtfully.

'You're never wrong,' Rigby moaned. 'Though how you can tell that is beyond me.'

'What's that in his left hand?' Sam asked, squatting down to get a better look.

Baird reached out with his gloved hand and picked up a small piece of paper, which he carefully unfolded. His eyes widened, then squinted, then he held out the paper for Sam to read.

'I hope he's left us the name of his killer,' Rigby stated.

'If that's what it is,' Sam stated, 'we're going to need help deciphering it.'

Unevenly scrawled, and probably with the pen Lloyd Marsden held in his other hand as his life left him, was the word:

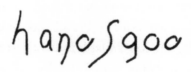

# Chapter Three

'OH MY GOD! HE WAS POISONED?' DALEY PRESCOTT SOUNDED LIKE ALL his worst fears and a couple of phobias had just invaded his personal space. He looked even worse. Sam was glad Rigby had waited till the man was sitting down before conveying Baird's suspicions.

'That's just the pathologist's preliminary report, Mr Prescott,' Rigby stated. 'It is *not* for general publication. We'll know more after the autopsy of course, but even if he wasn't poisoned, the man was certainly beaten.'

'To death,' Prescott snorted, almost as if Marsden's death was more of an insult to him, than a tragic end for the professor himself. Prescott swivelled his chair and stared blankly out the window.

Sam and Rigby, having left the forensics team to finish the crime scene investigation, had agreed it was time to question Prescott about what sort of 'ramifications' the murder of one of his colleagues was going to have – apart from the obvious ones – and why he had seen fit to contact the *Federal* Minister for Cultural Affairs. They had walked the two city blocks from the Library to the Museum's administrative headquarters on Exhibition Street and now sat with an agitated Daley Prescott in his office on the 18th floor.

While the Assistant Director tried to collect his thoughts, apparently by rubbing his fingers vigorously across his forehead, Sam gazed jealously out the huge window at the jigsaw of building facades, rooftops and patches of blue sky.

The view was a far cry from the windowless cubicle she shared with Ben Muldoon. A calendar of the world's most famous tourist sites, none of which she'd seen in person (nor was she ever likely to given the pathetic state of her savings account), was the only non-work-related item on those dreary blue-felt walls. September was the Pyramids of Giza which, as far as Sam was concerned, couldn't be further away if they'd been built on Mars.

'This is dreadful.' Prescott stated the obvious.

'Were you close?' Rigby asked, completely misunderstanding Prescott's anxiety. Sam, however, could tell there was little, if anything, personal intruding on the man's concern.

'Close? No, not really. Not at all, in fact,' Prescott replied. 'It's just that the international repercussions of this are, they're–'

'You keep saying that,' Rigby interrupted. 'What precisely *are* the repercussions or ramifications of Professor Marsden's death?'

'I can't begin to imagine,' Prescott said, annoyingly, and then frowned. 'Actually, I think I'm imagining the worst – in every possibly combination.'

'Do you think you could be more specific?' Sam asked.

'Marsden was on the ICOM committee,' Prescott stated, as if that explained everything.

'Which is what?' Rigby asked.

'The International Council of Museums,' Sam volunteered the information she'd been given by her boss. 'Melbourne is hosting the triennial conference – next month.'

'*Now* perhaps you'll understand why I'm in such a state,' Prescott explained. 'We've got close to 2000 delegates arriving in just over three weeks. They're coming from around the country and all over the world. This is a disaster.'

'All over the world? That explains the 'international' aspect of the ramifications,' Rigby noted. He looked at Sam. 'Probably explains why you're here too.'

Sam shrugged. 'I'm here because the Assistant Director called the Minister. Why exactly did you do that, Mr Prescott?'

Prescott started rubbing his forehead again. 'I took one look at Lloyd's body and realised a thing like this would send the media into a frenzy. I felt I had to act quickly to contain any possible fallout,' he explained. 'And the best way to do that was to go right to the top. To the Minister. *If* Lloyd had died from a stroke, as first thought, then I would simply have apologised for wasting your time. On the other hand if it was murder, which we now *know* to be the case, then my actions would have been, and in fact are, the right ones to ensure that a lid is kept on this whole affair.'

Rigby looked unimpressed by Prescott's logic. 'Why the *Federal* Minister?' he asked.

'This is an *international* conference, Detective. While it is being hosted by the Museum of Victoria *in* Melbourne, its success reflects on the entire nation. At the very least this will have a disastrous PR effect on the final preparations, and anything detrimental to the success of this conference is, in my opinion, of federal concern. Also, Jim Pilger is a friend of mine.' Prescott held up his hand to forestall any snide remarks about nepotism and turned to Sam.

'You are here, Special Detective Diamond. Whatever you may think, that says less about my 'connections' than it does about the fact that the Minister shares my concerns in this matter enough to send his representative. And you already know about ICOM '98, so I assume you have been briefed.'

'Brief being the operative word, Mr Prescott,' Sam admitted. 'I do, however, understand your concerns about the likelihood of the media turning this incident into a three-ring circus.

'I am authorised to work with both you and the police,' Sam glanced at Rigby, 'to exercise damage control and minimise the fallout. We can't make this go away, Mr Prescott, but we may be able to obfuscate matters so the media takes little or no interest.'

'Un-bloody-likely,' Rigby declared.

'I'm afraid I agree with Detective Rigby on that point,' Prescott's defeated tone seemed to be saying more than he was.

'There's something else, isn't there?' Sam asked.

'I believe that Lloyd Marsden's murder may have been a deliberate act of sabotage,' Prescott announced.

'Sabotage? Why?' Rigby was incredulous.

'I don't know.' Prescott searched his desk drawer for something. 'But there are a lot of sick individuals out there.'

And paranoid ones, Sam thought, leaning forward to inspect the postcard of the museum that Prescott passed across the desk. Typewritten on the back was a limerick:

You're failure will be my success
The confrence will be such a mess
One by one you will fall
Till theirs none left at all
And the hole thing will cause you distress.

'I received that last Wednesday,' Prescott said.

'And you didn't call the police?' Rigby raised an eyebrow. 'Or ring the Minister?'

Prescott smiled humourlessly. 'It is a dreadful limerick with atrocious spelling, but until this morning I thought it was merely a joke in extremely poor taste.'

'They may not be connected,' Sam said.

Prescott looked at her as if she was daft. 'You don't think 'one by one you will fall' is a threat now made manifest by the body of one of my curators lying down there in the library?'

'I'd like to ask you about that,' Rigby said. 'I'll have this analysed.' He picked the card up by the corner and slipping into his inside jacket pocket.

'Ask me what?'

'What was Marsden doing in the library? Wasn't the museum closed over a year ago?'

'Closed to the public yes, but the task of moving the collections is monumental and we have many staff, and that included Lloyd, who still spend much of their time in the old building. Our Collection Relocation Department is responsible for the move, but they have to liaise with the curators and collection managers to ensure the safe packing, labelling and cataloguing of all the items. So Lloyd has an office here, but his work is... was there.'

'But it's been 12 months, surely you don't have that much stuff to shift,' Rigby said.

Prescott laughed. 'You have to understand that, historically speaking, the curatorial staff of this institution have, primarily, been 'collectors' and they have been collecting for 150 years. We have about 16 million pieces of 'stuff', Detective. Moving them is not something that can be done overnight. It is a logistical nightmare, although it *has* provided us with a unique opportunity to assess, reorganise, catalogue and even photograph the entire collection. Everything is being moved in sequence to our storage facilities, and each transit lot is barcoded and the information scanned into a database so we know exactly where it is.'

'Storage facilities,' Sam noted. 'That's something I don't understand. Why close the old Museum before the new one is finished if it means everything is going into storage?'

'For the same logistical reasons. The new Melbourne Museum is not due for completion until the year 2000. Preparation for this move actually began over *two* years ago, long before we closed the doors on Swanston Street, and it will take another two. It's not simply a case of wrapping everything in old newspapers, packing them into cardboard boxes and wheeling them a couple of blocks across town.'

'I realise that—' Sam started to say, but Prescott was obviously on a roll.

'A great proportion of our collection is extremely fragile and irreplaceable. We have something like three million spiders, scorpions, ticks, mites, butterflies, beetles and other insects; over 30,000 mammal skins, mounts and skeletons; 70,000 reptiles, and the same number of birds including thousands of eggs and nests. They all require completely different handling and even the packing material itself has to be non-abrasive and acid free. As I'm sure you'll appreciate, we can't pack and move the ornithological or insect specimens in the same way we pack and relocate the dinosaur skeletons or a three tonne meteorite.'

'Naturally,' Sam managed to say. She noticed that Rigby, who had given up trying to get a word in edgewise, was sitting with his mouth half open.

'And, of course,' Prescott continued, 'before any actual moving happens, we have to tackle the problem of pest management – to ensure that the new storage areas, and ultimately the new Museum, are not contaminated by things like borers and moths from the relocated items. So, as you can see, it is not a simple procedure.'

'Besides, the library wanted the floor space, so you had to go somewhere,' Sam said.

'That is true,' Prescott agreed, 'but even so, it would never have been a case of closing the old museum doors on a Friday and reopening in the new building after a quick move on the weekend.'

A knock on the door brought Prescott's lecture on removal practices to a halt. 'Enter.'

Prescott's personal assistant, a personable young man with a large ruby stud in his ear who had introduced himself to Sam and Rigby as 'Call Me Anton', now ushered Constable Rivers into the Assistant Director's office.

'Excuse me, sir,' Rivers addressed Rigby. 'I've got a shortlist of people known to have had contact with, or who were seen talking to the deceased at some time yesterday. There may be others but you said you wanted something to go on as soon as possible.'

'Good work, Constable.' Rigby took the sheet of paper.

'Anton,' Prescott recalled his assistant. 'Did you manage to get in touch with Maggie?'

'Maggie has been in Paris for the last two weeks for a conference on new technologies and, I believe, she was involved in that Inca trinket fiasco. She is now on her way home; to Sydney, I mean.'

'A simple yes or no would have done, Anton.'

'Then yes and no, Mr Prescott,' Anton stated calmly. 'I left a message at Sydney University for her to call you the moment she returns.'

Sam watched Anton and Prescott as the latter tugged his earlobe then laced his fingers across his chest. Anton turned and left the room, so Sam figured that one of those gestures had meant 'that will be all', or 'thank you Anton, and I'm sorry for snapping at you'.

'Who can we talk to now?' Rigby asked.

'These four – Robert Ellington, Haddon Gould, Sarah Collins and Trevor Brownie – are all in this building,' Rivers said. 'Andrew Barstoc and Adrienne Douglas have allegedly gone sightseeing, and this guy, Enrico Vasquez, is over at the Exhibition Buildings in Carlton – so I sent a car to bring him back here. Vasquez was actually seen arguing with the deceased.'

Rigby looked up at Rivers. 'You sent a car?'

'Um, I thought it'd be easier to have everyone in the one place,' Rivers replied hesitantly.

'That's fine, good thinking. You can go back...' Rigby stopped and took another long look at the constable. 'On second thoughts, don't go anywhere. Half my crew are on leave so I've just seconded you to my team for this investigation; get you out of that uniform for the duration. What do you say?'

'That'd be cool sir,' Rivers grinned.

'Cool?' Rigby repeated, looking like he suddenly felt his age; or perhaps his youth repeating on him. 'Does that mean okay or groovy?'

'Both, sir.'

'Cool it is then,' Rigby agreed, then returned his attention to Prescott, to whom he passed the list of names. 'Can you fill us in on these people?'

'Let me see,' Prescott peered at the paper, 'Trevor Brownie... Brownie. Oh yes, he's one of our bean counters.'

'An accountant?' Sam asked, wondering how many of his staff Prescott actually knew.

'Financial administrator. Assistant,' Prescott replied. 'Sarah Collins is one of our public relations people and Haddon Gould is an Environment curator. Robert Ellington is senior curator in our Australian Society Program and shares, sorry shared, an office with Lloyd.'

'Which department did Mr Marsden work in?' Sam asked.

'Well, Lloyd was sort of his own man, really. His speciality was pre-Columbian Andean antiquities, but he was our only full-time authority on Central and South America so he was in charge of overseeing the resettlement of the whole collection. That's what he was doing in the old building. He was also, as I mentioned earlier, on the ICOM '98 committee *and* he had been assigned, as the Museum's representative, to assist Dr Marcus Bridger with his international travelling exhibition that is due to open in six days time.

'Which brings me to the other people on your list. Enrico

Vasquez, Adrienne Douglas and Andrew Barstoc are all visiting Melbourne with that exhibition. I can't recall their titles, I'm afraid, as I only met them briefly over dinner last week.'

'Who is Dr Marcus Bridger?' Sam asked.

'He's not on your list,' Prescott began and then realised he had mentioned the name. 'This touring exhibition, *The Rites of Life and Death*, is his project. It explores the fertility symbols and funerary rites of cultures and societies from around the world and across time, from ancient civilisations to the present day. It's a splendid collection.'

'But who is Dr Bridger?' Rigby asked.

'He is a renowned English archaeologist, primarily attached to the British Museum but who, through a variety of personal research projects and lecturing posts, also has affiliations with several other museums and universities in Britain, the Middle East and the United States. He arrived back in Melbourne this morning with the second shipment of artefacts for his exhibition.'

'Arrived from where?' Rigby asked.

'Paris. *The Rites of Life and Death* ended its run there at the end of August.'

'What do you mean 'back' in Melbourne?' Sam queried.

'He arrived with his colleagues and the first shipment last week; then returned to Paris so he could travel with the remainder of the exhibits.'

'Why two shipments? And why did Dr Bridger accompany both?' Sam asked.

'What does this have to do with Lloyd?' Prescott looked worried.

'Just background information,' Rigby replied casually. 'We never know what may be useful in an investigation of this kind. And you did bring it up.'

Prescott nodded. 'Firstly, this travelling exhibition grew out of a smaller one that Marcus put together from the existing collection at the British Museum. When he thought about taking it on tour he decided to broaden the scope and make it truly international. So, as well as the original collection, there are many artefacts on loan from museums and cultural institutions all over the world; brought together for the first time. Marcus is responsible for all of them, hence he insists on riding shotgun for both shipments.'

'He thinks someone is going to try and steal funeral relics?' Rigby asked, his tone implying there was no accounting for taste.

'No, Detective Rigby, though stranger things have happened. And in fact there was a hijacking of some valuable pre-Columbian artefacts in Paris just yesterday. In answer to your other question, having two or more shipments for exhibitions of this kind is standard operating procedure. The reason is not so much theft prevention as accident prevention; or, rather, reducing the odds against complete loss should, for instance, a plane carrying priceless and irreplaceable objects go down in the middle of the Pacific Ocean, never to be seen again.'

'Well,' Rigby stood before Prescott could launch into another aside, 'that will probably do for now. We'll be back if we need anything else.'

'And to keep me apprised of your investigation?' Prescott asked hopefully, glancing meaningfully at Sam as they both stood up.

'Of course, Mr Prescott,' she replied.

'Oh there was one other thing,' Rigby remembered. He opened his folder, pulled out an evidence bag and placed it on the desk. 'Do you have any idea who or what Professor Marsden might have meant by this?'

Prescott inspected Marsden's note and tried to make sense of the scrawl by mouthing the letters. Finally he tried a few combinations: 'hanosgoo, hancsgoc, hanfgoo,' and then shrugged. 'I'm sorry, I have no idea.'

Rigby reclaimed the bag. 'We'll need to look at your personnel records to see if there's any names that come close.'

'Of course. I'll get Anton to organise it for you.' Prescott showed them to the door.

Once they were out in the hallway Rigby consulted the list Rivers had given him and suggested they split the task to save time.

'I'd like to check out Marsden's office and talk to this Robert Ellington,' Sam requested.

'Fine,' Rigby agreed. 'I'll track down the others. Rivers, you go with Sam.'

Sam looked askance at Rigby. 'You seconded him to *your* team, Jack.'

Rigby gave her the same look back. 'There's no need to get your knickers in a twist. I need him with you because he *is* on my team. I know how you work, Sam. You keep too much up here.' He tapped his finger on his temple. 'I need a pair of eyes and a mind that remembers to write things down occasionally so I have *some* idea of what I don't see and hear first hand.'

'All right, already,' said Sam. 'Now whose knickers are all twisted?'

# Chapter Four

Melbourne, September 17, 1998

'YOU AND RIGBY SEEM TO KNOW EACH OTHER QUITE WELL,' RIVERS SAID as he followed Sam, who followed Anton's directions to Marsden's office.

'I haven't seen him for two years, but we worked closely together for six months on the Carjacker case,' Sam explained.

'The serial killer?'

'Yeah. The Bureau joined the hunt when it was discovered the killer hadn't confined his activities to Victoria. It was actually Jack and I who tracked Neville Strickland down to that fleapit hotel where he shot one of his hostages before turning the gun on himself.'

'I remember that siege lasted nearly three days,' Rivers said. 'Cultural Affairs must seem pretty tame, if that's the sort of work you were doing before – tracking serial killers.'

'You sound like you think it's an adventure, Rivers. It's not. It's awful work. I'd much rather there weren't any serial killers to track. Luckily Australia doesn't produce too many men like Strickland.

He was a really sick individual, and I don't mean insane. He knew what he was doing, and what he did to those women was indescribable. You'd have to see it to believe it and, believe me, it is not something you ever want to see. I transferred to the Anti-Drug Task Force after that case.' Sam glanced at Rivers.'Which I suppose, when you think about it, is really just a response to a different form of serial killing.'

'Ludicrous. Ludicrous,' came a voice from behind them. 'One would think they were professional enough to pay attention. I should have done it myself.' The words, delivered as if they'd been fired from a Gatling gun, were obviously being spoken *to* the person they were being spoken *by*. A man with unbelievably wild grey hair, and wearing a suit that looked like it had been retrieved from the still-to-be-ironed basket, overtook them in the corridor.

'I'm late, I'm late for an important date,' Rivers whispered to Sam, as the man, still talking to himself, darted into what turned out to be Marsden's office. Sam and Rivers followed him in.

Bookshelves, interspersed with filing cabinets, covered most of the walls, including the floor to ceiling window. Two desks, and their surrounding mess of things in boxes, sat on opposite sides of the room facing the centre. Framed photographs crowded a section of wall behind what Sam guessed was Marsden's desk, next to which was a cluttered pinboard hanging precariously from a bent coat stand.

'Robert Ellington?' Sam enquired.

'Of course,' he snapped, as he lost control of the manilla folders he was trying to stack on the other desk. Sam bent down to help him pick them up but it wasn't until Ellington was completely happy with the repositioned pile that he acknowledged her presence.

His eyes looked left, then right, then squinted at Sam. 'Do I know you?' he asked.

'No. I'm Special Detective Sam Diamond, from the Australian

Crime Bureau, and this is Constable,' she hesitated, but her new sidekick chose that moment to stare at the ceiling. 'Rivers,' Sam continued. 'We're investigating the death of Lloyd Marsden.'

'You mean murder. The word around here is that it was murder. Poor old Lloyd. Do you think he suffered? I hope he didn't suffer.'

'I don't know. But if I could ask you a few questions about Mr Marsden–'

'Professor,' Ellington interrupted. 'He liked to be called Professor; God knows why. It's a bit pretentious in this day and age, don't you think? Call me plain old Bob, I say. On second thoughts, I probably wouldn't answer since no one has ever called me Bob. I wouldn't know who you were talking to, would I? But Lloyd was a trifle old-fashioned, and just because the rambunctious old bastard is dead doesn't mean we ignore his wishes.'

'Robert.' Sam used his first name to try and get him back on track. When he smiled as if she'd recognised him in a crowd, she continued. 'We understand you saw Professor Marsden at some stage yesterday.'

'That would be correct, Sam,' he smiled. 'We had breakfast together, as usual, in a cafe near Flinders Street station. We walked together as far as the library, where I left him and continued on here. I also saw him just after lunch, about 2.30, when I had cause to go to the library myself. I'm researching blacksmiths and boilermakers at the moment for a future exhibit on trades during the early days of the colony. I just nodded hello to Lloyd on that occasion, as he was talking to that twerp Trevor Brownie.'

'The assistant financial administrator?' Sam wandered over to Marsden's desk.

'*One* of the assistants,' Ellington confirmed. 'A sycophantic, jumped-up little sluggerbug who acts as if the Museum's money comes out of his own piggy bank. Sorry. Sorry. But I don't have much time for middle-management types who have invariably, and inexplicably, risen above their limited talents.'

'It's a universal problem, Robert,' Sam agreed, sitting in Marsden's chair. The desktop was an inch deep in scattered clutter, some of which had spilled onto the floor, and one of the drawers was half open. 'Is this normal or has the Professor's desk been searched?'

Ellington glanced over. 'Quite normal, but that doesn't mean it hasn't been disturbed. Lloyd had a mind like a steel trap but no sense of order.'

'Do you have any gloves, Rivers?' Sam asked. The Constable stopped taking notes, fished in his uniform pocket and handed her a pair.

'You obviously knew the Professor well, Robert. Perhaps you could tell us about him.' Sam began picking through the leftovers of Marsden's working life. In a comparatively ordered pile on her right, topped by a shopping list, was a variety of museum-related invoices and inventories, plus a hardware store's catalogue, a pile of what looked like chocolate sprinkles, and a red phone bill bearing Marsden's name and a South Melbourne address. Sam scanned the phone bill and handed it to Rivers who dropped it in an evidence bag.

'Actually, I didn't know Lloyd all that well,' Ellington was saying.

'But you said you had breakfast with him 'as usual',' Rivers quoted from his notes.

Sam investigated the half-open drawer. It was full of chocolate bars and empty wrappers, and a box of half-eaten donuts and cakes; a sugar-junkie's variety of jam-filled, chocolate-topped or smothered in icing sugar or cream.

'Lloyd and I had been eating breakfast in the same establishment for 15 years. Earlier this year, when a busload of tourists invaded the place, we had to sit at the same table and discovered we share a passion for the horses. We've been breakfasting together ever since.'

'It took you 15 years to share a table?' Sam attacked the pile in front of her, finding newspapers, museum publications, and manilla folders filled with notes and printouts about the collection Marsden was responsible for relocating.

'That was Lloyd's choice. He was a private, thoughtful man not given to socialising.'

'But you were sharing an office as well,' Rivers commented.

'Only for the last two months. I've been working for this institution on and off, mostly on, for nigh on forty years. Lloyd has been here, but mostly off doing field work or fulfilling his teaching commitments at Melbourne University, for the past thirty. A long time yes, but our disciplines rarely connected. I know a great deal about his work and reputation but little about his personal life.'

Sam opened the long, deep drawer in the middle of the desk. 'Whoa!' she exclaimed.

'What is it?' Rivers stepped forward eagerly.

'Ah,' Ellington said. 'Lloyd's only other passion outside of his work. That I know of.'

'A man after my own heart,' Sam declared. The drawer was full of cryptic crosswords, all cut from newspapers and in various stages of completion. Sharing the space was a dictionary and a well-thumbed thesaurus.

As she shut the drawer, Sam noticed something protruding from under the large blotter that protected the surface of the desk from the paraphernalia and food scraps on top of it. Clearing everything back she lifted the blotter and set it down on the floor.

'Make a list, please Rivers. Three Mars Bar wrappers; an airline ticket dated for this Saturday, in Marsden's name – destination Lima, Peru; a dry cleaning bill – with pick-up for tomorrow; a prescription for malaria tablets – already filled; a catalogue for *The Rites of Life and Death* exhibition; and three betting slips from Sandown last Friday.'

Sam opened the full-colour catalogue which featured pictures of artefacts and photographs of "real-life" funerary and fertility rituals. On the inside cover, next to an article about the purpose of the exhibition, was a mugshot of a broodingly handsome man, of the Heathcliff variety. The caption read: Dr Marcus Bridger. MA, PhD, FSA.

Sam turned several pages of sponsors' ads, until the catalogue settled open, through previous use, on the captioned photos of the other exhibition team members and the show's worldwide itinerary. The fold was full of icing sugar, as if Marsden had eaten his lunch over it, so it was reasonable to assume that it had been he who used a marker pen to highlight some of the overseas tour dates.

Sam replaced the blotter on the desk and nodded to Rivers. 'Better get forensics in to check any prints found at the crime scene against any that shouldn't be here.'

Sam returned her attention to Ellington who had been patiently sitting at his desk. 'Do you know of anyone who knew Marsden well?'

'Pavel Mercier,' he replied instantly. 'And Maggie of course. They were the only people he spoke of with any kind of fondness or familiarity. They worked together over the years.'

'And who are they?'

Ellington scuttled over to the bookshelves next to Marsden's desk, drawing Sam's attention to two shelves of hard and soft cover publications, the spines of which wore the names Professor Lloyd Marsden, Dr Pavel Mercier and Dr Maggie Tremaine, either independently or as co-authors in various combinations. The titles ranged from the readily understandable – such as *Time Stands Still: An Exploration of Archaeology; The New Technologies of History; Inca Roads to Power; Aztec Glory, Aztec Blood;* and *Adrift in a Sea of Sand: The Ruins of Tanis;* – to the more esoteric: *An Interlude in Hatshepsut's Kitchen; Sipán and Chimú: Benefactors of Tahuantinsuyu?;* and *Anthropomorphic Entities and the Andean Supernatural Realm.*

'That's quite a body of work. Are they on staff here or do you know how to contact them?'

'Well, you can't contact Pavel at all; he died in Peru last year. That's him with Lloyd in the big picture behind you. It was taken a good 20 years ago though, so you wouldn't recognise him now even if he wasn't dead.'

Sam swivelled her chair to take a look at the gallery of framed photographs. 'What about Dr Tremaine?'

'Ah Maggie,' he sighed heavily. 'Formidable woman. Formidable. Endearing too, but formidable. And I mean that in the sense that she inspires admiration while being, quite often, well, difficult to deal with.'

'And she is where?' Sam prompted.

'Sydney University. She's actually on staff here at the Museum, but took a 12-month post in Sydney to teach archaeology while whats-his-name is on leave.' Ellington headed back to his desk but stopped abruptly, spun around and said, 'No, actually I tell a lie. She's in Paris. Yes, that's right. She went to a conference in Paris, from Sydney.'

'Is this the same Maggie who was involved in the 'Inca trinket fiasco'?' Sam asked, recalling Anton's conversation with Prescott.

'The very same. So you've heard about that then.'

'Not really,' Sam replied. And I don't need to, she thought. 'One of the pictures seems to be missing from the wall here.' She pointed out the empty hook.

'So it is,' Ellington agreed. 'That's odd. No, there it is on top of the cabinet beside you.'

Sam picked up what turned out to be an empty frame, labelled 'Manco City 1962'.

'That's odd,' Ellington said again.

'I've got one last question, Robert, and then we'll let you get back to work. Can you think of anyone who would have wanted to hurt Professor Marsden?'

'You mean did he have any *enemies*? Strong word isn't it? Lloyd had the tendency to rub people the wrong way. And he did a lot of rubbing, and pot-stirring, around here because he didn't exactly agree with the Museum's vision for the future; just ask Prescott. But enemies? No, not that I'm aware of. Certainly not anyone who'd want to stab him to death.'

'Stab him?' Sam echoed. 'He wasn't stabbed Robert.'

'Oh. Shot?' When Sam shook her head but wasn't forthcoming with the facts, Ellington shrugged. 'On the other hand, I'm wondering if Lloyd had some kind of premonition.'

'Why?'

'Last Friday, over breakfast, we were talking about families or at least I was; Lloyd has no living relatives. Anyway quite out of the blue Lloyd secured a promise from me, gladly given, that should anything ever happen to him I was to contact his lawyer. Immediately.'

'To do what?' Sam asked.

'I've no idea,' Ellington replied, searching his pockets. 'I was simply to contact the man and inform him of "whatever had happened".' Ellington handed a business card to Sam.

'Have you spoken to this James T. Hudson yet?' Sam asked, noting Hudson & Bolt had offices in Melbourne and Sydney.

'Of course. Lloyd had said 'immediately'. As soon as I had confirmation that the rumour of his demise was true, I rang Hudson.'


'So, what *is* your first name,' Sam asked Rivers as they left Ellington to his mutterings and went in search of Rigby.

Rivers groaned. 'You promise you won't laugh?'

Sam crossed her heart.

'Hercules.'

'Really?' Sam raised her eyebrows and tried not to laugh. 'And how did you come by that?'

'My father. Never read a book in his life but, remember *Epic*

*Theatre* the old Sunday afternoon TV series of movies about blokes like Ulysses and Jason and the Argonauts?'

'Dubbed into English, as I recall.'

Rivers nodded. 'My Dad loved those movies. He was a Championship Wrestling fan too, so I guess I'm lucky I didn't get named after Titan the Terrible. It's useful on the Internet though. I can use my own name and people just think I'm a nerd with a hero complex.'

'Dia...mond.' Rigby's bellow bounced off several walls as Sam and Rivers rounded a corner. 'Oh, there you are.'

'Jack, this is not a squad room. It would be courteous to keep your voice down.'

'Good idea,' Rigby nodded. 'Now, I've spoken to Brownie and the PR lady, but Gould, the curator, is off sick today. Anton has just directed that Vasquez guy to a room down the hall. So what do you say we do him together and compare notes on the others later. Rivers, you can chase up that personnel list.' Rigby headed off down the hall.

'We found a plane ticket in Marsden's name,' Sam said, jogging to keep up with Rigby's long stride. 'He was flying to Peru this Saturday.'

'Was he now?'

'And, I think we should check out his home next. He had no family but he may have a cat or something that should be informed.'

'Already organised. I sent some guys there fifteen minutes ago.'

Enrico Vasquez looked like he expected to be put through a clichéd 'good cop, bad cop' routine. He kept flexing his shoulders, as if he was preparing himself for a good whack with a phone book, yet his expression was composed and determined. There was no guessing what was going on behind his dark eyes which, while they seemed to be looking everywhere at once, did so without making him appear nervous.

His dark hair, thin moustache and pleasant face brought Zorro to Sam's mind, except that Señor Vasquez was short and stocky. While his expression had registered amused indifference when introduced to her, his reaction to Rigby was typical of a phenomenon that Sam had always found curious. Shaking hands was not something cops do, as a rule, with suspects or witnesses, but Sam had noticed on many occasions that men shorter than about six foot felt they had to bond with Rigby. Vasquez was no different. He offered his hand automatically, although he stepped back as he did so, as if increasing the space between them would make him feel taller. Sam had yet to figure out the psychology of this, whether it was deference, submission or merely an attempt to stake out some territory.

'Would you care to explain why I am here?' Vasquez demanded of Rigby. 'The other officer refused to say anything except that someone had died. What could I know?'

'Do you know who has died, Mr Vasquez?' Sam asked.

'No, I just said,' he frowned and returned his attention to Rigby. 'Is it one of my colleagues? Is that why I'm here? What has happened?'

'Professor Marsden's body was found in the State Library this morning,' Rigby stated. 'He was murdered.'

'But I know nothing of this.' Vasquez was horrified. 'You think I know something? How can I? I barely know Professor Marsden and I have no idea where your Library is.'

'But you were seen arguing with Professor Marsden yesterday,' Rigby said. 'Do we have our facts wrong?'

'Yes. No. Your facts are incomplete,' Vasquez replied, regaining his composure. 'I did see Professor Marsden yesterday. But not in your Library. Between 3 pm and 4.30 we were working out some details at the Exhibition Building. And we were not arguing.'

'You did not have an argument of any kind with the Professor?' Sam asked.

'No! Ah, wait. We did have a discussion, which may have *appeared* um...heated. Our views on the subject of cultural artefacts and their repatriation could not be more opposite.'

'Can you explain what you mean by that,' Rigby requested.

'The Professor was a dinosaur, a dedicated collector whose thinking has not changed with the times. He was as much of a relic, in terms of current international museum practices, as the things he collected. He still believed in an institution's right to hoard the artefacts of other countries, thus denying those countries their own cultural heritage.'

'And that's what you were arguing about?' Rigby asked.

'Discussing, yes. The return of such items to their rightful owners is something I am most passionate about. My part of the world has been plundered by outsiders for centuries.'

'Where are you from?' Rigby asked.

Strangely, Vasquez looked like he had to think about that question. 'I have come from Colombia,' he replied. 'Things are changing though and maybe, one day, we will get everything back – what little there is left of our histories in South America.'

'This desire of yours to get your stuff back seems pretty strong,' Rigby suggested bluntly.

Vasquez laughed. 'There was nothing personal in our discussion, Detective. Debates like the one we had go on every day in museums the world over. It's a sign of the times. I did not kill Professor Marsden because we had a difference of opinion. In fact we ended up agreeing – and laughing, I might add – about the rather dubious merits of the *Life and Death* exhibition.'

'You were laughing about your own exhibition?' Sam asked.

Vasquez shrugged. 'What can I say? It is Dr Bridger's exhibition. I am simply the working curator, which means I do all the work. For me it is just a job, but career-wise it is a little embarrassing. Don't get me wrong, it's a good show but 'show' is the best word for it.

'Our artefacts may draw in a public curious to see a collection of exotic phallic symbols and mummified cats, but it is a questionable concept for a serious exhibition. Marsden and I agreed it was simply an excuse for Marcus to travel the world – and make money.'

'Andrew Barstoc and Adrienne Douglas,' Rigby read the names from his list. 'We understand they went sightseeing together today. Do you have any idea where?'

'Sightseeing?' Vasquez snorted. 'I find that... unlikely. And wherever they are, I doubt they're together. Knowing Adrienne she's probably visiting your casino.'

'What is her job with the exhibition?' Sam asked.

'She's our public relations expert, and Andrew is our expert in logistics. It's his job to make sure everything runs smoothly, that in each new city – and we've been in eight in the last year and a half – we have everything we need to set up the show. But while we've been waiting for the second shipment Andrew has been off making business wherever he can.'

'What sort of business?' Rigby asked.

'I have no idea. That is what he *does*. He's a business man. He'll be on site when the rest of the exhibits get delivered tomorrow and is always on call, but he will spend the rest of his time, as usual, taking care of his own personal...' Vasquez shrugged, 'business.'

Sam rubbed the back of her neck to stem the annoying prickling sensation she always got when a seemingly unrelated fact surfaced from somewhere in her memory, prompting her mind to leap to a most unlikely conclusion. Failing to convince herself that her suspicions were based purely on coincidence she was half-way out the door before she realised she moved.

'Are you all right, Sam?' Rigby asked. 'You look like you've just remembered you left the iron on at home.'

'Sorry. Something *did* just occur to me. I have to check it out straight away.' She turned to Vasquez and asked, 'When did you arrive in Melbourne with the first lot of exhibits?'

'Last Wednesday.'

Sam returned to Marsden's office and, relieved to find it empty, sat down at his desk. She put the gloves back on, took her phone out of her jacket pocket and rang her office. While she waited for Ben Muldoon to answer, she removed the blotter from the desk top again and opened *The Rites of Life and Death* catalogue to the contents page.

'Muldoon here.'

'Hi Ben, it's me,' Sam said, cradling the phone awkwardly with her shoulder while she used a pen to scrape some of the icing sugar into an evidence bag. 'Have you had any leads on the origin of that new stuff that hit the streets last weekend?'

'Nothing concrete. Just a rumour that it's a brand new source,' Ben replied.

'Well, I may have news for you. I've got something for the lab to check first.'

'Where are you?'

'I'm still at the Museum.'

'You found something *there?*'

'It's a long story. I'll explain when I get back. In the meantime get the squad to check out a shipment of exhibits that came in by plane from Paris today. Make a call to stop it leaving the airport if it hasn't already.

'It's for a show called *The Rites of Life and Death*, though it might be registered in the name of Dr Marcus Bridger – or for delivery to the Exhibition Building.' Sam disconnected the call.

'What the hell was that little performance back there about?' Rigby demanded as he strode through the door. Rivers was close behind him trying to get his attention.

'I think the late Professor may have stumbled onto a smuggling operation,' Sam stated.

'Smuggling what?'

She waved the bag. 'Cocaine.'

'You're kidding.'

'We won't know for sure till we get this tested. I'll take it to our lab to compare it with a sample that turned up on Sunday.'

'There's something else you should know,' Rivers said. 'The guys that went to Marsden's place just rang in. His house has been trashed. They said things like the TV and video were broken, not stolen, and that it looks like someone was seriously looking for something specific.'

# Chapter Five

Melbourne, Friday September 18, 1998

'DON'T DO THIS TO ME,' SAM BEGGED, POUNDING THE STEERING WHEEL. A sharp rap on the window nearly frightened the life out of her. The bizarre appearance of her sister completed the job.

Jacqui's hair was littered with sequins, teased outwards in all directions and frozen in space and time by what could only have been the contents of 23 cans of hairspray. She wore a gold mini-skirt, a leopard-skin singlet, fishnet stockings and very high heels.

Sam struggled out of her seat belt and out of the car. It was eight o'clock in the morning and her sister looked like a tart. Correction. She looked like a drag queen dressed as a tart.

'I'm afraid I have to arrest you,' she said. 'You can*not* go out looking like that.'

'I'm not going out, I'm coming home.'

'Oh my god! In that case, I'll have to shoot you,' Sam stated. 'Right after I've emptied a clip into this useless bloody car of mine.'

'I'll give you a lift to work *if* you can resist making further comments about my attire,' Jacqui offered, flouncing back to her car which was parked behind Sam's outside their house.

Sam locked her clapped-out Mazda, got into Jacqui's brand new Celica, put her sunglasses on even though it was overcast, and tried to pretend she was in a taxi with a total stranger.

'I had the *best* time last night,' Jacqui volunteered after several minutes silence.

'Did you go out with Ben dressed like that?' Sam braced herself, as Jacqui swung out into the traffic on Beaconsfield Parade and headed towards St Kilda.

'Don't be ridiculous,' Jacqui declared. 'Ben and I have a date on Friday. *Last* night I went around to Leo's for pasta and got picked up by an absolutely gorgeous American sailor.'

'I'm not surprised a sailor picked you up if you trawled Fitzroy Street dressed–'

'I was wearing jeans and a shirt, Sam,' Jacqui interrupted.

Sam decided it was too early in the day to be dealing with her sister's habit of providing only half the information necessary to make a conversation understandable. She stared out the window at the dreary sky which was hanging lower than usual, making everything dull and lifeless. In the distance she could see a red supertanker, ploughing towards the Heads, and one determined shaft of sunlight that provided the only light and colour on the flat, grey-green expanse of Port Phillip Bay.

'Reuben, his three friends and I had a few drinks at Leo's,' Jacqui explained, while Sam silently questioned the common sense of the four joggers who were pounding along the footpath breathing in toxic peak-hour car fumes. She watched, impressed, as a windsurfer demonstrated perfect control by leaping off his board as he ran it into the sand of St Kilda beach; and astonished, as a middle-aged man in an expensive suit lost control of his morning completely by rollerblading face-first into a No Standing sign.

'...and then we went to a gay bar in Commercial Rd.'

'A gay bar? What on earth for?' Sam asked.

'Reuben and his mates wanted to check out the local scene,' Jacqui replied, turning left into Fitzroy Street. 'That's what gay guys like to do, Sam. There's no need to look so amazed.'

'I'm not amazed, I'm confused. You said you were 'picked up' by a gorgeous sailor.'

'Yeah. We went drinking and dancing, then we met these drag queens and went back to someone's penthouse and put on a fashion parade. Hence the outfit. It was a real hoot.'

'No wonder you have trouble finding 'the right man',' Sam remarked, shaking her head.

'Well, not that you'd know Ms Workaholic, but the only men out there these days are married, gay or desperate. And the gay guys are, without doubt, the most fun.'

'I think you're looking in the wrong places,' Sam remarked.

'Oh yeah? When was the last time you had a date?'

'I'm not looking,' Sam stated.

'There you go then.'

'There I go where?'

'To an old policemen's home where you can while away your dotage with other socially retarded cops, reliving old cases and wondering whatever happened to your sex life.'

'Well, at the rate you're going, Jacqui my sweet, you'll end up in charge of the geriatric make-up and karaoke sessions at the old queens' disco,' Sam retorted.

Ten minutes later Sam stood with a small crowd, in the foyer of the Anato Building on St Kilda Road waiting for the lift. The lower twelve floors of the 14-storey building accommodated a variety of organisations including law and accounting firms, a psychiatrist or three, a couple of dentists and doctors, a firm of private investigators and a publishing house that produced what Sam called 'woo-woo' publications – books and magazines about crystals, angels, spirit guides, and out-of-body encounters with aliens from the Pleiades. The top two floors belonged to the high security offices of the Australian Crime Bureau, Melbourne branch.

Sam squeezed into the lift, waited while buttons were pushed by the other occupants, then pressed 12A. By the time the doors opened on the 13th floor the lift was empty except for Sam and two detectives she recognised but didn't know. While they waited for the officer on the other side of the bullet-proof security door to okay each of them as they swiped their ID cards, Sam wondered whether her companions were also 'socially retarded' or had wives and children to go home to each night.

One of the pitfalls of being on the force was that the most suitable partner for a cop was another cop – someone who understood the hours and the unique stress of the job. But the odds were against finding the right someone in such a limited pool. That's why so many cops retreated to the pub after work, to debrief with mates who shared the same daily crap, so they didn't have to take it home to a civilian husband or wife who could not possibly empathise.

Sam's own experience of the cop/civilian tango had been three times unsuccessful. One guy found he couldn't date a cop; one had offered to support her so she didn't have to be a cop; and the last had given the ultimatum – him or the job. The job was far more interesting. She then tried dating a fellow officer but that ended in disaster when his concern for her safety, because she was a woman, jeopardised an assignment.

So Sam decided there was nothing wrong with being single. It made her career choices easier and her social life freer. She was still open to taking a chance should a potential someone enter her world, but she wasn't desperately seeking anyone. Besides, judging by the trouble her sister and half her friends, also in their thirties, were having finding a compatible partner it obviously wasn't her *job* that was the problem. It was her generation; it was the gains of feminism versus the stagnation of masculinism; it was life at the arse-end of the millennium; it was the hole in the ozone layer; it was–

'Morning, Sam. You're in deep shit.'

Ben Muldoon – case in point, Sam thought. Thirty-six years old, good prospects, not bad looking (in a scrawny sort of way), never married and prepared to date Jacqui – a lunatic masquerading as a sister – just for something to do.

'Morning, Ben. You're looking pretty good yourself,' Sam smiled, depositing her gun and holster in her desk drawer.

'I mean it. You know that cocaine you sent for testing?' Ben pushed his chair back and crossed his arms. 'It was icing sugar.'

'Damn.'

'That's not all. That shipment you sent us to examine? Carved penises,' he said, as if it was business as usual. 'Some were attached to little goblin-type figures, but most of them stood alone. Made all us blokes feel pretty inadequate.

'Oh, there were also some sticks and stones, ceremonial items I believe, a bunch of huge photographic displays and the ashes of some dead geezer from Persia, but mostly there were penises. The sniffer dogs had a good time with the mummified cat though.'

Sam took a deep breath, ran her hands through her hair and sat down heavily in her chair.

'The Boss is ropable,' Ben added, unnecessarily. 'And the guy, that Dr Whatsit in charge of the exhibition, he's as mad as hell; although he took it out on his own staff instead of us, which made a nice change.'

'Muldoon! Is that ex-partner of yours here yet?' Dan Bailey, the ACB's Chief Inspector, otherwise and universally known as 'the Boss' and who, until probably this very minute, was Sam's mentor in the Bureau, stuck his head over the partition. 'You two. My office. Now.'

Bailey closed his office door calmly, waved them to the spare chairs, sat down at his desk and smiled benignly at Sam.

'Special Detective Diamond, would you care to explain, precisely, why you sent Muldoon and the squad on a wild willy chase to the airport yesterday, and why you wasted valuable lab time on a substance commonly, and legally, used in the making of fairy cakes.'

'I'm sorry Boss but, at the time, the facts I had pointed to the possibility that the exhibition was being used as a cover for drug smuggling. Professor Marsden's murder itself appeared to indicate that he had stumbled on something.'

'Which 'facts' were these?'

'I suppose, in retrospect, it was a hunch based on a set of coincidences,' Sam admitted.

'It's not often that Sam is wrong, Boss,' Ben volunteered.

'Granted. But all her other miraculous flashes of intuition put together do not make up for this bloody disaster.'

'Despite the outcome, Boss, I'm convinced that the Professor's murder has something to do with the exhibition or those involved in it. And just because Ben found nothing yesterday, doesn't mean there wasn't something in the first shipment.'

'That's possible,' Bailey conceded. 'And I can see the headline: 'Drug lord arrested; famous archaeologist charged with operating icing sugar ring.'

'Okay, so I jumped to conclusions on the drug thing. I'm sorry, it *was* a bit far fetched.' Sam felt suitably chastened but not convinced her theory was wrong as the prickling sensation in the back of her neck had not dissipated.

'Actually, it's not all that far-fetched,' Ben stated. 'After I had rejected the notion that Sam sent us to check out those things in order to get revenge for the girlie calendar in the lunch room, I figured there must be something to her request, so I did some checking – internationally.'

'And?' Bailey demanded impatiently.

'A sudden, and unexplained, influx of cocaine has coincided with a visit from this *Life and Death* show in Paris, London, Anchorage, San Francisco and now Melbourne.'

'I knew it!' Sam exclaimed.

'That doesn't mean diddly,' Bailey said.

'We're not going to ignore this are we?' Ben argued.

'No. But what we are going to do, is exercise a little discretion. Do you actually have a suspect Sam, or does your hunch involve everyone at the Museum?'

Sam ignored the patronising tone. 'The show's manager, or logistical expert, apparently engages in extra-curricular business in every city they visit. According to the exhibition curator, Enrico Vasquez, Andrew Barstoc is a businessman – and his business is private.'

'Barstoc?' Ben interjected. 'He was the one the boss cocky was venting his anger at.'

'Dr Bridger was angry with Andrew Barstoc?' Sam asked.

'Yeah.'

'Elaborate, Muldoon.'

'The Customs guys moved the crates into a small warehouse so we could go over them. This Dr Bridger was irate but, given the circumstances, he was reasonably cooperative. We told him it was a routine search, by the way. So he asked to oversee the unpacking, and insisted on attending to some items himself. He was afraid we'd break his precious phallic things. Anyway when the job was nearly done, this Barstoc bloke turns up. I honestly thought the good doctor was going to deck him. He shoved him against a wall and got right in his face about something. I couldn't hear what it was, but he was mighty pissed off.'

'And you think Barstoc killed the Professor,' Bailey addressed Sam.

She shrugged. 'I honestly don't know, Boss. I had a hunch about the drugs – which may still prove correct. Because if there was cocaine in that first shipment of artefacts, and if Professor Marsden found out about it, then it stands to reason that he was murdered because of it. In that case Andrew Barstoc would be my prime suspect. Jack Rigby, on the other hand, thinks it was the workplace equivalent of a domestic argument.'

'Ah, a voice of reason surrounded by conspiracy theories,' Bailey remarked.

'You may be right,' Sam agreed. 'But that wouldn't explain why Marsden's house was searched by someone who didn't care about cleaning up afterwards.'

'What was the cause of death?'

'We're waiting for the autopsy results, but Ian Baird thinks he was poisoned. He was also bashed but Baird found puncture marks and traces of a sticky blue residue on the face.'

'That's a bit Agatha Christie isn't it?' Bailey shook his head. 'Do *not* let the press get hold of that detail, Sam.'

'What do we do now?' Ben asked.

'Now? You can look into this cocaine *coincidence* Muldoon. You may have two squad members to keep Barstoc, and only Barstoc, under surveillance. There will be no more raids, in fact no contact of any kind with the alleged suspect unless you observe him red-handed with the goods. You got that?'

'Yes Boss.'

'And you, Sam, stay away from the drugs angle. You get any more wild hunches, you run them by me first. Understood? Your *assignment* is to continue the joint murder investigation with Rigby; but your *priority*, as far as Cultural Affairs go, is to contain this incident. Damage control, okay? Keep that Museum boffin happy and off the phone to the Minister. Discourage this delusion about a conspiracy to wreck his conference, or the silly bastard will discover that publicly voicing his own paranoia will have the same effect.'

Sam returned to her desk, checked the business card Ellington had given her and dialled the number for James T. Hudson, of Hudson & Bolt. She was put through immediately but Mr Hudson, citing client confidentiality, asked if he could ring her back – to ensure that he was, in fact, speaking to someone from the ACB. Her phone rang a few minutes later.

'I apologise for the runaround, Detective Diamond, but please understand you could have been anybody. The press, for instance.'

'The press? Are you expecting them to call in regard to Professor Marsden?'

'Not particularly. But you never know what prompts them to do the things they do.'

'I guess not,' Sam said. 'Robert Ellington said the Professor asked him to contact you *immediately* should anything ever happen to him. Obviously, unless it has a bearing on the case, you're not required to divulge the details of his will but can you explain the urgency?'

'No,' Hudson said.

'You are aware this is a murder investigation?'

'Perfectly aware, Detective. I am not being difficult, I simply cannot answer your question. This has nothing to do with Lloyd's will, it was a separate matter. He came to see me last Thursday and entrusted me with a package that was to be delivered *immediately* to a certain person should anything ever happen to him. They were his words, and it seems he used the very same with Mr Ellington, but he did not explain the urgency.'

'Do you know what was in the package?'

'No. But I suppose I can tell you that it is currently with a colleague who is waiting to deliver it personally, as per Lloyd's instructions, to a Dr Maggie Tremaine at Sydney University. Perhaps she will be in a position to help – *if* it is relevant to your investigation.'

What's with this Maggie Tremaine popping up all over the place, Sam wondered as she ended the call and sat back in her chair. Her phone rang again, this time it was Rigby.

'You're not going to believe this,' he said.

'Jack, I think I'm ready to believe anything.'

'The cause of death *was* poison, but get this, Baird thinks the stuff was injected with one of those poison ring gadgets you see in spy films.'

'You're right, I don't believe it.'

'It's fair dinkum. The doc says the tiny punctures are too wide and too shallow to have been caused by a syringe; *and* there was an oval mark around each of the holes in the cheek, the jaw and the jugular vein.'

'The Boss just said this was very Agatha Christie.'

'That ain't the half of it. The poison was a mean and bizarre little cocktail of curare and peyote. Weird, huh?' Rigby had a knack for understatement.

'Peyote?'

'Yeah, you know mescal, peyote. Indians use it for their vision quest things.'

'I know what it is, Jack. It's an hallucinogen. You can remind me about curare though. What does it do exactly?'

'Used medicinally, it's a muscle relaxant. As a poison it attacks the motor nerves and causes muscular paralysis. The South American Indians use it on their arrows.'

'Arrows, poison rings, peyote. Great,' Sam moaned. 'Consider our possible suspects, Jack. We've got one certifiable South American, Señor Vasquez the Colombian, plus a whole swag of archaeologists and their ilk, who have probably *all* traipsed round that part of the world at some time in their careers.'

Rigby grunted. 'Let's start with Barstoc and Douglas,' he suggested. 'They're at the Exhibition Building waiting for the rest of their stuff. What happened with your cocaine theory, by the way?'

'Don't ask,' Sam pleaded. 'I have to talk to Prescott again, if you want to join me later. And we still haven't interviewed Haddon Gould, the other curator.'

'We can't talk to Gould till later this afternoon. He was rushed to hospital yesterday for an appendectomy. Rivers can sit in on your chat with Prescott. We'll meet you at the Exhibition Building in half an hour.'

Rigby hung up before Sam could object to being nursemaided by Constable Hercules Rivers. She snapped her gun and holster in place on the belt of her slacks, dropped her phone into the pocket of her black jacket and then slipped that on over her white shirt.

# Chapter Six

When Sam left the Anato building, into brilliant sunshine, she stared in amazement at the clear blue sky and wondered where on earth, literally, the rain clouds had gone. She hopped on a tram and relaxed while it trundled its way beneath the canopy of plane trees on St Kilda Road towards the city centre. It made only two stops, at the Art Gallery and the Concert Hall, before crossing the Yarra River where it got stuck in a snarl of traffic caused by motorists slowing to check out a film crew under the clocks of Flinders Street Station.

Sam left the tram outside the State Library, strolled up LaTrobe Street, across Victoria Parade and into the comparative peace of the Carlton Gardens. Beyond the splendid domed edifice of the 118-year-old Royal Exhibition Building, Sam could see the modern structure, still a work in progress, of the site's latest addition. The last time she'd been here, over a year ago, that construction had been nothing but a huge hole in the ground, into which the bowels of the new Melbourne Museum would be buried. Now the futuristic lines of the new building rose in stark contrast to the squares, domes and arches of its historic neighbour.

Sam decided her imagination was not up to translating the seemingly odd angles of the Museum's framework into a finished product that didn't seem incongruous to the location. She cast her mind back to the scale model, complete with landscaping, that she'd seen outside Prescott's office, and overlaid that image on the view before her. Now she could see how the old and new, the past and the future, would complement each other.

'It's a sight to behold; the old and the bold.'

'Yes,' Sam acknowledged automatically before glancing to her right to find a middle-aged man, dressed in a three-piece suit and carrying a hockey stick, nodding at her.

'Do you like my hair?' he asked. 'I've just had it replanted. Can you tell it's not real?'

'Ah, no. It looks great,' Sam lied.

'My son says I look like a cockatoo, and that I'm too old to be so vain.'

'Yeah? Well let's hope the hair loss is hereditary,' Sam said.

'Yes indeedy!' the man cackled, as he walked away. 'Then he'll know what's what.'

Sam shook her head and decided to take cover before anyone else accosted her. She found, or rather heard, Rigby in the main hall, where temporary walls and a false ceiling, of different levels and shapes, had been erected to enclose most of the huge exhibition space. Access to *The Rites of Life and Death* was via a ramp and through the central and monstrous fibreglass jaws of Cerberus. The second and third mechanical heads of the watchdog of the infernal gates snapped and snarled every few seconds.

A workman, inspecting an electrical panel inside, handed Sam a token and pointed to the gnarled, outstretched hand of the skeletal, cloaked Ferryman. Once the price was paid to enter the Realm of the Dead, a panel in the wall behind slid back. Sam headed into

The Catacombs – a maze of 'rock' walled tunnels, complete with niches for skeletons, and intersected with vaults containing coffins, and alcoves with life-size dioramas of human sacrifices and bodies on funeral pyres. She had to duck her head to pass into the replica of a pharaoh's tomb, where artificial torches flickered eerily over a stone sarcophagus and the hieroglyphs on the walls.

Sam began to wonder if her imagination was working overtime or whether Dr Bridger and his team had managed to infuse the claustrophobic tunnels and tombs with the distinctive odour of must and decay. Whatever the cause, she was glad after passing the zombies and weird fetishes in the Voodoo exhibit to emerge into the light and fresh air of the main exhibition area. This was partitioned into areas of fertility and life, death and the afterlife, by walls of fibreglass rock, fake marble pillars or panels of thatch. Much of the space was still empty, awaiting the relics and photographic displays that would, as Prescott described, 'explore the fertility symbols and funerary rites of cultures and societies from around the world and across time'.

Sam felt like she'd just traversed Indiana Jones territory. The concept was fun, but she could see why Marsden and Vasquez questioned its merits as a serious exhibition.

'You get lost in the Underworld?' Rigby asked, as he strode towards her.

Sam curled her lip at him, but then did a double take as she realised the guy in the suit keeping pace with Rigby was the plain-clothed Hercules Rivers.

'You scrub up well,' she said to him. The constable grinned.

'*Miz* Douglas is waiting for us over there,' Rigby said, ushering Sam ahead of him. 'And Herc here tells me *Mister* Barstoc refused to give him a statement because he knew he'd only have to give another one to us.'

'Really,' Sam commented wryly. 'It's been a productive morning so far then.'

Adrienne Douglas, blonde-haired and fresh-faced, was sitting, coffee cup in hand, on a stool in front of a partly constructed shrine. She stood when Rivers made the introductions, looked up at Rigby, as if this was the most tedious experience of her life so far, then smiled warmly at Sam and offered her hand.

'How can I help you detectives?' Although she included Rigby and Rivers in the question it was addressed to Sam.

'We understand you saw Professor Marsden on Wednesday, Ms Douglas,' Sam began.

'Adrienne, please,' she interrupted. 'And the answer is Professor Marsden was here, I was here, we had a few conversations. That's about the extent of it.'

'You're American,' Rigby remarked. When Adrienne gave him a 'you don't say' look he added, 'Conversations about what?'

Adrienne waved her right hand at the space around her. 'The exhibition, what else. To be precise we were consulting each other rather than conversing.'

'Did he seem preoccupied or worried about anything?' Sam queried.

'I hardly know – knew the man,' Adrienne corrected herself, gave Sam a long searching look and then shrugged. 'I really don't know. I met him for the first time less than a week ago. I could say, in *my* experience, he was no more preoccupied than usual. But it's my guess that if you ask someone who knew him, they'd say that's just the way he was. Whether it was a recent occurrence that made him irritable or some lifelong problem that gnawed constantly at his temperament I couldn't say. I quite liked him, but he was a testy old gent.'

'And you last saw him, when?' Rigby asked.

Adrienne shrugged again. 'Enrico and I were here till about six on Wednesday. The Professor left some time before that; maybe 4.30.'

'*There* you are!' The owner of the interjecting voice, who now had his back to Sam, had pushed his way unceremoniously into the space between her and Adrienne. 'Do you know–'

'Marcus,' Adrienne snapped, as if she was talking to a child. 'Can't you see I am otherwise occupied?'

'What?' The man's tone was short but a little vague, and as he turned around it was obvious he hadn't even noticed that Adrienne had company.

*The Life and Death* catalogue photo she'd seen, had definitely not done justice to the blue-eyed, tall, dark and to-die-for handsome Dr Marcus Bridger. Sam suffered a complete Mills and Boon moment, weak knees and all, for a good three seconds before she gathered her wits and realised it was *not* love at first sight but the fact that the man was the spitting image of Timothy Dalton.

She had recovered her mistaken-identity senses by the time Rigby's introductions got around to her, but then had to fight a completely different reaction as Marcus Bridger gave her the once over, and then smiled approvingly as he onced her over again.

Sam acknowledged the introduction with a nod, told Adrienne they were finished – for now anyway – excused herself *and* Rigby and led him away. Rivers followed.

'You okay?'

'I'm fine, Jack. Just fine,' Sam declared. 'Though I could do with a caffeine fix.'

'I'm surprised you didn't deck that bloke for perving at you.'

'Hence the need for a coffee break.'

'There's an urn over there, I'll get you one,' Rivers offered.

'My hero,' Sam smiled. 'Black with no sugar, and the same for Jack.'

'That bird did *not* like me,' Jack said, as if he couldn't understand why anyone wouldn't take to him immediately.

Sam squinted at him. 'She probably guessed you were the sort of man who'd call her a bird. Or she might just not like cops.'

'Oh I don't know, she took quite a shine to you,' Rigby noted.

'It takes some people a long time to process the fact that I *am* a cop,' Sam said. 'But if she makes you uncomfortable, I'll deal with her in future, on the condition that you take care of the equally judgemental Señor Vasquez.'

'I think that's a Latin thing,' Rigby suggested. 'All that macho blood in his veins, he probably thinks you should be home with the bambinos.'

'Speak of the devil,' Sam muttered as Vasquez, who had just emerged from the Voodoo exhibit, made a beeline for them. Correction: a beeline for Rigby; he ignored Sam completely.

'Detective Rigby,' he pronounced. 'I was wondering whether you were aware that Professor Marsden was planning to fly to Peru tomorrow?'

'Yes, we were aware of that.'

'Ah, good,' Vasquez ducked his head. 'It's just that I recalled, last evening, overhearing the Professor tell Adrienne, on Wednesday, that he was off to Peru this weekend.'

'Thank you, Mr Vasquez,' Rigby said.

'I am trying to be helpful, as best I can.' Vasquez gave a crisp nod and headed off to a group of workmen who were fitting in place the last metre-square section of a giant photograph of a Hindu ceremony.

'I do *not* trust that man,' Sam stressed. 'What do you suppose is motivating him to cast so many aspersions on his colleagues?'

'That information wasn't particularly aspersive,' Rigby disagreed.

'The info about Marsden going to Peru, no, but did we need to know the Professor had told Adrienne *on Wednesday,* which just happens to be the day he died? Are we suppose to read something into that? It's like letting us know, in no uncertain terms, that Andrew Barstoc carries out business, unrelated to the exhibition, wherever he goes.'

'He's trying to be helpful,' Rigby repeated in a bad impersonation of Vasquez's accent. 'But, it's hardly his fault if your wild cocaine theory didn't pan out.'

'It's not that wild, Jack.' Sam was about to explain when she noticed that Rivers, carrying three cups of coffee, was escorting Andrew Barstoc in their direction.

'Will this take long?' Barstoc asked impatiently. 'I am rather busy.'

Rigby gave a deep shrug and took his coffee from Rivers. 'You could have given your statement to my constable half an hour ago, Mr Barstoc.'

Barstoc gave a supercilious smile. 'I would rather speak to the superior officer from the outset. It saves time – ultimately.'

'When did you last see Professor Marsden?' Sam asked, getting right to the point so she didn't have to spend too much time in the same room as Barstoc.

'Wednesday afternoon, at about 3.30.'

'Ms Douglas said the Professor was here until 4.30.'

'He may have been. But *I* left at about 3.30.'

'Where did you go?' Rigby asked.

Barstoc looked taken aback. 'I don't see how that is relevant to your inquiry.'

'Everything is relevant Mr Barstoc,' Jack enunciated cheerfully. 'We have to account for everyone's whereabouts on Wednesday. The Professor was last seen, alive, just after five. As he wasn't found *here*, we need to know exactly where you went when you left here.'

Barstoc made no attempt to hide his irritation. 'I met with some colleagues, after which we went to a Thai restaurant for dinner. I returned to my hotel room at about midnight.'

'Were these colleagues from the exhibition?' Sam asked.

'No. They were business associates.'

'Is this your first visit to Melbourne?' Sam queried.

'Yes.' Barstoc straightened his suit jacket.

Sam nodded. 'Yet you have associates who are not connected with this exhibition.'

'I have business interests quite separate from my position here.'

'And what would they be exactly?' Rigby prompted.

'Importing, exporting. I have a passion for precious stones, the older and rarer the better.'

'Were you meeting with these same associates yesterday as well?' Sam asked.

'No, not the same, but I was in meetings for most of the day. I wasn't needed here.'

'You *were* expected at the airport, though, for the arrival or your second shipment.' Sam hesitated just long enough for Barstoc to frown. 'I imagine your being so late for that duty would explain why Dr Bridger was, reportedly, so... displeased with you.'

Barstoc ran his hand through his wavy black hair, as his eyes widened in surprise. 'I was under the impression that was a random, routine inspection.'

'Oh, it was, Mr Barstoc. The ACB carries them out quite randomly and routinely. One of my colleagues mentioned the inspection when he heard I was working on this investigation. But you haven't answered my question about Dr Bridger.'

Barstoc took a settling breath. 'I was *very* late,' he explained. 'And Marcus does not cope well, at all in fact, with bureaucratic red tape, particularly the kind he was subjected to yesterday. He was not displeased; he was angry with me for not being there to deal with it.'

Sam nodded understandingly but said nothing more, so Rigby wrapped up the interview by asking Barstoc to give the names of his business associates to Rivers.

'Jumped-up Pommy git,' Rigby said as he led Sam away.

She tried not to laugh. 'I agree, except that I don't think he's as 'terribly British' as he makes out. And Jack, you *have* to do something about your appalling ethnic stereotypes; not to mention the fact that you're still a sexist bastard. In half an hour you've insulted half the known universe with your references to Latin machos, Pommy gits and birds.'

'Hey, if the shoe fits,' he protested. 'And you know I'd never call *you* a bird.'

'That's because you know exactly where I'd shoot you if you did.'

'Speaking of types, stereo or otherwise,' Rigby said, standing with his arms akimbo, as he surveyed the room. 'Have you noticed the size of all these egos?'

Sam noted that Barstoc was still giving details to Rivers, Adrienne Douglas was talking on a mobile phone, and Dr Bridger was haranguing Enrico Vasquez about a missing something.

She studied Bridger's body language and recalled Ben's report about how the good doctor had shoved Barstoc up against a wall at the airport. She realised the characteristic reserve of the English gentleman was probably as mythical as the notion of the tall bronzed Aussie, for there was no sign of formality in Bridger's manner, at least not at the moment. His expansive hand gestures said as much about his annoyance as his words probably did.

It must be the Heathcliff factor, Sam decided, remembering her initial reaction on seeing his photo in the catalogue. In person, the man oozed a brooding and exotic sensuality, which was overlaid by the impression that he stood confidently and powerfully at the centre of his own private universe. Sam fancied that in another time and place he'd have been the leader of a band of outlaws or pirates.

'You can sort of understand it with Prescott and maybe Bridger and those other over-educated Museum types...' Rigby said. He dropped his shoulders when he saw the look on Sam's face. 'All right already. But,' he continued, 'even that financial assistant and the PR woman yesterday had seriously over-inflated opinions of themselves. It's like they've all got a throbbing aura of conceit.'

'Oh my god, you do exaggerate, Jack,' Sam declared. 'And that attitude says more about you than them. Some of them. Anyone would think they refused to let you into university the way you carry on.'

'Well, I wish they had; I hated it. But that's not the point. These Museum people have all got their own not-so-hidden agendas. Prescott told me this morning, for instance, that Haddon Gould was always pissed off with Marsden because the late Professor usually got funding for his pet projects while Gould was usually overlooked.'

'I bet Prescott did *not* say 'pissed off',' Sam stated. 'What's your real point, Jack?'

'I think it's time to stop looking for grand conspiracies amongst these... these tourists,' he said waving his arm at the room. 'They don't have any history with Professor Marsden.'

'That we know of,' Sam interrupted.

'That we know of,' Rigby acknowledged. 'But they've been here less than a week. Marsden couldn't have been be so obnoxious that one of them was provoked into knocking him off.'

'You still think it was a domestic, don't you? A flash of anger with no premeditation?'

'Yes I do. The man was beaten up, Sam.'

'Yeah,' she laughed derisively. 'And then he was poisoned. And it's not like his attacker reached out for a handy pack of Ratsack. This has to be premeditated, Jack. A curare and peyote cocktail is a pretty bizarre thing to use on the spur of the moment.'

'Granted, but in my opinion we should be concentrating on Marsden's own colleagues.'

'Okay. What about the other conspiracy – the one to sabotage the ICOM Conference?'

'That's way out there with all those sightings of Elvis at the 7-Eleven.'

'What about the portentous limerick?'

'We matched the dropped capital T to an old typewriter in a room that any member of staff in that head office could access. The only fingerprints on the note were Prescott's, and it was posted in the city. There were no other distinguishing features except a trace of a strange fungus which turned out to be something that had been growing in *my* pocket.'

Sam rolled her eyes. 'Where are you going next?'

'Back to the library to talk to the security blokes again. I want to know why no one wondered why Marsden hadn't signed out of the building. What about you?'

'Prescott,' Sam answered. 'I gather you're with me, Rivers.'

'Detective Diamond,' Rivers began, as he and Sam followed the exit signs through a section of maze and around an Apache burial ground, 'you might be interested to know that Dr Bridger did not take his eyes off us the whole time you were interviewing Barstoc.'

'Really? Was he watching us or Barstoc?'

'Well, mostly Barstoc, but also you in particular.'

Sam raised an eyebrow and hoped like hell she wasn't looking as embarrassed as she felt. It was time to change the subject. 'You said yesterday that you're on the Internet.'

'Yeah. I'm a bit obsessed by it at the moment.'

'It's possible to access foreign newspapers or news services, isn't it?'

'Of course.'

'Great. I've got a favour to ask. Could you cross reference the international tour dates for this show with any odd, even vaguely related, incidents that happened to coincide with the Exhibition's time in those other cities.'

'Like Professor Marsden in the Library with the poison ring,' Rivers grinned.

'Exactly,' Sam laughed. 'I like the way you think, Rivers. And please, call me Sam.'

# Chapter Seven

Melbourne, September 18, 1998

'CURARE AND PEYOTE? GOOD GOD. POOR LLOYD,' DALEY PRESCOTT slumped into his desk chair.

'Not a nice way to go,' Sam agreed, as she and Rivers sat down. 'There's no telling what the poor man was seeing while he was lying there paralysed and dying.'

Sam picked up the coffee that Anton had delivered and studied Prescott who, for the first time, displayed genuine sympathy for Marsden rather than worry over how his death would impact on the Museum and the Conference. It didn't last long.

'This is worse than we thought. Imagine the to-do if this should get out.'

To-do? Sam thought, raising an eyebrow. Suspecting Prescott was his own worst enemy, she said, '*You* haven't told anyone about the poison, I hope.'

'Only Jim,' Prescott admitted, as if it was a perfectly logical thing to do.

Sam raised an eyebrow. 'Jim?'

'Jim Pilger.'

'Mr Prescott, the Minister does not need to know the finer points of this investigation. That's why *I'm* here, as his delegate. And unless you informed Mr Pilger that we had asked you not to mention the cause of death to *anyone,* then he's not to know that withholding that information is one of our strategies for keeping this off the front pages.'

'Jim wouldn't tell the media.' Prescott was indignant.

'Of course he wouldn't. But he might mention it to a colleague, then it's out there isn't it.'

'I'll ring him immediately and ask him to keep it to himself.'

'No.' Sam gripped the side of her chair in frustration. 'That's my point. We don't want you to contact him. That is my job, *if* and when it's necessary.'

Prescott resettled himself in his chair. 'Is there any progress on the threatening note?'

'Yes and no,' Sam replied. 'We know only that it was sent by someone who has access to these premises. Personally I think the note and Professor Marsden's death are unrelated.'

'Oh, I pray you're right Detective Diamond, but I am nonetheless fearful that there is a saboteur at large bent on ruining our Conference. Lloyd's death alone is proof of that.'

'The Professor's death is proof of nothing Mr Prescott, except that there is a murderer out there. He or she may have no connection to, or beef with, your Conference. Detective Rigby believes it's a case of anger gone too far, maybe arising out of professional jealousy or some personal issue. It may have nothing to do with the Museum at all.'

'Detective Rigby thinks that. What do you think?'

'I think that until we find out who is responsible we can only guess at the motive. Regarding a plot to ruin the Conference I will ask you this: would you be so concerned about the ramifications of this murder if Professor Marsden had not been on the ICOM '98 committee?'

'Of course,' Prescott asserted. 'That *fact* just makes it worse. Let me try to explain. Lloyd's death reduces years of hard work preparing for this prestigious event to a base level, and makes a mockery of our promotion of this city as a beautiful, liveable and peaceful place to visit.'

Sam wanted to tell him that was a pessimistic overreation to one man's death but Prescott was on a roll.

'You have to understand that, for the museum community, being selected as the Host Institution for the ICOM Conference and General Assembly is akin to being chosen to host the Olympics. We had to compete against two other countries so this is an honour not only for the Museum of Victoria and Melbourne, but for Australia as well. It is the first time the triennial conference has been held in the Asia-Pacific region and only the second time in the Southern Hemisphere.'

'I understand that, but–'

'We'll be on show, Detective. The theme of ICOM '98 is *Museums and Cultural Diversity, Ancient Cultures, New Worlds.* And the world is coming here, to us, to see how we stack up, how we care for our culture and heritage. The Museum of Victoria is a leader in many fields and the success of the Conference *will* have an effect on the country's esteem and reputation.'

Yes, but *what* does this have to do with Marsden's murder, Sam wondered desperately.

'Our Conference,' Prescott continued excitedly, 'will be addressing the resolution of international issues such as the repatriation of cultural material, and will focus on the latest uses of technology in museums, unique collections in Australia, and World's Best Practice, as exhibited by *Australian* institutions.

'Two thousand delegates from 138 countries, including some of the most influential members of the museum community, will be meeting to debate these issues in a host of specialist meetings, and then vote in General Assembly on the resolutions that come from those meetings.'

'I don't see how the Professor's death could affect any of that,' Rivers said hesitantly. He glanced at Sam, who gave him a reassuring smile.

Prescott took a breath. 'When our successful bid to host ICOM '98 was announced three years ago, the ICOM Board in Paris said Australia had a unique chance to do something different and extraordinary. I don't think a murder in our museum was what they had in mind.'

'One would hope not,' Sam stated. 'Mr Prescott, I can only repeat that we will do all we can to contain this incident, to keep it out of the media and limit its impact on the Conference. But you have yet to convince me that this murder is part of a greater plot of sabotage, mostly because I don't understand what purpose it would serve. *Why* would someone want to sabotage the Conference and, more to the point, why wait till now? Wouldn't it have been more damaging at the time your proposal was being considered by the ICOM Board?'

'You mean to stop us being chosen in the first place?'

'Yes.'

Prescott rubbed his forehead. 'The perpetrator may have had no reason three or four years ago; or maybe he is completely perverse and thinks that more obvious and lasting damage can be done now. Lloyd's murder may well be just the start in a campaign to–'

'Mr Prescott,' Sam interrupted, 'bizarre poisons aside, I don't think we are entangled in a Hercule Poirot plot where all the main characters get bumped off one by one, do you?'

'No. I guess not.'

'Then let's concentrate on what we *do* know and on the things that *have* happened. I am not dismissing your concerns but in order to investigate your theory I will need a list of anyone and everyone you can think of who may want to disrupt the Conference.'

'I'll get Anton right on it,' Prescott said, reaching for his phone.

'This is not a task you should delegate. You will have to consider present employees who may have an axe to grind, including any problems with you personally, and past employees who may have a grudge against the Museum because they *are* past employees.'

'I see, a confidential list.'

Sam nodded. 'Confidential and comprehensive. I also need to know more about Marsden. I believe a Dr Maggie–

'Excuse me,' she pulled the ringing phone from her pocket.


### Sydney University, Friday September 18, 1998

'I AM *NOT* HERE,' MAGGIE TREMAINE INSISTED AS SHE STRUGGLED through the doorway of the office she temporarily shared with Professor Carmel Ward. Maggie dropped her laptop, a travel bag and box on her desk. 'I'm just dumping these and then I am really not here.'

'Ah, you might have to be,' Carmel said, waving a hand to get Maggie's attention. 'A man has been waiting to see you for five hours. He was here most of yesterday too.'

'A man, indeed? Well he can wait till Monday,' Maggie declared.

'I'd rather not.'

Maggie turned to find a tall, angular man rising from the arm chair behind the door.

'My name is Richard Avonscroft,' he said, offering his card. 'Of Hudson & Bolt.'

'And?' Maggie prodded.

'You *are* Dr Margaret Selby Tremaine?'

'Yes.'

'Do you have identification?'

'I can verify she is,' Carmel stated, but the man ignored her.

Maggie scowled at him and rummaged around in her traveller's belt pouch for her passport.

'We have been instructed,' Avonscroft stated, after holding the picture up to compare it to the real thing, 'by Professor Lloyd Marsden to deliver this personally to you.'

Maggie accepted the audiotape-sized package and tore off the paper. Written on the lid of a slim cardboard box were the words:

*If you are reading this my fears have been realised. I am no more.*

Maggie read it again and then looked up at Richard Avonscroft. 'What's happened?'

'Professor Marsden was apparently found murdered in Melbourne yesterday morning.'

'Um, to which part of that sentence does the word 'apparently' actually apply?'

'The Professor was found dead in the State Library. It is apparently a case of murder.'

Maggie dropped into her chair. Her hands were shaking as she removed the lid of the box. Inside was a door key, and a note which read:

*Check the odyssey of Ouroboros.*
*Safe no more.*
*Return to the finder, from the words of the Bard.*
*Sweet bugger all back here is the key to Thomas's clue.*

'What is it, Maggie?' Carmel asked.

'I have *absolutely* no idea,' Maggie stated. 'But I have to go to Melbourne.'

# Chapter Eight

Melbourne, September 18, 1998

'No worries, we'll do that next, Jack.' Sam ended the call and snapped her mobile shut. 'Were was I? Oh yes. If we can assume, for the moment, that Professor Marsden's murder has nothing to do with the ICOM Conference then, in order to narrow down the field of possible suspects, I need a better understanding of the man himself. You can help to a certain extent, Mr Prescott, but I believe a Dr Maggie Tremaine knew him quite well.'

'Better than anyone, I'd say,' Prescott nodded. 'But Maggie's in Sydney. Or, rather, she's due back there from Paris today. I could have Anton check to see if she's put in an appearance at the University. He could arrange a time for you to call.'

Prescott pushed the speaker button on his phone, dialled Anton and asked him to ring Maggie.

'Dr Tremaine just rang *you,* Mr Prescott,' Anton stated.

'Why didn't you put her through?' Prescott demanded.

'You said to hold all your calls.'

'Oh. Well, call her back will you, there's a good lad.'

'It's probably too late, she was just leaving. She already knew about Professor Marsden, and said to tell you she'll see you tomorrow. She's catching a morning flight to Melbourne.'

'It seems, Detective Diamond,' Prescott said, switching off the speaker without further ado, or anything resembling a 'thank you Anton', 'that I may be able to arrange a time for you to meet with Maggie, in person.'

Sam nodded her thanks but decided if Prescott's treatment of Anton was anything to go by, the Assistant Director's entire staff probably wanted to ruin his precious Conference – just to see him squirm. She decided it would be more profitable to ask Anton for a list of people who were ticked off with Prescott or the Museum.

'Can you tell me about Professor Marsden's trip to Peru?'

'Which one?' Prescott asked.

'His next one,' Sam replied. 'He was supposed to fly to Lima tomorrow.'

'Was he?' Prescott reached for his phone again and for a moment Sam thought he was going to get Anton to explain *that* hitherto unknown fact, but he spoke this time to someone in personnel. Hanging up, again abruptly, he said, 'Lloyd asked, at short notice, for three weeks leave. This Peru trip had nothing to do with the Museum, at least not directly. Knowing Lloyd though, he would have returned with a request for funding to acquire some 'thing' or other.'

Sam looked puzzled. 'Marsden was liaison for the visiting exhibition, which starts next week, and on the committee for the Conference, which starts in three weeks, and yet he was just going to fly off to Peru for a holiday?'

'Lloyd pretty much did what he felt like around here,' Prescott said.

'You said short notice,' Rivers said. 'When did he apply for leave?'

'Apply? Last Friday he *told* personnel he was taking three weeks, from the end of today.'

Rivers consulted his notebook. 'That was the day he spoke to Ellington about the lawyer.'

'And the day after he saw the lawyer himself,' Sam said. 'Mr Prescott, I believe you said that Haddon Gould was pi... um, resentful of Marsden over funding issues.'

'Yes, but that's old history,' Prescott qualified. 'Lloyd was simply more eloquent than Haddon and better able to state his case for research funding or money for acquisitions. That changed completely with the restructure of the Museum a couple of years ago. Lloyd was getting less for his pet projects while Haddon's field of expertise became encompassed in the Environmental Conservation Program, one of our key areas of development. In fact Lloyd's whole collection, South American antiquities, is something of an anomaly within the new structure. We're still trying to find a place for it.'

'You mean in the new Museum when it's finished?'

'No. I mean in the grand scheme of things, young man. New technologies, especially in the arena of information gathering, storage, dissemination and access, are radically changing the way the world communicates. It's already had and, as we approach the threshold of the new millennium, is still having a revolutionary impact on the role of museums in society.'

'But why should that adversely affect Marsden's collection?' Sam asked, trying to avoid another lecture on museum practices.

'With its restructure, the Museum of Victoria has developed a unique philosophy and mission to improve the understanding of ourselves and the world in which we live.'

'That's nice and vague,' Sam commented. 'I thought museums have always done that.'

'Well, yes,' Prescott bristled. 'But the new Melbourne Museum will be a living museum, a place full of activity and interaction. Much like Scienceworks. Have you been there?'

'Yes, it was quite an experience.' Sam gave up trying to keep

Prescott on track. She watched his hands, noting the gestures were quite deliberate as if he'd had lessons in motivational speaking.

'Then you should understand the difference between the static 19th century style of specimens and artefacts in glass cases, and the interactive exhibits of the modern museum. Museum policy has historically been driven by research, education and collections. While research and education are still paramount in our mission for the future, our traditional role of collecting, preserving and displaying artefacts is evolving to fit the new philosophy of providing an institution that will benefit the whole community, not just those who work in it. The new Melbourne Museum will be deliberately outward looking and audience focussed, with an emphasis on public programs that are relevant, involving and educational.'

'But how did this affect the Professor?' Rivers took a turn at guiding Prescott to the point.

'It's been a giant leap in thinking and application from those inanimate institutions of the past to the dynamic museums of the future,' Prescott continued, undeterred. 'Lloyd didn't want to make that leap. He was a traditionalist, a collector, and he hated change. I think the future frightened the hell out him.'

'So Marsden's collection was denied a place in the new Museum because he refused to change his thinking.'

'Of course not,' Prescott pronounced. 'But our new charter provides for priority areas in which to deliver broad-based public programs with the best possible research, information, and content. We have six programs, Environmental Conservation, Indigenous Cultures, Australian Society, Human Mind and Body, and Technology in Society. Lloyd's collection as you can see fits none of these categories.'

'What was going to happen to it?' Sam asked.

'It will still go into storage until a suitable home can be found for it.'

'It seems like Professor Marsden had a better reason for being a murderer than meeting his death at the hands of one,' Sam noted.

Prescott actually laughed. 'It may seem that way, but it didn't particularly worry him where his collection was housed as long as it was kept intact. Lloyd was a bit of a bower bird, if the truth be known, but his collection is priceless in terms of historical significance. We had no intention of giving it up or keeping it in storage but when he threatened to resign, during the restructure, we gave a firm commitment that a permanent space would be found by the end of 1999. We simply couldn't afford to lose his expertise.'

'You said the Professor didn't care where his collection was kept, yet he threatened to resign over it,' Sam noted.

'It wasn't over that. Lloyd just didn't approve of the new direction. I suppose you've noticed that museum people are passionate about what they do. Lloyd, unfortunately, was passionately old-fashioned. *I* assigned him to the ICOM committee in the hope that involving in him in the preparations would help him understand our vision for the 21st century.'

'That could have been risky,' Rivers commented.

'No, not really. Lloyd could always be counted on to put his heart and soul into whatever he was doing. He was also a pragmatist; he knew he couldn't stop progress. So he did what he always did – worked tirelessly and argued like mad.'

'What is Haddon Gould's story?' Sam asked.

Prescott hesitated a moment, as if he had to retrieve the name from a filing cabinet located in the depths in his mind. 'Haddon thinks the Museum is here for him. He's a collector, much like Lloyd, but less talented and with a tendency to whinge. Needless to say, he was quite pleased with the restructure.

'The term 'living museum' that I used before, applies particularly to a key environmental feature of the new Museum – an interpretive area we're calling the Gallery of Life. This will be a living temperate forest with plants, birds, fish and insects.'

'And this was Dr Gould's idea?' Sam queried.

'Good heavens, no,' Prescott exclaimed. 'Haddon hasn't had an original thought in decades. But we will be using some of his plant collection.'

'Did the restructure affect anyone else apart from Professor Marsden?' Sam asked.

'Yes and no,' Prescott smiled. 'Morale within the museum community is bound up with issues like whether the institution is supporting or betraying individual ideals. The pay is never good, but as I said earlier our staff are passionate; they work for the love of it. When we announced that changes were on the horizon, everyone – and I mean everyone – went into a flat panic. Understandable you might think when, in the outside world if an organisation the size of ours announces a restructure it means downsizing, or whatever euphemism they're using this year. But here, not one single person lost their job, they simply got new titles and that caused a great deal of angst.' Prescott seemed to find this highly amusing.

'You said earlier that the Conference will be addressing the resolution of international issues such as the repatriation of cultural material...' Sam hesitated because she noticed that Rivers seemed to have lost his place in his notebook. He was flipping back the pages and looking quite puzzled. 'Are you okay, Rivers?'

'Yeah,' he nodded. 'Sorry.'

'The return of cultural property is a key issue,' Prescott replied, 'But I think Julia Cooper from our Indigenous Cultures Program could best explain the concept for you.'

'I understand the concept, I simply wanted to verify whether this was another thing that Professor Marsden had a problem with.'

'My word, yes. Giving things back is quite an alien concept for a professional collector.'

Sam called into Anton's office after leaving Prescott and asked him to compile a list of past and present employees with possible grievances.

'You don't really think one of us killed the Professor?'

'It's a sad fact, Anton, that murderers usually kill someone they know. But I need this list for something else. Are you aware of the postcard Mr Prescott received?'

'Everybody knows about that,' Anton replied. 'He thought it was a sick joke but it upset him enough to send an office email stating that he did not appreciate the humour, *and* if he ever found out who sent it, that person would be jobless. Is the postcard connected to the murder?'

'We're not sure. I've asked Prescott for a list but I suspect–'

'The Assistant Director wouldn't know what to look for or who to consider,' Anton agreed.

'That reminds me,' Sam said, 'why are we dealing with the AD? Where is the Director?'

'Mr Buchanan hasn't been well. He took long service leave and left Mr Prescott in charge.'

'Detective Diamond, I mean Sam,' Rivers began, as they took the lift down to the carpark. 'I hope I wasn't out of line asking questions when you were interviewing Prescott.'

'No, of course not,' Sam assured him. 'That's what we're here for – to ask questions.'

'Good, because I have to say my money's on that windbag Prescott being the murderer.'

'You're not serious,' Sam laughed.

Rivers shrugged and grinned. 'There's something really sus about a bloke who's so obsessively neat. There was nothing on his desk, it makes you wonder what he does all day.'

'It doesn't mean he goes around knocking off his staff,' Sam said. 'Personally I think the man is a victim of the end-of-the-century paranoia virus. He's got the particularly virulent strain that makes him irrationally suspicious but completely clueless.'

Sam rubbed her forehead and lowered her voice: 'I am nonetheless fearful that there is a saboteur at large bent on ruining our conference. Lloyd's death alone is proof of that.'

'How the hell do you do that?' Rivers asked as they exited the lift and headed for his car.

'Do what? I didn't sound anything like Prescott.'

'No, how do you remember all that stuff? I can recall the gist of something but I have to refer to my notes for the specifics. But you remember names, titles, dates and when you refer to what someone said you repeat it verbatim. I know, because I checked when you asked Prescott about the cultural stuff on the conference agenda.'

'The cultural *stuff*? See, you do remember what he said.'

'Yeah,' Rivers snorted, 'the *stuff* but not the substance.'

Sam smiled. 'Well, I'm good with the substance. I don't take notes because I don't need to, that's why Jack assigned you to do the rounds with me. Mind you, I doubt he meant for you to record every word of every conversation. He just wants the facts.'

Rivers unlocked his car. 'I haven't worked with Rigby before, so I don't know what he wants. He did, however, tell Barstoc that everything is relevant. So until I know what is and isn't...' he shrugged. 'Besides, it's good practice.'

'True, but while you're practising, you're listening and writing, not hearing and processing.'

'Processing? Is that something they teach you at the Bureau?' Rivers asked.

'No, I've always been a processor. Plus I've got a lot of RAM and a huge hard drive.'

Rivers laughed, and made a left turn out of the carpark onto Lonsdale St. 'Where to now?'

'The Alfred Hospital. Jack wants us to talk to Gould.'

Haddon Gould appeared remarkably fit for someone who'd undergone an emergency appendectomy the day before, but then the man was also considerably younger than Sam had expected. She'd wrongly assumed that the three 'professional collectors' were peers in age as well as occupation. Marsden had been 61; although his face, wracked as it was by the poisons that killed him, made him look closer to 80; and Robert Ellington had muttered something about what he'd do with his retirement package in three years.

Gould, on the other hand, wasn't a day over a hale and hearty 50-ish. His hospital gown, usually an item of clothing about as far removed from a fashion statement as a garment can get, looked like it had been designed especially to let him show off his tanned and muscled arms. His blue eyes matched his Nordic blonde hair but his face was otherwise quite plain.

'Ah, the police, I assume. My wife said you'd be calling to talk about Lloyd.'

'I'm Detective Diamond, this is Constable Rivers. I promise we won't take too much time.'

Gould waved his arm towards the visitors' chairs. 'I'm not going anywhere.'

'We'd like to verify the time you saw Professor Marsden on Wednesday.'

'Well, we ignored each other while having coffee in the tea room around 2 pm,' Gould stated. 'Duncan Jones was there too, because I remember Lloyd telling him he had to go over to the Exhibition Building to see the curator and Peter. Lloyd then left with Sarah Collins. Later–'

'Just back up a sec, please Mr Gould,' Sam interrupted. 'Peter who?'

'Oh, what's his name?' Gould drummed his fingers on the tray table. 'Ah! Gilchrist. Lloyd's assistant. He's a student. A very focussed and driven young man, but a tad peculiar.'

Sam glanced at Rivers whose expression indicated he'd never heard of Gilchrist either.

'You said "later". Did you see the Professor again that day?' Rivers asked.

'Yes. Later in the afternoon I went looking for him to talk about his Peru trip.'

'What time was that?' Sam asked. They'd only known about Gould, and indeed Sarah Collins from the PR department, because of the statement given by Duncan Jones, after he'd found the Professor's body the next day.

'Maybe just after 5.30,' Gould said vaguely.

'Really?' Sam said, unable to mask her surprise. 'Did anyone see you talking?'

'Not that I'm aware of. Why, what difference does it make?'

'Until now, the last known person to see the Professor was a security guard at 5.20. You may have been the last to see him alive.'

'Oh dear. Um, I should perhaps tell you then, I don't know whether anyone heard us, but Lloyd and I had a very loud argument. Well, *I* was loud; Lloyd was being irritatingly pacific.'

'What were you arguing about?' Sam asked.

Gould ran his hands through his hair. 'I was just about to go home when I heard, from Sarah, that Lloyd had decided to up and fly off to Peru. I was annoyed. No, I was extremely angry. I let him know, in no uncertain terms, how irresponsible he was. He was on the ICOM committee yet he was just going to piss off to South America on a whim.'

'I take it you're on the committee,' Sam commented.

'No I'm not,' Gould replied bitterly. 'That's was why I was angry. Lloyd got *my* place on that committee, yet he didn't give a damn about it.'

'I see,' Sam said. 'During this loud argument, Mr Gould, did you strike the Professor?'

'Of course not!' Gould was appalled. 'And I certainly didn't kill him, if that's what you're implying. Lloyd was very much alive when I left him, at about quarter to six.'

'Do you recall if anyone saw you leave?'

Gould closed his eyes for a moment. 'There may have been a couple of people left in the offices on the way out and there were a few milling in the Library foyer.' He shrugged. 'I can't remember anyone specifically and I've no idea whether they noticed me.'

'Why do you suppose he volunteered that information?' Rivers asked, feeding coins into a drink machine in the hospital hallway.

'Because he's got nothing to hide,' Sam suggested. 'Or because a witness to that argument may turn up, and he no doubt thinks it's sensible to be up front from the start.'

'I'd say he just made the top of the suspect list,' Rivers whispered.

Sam nodded. 'He's got motive, petty as it might be, and obviously opportunity. It's the means we have to investigate now. Gould certainly has the physique to be able beat the crap out of someone like Marsden, but the poison is another issue.'

'Search warrants?' Rivers asked.

'Search warrants,' Sam agreed. 'But not yet. I think we – Jack, you and I – need to go over everything we've got first. Gould is almost too obvious for my liking.'

'And there's the guy, the student,' Rivers reminded her.

'Yeah, the Peter Gilchrist guy,' Sam enunciated, reminding Rivers he'd been note-taking instead of processing again.

# Chapter Nine

Melbourne, Saturday September 19, 1998

'DETECTIVE DIAMOND, YOU LOOK LIKE YOU COULD DO WITH A GOOD strong coffee.'

Sam had been quite lost to her surroundings as she examined a life-size photograph of a burning body on a small funeral pyre beside a river, in which red-saried women were washing their hands. She turned to find Adrienne Douglas offering her a mug.

'Black, no sugar,' Adrienne verified. 'I heard you tell your offsider yesterday.

'You're a lifesaver, thank you.' Sam accepted the mug.

'I gather you don't get Saturdays off when you're investigating a murder.'

'Not this early in the investigation,' Sam stated. 'I don't suppose you've seen my offsiders?'

'The big guy *was* with Enrico near the yoni display, but I don't know where they went.'

'Did Professor Marsden mention his trip to South America to you, Adrienne?'

'Yes. I think it was the same day, you know the day he died.'

'What did he say exactly?'

'We're hosting a dinner tomorrow night. It's a PR exercise, sort of a pre-opening thank you to all the people who've helped with the exhibition and to your Museum for having us here. I asked the Professor if he was bringing his wife, or whatever, and he said he couldn't make it, because he was flying to Peru on Saturday. That's today.'

'Did you think it odd that Marsden was planned to leave town like that when he was supposed to be helping you get this show off the ground?' Sam asked.

'Not at all. The Professor was basically a liaison officer; an efficient one, but that's all. We'd gone over all our concerns with this site, and talked about the things that had gone right and wrong in other cities. He introduced us to everyone who could provide help or support at short notice.'

'I see there's no rest for the forces of law and order.' Dr Marcus Bridger had appeared by Sam's side without warning. 'Detective Diamond isn't it?' he said.

'Yes, Dr Bridger,' Sam said. 'I must say I'm impressed by how fast the exhibits are being put together.'

'We've had a lot of practice.' He smiled warmly. 'This is our eighth venue in 18 months, and we've still got Wellington and Montreal to go.'

'It helps that we're ahead of schedule because you managed to get the exhibits here a day earlier than expected,' Adrienne commented.

Dr Bridger acknowledged the statement, but returned his attention to Sam. 'I was most distressed to learn of Professor Marsden's tragic death,' he said. 'He was such a gentleman, a rare breed indeed, and most generous, I hear, with the time he gave to our exhibition.'

'You did meet him then,' Sam said.

'Yes, we all dined together on... What day was that, Adrienne? I've lost track.'

'Wednesday. The day we all first arrived, and the night before you returned to Paris.'

'Who was at this dinner?' Sam asked.

'My team, the Professor of course, Daley Prescott and a few other people whose names escape me I'm afraid,' Dr Bridger replied.

'I spoke to a dear old fellow called Robert for a while,' Adrienne volunteered. 'But the Professor himself didn't stay very late. He left about nine because he wasn't feeling well. Remember Marcus? It was just after you and he had been talking.'

Dr Bridger looked like this was news to him. 'I don't recall. I do remember having my ear all but talked off by Daley Prescott,' he said, and then smiled. 'Ah, I gather you've had a similar experience, Detective Diamond.'

Sam had tried unsuccessfully not to laugh so there was no point denying it. 'The full treatment. I know more than any detective ever needs to know about museums.'

'There's your partner in crime detection.' Adrienne pointed over Sam's shoulder.

Sam thanked Adrienne again for the coffee before excusing herself to join Rigby.

'I hear Enrico,' Sam said, rolling the 'r', 'has been bending your ear yet again, Jack.'

Rigby sighed. 'He told me Barstoc returned to their hotel just on 2 am the night of the murder.'

'*Why* did he tell you this?'

'Because he overheard Barstoc telling us he'd returned at midnight.'

'And because he's trying to be helpful,' Sam added.

'As best he can,' Rigby laughed. 'Why are we here again, Sam?'

'To track down a Peter Gilchrist. Didn't Rivers tell you about him?'

'I haven't spoken to him today. I left instructions for him to go over Marsden's office again, to see if there's anything we overlooked.'

'Like what?'

'Like, I don't know. If I did, we wouldn't have to search for it,' Rigby said. 'But if he was into the horses he might have owed money. Maybe his bookie bumped him off. This Gould character has gone to the top of my list though.'

'I thought you said you hadn't spoken to Rivers,' Sam said.

'I haven't,' Rigby stated. 'But yesterday I spoke to a researcher who wasn't in the old Museum the day Marsden's body was found, but *was* there late on Wednesday. She overheard–'

'An argument between the Professor and Haddon Gould,' Sam finished. Rigby looked like his thunder had been stolen. 'He told us all about it, Jack.'

'Did he admit to a lot of shouting and abuse and then storming out?'

'Yes. Did this researcher see Marsden afterwards?' Sam asked.

'No, but she said it was very quiet down that end of the hall after Gould left.'

'Gould was doing all the shouting, so I'm sure it was. Marsden could still have been alive and working quietly.'

'Or hallucinating and dying in paralysed agony,' Jack argued. 'Did Gould tell you what they were arguing about? Can we find a motive for this guy?'

'He said he was angry about Marsden taking off for Peru when he had commitments here. Gould believed the Professor got *his* place on the ICOM '98 committee. But I spoke to Prescott this morning and he claims Haddon Gould would only have got a position on that committee if everyone else in the Museum, including the cleaning staff, had turned it down first. Not that that matters. It could be enough that Gould *thinks* he lost his place to Marsden. I reckon there's more to Gould's resentment of the Professor than we know, but I'm not sure it translates into making him capable of murder.'

'Well he's odds-on favourite for me. I've organised warrants to search his home and office. I suppose you still think it's one of this lot,' Rigby waved his hand around at the Exhibition.

Sam gave a noncommittal shrug. 'How do you suppose Bridger managed to get the second lot of exhibits here a day early?'

'Um, obviously he put them on an earlier flight. What difference does it make? He still didn't arrive early enough to be a suspect, so why do you care?' Rigby asked.

'Because it's odd, Jack. Remember Prescott's rave about transporting shows like this? It's not like Bridger could just turn up at Paris airport with all his stuff and hope to get on the next available flight.'

'If it's bothering you, Sam, why don't you ask him how he managed it? But it's my guess he probably just knows the right people.'

'Maybe. Oh, that reminds me.' She pulled out her phone and dialled Rivers' number. 'Hi, it's Sam. Are you still in Marsden's office?'

'Yep. And I think someone other than our forensics team has been here too.'

'Great,' Sam moaned. 'When you've finished could you track down Robert Ellington and–'

'He's here, Sam.'

'Oh. Good. Could you ask him about the dinner he went to on the Wednesday before last, the 9th, with Prescott and the bods from *The Life and Death* show. See if he remembers hearing any part of the conversation between Dr Bridger and Professor Marsden.'

'Sure. Do you want to wait while I ask?'

'No. Prescott has arranged for me to see Dr Tremaine at 6 pm in the bar of the Regency Hotel. Can you meet me there at 6.30?'

'Okay. I've got that info you wanted from the internet. I'll bring it with me.'

'Excuse me, are you the police officer who's been looking for me?' A gangly young man, with receding blonde hair and a pitiful excuse for a moustache, stared earnestly at Sam through a pair of round-rimmed glasses. He was wearing jeans, and a T-shirt with the slogan: *Archaeologists Dig Deeper*.

'Peter Gilchrist,' he stated, tapping his own chest.

'Ah, yes, Mr Gilchrist.' Sam introduced herself and Rigby. 'We wanted to ask you about your association with Professor Marsden, and when you last saw him.'

'Yeah, the poor old bloke. What a way to go, eh?' Gilchrist shoved his hands in his pockets and stared around the room for a moment. 'I'm, or I was, one of Professor Marsden's students. I'm studying archaeology at Melbourne Uni. The Prof was generous enough to take me on earlier this year as his assistant, part-time.'

'Where have you been all week?' Sam asked.

'At home studying. I worked for the Prof on Tuesdays, Wednesdays and some weekends. Like this one and the last; helping out here. I only found out about him dying yesterday, when he didn't turn up for our tutorial.'

Sam found she was irritated by Gilchrist's habit of either studying her face as if she was an interesting specimen or not looking at her or Rigby, at all, while he spoke.

'So you saw him on Wednesday,' Rigby said.

'Yeah. At the old Museum in the morning. We were cataloguing stuff. Then after lunch we met up here to help out with a problem Enrico was having with the fittings for the photo displays. The Prof was in a pretty grumpy mood in the afternoon.'

'Was he?' Sam noted. 'Did you know he was supposed to fly to Peru today?'

Gilchrist dropped his gaze to concentrate on Sam's chin. 'Nah, didn't know about that.'

'When did you last see the Professor?' Rigby asked.

'We finished up here at about 4.30 on Wednesday. He was going back to the Library but said he didn't need me. So I went to the pub and met up with some mates from Uni.'

Rigby grunted as Gilchrist walked away inspecting the floor, the walls, the ceiling and the floor again as he did so. 'These museum types keep getting weirder,' he complained. 'I'm gonna check his alibi. I don't trust a bloke who can't look you in the eye when he's talking.'

'Marsden had *words* with him on Wednesday.' Vasquez had materialised as if from thin air.

'What sort of words, Señor Vasquez?' Sam asked, politely.

'Harsh words,' Vasquez nodded. 'I believe you call it a dressing down. I gather Peter had *again* not carried out a task the Professor had set him. Something to do with a late paper. Marsden was most annoyed. He told Peter that he'd better pull up his socks or even the extra work he was doing would not help him pass.'

'Why didn't you tell us this before now?' Rigby demanded.

Vasquez turned his palms up in apology. 'He is, wouldn't you say, an instantly forgettable young man?'

# Chapter Ten

THE BAR OF THE REGENCY HOTEL WAS LIT TO PROVIDE MAXIMUM RELIEF for tired eyes without leaving patrons completely in the dark. Sam took a seat at the bar, ordered a beer and surveyed the rest of the clientele.

In front of the large tinted window that faced Lonsdale Street, a dozen businessmen had pushed four tables together and were noisily giving drink orders to a waitress who looked like she'd already had enough of customers like them for the day. Two tizzied-up socialites were sitting in a booth besieged by shopping bags, and the only other woman in the place looked like she'd been outfitted by the same drag queens Jacqui had met on Thursday night. Her shoulder-length auburn hair had been given electric shock treatment and she was wearing a loose purple shirt, gold leggings, and black runners – fine attire for a 20-year-old but this woman was fast approaching 50. Sam hoped the woman was waiting for a loving husband because if she was on the prowl for Mr One Night Stand she'd probably only end up with a vice cop.

She sent up a prayer to the goddess of single women that she'd never have to hang out in hotel bars to... She slapped herself mentally. The woman she was being so ageist and judgemental about had a delightfully charming face, looked fit and braced with energy, and probably had better luck with men than Sam ever did.

'Isn't it a sign of madness, or something, to drink alone?'

'Adrienne?' Sam said in surprise. 'What are you doing here?'

'We're *all* staying here at this hotel.' Adrienne slipped onto the stool beside Sam. 'Is this where you hang out?'

'No,' Sam laughed. 'I'm waiting for someone.'

'Damn. I was going to offer to buy you a drink, Sam. Can I call you Sam when you're obviously off duty, and...' Adrienne glanced around the room. 'And we're in a bar?'

Sam smiled. 'Sure. You can buy me a beer too if you like.'

'Good. Oh damn!'

'There you are, Adrienne, I wish you'd stop wandering off,' Marcus Bridger said, loudly, as he manoeuvred his way around the tables to the bar.

'Oh, Detective Diamond,' he added brightly. 'This *is* a pleasant surprise. Or are you following us?'

'Should I be?' Sam asked.

Bridger smiled suggestively. 'Only if you have nothing better to do.'

'Well in that case I'll have to give it a miss. I'm taking my grandmother on her first moonlight parachute jump tonight.'

Bridger's taken aback expression dissolved into laughter; a warm, rolling laugh. He clasped his hands to his chest and gave a slight bow. 'I am *truly* devastated that we cannot stay,' he said, taking Adrienne by the elbow. 'But no doubt we'll be seeing you again.'

Sam watched them walk away then swivelled back to the bar.

'It seems we are about to have our preconceptions dashed on the rocks of reality.'

Oh no, not again. Why do I *always* attract *all* the nutters? Sam wondered.

The wild-haired woman, all five-foot-four of her, had moved from the other end of the bar to stand beside her.

'I beg your pardon?' Sam asked politely.

'You were no doubt expecting Margaret Rutherford, or a similar large-breasted, tweed-suited 'Miss' of the jolly-hockey-stick type,' she stated.

'Dr Tremaine?' Sam was flabbergasted, and there was nothing she could do to hide it.

'Indeed. And you my dear look more like a dark-haired Meg Ryan than the Humphrey Bogart of my expectations. Clearly I should read or watch more contemporary crime fiction.'

'What should I do?' Sam asked, worried that if the wind changed now she'd be wide-eyed and open-mouthed forever.

'Buy me a whisky, dear. And call me Maggie.'

Fifteen minutes later, having retreated to a booth together, Sam had somehow given Maggie a complete rundown of the investigation so far, minus the details about the actual cause of death and likely suspects, but hadn't asked a single question herself.

'I was wondering how you knew Phineas,' Maggie said, when Sam mentioned interviewing *The Rites of Life and Death* team.

'Who?' Sam asked.

'Marcus; you know, Dr Tall Dark and Obvlious. He's known, within the museum community, as P.T. Barnum. The 'P' stands for Phineas.' Maggie explained. 'Is he a suspect?' She seemed quite taken by the idea.

Sam shook her head. 'He wasn't even in the country.'

'So who are your suspects?'

'That's what I need to talk to you about,' Sam said, trying to regain – no, gain – control of the conversation.

'You seem to be the one person who might know if Professor

Marsden had any enemies, if he owed money, why he'd suddenly decide to go to Peru, what that trip has to do with his murder – if anything, what *hancsgoc* or *hanosgoo* means, why–'

'What what means?' Maggie asked.

'I'll get to that in a minute,' Sam said. 'Can you think of any reason why anyone would want to kill the Professor?'

Maggie shook her head thoughtfully. 'He was a cantankerous old so-and-so but I've no idea why someone would want to poison him to death.'

'Poison? Who told you that?'

'Daley, he–' Maggie stopped when Sam groaned and bumped her forehead on the table.

'That idiot man!' Sam growled. She sat up. 'He's convinced there's a mysterious plot afoot to ruin ICOM '98, that Marsden's death is just one gory part of it, and that if the press gets hold of the story they'll be going through his sock drawers to get all the juicy details – yet he's the one who *can't* keep his mouth shut. He may as well hire a float and tell the whole city. I could *strangle* him.'

'I know how you feel,' Maggie laughed.'I have often been tempted to defenestrate him.'

'To do what?'

'Chuck him out the nearest window, dear. Just to shut him up.'

Sam was still laughing when she noticed Rivers enter the bar. She motioned to him to get a drink before joining them. 'You won't tell anyone about the poison will you, Maggie?'

'Pah! Who would I tell?' Maggie assured her.

'Dr Maggie Tremaine, Constable Hercules Rivers,' Sam said, as the latter slid onto the bench seat beside her. 'Don't ask,' Sam said, when she noticed Maggie's questioning look.

'You can tell me later, *Hercules*,' Maggie suggested, leaning over to Rivers. 'Especially seeing you look as surprised by *my* appearance as I am... delighted by yours.'

'Sorry for staring,' Rivers stated. 'It's just that Robert Ellington kept saying "formidable woman, formidable", like you were some scary thing. I expected you to be seven feet tall.'

'Ha! The silly old fart,' Maggie chuckled.

'So, what have you got, Rivers?' Sam asked, wondering if it was her imagination or whether Maggie Tremaine was indeed flirting with the constable.

'First off, Ellington said he was sitting at that dinner between Dr Bridger and Ms Douglas. He says Bridger and the Professor were talking about an archaeological dig in Peru, and some Inca called... hang on.'

Rivers shrugged at Sam as he pulled out his notebook. 'I'm trying to get the hang of this processing deal, but this one I have to look up. Right, an Inca dude called Teepackamoo.'

Maggie nearly choked on her drink. 'You needn't have bothered looking it up, Hercules. The *dude's* name was Tupac Amaru.'

'Is there any reason why this topic would have made the Professor claim he was ill so he could leave the dinner early?' Sam asked Maggie.

'Not unless he was suddenly grief-stricken over the murder of the last Inca king by the Spaniards over 400 years ago,' Maggie said. 'Lloyd was not a social man. He probably just wanted to go home.'

'Oh.' Sam was getting depressed and wondering if Rigby was right about Marsden's death being a domestic affair. It was obviously time to get her intuition sent somewhere for a reality check. 'What about the Internet stuff?' she asked hopefully.

'Ah, now *this* is interesting,' Rivers stated, placing a printout on the table. 'The first two are pretty wacky but I haven't found any connection except the dates. A guy was killed in a hit-and-run snowmobile accident in Anchorage on July 6 last year; and a suicidal Scotsman leapt off the roof *next* to the museum in Edinburgh on December 23. He lived, by the way.

'The rest of these are probably more relevant. An art broker died of smoke inhalation in a gallery fire in New York on March 15, 1997; some Egyptian scrolls and Roman coins were stolen in a burglary at an archaeological museum in London on October 10; and lastly, a van carrying South American treasures was hijacked in Paris four days ago. That last one doesn't *really* fit though, because the Exhibition had already left.'

'Not *all* of it,' Sam stated, feeling her intuition sparking on all cylinders again. 'I believe you know something about the Paris hijacking, Maggie.'

'Yes. And, as it happens, the burglary in London. What has all this got to do with Lloyd?'

'Nothing directly, but each of these bizarre little incidents occurred during a visit to those cities by *The Rites of Life and Death* exhibition.

Maggie smiled. 'So Marcus *is* a suspect.'

'No. As I said before, he wasn't here when Marsden was murdered. Although he *was* probably still in Paris during the hijacking.'

Maggie roared with laughter. 'I can imagine Phineas doing away with a competing colleague, but I *can't* see Dr Marcus Bridger carrying out an armed robbery in broad daylight,' she said. 'What on earth made you look into all this?'

'Coincidences,' Sam stated. 'I hate them, and they're cropping up everywhere in this investigation.'

'Well I've another one for you,' Maggie offered. 'A dear friend of mine, Dr Alistair Nash, was curator of that burgled London Museum. He died in a car crash on the day of the robbery.'

'Whoa!' said Sam.

'It's just a coincidence, Sam dear. They do happen.'

'Not without a reason they don't,' Sam pronounced, and explained her theory about a smuggling operation.

Maggie was highly amused. 'An intriguing possibility, but not very likely.'

'Do you need me any more tonight, Sam?' Rivers asked. 'It's just that I'm supposed to be playing pool in the inter-department comp tonight.'

'No, that's fine. Thanks for all this info.' Sam pocketed the printout. 'And good luck.'

'I'll just get us another drink,' Maggie said. She got up and followed Rivers. 'Pool?' Sam heard her say. 'I would have thought you'd play football.'

Rivers, who looked like he was being completely charmed by Maggie, continued to chat with her at the bar until the drinks had been served.

'There's nothing like a handsome, strapping young man to get my wires all abuzzing,' Maggie announced, returning to her seat.

Sam laughed. 'He's got to be 20 years younger than you.'

'I thank you for the compliment Sam, but it's closer to thirty years. I turned 58 last month. And there's no need to look so amazed, you don't look 35 either.'

'How do you know how old–'

'Oops,' Maggie muttered. 'I'll have to come clean now, if I'm going to ask for your help.'

'*My* help?'

'Yes. I confess that after Daley arranged this meeting I did a little investigating of my own.'

'You checked *me* out? Why? How?'

'Suffice to say I know a lot of people. It wasn't difficult. So, although I didn't know what you looked like, I *did* know that Sam Diamond had achieved a few firsts in the Bureau: the youngest woman to earn the rank of Detective, and the youngest anything to be promoted to Special Detective. I also know you have a Masters in Criminology, that you usually beat the boys at the shooting range, and I'm told you're smart, intuitive, analytical and prepared to take risks.'

'I am?' Sam said warily, realising she'd pressed her whole body back into the bench seat.

'Don't look so worried.' Maggie searched her bag for something. 'I simply have a mystery that needs unravelling, and I suspect you're good with mysteries.'

'Yeah? Well, my old boss thinks I'm good at inventing them.'

'Good. Because if you can make them, you should be able to break them.' Maggie placed a small box on the table.

'*If you are reading this my fears have been realised. I am no more,*' Sam read aloud. 'Good grief! Is this what Marsden sent you?'

'You know about this already,' Maggie said in surprise.

'I knew about the package but not what it was. I spoke to the lawyer after Ellington said Marsden had asked him to contact Hudson and Bolt if anything happened to him.'

Sam removed the lid of the box and stared with disappointment at the contents. 'A key? Is that all?'

'And that ridiculous note,' Maggie said. 'Lloyd knew I wasn't much of a lateral thinker, so I don't know what possessed him to send this to me.'

Sam shuffled around the bench seat until she was sitting next to Maggie, and placed the note on the table between them. She read aloud, but softly:

'*Check the odyssey of Ouroboros. Safe no more. Return to the finder, from the words of the Bard. Sweet bugger all back here is the key to Thomas's clue.*'

'Fascinating isn't it?' Maggie said sarcastically. 'I don't have the faintest idea what it means.'

'Who's Thomas?' Sam asked.

'No idea. And the only Bard I know of is a dead playwright so he's not going to be much help, is he?'

'You don't know who Ouroboros is either, I take it,' Sam said.

'What, not who,' Maggie corrected. 'And that I do know. It's a symbol found world-wide and means different things, for instance: "my end is my beginning". In Orphic cosmology it encircles the Cosmic Egg; the Egyptians saw it as the circle of the universe, the Greeks as "all is one", and the Hindus and Buddhists as the wheel of samsara. In alchemy Ouroboros symbolises the unredeemed power of nature.'

'Oh, well that's helpful,' Sam said mockingly. 'What does this symbol look like?'

'It's often depicted as a serpent or dragon biting its own tail, symbolising self-sufficiency and the eternal cycle, wherein the serpent begets, weds, impregnates and kills itself.'

'It's life and death,' Sam said excitedly.

'Yes exactly. Ouroboros the serpent perpetually injects life into death and death into life.'

'No, yes, I mean look at the first sentence,' Sam babbled, pointing to Marsden's note. 'He's telling you to "check the odyssey of Ouroboros". That *has* to mean the itinerary of *The Rites of Life and Death*. I *knew* I was right about that Exhibition.'

'Well I'll be damned,' Maggie declared. 'That doesn't mean they're smugglers.'

'No, but I'll bet *anything* it means that at least one of them is a murderer.'

'None of this explains why Lloyd suddenly decided to go to Peru. That's not like him at all. He usually put a lot of planning into his field trips.'

'Maybe it wasn't a field trip,' Sam suggested. 'The Professor set this whole mystery in motion the day after the exhibition arrived in Melbourne. Perhaps he was threatened and simply decided to go somewhere safe.'

'Surely he'd have left straight away, instead of applying for leave and waiting a week.'

'Unless it was Dr Bridger who threatened him. Marsden bought the ticket and delivered this package to his lawyer the day Bridger flew to Paris. The Professor's flight to Peru was for today, when Bridger was *supposed* to return to Melbourne. He came back early though.'

'But not early enough to kill Lloyd.'

'No, that's true. But perhaps someone else from the team is involved too; or all of them.'

'Sam dear, I believe you're creating your own plot and losing it as you go. You're supposed to be solving, not creating a mystery.'

Sam sighed. 'I know.'

She picked up the key. It just was an ordinary door key. She bent over the note again. 'Hah! Maggie, this is a *cryptic* clue.'

'I know, dear. It's all very cryptic.'

'No. Most of it is straightforward; it's obscure but directly translatable. The last sentence though is an actual cryptic clue.' Sam held up the key. 'And I bet *this* will open the answer to the clue.'

'That much I did work out,' Maggie stated. 'It's obviously the key to the clue.'

'No, it's the key to the answer. 'Thomas' is the key to the clue. But who is Thomas?' She picked up her beer.

'I have no idea what you're talking about.'

Sam sat bolt upright and loudly gulped the mouthful she'd taken. 'Yes! 'Sweet bugger all' is the answer. Oh Maggie, this is really clever,' she said admiringly. 'It's *Clarreguf.*'

'Really? You sound like you've got whooping cough.'

'It's Welsh, Maggie. It's *Dylan* Thomas. And the word 'back' tells us to reverse the letters of 'bugger all'. Have you got a pen?'

Maggie found a pencil in her bag and Sam wrote the word 'Llareggub' on a paper napkin. 'Bugger all, backwards,' she said. 'It's the name of the town in Dylan Thomas's *Under Milkwood.*'

'Oh. And all this time I thought the name of Lloyd's retreat was pronounced *Lara-gub*.'

'What retreat?' Sam asked.

'Lloyd had a little mud brick cottage that his sister left him when she died 15 years ago. It's in Eltham.'

Sam held up the key again. 'This will open the answer to the clue,' she repeated.

# Chapter Eleven

Melbourne, Sunday September 20, 1998

'SAM? YO, SAM.' JACQUI TAPPED HER FINGER ON THE KITCHEN TABLE.

'Go away, Jac, or at least be quiet. Please. It's too early.' Sam remained motionless, her head resting on the crook of her arm on the table.

'Why are you up?' Jacqui poured herself a coffee from the pot and refilled Sam's mug.

Sam opened one eye, then sat up before opening the other one. '*What* are you wearing?'

'Reuben's long johns,' Jacqui replied, turning to show off the *USS Detroit* stamp on the back.

'You're wearing a gay sailor's underwear?'

'Cool aren't they?' Jacqui said adjusting the sleeves.

Change the subject, Sam thought. 'So, how did your date with Ben go on Friday night?'

'It was great. Last night too. We all went to an amazing party.'

'Who all?'

'Ben and me and Reuben, and Josh, Peter, Leo, James and Elvira.'

'Elvira?'

'Yeah. His real name is Brandon but he's Elvira when he's all frocked up.'

'I'm sure he is,' Sam said. 'You took Ben, my Ben, out with a bunch of gay boys?'

Jacqui gave Sam her best 'which planet are you from?' look. 'On Friday *I* took Ben out with a bunch of gay boys. Last night *your* Ben and *his* Elvira took *me* to a warehouse party.'

'I knew I shouldn't have got up this morning,' Sam groaned.

'Well, go back to bed. Try getting up when you're less grumpy.'

'I'm not grumpy, I'm gobsmacked.'

'You don't need to get all self-analytical about why your famous intuition failed you or you weren't astute enough to work out your partner was gay. Ben wasn't sure himself, until he met Brandon.'

'I was *not* questioning my prodigious powers of perception,' Sam lied. 'I was wondering what Ben's going to do when his American sailor heads for ports unknown.'

'Brandon's not an American sailor, he's a Melbourne architect. He lives in Yarraville,' Jacqui said. 'Now, are you going to tell me why you're up so early on a Sunday?'

'I've got a date with an archaeologist for breakfast, and I'm trying to figure out what–'

'To do with your life?' Jacqui interrupted. 'Honestly Samantha! Breakfast is what you do *after* you've had the date and spent the night together.'

Sam scowled at her sister. 'It's a business breakfast and *Maggie* is not that kind of date.'

'Oh. What are trying to figure out then?'

'Maggie has provided some *possibly* relevant information about this case I'm working, but she's asked that I keep it to myself, or between us, until *we* check it out.'

'So? What's wrong with that?'

'Nothing. Everything. I'm a cop, I can't withhold information from the investigating team.'

'I dunno, Sam. It seems to me you'd better check out this *possible* lead with this Maggie person rather than calling the squad in too early,' Jacqui advised seriously. 'Your detective mates might get really pissed off if they have to inspect another crate of stone penises.'

'Bloody Muldoon,' Sam laughed. 'I am *never* going to live that down. But you're right about this lead, Jac. They can wait till I verify it.'

Sam scanned the Regency Hotel's dining room and saw: Marcus Bridger breakfasting with Enrico Vasquez at a table by the window; Adrienne, in sunglasses, sitting alone; Barstoc with a newspaper, also alone; and – no Maggie.

Oh. On second glance, she just hadn't recognised Maggie Tremaine who was sitting, with another woman, on the far side of the room. This morning Maggie was dressed much the same as Sam, in jeans and a cotton shirt, but it was her neat, elegantly brushed-back hair that made her all but unrecognisable.

'Good morning Sam,' Maggie said cheerfully, as Sam pulled out a chair. 'This is my dear friend Julia Cooper. Julia this is Special Detective Sam Diamond of the ACB.'

Sam shook Julia's hand. 'Are you *Dr* Cooper, curator of the Indigenous Cultures Program?'

'That's me,' Julia said.

'I have a bone to pick with you, Sam,' Maggie stated, as she spread Vegemite on her toast.

'With me, why?'

'You might have told me last night that I looked like I was wearing a fright wig.'

Sam shrugged apologetically. 'My sister does things like that to her hair on purpose.'

'Oh, well, just so you know, *this* is the real me. Last night I had some kind of static reaction to my new hair dryer, or the lift coming down from my room, or something. Okay?'

'Yes, Maggie,' Sam said.

'We've just been talking about poor Lloyd,' Julia said.

Sam flashed a warning glance at Maggie and then turned to the waitress who had appeared at the table. 'Eggs Benedict and black coffee, please.'

'It's okay,' Maggie said. 'I haven't divulged anything I shouldn't.'

'I've been doing most of the talking,' Julia assured Sam. 'I was saying how surprised I was to learn that Lloyd was going to Peru. We had lunch together a couple of weeks ago and he made no mention of it.'

'It seems he only decided last week,' Sam stated.

Julia shook her head slowly. 'That's what I find unusual. Lloyd planned his trips meticulously, for weeks in advance. And he was usually excited and voluble, even if he was going somewhere he'd been before. It was always a new adventure but everything *had* to be perfect.'

'Lloyd hated surprises,' Maggie stated.

'Were you and Marsden friends, Julia?'

'Yes, I suppose we were. Lloyd was a dear old soul but he wasn't the sort of person you'd invite over for a Sunday barbecue. Well, you would, but he'd never come. But at work, yes, we were more than colleagues. We had lunch once a month and he was always generous with his advice or assistance.'

'You look puzzled, Sam,' Maggie commented.

'I'm a little confused about Museum politics.'

Maggie and Julia burst into laughter.

'Okay,' Sam acknowledged, 'I suppose it's no different to any other organisation. But it seems odd, given the inter-department rivalry, that there's so much generous collaboration between the curators of those different departments.'

'There's actually very little inter-department rivalry,' Maggie said. 'It's usually much more personal than that.'

'Absolutely,' Julia agreed. 'It rarely comes down to Indigenous Cultures versus Technology in Society. It's more likely, for instance, to be me arguing a new policy, or Maggie battling Daley over some idiotic red tape, or three or four researchers competing for a limited pool of money.'

'Or Professor Marsden disagreeing with the restructure,' Sam suggested.

'Exactly. Lloyd felt he'd been personally betrayed. And not because his collection wasn't to be included but because his whole world, the Museum, was changing,' Julia explained.

'Despite all that, the Professor was still willing to join the ICOM committee, be liaison for this visiting exhibition, and give you and anyone else advice and assistance.'

'Lloyd didn't have a vindictive bone in his body,' Maggie said. 'It's hard to explain but although he felt personally betrayed he didn't take it personally. Sometimes I think he argued about things simply because he thought someone should. It was his way of ensuring that every conceivable angle of something had been properly thought through.'

'What about his rivalry with Haddon Gould?' Sam asked.

'That stupid posturing peacock!' Julia exclaimed. 'Excuse me, but any *rivalry* between those two was all in Haddon's otherwise unimaginative little mind. Although I suspect his antagonism towards Lloyd actually had nothing to with the Museum, at least not originally.'

'Do you have any idea what caused it?'

'No, I just got the impression it wasn't professional jealousy, that it was *really* personal.'

'Marsden apparently had quite a disagreement with Enrico Vasquez, from the touring exhibition, about the repatriation of cultural artefacts,' Sam said. 'Was he genuinely against the idea or was that something else to argue about just for the sake of it?'

'Oh no, he was dead against it,' Maggie stated, 'depending on the circumstances. He considered his own collection to be unreturnable, not because he was selfish so much but because who the hell would he return it to? The Incas? The Aztecs? He would mount the same argument in defence of say ancient Egyptian artefacts. 'That culture is dead and gone', he would say.'

Julia picked up her coffee. 'On the other hand, he acknowledged without hesitation that the Museum's collection of indigenous artefacts come from a people as old as the human race itself but *belongs* to a living culture. And this was an attitude he held even before he discovered, only 10 years ago, that his great-grandmother was a Koori.'

'So he was in favour of the return of Aboriginal cultural property?' Sam asked.

'Oh yes. In fact since discovering his own heritage he also took an active, though limited, role in the curatorial assistance that we offer Aboriginal cultural centres around the state. On occasion this included the management of cultural material we have on loan to those centres.'

'On loan?' Sam leant back so the waitress could place her breakfast on the table and thanked her before continuing. 'So you don't actually give things back?'

'Yes we do,' Julia said. 'It's our policy to return all human remains and secret/sacred objects on request. Once we verify that it is being returned to the right people it is repatriated permanently. We then offer that community our expertise should *they* want any further work or documentation done on those remains or objects. Some do, some don't. Appropriate and respectful management of secret/sacred material is one of our highest priorities. But we also have a huge collection of other cultural material that we lend to Aboriginal centres or museums.'

'Mind you,' Maggie said, 'this is a recent innovation. Our Museum has long been renowned for its collections relating to indigenous Australians but, as is the case with institutions the world over, those human remains, sacred objects and artefacts were *acquired* and donated by white anthropologists and collectors. It's only been in the last 15 years that Aboriginal people have had an active role in the Museum and a say in the proper and respectful management of the collections.'

'And believe it or not,' Julia added, 'the bulk of that *renowned* collection came from anthropological work carried out in northern and central Australia. Until the Museum began employing Koori staff in the early 80s there had been very little research of our own Victorian Aboriginal culture.'

Sam shrugged. 'That's not so odd, when you think about. How often would any of us take a sightseeing tour of Melbourne, unless we were showing our city off to visiting friends. It's almost like when it's right under your nose it's not exotic or worth investigating.'

'It's hardly the same thing,' Julia stated, taking offence. 'The history of this city and state is well documented, yet we barely rate a mention.'

'I'm not disputing that, Julia, and I certainly didn't mean to be insulting. But it's a fact that the white settlement of Melbourne was chronicled by white people who were completely ignorant and uncaring of the impact they had on your ancestors. And when they recorded their daily lives, those settlers were concerned with their own stories, hardships and achievements – not yours. It was always up to you to be the ones to tell your own story – no one else could do it justice. It may have taken over 160 years to be heard, but in the last 15 or so you've gone from being the subjects of a museum collection to being the researchers, caretakers and managers of your own culture and history. That has to be pretty unique in the world.'

'The Museum *is* a leader in how it works with the indigenous community,' Maggie stated.

'You're quite right,' Julia smiled. 'I'm sorry I snapped, but I am wary of people's attitudes so I tend to bite when perhaps I shouldn't.'

'Please don't apologise. I'd be doing a hell of a lot snapping if I were you,' Sam said. 'Speaking of change though, wasn't there a special ceremony before work on the new Museum began? I seem to remember the Premier being presented with something that symbolised the collaboration of the Koori community and the Government.'

Julia smiled in surprise. 'Yes, it was a cleansing of the site for the Museum's Aboriginal Centre with smoking fires, music and dancing. The Wurundjeri people, the traditional land owners of Melbourne, organised it and the Elders presented the Premier with a Message Stick and invited him and the Museum President to share water. You've got an amazing memory, Sam, for something that doesn't directly concern you. That was nearly two years ago.'

Sam shrugged. 'I am blessed, though it often feels like a curse, with an eidetic memory. Consequently I have a very eclectic store of info up here,' she explained, tapping her head.

'That must be useful in your line of work,' Maggie noted.

'It is, but you've no idea the amount of litter I pick up along the way. For instance a completely useless fact that I've been carrying around for 10 years, is that a petty crook I arrested for burglary had a girlfriend called Marge who collected matchbooks. Now, I never met Marge, never saw her collection and matchbooks are not an unusual thing to collect, so *why* do I need to remember that? Or the entire contents of a bookie's briefcase that I inspected 1987?'

'What was in it?' Maggie asked intrigued.

'A pack of Marlboro, a bottle of Brut aftershave, an address book, *three* nail clippers, a return plane ticket to Brisbane, a Surfer's Paradise postcard from his wife, Shirley, $1837 in cash, an unregistered Colt .45 and 13 bullets.'

'Good heavens, it's a wonder you can remember ordinary things, like where you live, with all that clutter in your brain,' Maggie laughed, although she seemed to be distracted by something going on behind Sam. 'Good morning Phineas,' she said.

'Good morning *Margaret*,' he replied pointedly, 'Detective Diamond, and...'

'Julia Cooper,' Julia replied, offering her hand.

Sam noticed that Julia seemed to be fighting to hide any outward signs of the romance-novel reaction that she'd experienced on meeting Marcus Bridger. Sam was relieved she wasn't alone in this regard, although now she worried it might be a virus.

'May I join you for a moment? There is something I would like to ask Detective Diamond,' Bridger said.

'Sit, Marcus,' Maggie commanded waving at the empty chair.

Bridger did just that and turned immediately to face Sam. 'This may seem an unusual request Detective, and I apologise for being so forward, but would you do me the honour of being my guest at a formal dinner we are hosting this evening?'

'Your guest?' Sam repeated, mostly because it was all she could manage.

'Yes. If it is not appropriate, given the circumstances, I understand but I don't know anyone in Melbourne and to be perfectly honest I am tired of attending such functions alone.'

'Um, I don't know—'

'She'd love to,' Maggie interrupted. 'Don't look at me like that, Sam. Half the Museum staff are going to be there, so you can pretend it's work related if you want to. Besides your offsider will be there as *my* escort for the night, so you may as well join us.'

Bridger gave Maggie a look that said he could manage his own business thank you very much, and Sam gave her a look that said mind your own business.

'What?' Maggie asked looking from one to the other.

'I would love to, Dr Bridger,' Sam finally said.

'Splendid,' Bridger exclaimed. 'If you write down your address I will pick you up at 6 pm.'

Sam wrote her address and home phone number on the back of one of her business cards, all the while thinking how stupid it was to pretend this was work-related, or even a vaguely sensible thing to do in the middle of an investigation. You can't date a possible suspect, Sam, she told herself, even if you're the only one who suspects him. She handed him the card.

'My god,' Julia exclaimed after Bridger left the table. 'What a gorgeous specimen that was.'

'Now girls, control yourselves,' Maggie teased. 'I will tell you now, before either of you get too charmed by his er, attributes, that Marcus Bridger is as arrogant as an English Setter and not nearly as clever or faithful.'

'Who cares!' Julia stated. 'If you can't make the date for any reason, Sam, give me a call.'

'It's not a date,' Sam emphasised. 'Maggie, did you say that Rivers is escorting you tonight?'

'Not in so many words, but yes, the delicious young Hercules is *my* date for the night.'

# Chapter Twelve

Trees, Sam thought with delight. She wound down her window to let the smell of wattle and eucalypts flow through Maggie's hire car as they turned off Eltham's unimaginatively named Main Road. 'I'd forgotten how beautiful it is out here,' she said.

One of Melbourne's outer suburbs, Eltham was surrounded by inner and outer-outer suburbia but managed to retain its natural beauty. Artists had settled in the area in the 1920s and 30s to escape the growing city and to capture on canvas the unique light and colours of the Australian bush landscape. Artists, bohemians and hippies had been followed by others seeking an alternative or country lifestyle, who built here because of the environment and still fought to keep housing developers or rampant construction at bay.

'I just love the peace and quiet,' Maggie agreed. 'It's hard to believe we're only 20 kilometres from the city centre and that there are houses somewhere in amongst all these trees.' She made a right turn onto a dirt road, then another onto a narrow, deeply rutted track. Half a kilometre later, she stopped and waited while Sam opened a gate on which hung a rusty metal sign bearing the number four.

Sam closed the gate again after Maggie had driven through and then followed on foot, around a sharp bend and into a small clearing where a mud brick cottage sat looking like it had literally grown out of the surrounding bush. Maggie was already out of the car and waiting patiently by the front door which was engraved with the name 'Llareggub'.

'This is ridiculous,' Maggie said, slipping the key in the lock, 'I've been here a hundred times but I feel like we've just discovered a long-lost tomb.'

The door opened into a confined space lined with shoes, and crowded with coats on a wall rack. Maggie picked up a torch from a shelf, whacked it on the wall to get it working and then opened the interior door.

'Hang on while I brighten things up a bit,' she suggested, using the dying torch to pick her way across the dark room. 'What are we looking for exactly?'

'Well, the note said 'return to the finder from the words of the bard',' Sam reminded her. 'So I'd say we're looking for a copy of Shakespeare. That shouldn't be too hard.'

Sam heard the sound of a match being struck, then slowly the room seemed to come alive, with the furniture apparently moving as the light grew around her, beginning with a dim flicker along the walls and ending with a flash above her head.

'Oops, sorry,' Maggie said. 'I think I turned it up too high.'

'Gas lighting?' Sam said, inspecting the lamp on the wall.

'Oh yes, Lloyd's got all the mod cons.'

'Oh my god,' Sam breathed, facing the room. 'We could be here for weeks. This isn't a tomb, it's the long lost repository of a committed bibliophile.'

She stared open-mouthed at the thousands of books that were crammed into the shelves that lined the room and overflowed into piles that covered the floor.

The room was large but even without the books would have been crowded. A huge desk, filing cabinet, a small table with an old Remington typewriter, and a large free-standing globe were arranged in a semi-circle in front of a small bay window with drawn curtains. A few steps away, two raggedy armchairs, a couch and a coffee table were set up in front of a huge open fireplace. Between them and where Sam was still standing near the door was a cedar dinning table with eight chairs and, against the wall behind them, an antique dresser and a wardrobe.

'I'm afraid to ask how many rooms there are,' Sam said.

'This one, two bedrooms, a bathroom, an enclosed verandah out the back, and the kitchen through there,' Maggie pointed to a door behind her. 'But the books are mostly in here.'

'Thank heaven for small mercies,' Sam stated. 'Pick your spot, Maggie. I'll start here,' she added, taking a seat at the dining table to go through the books that covered it.

Maggie sat down at the desk. 'You know, the more I think about your smuggling theory, the more far-fetched it seems.'

'I *know* it's far fetched. My so-called clue was icing sugar and the search at the airport was an embarrassing waste of time but the coincidences are just too–'

'Coincidental?' Maggie suggested.

'Yes,' Sam agreed testily. 'But the timing of the Exhibition and the influx of cocaine in Melbourne and those other cities *has* to be more than coincidence.'

'Perhaps,' Maggie agreed, rifling through the desk drawers, 'but you keep adding two and two together and then trying to justify that the answer keeps coming out at five.'

'That's because I haven't found the missing 'one' yet.'

'Think about it, Sam. You already knew about the cocaine, then you found a suspicious substance that turned out to be innocent, and you carried out a search that found nothing yet you're still trying to fit the facts of these two unrelated cases together. Are you sure you're not trying to make too much out of a simple murder?' Maggie rolled her chair across to the nearest bookshelf and began checking the titles on the spines.

'I don't think so, besides a simple murder is a rare thing,' Sam said. 'Bingo! A copy of *Macbeth,*' she exclaimed. She flicked through the pages, shook the book, started from the beginning again to look more carefully and found nothing.

'What I mean,' Maggie said, 'is that, logically, there is no reason to believe that Marcus's show has anything to do with smuggling. If you forget the cocaine thing and take the investigation of the itinerary in a different direction you'd probably find it also coincides with archaeological symposiums, touring rock concerts or strange weather patterns.'

'Or hit and run accidents, gallery fires, museum robberies and hijackings,' Sam reminded her.

'Exactly. Odd things indeed, but they happen all the time. I'm sure young Hercules could search the internet and match the itinerary with mysterious crop circles or alien abductions.'

Sam laughed. 'I get your point. But if Marsden's death is so simple why would he cryptically ask you to check the "odyssey of Ouroboros". And, more to the point, *why* are we here?' Sam moved over to tackle the books on the coffee table and the floor around the couch.

'Given the circumstances I admit it's unlikely, but perhaps we should consider that his murder is not related to this; whatever this is we're looking for here.'

'Now *that* is far-fetched. "If you are reading this my fears have been realised. I am no more",' Sam quoted.

'Yes yes,' Maggie acknowledged. 'But tell me what you know about Lloyd.'

'He was dedicated, professional, generous, argumentative, not very social and obviously loved a good mystery,' Sam stated. 'And I've found a Complete Works.'

'Me too.' Maggie sat down on the floor to reach the leather bound book on the bottom shelf.

'Find anything yet?' asked Sam, turning the pages carefully.

'No. Getting back to Lloyd; he was also practical, analytical, and usually quite down to earth, except that he believed strongly in premonitions, of which he claimed to have had more than a few,' Maggie continued, as she too flicked the pages. 'He was also scared of flying. He may have had a premonition that he wouldn't make it home from Peru.'

'That might be a workable theory if he had left the package for you with his lawyer a year or 10 years ago and not, coincidentally, in the same week he turned up murdered.'

'I suppose,' Maggie muttered, fiddling with some pages that appeared to be stuck together. She prised the top corner away and discovered the entire mid-section of the book had been glued to conceal the cut-out hiding place of a long narrow, black box.

Maggie lifted the hinged lid and stared in disbelief at the contents. She glanced at Sam and, making what she hoped was the right decision for the time being, removed the long and heavy object. She slipped it into her pocket and closed the box again.

'I've found something, Sam,' she said excitedly. 'A secret compartment, with a box.'

'What's in the box?' Sam asked leaping up to join her.

'Oh. Nothing,' Maggie lied dejectedly, standing to place the heavy book on the desk.

The box, about 16 centimetres long by six wide and lined with red velvet, was indeed empty. Sam reached over and removed it from the cavity in the book. Underneath was a small printed card. It read:

*Talk to Hamlet's late messengers.*

'Bloody hell,' Sam complained. 'This is never ending.'

'I wonder what the box was for.' Maggie tried to sound innocently curious.

'Well, unless someone beat us to it,' Sam said, 'it's my guess the box is a decoy to hide this latest clue. We are now, I think, looking for a copy of *Rozencrantz and Guildenstern are Dead.*'

'Oh great,' Maggie said, turning back to the shelves. She felt awful but it was obvious there was a hell of a lot more to all of this than just Lloyd's murder.

Sam returned to the couch. 'You know, what with the murder, exotic poisons, sabotage fantasies, and all this literary legerdemain I feel like I'm being dragged into a cliché.'

'A what?' Maggie asked. 'Found it,' she added, waving a copy of Stoppard's play.

'A B-grade movie cliché; one of those dangerous *webs* of murder, deception and intrigue.'

'Well,' Maggie laughed, 'I think it just became an *international* cliché.' She collapsed onto the couch next to Sam. 'Unless of course this is just a bookmark.' She handed Sam an envelope, addressed to Marsden and posted from Cairo on the May 28, 1998.

Sam lifted the flap and removed a piece of cardboard, on which was taped a key. 'It looks like a safety deposit box key,' she said. 'Oh, and this is useful.' She removed the only other thing in the envelope. 'A postcard of the Nile Hilton. Just what we need.' She turned it over to find yet another enigmatic message, this time scrawled in purple ink:

*Safe no more. Inform MM. Am going to seek the finder.*

*N.W.*

Sam growled. 'This is getting tedious. Who the hell are MM and the finder? Marsden's note also said: 'safe no more' and 'return to the finder'.

Maggie shook her head. 'I don't know, but N.W. could be Noel Winslow. He's a mystery writer and an old friend of ours. He lives in Cairo but it could take a bit to track him down.'

'Where do we start?' Sam asked.

'The telephone. There *is* one here, somewhere. Lloyd could do without power but not a phone.'

Sam glanced around the room and then stood up. 'The phone plug,' she said, following the cord along the wall, under one of the armchairs, around the leg of the desk to the window seat, where she found the phone buried under a pile of magazines. 'Who do I call first?'

'The international operator for the number of the Cairo Museum.' Maggie wandered over to sit in the desk chair. 'You'd better check what time it is there too.'

Sam did as suggested and wrote the number on a notepad by the lamp. 'It's 5 am today. It's a bit early to be calling anyone. But if this guy's a writer why are you calling the museum?' Sam pushed some of the piles aside so she could sit down on the window seat but then had to cope with a landslide of magazines as she tried to move something hard that was jabbing her in the leg.

'Noel is also an anthropologist but he found he was a much better fiction writer than he was a scientist. So he combined the two passions of his life into a series of anthropological detective novels. The last time I saw him he was still doing some consultancy work at the Cairo Museum so Ahmed Kamel, one of the curators, may know where to find him. Noel might, however, be off researching his next book, so he could be in Turkey or South America or god knows where.'

'Manco City,' Sam said.

'Never heard of it,' Maggie said absently, as she flicked through

Marsden's address book. 'But then I suppose Noel is writing fiction so anything is possible. What made you suggest that?' she asked, finally looking up to find Sam holding a picture frame.

'This. It seems to be a picture of a bunch of people standing in a place you've never heard of.' Sam turned the frame around. 'It says Manco City 1962. There was one of these in the Professor's office but the picture was missing.'

'How very odd.' Maggie studied the photograph in which 16 people, men and women, had posed to record what was apparently a significant event. They were standing or kneeling, in three rows, in front of a stone archway through which could be seen the overgrown ruins of a multitude of buildings. The camera had captured a variety of expressions in that moment in time, but there was no doubt they were all extremely pleased with themselves.

'Do you know any of them?' Sam asked.

'Yes, I worked with some of them the year before this was taken, and with various combinations of them at other times since.'

Maggie pointed to a young man standing in the back row. 'That's Lloyd. He would have been 29 years old. Good-looking wasn't he? Next to him is Noel Winslow; in front of them is Jean McBride – she recently retired from the museum in Edinburgh. Beside her is Alistair Nash, the friend I told you about who died in the car crash; and that bear of a man looking smug on the end there is Pavel Mercier. He's–'

'The author of *Anthropomorphic Entities and the Andean Supernatural Realm,*' Sam said. 'I saw it in the Professor's office,' she added, in answer to Maggie's questioning look.

'The weird thing,' Maggie continued, 'is that I don't know where this photo was taken. There really is no such place as Manco City. Unless... 1962?' she asked herself. 'Unless they *thought* they'd found Vilcabamba.'

'What's that?'

'Do you know anything about the Inca?'

Sam shrugged. 'Just what I learnt in primary school.'

'Ah well, make yourself comfortable Sam, but do tell me if you think I'm just rambling on like Daley Prescott,' Maggie smiled.

'In 1532 the Spanish led by Pizarro conquered the Incas at Cajamarca, held the 13th and reigning king, Atahualpa, to ransom for a room full of gold; and then executed him anyway on the spurious charge of treason. Their conquest succeeded for two reasons. One was horses and superior weaponry, the other was the fact that Tahuantinsuyu itself was in political turmoil.'

'Tahuantinsuyu?' Sam queried.

'The Incas called their empire Tahuantinsuyu or 'Land of the Four Quarters'. It was an administrative name referring to four huge sectors, aligned to the cardinal points and arranged around Cuzco, the capital. The word was also symbolic of the immense size of the empire which included modern-day Peru and vast areas of what is now Ecuador, Bolivia, Chile and Argentina.

'Prior to his death Huayna Capac, the 11th Inca, divided the empire between his two sons, giving the north around Quito, which is now in Ecuador, to his bastard son Atahualpa, and the south around Cuzco to the rightful heir, Huascar.

'The sibling rivalry of these two kings degenerated into a fratricidal civil war of which Atahualpa emerged victorious, after drowning his half-brother – just before the arrival of the conquistadors. So, although Atahualpa had reunited Tahuantinsuyu, there was resentment amongst the Incas of Cuzco who believed Huascar was the rightful king.

'Pizarro took advantage of that, *and* enlisted the support of Indian tribes who had been subjugated by the Inca, so that when he and his tiny army, of only 168 Spanish soldiers, marched on Cajamarca they were actually accompanied by a great many Indian auxiliaries.

'As I said before, Atahualpa was put to death but Pizarro recognised the advantages of having an Inca ruler under Spanish control, to ensure the obedience of the native people, so he enthroned one of Atahualpa's younger brothers as Sapa Inca.

'When this child-king was poisoned, Pizarro appointed Manco Capac, the brother of Huascar, as 15th Sapa Inca. This was a smart move because the Incas of Cuzco opened their gates to the invading Spaniards, believing them to be liberators because they had defeated Atahualpa, and restored the rightful Inca line.

'Manco Capac, who by the way is the father of that *dude* Tupac Amaru that Hercules mentioned last night, was given his own palace, the conquistadors took over most of the other Inca palaces in Cuzco, and things were relatively peaceful in the empire for about three years. In fact when Quisquis, one of Atahualpa's surviving loyal generals, tried to invade Cuzco the Spanish *and* Manco Capac's Inca warriors fought side by side to drive him back beyond Quito. Am I boring you yet, Sam?'

'No, not at all.'

'Good. Apart from looting the empire of all the gold they could find, the Spanish began dividing up the Land of the Four Quarters between themselves, becoming governors of regions that would later become Peru, Chile, Bolivia and Ecuador. When Manco realised the Spanish were never going to leave his land, he escaped from the city, rallied tens of thousands of Inca warriors and laid siege to Cuzco for 12 months. When Spanish reinforcements arrived, Manco and about 20,000 followers retreated to the central Andes of Peru from where they continued to provoke uprisings.

'Manco founded a new Inca capital in a region of almost impenetrable jungle northwest of Cuzco, where he built a city called Vilcabamba. He fought the invaders for nine years before being murdered by a supposed ally. Three of his sons, in succession, ruled Vilcabamba and waged irregular guerilla warfare for three decades.

'In 1572 a large Spanish force set out to destroy Vilcabamba but the Incas set fire to and abandoned the city. However the last Sapa Inca, Tupac Amaru, was captured and taken back to Cuzco where he was put through a show trial and beheaded in the town square.'

'What happened to Vilcabamba?' Sam asked.

'The jungle reclaimed it and it became the stuff of legends – a lost city, the last stronghold of the last Inca kings.'

Sam tapped the photograph. 'And *you* don't think this Manco City is Vilcabamba?'

'Maggie shook her head. 'Not unless Pavel, and all the people in this photo, decided *not* to tell the world of their discovery. Archaeologists had been looking for the city since the 1830s. Hiram Bingham thought he'd found it when he discovered Machu Picchu in 1911. In fact he almost *did* find it but his guides wouldn't take him further than Espíritu Pampa – the Plain of Ghosts.

'In 1964, two years *after* this photo was taken, an American explorer named Gene Savoy retraced Bingham's steps to Espíritu Pampa but went just a bit further and actually found the lost city of Vilcabamba. The ruins covered two square miles and were, in turn, covered in trees and vines.'

'So where do you suppose this picture was taken?' Sam asked.

'I've no idea. It's definitely Inca architecture though, the stonework is unmistakable. I know Pavel's team found a couple of ceremonial centres northwest of Machu Picchu in 1962. Maybe they *did* think this one was Vilcabamba, or Manco's city, but further research proved them wrong.'

'Why weren't you with them?' Sam asked.

'I was in Luxor. I went into archaeology because of a passion for all things Egyptian but in 1961 Jean McBride asked me to travel with her to meet up with an expedition she was joining in Peru. I ended up staying for the duration, becoming enthralled with that part of the world and its history and consequently changing the course of my life. I blame Pavel entirely for that. But I had to finish some work in Luxor in 1962 before I could embrace my new passion and all the study that went with it.'

'That explains *An Interlude in Hatshepsut's Kitchen,*' Sam smiled.

Maggie laughed. 'I would kill for a memory like yours, Sam.'

'I would kill for a cup of coffee.'

'Well if you think we've found all there is to find here, we may as well head back to town.' Maggie checked her watch. 'You'll have most of the afternoon to get ready for your date.'

'It is *not* a date, Maggie.'

'Whatever you say, dear.'

'Oh please don't. My sister Jacqui gives me that look when she thinks *she* knows better.'

'Perhaps she does, Sam. Does she share your gift for remembering things?'

'No, she shares my house. We couldn't be more different. She dresses like a tart, goes out with gay sailors and reads romances. I'm still trying to work out which of us was switched at birth.'

'Interesting,' Maggie commented. 'I think I'd like to meet her sometime.'

'Oh no you wouldn't,' Sam insisted, 'she's quite deranged.'

# Chapter Thirteen

Melbourne, September 20, 1998

Sam had tried on her entire wardrobe three times before finally settling on a close-fitting, elegant black cocktail number with a dark purple flash that began discreetly at the waist on the right hand side and swept around to the hemline at the front. Shoes were going to be a problem though; she hadn't worn heels in three years.

'Well, well, so you *are* a girl,' Jacqui said from the doorway.

'I'm surprised you can tell the difference any more, Jac,' Sam returned.

'Funny. Where are you going on a Sunday dressed liked that?'

'I've got a date with an archaeologist.'

Jacqui raised an eyebrow. 'I thought you said whats-her-name wasn't that sort of date.'

'She isn't. This is a different archaeologist. Ah, the doorbell. Would you let him in while I finish.'

Jacqui disappeared but returned moments later, her eyes wide. 'Sam. There is *the* most gorgeous man standing in our lounge room.'

'Well don't leave him all by himself, Jacqui. I'll only be a minute.'

'I wouldn't know what to say to him.'

You and me both, Sam thought. 'Ask him about his exhibition,' she suggested; which is exactly what Sam did the moment she was alone with Marcus Bridger in his car.

Discussion of his show maintained the conversation almost all the way to the Regency. And Rigby had been right, Bridger *did* know the right people to ask about getting his exhibits on an earlier flight from Paris.

'I'm quite passionate about de-accessioning,' Bridger said in response to Sam's question about where he stood on the issue of the return of cultural property. 'It's my belief that countries should be in possession of their own cultural heritage. But there are still museum curators and private collectors all over the world who, inexplicably, believe they have the right to horde the treasures and artefacts of cultures not their own.'

'What happens with something like Inca artefacts though? *Whoa!* Watch out,' Sam cried as Bridger took too sharp a turn into the hotel's carpark, narrowly missing the booth.

'Sorry,' he apologised, though he looked more shaken by the near miss than Sam did. 'I've spent the last couple of months driving on the other side of the road. You were saying?'

'If the Inca Empire encompassed what is now five different South American countries, which one do you return the cultural material to?'

'That situation does pose a dilemma. The same applies to relics from the Persian Empire which at its height extended from Iran to India and Europe. And I'm not suggesting museums give everything back. Rightful ownership would have to be verified. But why are you interested in Inca artefacts?'

'I'm not really,' Sam fibbed, as they got out of the car. 'It's just that Marsden was dead against returning any of his Andean antiquities. And Maggie has been in Paris mediating a dispute between museums in Chile and Peru over the ownership of an Inca artefact – which was subsequently hijacked.'

Bridger laughed. 'Ah, the now infamous "Inca trinket fiasco". That dispute, even before the theft, indicated the concept of returning cultural property is saddled with a host of problems. If Peru and Chile can't agree on who really owns a bracelet that one of them already possesses, then you can imagine how hard it is to make decisions about the collections held by foreign institutions.'

'So do you advocate returning only those things that are requested?' Sam asked.

'Yes. Doing anything else would be nigh on impossible, but doing anything less would be unenlightened. Don't you think?' Bridger ushered Sam into the lift.

'Oh I agree,' Sam said. 'But what about the argument that if all Inca artefacts were returned then the rest of the world would be denied easy access to the remnants of an incredible civilisation?'

'That's where exhibitions like mine become so important,' Bridger stated. '*The Rites of Life and Death* features treasures from all over the world, mostly on loan from their places of origin. My aim is to take the world to the world. More people have seen some of the Hindu relics that were lent to our show *after* their return to India, than ever saw them in the museum in London.'

'I know that's true, Marcus,' Sam said. 'I was entranced by the Gold of the Pharaohs exhibition that came here a few years ago, partly because I knew it might be as close as I'd ever get to Egypt.'

Bridger smiled. 'I was lucky. My father was also an archaeologist, so my entire childhood was submerged by other times and places.'

'You know,' Sam caught her breath as Bridger's hand brushed against the small of her back to direct her from the lift to the reception room. 'You know,' she repeated, 'I come across people from all walks of life during my investigations but I have to say I have never met a group who, collectively and individually, are as passionate about their work as you all seem to be.'

'It gets in your blood,' Marcus stated. 'It's not work, it's much more than a job, it's a life.'

'In your case, Marcus, it really is in the blood. Your career choice seems to be inherited.'

'Yes, my father's passion for his life's work was quite inspiring. He once organised a protest, long before the 60s made it popular, to prevent a golf course being built next to a sacred site. But I feel *I* have to say, and I don't mean to sound old-fashioned Sam, that *your* career choice seems a strange one for a woman.'

Sam shrugged; she was accustomed to this attitude. 'I've always loved figuring things out, solving puzzles. In a sense, Marcus, our work is similar. We're both detectives rummaging around in the lives of dead people. Mine just happen to be more recently dead than yours.'

'True,' Marcus acknowledged. 'I've never thought of it like that, and I admit I never thought it strange that women wanted to be archaeologists. Speaking of driven professional women, is that your young constable with Maggie? I thought she meant the older detective was escorting her.'

Sam snorted. 'Jack? He wouldn't be seen dead at a shindig like this.' She looked over at Maggie and Rivers who were seated at a large table with Prescott, Adrienne, Andrew Barstoc, the dreaded Enrico Vasquez, Robert Ellington and three people Sam had never seen before. Glancing around the other tables in the intimate dining room she recognised several museum staff, including Peter Gilchrist and Anton, as well as people she'd seen working at the Exhibition Building.

There were two spaces left at the main table, between Rivers and Adrienne. Bridger, ever the gentleman, pulled Sam's chair out for her before sitting down himself.

Ellington introduced Sam to his wife Miriam, and to Joan Harris, head of Museum PR, and her husband Paul. 'I believe you know everyone else.'

'We're so pleased you could join us, Sam,' Adrienne smiled, although she'd given Bridger what could only be described as a filthy look.

'Sam dear, you look stunning,' Maggie stated.

'And you look like a million dollars,' Sam said, admiring Maggie's gold silk frock-coat.

'Not quite a million, but it was the only thing I splurged on while in Paris.'

'Any progress on the case, Detective Diamond?' Prescott asked.

'He's already tried me,' Rivers muttered to Sam.

'This is a social evening, Mr Prescott. Officially, I am *not* here.'

'Ah yes, of course,' Prescott murmured, his immaculate exterior barely concealing his impatience; or his curiosity as to why, in fact, Sam *was* there.

When the drink waitress arrived to take orders Sam motioned to Rivers to lean back a little so she could address Maggie. 'Did you manage to get in touch with–'

'My friend?' Maggie said. 'No. But I made several calls throughout the afternoon and I'm expecting at least one to be returned this evening,' she replied.

'Yes, Miriam, it is indeed tragic,' Prescott was saying. 'And I'm just praying it doesn't reflect too badly on the Conference.'

Maggie tried not to laugh at Sam's expression. She leant across Rivers, her hand on his knee, and whispered, 'He really only opens his mouth to change feet, you know.'

'What with ominous postcards and–'

'Mr Prescott,' Sam interrupted before he could spill the beans about poisons and suspect lists. 'There's something I've been meaning to ask – someone.' Preferably someone else, she thought, hesitating as a waiter informed Maggie she had a phone call.

'And what would that be?' Prescott asked.

'How can the Museum of Victoria host an international museum conference when Melbourne doesn't actually have a museum at the moment?'

Uproarious laughter from everyone at the table, except Rivers, made Sam wish she'd kept her mouth shut. She raised her hands, 'Okay, obviously I have *no* idea what I'm talking about.'

'The new Melbourne Museum may not be finished,' Prescott said, 'but it *is* a prime example, in production, of just where museums are heading in the 21st century. The old idea of a museum as *one* building able to display only a small part of its collection at any one time, has given way to the multi-campus concept – a network of museums and galleries which focus on different aspects of culture, science, and natural and social history.'

'Part of the new Museum *is* open,' Joan Harris said. 'The IMAX theatre has been operating for a while now.'

'What's that?' Rivers asked.

'It's an experience and then some,' Joan enthused. 'The screen is six-stories high and designed to show, in amazing fidelity, the latest films on technology, human history and nature.'

'Getting back to what I was saying,' Prescott said, 'we *do* have Scienceworks, the Immigration and Hellenic Archaeological Museum and the National Wool Museum, not to mention a reputation within the museum community for our superb natural history collection – even if it is in storage.'

'And work is proceeding on the National Air and Space Museum at Point Cook,' Ellington volunteered. 'We also have heritage buildings, parks, cultural sites, folk museums like Sovereign Hill at Ballarat, even the Old Melbourne Gaol. And of course the term *museum* covers the Botanic and Zoological gardens and the National Gallery.'

'I surrender.' Sam laughed along with everyone else who was still amused at her expense.

'Did they put you back in your box, Sam?' Maggie asked, as she returned to her seat.

'They certainly did,' Sam declared. 'What's with you? You look like the cat who–'

'That was the call I've been waiting for,' Maggie smiled. 'Everything is arranged, Sam.'

'What everything?' Sam asked.

'The arrangements for our trip.'

'Our trip? What trip?'

'You and I are flying to Cairo tomorrow.'

'We *are*?'

# Chapter Fourteen

Melbourne, Monday September 21, 1998

'HAVE YOU GOT YOUR TOOTHBRUSH?'

'Yes, I've got my toothbrush. My toothbrush is not the problem,' Sam growled, tipping everything she'd just packed out onto the lounge floor. 'The problem is this backpack is too small. Why did you let me buy this fiddly little handbag thing?'

'Hey, I was all in favour of that triple-decker sea trunk contraption,' Jacqui said. 'Let me have a go while you see who's at the front door.'

Sam did as she was told, tripping over several pairs of shoes on the way out of the room. She opened the front door to find Maggie and a perfectly strange young man in a black suit.

'Thank god you're here,' she said to Maggie. 'I'm having a luggage crisis.'

'That is not a good way to start the day,' Maggie said. 'Have you got your passport?'

In a nanosecond Sam's expression changed from exasperated to dumbfounded. 'Bloody hell. Maggie, I don't *have* a passport. I don't know what I was thinking. I can't go anywhere. I shouldn't be *allowed* to go anywhere; I'm an idiot. Jacqui's quite right about me not coping with spontaneous acts. I mean how the hell can I when it requires so much forward planning?'

'Sam, please stop babbling,' Maggie pleaded.

'Excuse me,' said the guy in the suit. 'Are you Detective Samantha Diamond?'

'No, she left town on the Stupid Express last night,' Sam declared. 'I'm her alter ego.'

'I've got a package from the Bureau for a Detective Diamond,' the guy said hesitantly.

Sam pulled out her ID, accepted a small envelope and signed for it. 'What is it?' she asked.

'No idea,' he said, heading off down the path.

'Please come in, Maggie. Last door on the right,' Sam directed, ripping open the package as she followed Maggie down the hall.

'It's a passport,' she said. 'It's *my* passport,' she added in amazement, turning the page which featured her personal details and standard Bureau photo, to find a freshly stamped Egyptian visa.

'You did this, didn't you Maggie? Is this a forgery? I'm sure the ink's still wet. Who the hell are you, Mata Hari's daughter or something?'

'I told you I know a lot of people,' Maggie stopped dead in her tracks. 'Heavens above, Sam! No wonder you're in a tizzwoz. You've got everything here including a redhead.'

'I'm the sister,' Jacqui pronounced. 'And I assume you're the breakfast archaeologist.'

'The what?' Maggie asked.

'Just say yes, Maggie,' Sam suggested.

Maggie nodded vaguely and then waved her hand at the piles of clothes on the floor. 'Honestly Sam, we're only going to Cairo for a few days. Why have you got that gargantuan backpack?'

'It's not *that* big,' Sam protested. 'It only fits half my stuff.'

'You don't *need* all that stuff. Get rid of all the warm clothes for a start. It's *hot* in Cairo. Just pack underwear, socks, three T-shirts, *one* pair of jeans, some loose trousers, a couple of long-sleeved shirts, walking boots, a pair of sandals, one windcheater, a lightweight jacket, basic toiletries and a towel. And make sure you're comfortably dressed for the plane. Wear runners.'

'What if we're there for more than a few days?'

'That's enough for a year, Sam. If I was *sure* it was only going to be a few days you'd be taking *half* what I said. And I have everything else we need including a first aid kit, so you can put that emergency field hospital back in your warehouse.'

'What if we get separated or I get lost or–'

Maggie glanced at Jacqui. 'Is she always like this?'

'Yep. And she *will* get lost too. She's got no sense of direction, unless of course she's memorised the map and can manage to find one recognisable landmark.'

'Do you mind,' Sam objected. '*She* is in the room, you know.'

'I just want to know what I'm in for, Sam. You seemed so level-headed yesterday.'

'I was, I mean I am. I'm–'

'She's cactus,' Jacqui stated. 'She'll get over it, round about the third whisky on the plane.'

'How about you trot off and make us some coffee, sister dear,' Sam suggested sweetly.

'Good idea. Maggie's going to need it.' Jacqui quipped.

'Here, Sam, this is for you. It's a money belt. Put your passport, travellers' cheques, credit card and drivers' licence in it,' Maggie said. 'You wear it *under* your clothes,' she added as Sam put it on over her jeans.

'Under? With all that stuff in it?'

'You strap on a gun everyday, Sam, I'm sure you'll get used to this.'

'Speaking of guns, which we weren't really, but it reminds me

I have to go and see Jack Rigby from Homicide before we go. I can't run off to Cairo without filling him in on the case.'

Rigby was wrapping up a team briefing as Sam and Maggie approached his office at the end of the squad room. He motioned for them to enter and then dismissed everyone else except Rivers, who leapt to his feet, said good morning to Sam and grinned idiotically at Maggie.

Sam looked questioningly at Rivers, who sat down again and gave his undivided attention to his notebook, and then glanced at Maggie, who smiled suggestively.

Sam shook her head in bemusement and then said, 'Jack, I'd like to introduce to you Dr Maggie Tremaine: archaeologist and lecturer at Sydney Uni; long-time friend of the late Professor; and connected, it seems, with everyone in the known universe who has influence.'

Jack smiled. 'I'll just pretend I understood that last bit,' he said, nodding at the empty chairs. 'Are you the Maggie responsible for the Inca trinket thing Prescott mentioned?' he asked.

'Fiasco is the term that's being bandied around and I most definitely was *not* responsible.'

'Sorry, I didn't mean to imply, um... I'm glad you're here Sam,' Rigby changed the subject. 'We've got a few more leads. For a start, Gilchrist's alibi sucks. Excuse me, Doc,' he said, glancing at Maggie, before continuing. 'Could you and Herc talk to him again this arvo?'

'I can't, Jack, I'm going to Cairo today,' Sam said, as if it was a perfectly ordinary thing to do.

'You're going to Cairo.' Rigby frowned as if he thought he'd misheard. 'Which Cairo?'

'There's only one as far as I know,' Sam stated.

Rigby shook his head. 'You can't go just *go* to Cairo, Sam.'

'Why not?'

'Why, would be a better question.'

'Maggie and I have some leads of our own, which I'll give you, that necessitate a trip to Egypt.'

'They *necessitate* a trip to Egypt?' Rigby repeated. 'What the hell does that mean? Are you saying the murderer has left the country and nicked off to Cairo?'

'No, but we believe the answer to *why* the Professor was murdered might be in Cairo.'

'The answer might be in my garden shed too, but I'm not going to spend the week in there looking for it,' Rigby snorted, eyeing Sam as if he thought she'd gone completely mad.

As Sam had spent most of the previous night wondering the very same thing, she could hardly take offence. She smiled and filled Rigby in on the details about the package Marsden had sent to Maggie, their search of the cottage and the details about the postcard from Cairo. She didn't mention the photograph of Manco City or anything about Incas, partly because it was probably irrelevant but mostly because she knew Jack would still be laughing next week if she had.

'So, Sherlock, you're telling me that you and Dr Watson here are just going to flit off to Cairo on the basis of this flimsy load of old cobblers,' Rigby asked, waving his hand at Marsden's cryptic notes and the key to his cottage which Sam had laid out on the desk as she spoke.

'Yes, Jack, and what's more, odd as it may seem,' Sam said, casting a sideways glance at Maggie, 'I am under orders to do just that.'

'Whose orders?' Jack demanded as if that person had also lost their mind. 'Pilger's? Blimey Sam, I realise your or rather the ACB's interest in this case is primarily one of damage control because of the conference, but this is crazy. What's the man thinking? We're up to our armpits in suspects right here in Melbourne.

'Gilchrist is failing his degree, apparently suffers some

personality disorder that makes him resent anyone, like Marsden for instance, who tries to help him, *and* has an alibi you could drive a truck through. Some bird in publicity had a mile-wide crush on the Professor and, allegedly, has a tendency to overreact when rejected. And Marsden *did* owe money to a Melbourne bookie, about eight grand worth.

'Then there's my prime suspect, Haddon Gould, who apart from having a questionable sense of reality and a big-time grudge against the Professor, was also the last known person to see him alive. To cap it off *his* museum plant collection just happens to include varieties of the genus *Chondrodendron* from which curare can be extracted.'

'Really, Jack? Is Gould the only one who has access to those plants?' Sam asked.

'No, but I doubt Marsden's bookie slipped in and cooked up a batch of poison,' Rigby snarled.

'It's your case, Jack. I'm sure you'll cope while I'm away for a few days,' Sam remarked.

'Of course I will, but it's beyond me what it was about these silly notes that convinced the Minister to send you half way round the bloody world.'

'Not what, who,' Maggie corrected. 'I convinced Jim Pilger of my belief that there is much more to this whole thing than just Lloyd's murder.'

'Oh you did, did you? And what is the basis of that belief exactly?' Jack asked.

'I'm not *exactly* sure,' Maggie admitted. 'But I think it has far-reaching implications.'

'Far-reaching implications?' Rigby echoed, eyeing Maggie warily. 'You're not related to Prescott are you? Speaking of the Director of Conspiracy Theories, isn't it your job to keep him reigned in, Sam? And, not that I think it's connected with the murder, but what about the limerick sent by that illiterate whacko?'

Sam grinned. 'You *are* going to miss me, aren't you Jack?'

'Don't bet on it,' Rigby said. 'I just don't want to see Prescott on the evening news denying sabotage rumours of which the media had no previous knowledge.'

'I don't mean to throw a spanner in your works Jack, but I think the limerick *is* related to the murder, not as a threat of sabotage, but as a device to throw us off the scent.'

Rigby closed his eyes and pinched the bridge of his nose in frustration. 'Why, pray tell?'

'Because I think it was sent by an educated someone who *wanted* us to think it was written by an illiterate whacko.'

'Lovely, that brings us back to everyone at the Museum,' Jack complained. 'So when are you coming *back* from Cairo?'

Sam looked at Maggie who replied, 'Friday, if all goes well.'

# Chapter Fifteen

Cairo, Tuesday September 21, 1998

SAM STILL COULDN'T BELIEVE IT. SHE WAS ACTUALLY IN EGYPT.

Everything had happened so fast that halfway through the interminable 21-hour flight she was still trying to process the fact that she'd even left home for the first time in her life. She couldn't believe that she was now being driven through the streets of a city she'd only ever dreamed of visiting and that she *really* was within cooee of the pyramids. But mostly she couldn't believe that having come all this way, she was going to die on her first day in Cairo because her life was in the hands of a maniac driver who was watching the road ahead with his left ear, while he talked in Arabic to Maggie who was in the *back* seat.

'Truck,' Sam pointed out, gripping the dashboard. 'Truck!' she yelled.

'Yes, truck,' the driver agreed, zigzagging back onto the correct side of the road. 'Is okay.'

'Is not okay,' Sam stated, rubbing her arm where it had been slammed into the door.

'Camel truck,' the driver informed her, turning to point behind.

'Is that what they were?' Sam said flatly. 'All I saw were five furry heads screaming "car, car!" Do you think you could watch where we're going instead of where we've been?'

'I don't think his English is a match for your hysteria, Sam.' Maggie said something in Arabic and the driver turned to face the front, grinning madly. 'Emil is actually one of the better Embassy drivers. You're lucky we didn't have to take a service taxi.'

'Ser-veece taxi, very bad drives,' Emil proclaimed, then added *'ismik eh?'*

'He wants to know your name,' Maggie translated.

'Sam.'

'Sam,' he repeated, then handed her a business card and said, 'Emil best drive, try me all times. No taxi. Is okay?'

Sam nodded. 'Whatever you say, Emil.' She turned to Maggie. 'Are you going to tell me how we were ushered straight from the plane to an Australian Embassy car chauffeured by Mad Max?'

'My friend, Michael Frank, who is sort of a cultural attache at the Embassy, expedited our passage through customs and immigration.'

'We didn't pass through customs and immigration,' Sam reminded her.

'Exactly,' Maggie said. 'And I imagine that when Michael doesn't need him, Emil is at our disposal.'

'Wonderful. Oh, this is amazing,' Sam noted, holding her breath as three oncoming cars, a motor cycle and another camel truck veered out of the way as Emil overtook a rickety donkey-drawn cart. 'The traffic is much worse than Melbourne peak hour, yet it's actually moving.'

'Cairo has upwards of 15 million inhabitants, Sam, it doesn't have time to stop,' Maggie said. 'Emil, *Sharia Talaat Harb.*'

Sam gripped the seat as Emil swung the car through a huge intersection. 'Dammit Maggie, what the hell did you say to him?'

'I asked him to take Sharia Talaat Harb. This is your first

orientation lesson, Sam. Sharia means street, and Talaat Harb is one of the main streets in central Cairo. Everyone knows it, even other travellers, so pay attention to the things that *aren't* moving out there so you'll recognise something if you get lost.'

'I'm not leaving the hotel,' Sam stated categorically.

Maggie chuckled. 'Cairo is a city that won't be denied, Sam. It will drag you out by the bootstraps if necessary, to thrill and enthral, annoy and amaze you. You'll be overwhelmed by the sheer weight and splendour of its history, and by the sights, sounds, smells, colour and movement of its living, breathing fabric. It's like a vampire; it *will* get in your blood and you'll spend the rest of your life wanting more of it. Or you'll hate it, passionately. But there are no half measures.'

'Midan Talaat Harb,' Emil announced as he rocketed the limo through a six-street intersection, before screeching to a halt to avoid joining a three-vehicle pile-up that had already happened. Emil put the car in reverse, backed up about 10 metres, then swung across the road and down a narrow side street draped with multi-coloured fabrics, lined with shops displaying food and basketware on the narrow pavement, and crowded with people, motor bikes and the odd donkey or two.

'Well I'm really lost now,' Sam joked, after Emil had made a couple more turns. Maggie smiled broadly and directed Sam's attention to the view ahead.

'Wow!' Sam exclaimed. 'Oh wow. That's the Nile.'

'Very good, Sam. See, you're not lost at all.'

'Old Hilton here. New one much better, Maggie,' Emil stated, pulling up in front of the hotel that Sam recognised from the postcard that had brought them half way round the world. 'Now you see, I take you to Ramses Hilton yes?'

'No Emil, *la'shukran*. This is the one we want.' Maggie opened the car door and struggled out.

Sam did the same, with great relief, and then stood open-mouthed, staring at the Nile and the graceful single-sailed boats that skimmed the surface of its dark blue water.

'You want me drive more, Maggie?' Emil asked, removing their packs from the back seat.

'Maybe later, okay. *Shukran* Emil. Are you coming, Sam? Because if I don't get a shower, a beer and some food, in that order and very soon, I will be completely unmanageable.'

Half an hour later, having showered and changed, Sam sat captivated by the view from the window of their spacious room on the 12th floor. The River Nile passed from left to right below and the white-sailed *feluccas*, as she now knew the boats to be called, looked like waltzing butterflies.

Opposite, the Cairo Tower loomed out of the skyline of Gezira Island which, according to Maggie, was the home of Cairo's elite. Looking further west, through a haze of smog and dust, Sam was sure she could see the desert; the actual Sahara Desert.

'Are you ready for lunch, Sam?' Maggie asked, 'or are you still full of trepidation?'

'Nope, I'm ready,' Sam declared as she turned away from the view. She slapped her hand over mouth to control a fit of laughter. 'Um, but I doubt you'll speak to me if I let you go downstairs looking like that.'

'Oh god, not again,' Maggie moaned, running her fingers through the static in her wild hair. She grabbed a wet towel from the bathroom and wrapped it around her head. 'Do you suppose this is a manifestation of some kind of dementia?' she asked.

'No,' laughed Sam, 'but you should chuck your dryer out. I think it's possessed by the demon god of bad hair days.'

'Do you think the key is to a safety deposit box here in the hotel, or the postcard was simply asking the Professor to meet Winslow here?' Sam asked as the lift doors opened into the lobby.

'There's only one way to find out.' Maggie headed for the reception desk. She produced the key and informed the concierge that she wanted to check her safety deposit box.

'Well, that went smoothly,' Sam commented, when the concierge simply checked the number on the key, nodded politely and disappeared through a doorway behind.

Sam turned, leant against the counter and gazed around at the lobby which was furnished with plants and arm chairs set around low coffee tables. Three elderly women in white linen dresses and wide-brimmed hats sat together drinking iced tea; a swarthy-looking man in an ill-fitting suit snapped his newspaper up in front his face; a man with a moustache and bad acne scars was trying not to fall asleep next to a potted palm; and an American in a very loud shirt was escorting a blonde woman into the bar. 'I think we're on the set of *Casablanca*,' Sam whispered. 'There's even a guy wearing a fez.'

'They do that a lot here,' Maggie said, turning to survey the room. 'But the scene is more reminiscent of *Death on the Nile* don't you think?'

'God, I hope not,' Sam laughed.

'Excuse me, Madame.' The concierge had returned with a long metal box. 'Would you care to step to the side, it is more private,' he said, scanning the room for possible spies and assassins.

'Thank you,' Maggie said, taking his advice. Sam hung over her shoulder as she unlocked the box and lifted the lid. 'It's empty.'

'It can't be,' Sam objected, reaching over to tip the box on its end. A small white envelope slid into view. 'If this is another cryptic note I think I'll scream,' she said.

Maggie removed the envelope, slipped it in her pocket, closed the box again and thanked the concierge. 'We can't have you creating a scene in the lobby, Sam. Let's get a beer.' She led the way into the bar, ordered two Stellas and chose a table well away from the other patrons.

'Okay, let's see which garden path we're going to be led up next,' Sam prompted. As she resettled her chair next to Maggie, she noticed that the guy in the fez had given up on his nap and had taken a seat at the bar, and the Miss Marple triplets had obviously decided the sun was far enough over the yard arm to warrant something stronger than tea.

Maggie opened the envelope, peered inside and closed her eyes. 'Please don't scream, Sam,' she said tipping the contents onto the table. It was another safety deposit box key. 'You'll be pleased to know there's no note at all this time.'

'Great! Now is when we need one. It's not the same sort of key either. So now what?'

'Now we eat, drink, and then go to the museum to see if Ahmed Kamel has managed to track Noel down for us.'

'That was a very nice lunch but I can't believe I came all the way to Egypt to eat pizza,' Sam said, putting her sunglasses on as she and Maggie strolled along Corniche el Nil beside the river.

'Tonight we'll do Cairo, Sam. We'll go to my favourite eating place on Talaat Harb. And if we have time while we're here I'll also take you to the mind-blowing Khan el Khalili for a bit of shopping. The Khan is one the largest bazaars in the Middle East.'

'And the pyramids?' Sam said hopefully.

'The shopping's no good there,' Maggie said, giving Sam a sidelong smile. 'I promise, Sam. You will see the pyramids. But right now it's time for what – in my humble and biased opinion – is the greatest museum on earth, the Museum of Egyptian Antiquities.' Maggie waved ahead to the huge sandstone-coloured, neo-classical building fronted by palm trees and sphinxes. 'Do you want the lowdown?'

'Definitely, I'm not going to pass–'

'Hello, hello, welcome to Egypt.' A young man, wearing the traditional long-sleeved, ankle-length gown, fell in step with Sam.

'Thank you,' Sam replied politely.

'Ignore him,' Maggie urged.

'You want change money, yes?' he asked.

'No thank you,' Sam said.

'Ah, you want museum guide? Mohammed best guide, know everything. Only five pounds.'

'*La'shukran*, Mohammed,' Maggie said firmly.

'Maybe pyramids, *bukra*, tomorrow yes? My uncle has best camels for riding. Only 10 pounds.'

'Don't say a word, Sam,' Maggie warned and then rattled off something in a particularly formidable tone. It scared the hell out of Sam and she had no idea what Maggie had said.

Mohammed grinned widely, however, and bowed slightly. '*Insha-allah, insha-allah*,' he said and turned to try his routine on a middle-aged couple approaching the museum steps.

'What did you say to him?'

'I told him if he didn't leave us alone immediately I would follow him everywhere and ruin his business by claiming my *husband's* camels only cost five pounds.'

'That's a bit harsh. What did he say?'

'He said *insha-allah* which means 'if god wills it'.'

'How many languages do you speak?'

'Five. English, oddly enough, French, Spanish, Arabic but not very well, and Quechua which is the Indian language of Peru.'

'I'm no good with languages,' Sam admitted. 'I *memorised* French at school, so I can understand it, but when I open my mouth I'm sure it sounds like Klingon.'

'That's just a lack of confidence, Sam. You could try your French here, a lot of Egyptians speak it, and it's certainly easier than Arabic. But if you want to get into the lingo during our limited stay, I'll teach you the basics of ordering food and drinks. Apart from that there are only three things you need to know for a brief visit like ours – and I've discovered this applies in India, South America and parts of Indonesia – and they are: please, thank you, and bugger off. Although if you wish to be polite, "no thank you" is a good substitute for that last one.

'I don't know, *insha-allah* seems pretty useful,' Sam said.

'It is that,' Maggie agreed. 'Now where was I? Oh yes. The Service de Antiquities le l'Egypte was established by the Egyptian Government in 1835 partly to exhibit its own collection of artefacts but mostly to stop the plundering of archaeological sites by foreigners. This museum was finally built in 1900 to house the Government's collection and that of the French archaeologist August Mariette. There are some 120,000 objects in the museum, including the mummies of various pharaohs, such as Tuthmosis I, II and III, Seti I and Ramses II through VI. These were found in the late 1800s, not in their own tombs but reburied in ancient times in a shaft at Deir el Bahri, which was Hatshepsut's Temple, and in the tomb of Amenhotep II in the Valley of the Kings. The museum also has artefacts from the time of Akhenaten at Tell el Armana, the contents of several royal and private tombs at Tanis, and of course the incomparable treasures of Tutankhamun. So, are you ready?'

Sam nodded as they passed through the front doors but was instantly overwhelmed by the stony visages of the colossi that towered over her. She wondered how on earth they'd got the mammoth seated statues inside the building.

Maggie watched Sam in amusement, remembering her first visit here, and was disappointed they didn't really have the time to explore it. 'We should get our priorities straight, Sam. We *are* on a mission, so perhaps we should find Ahmed, then find Noel and return here later.'

'Maggie, what if we can't come back? I have to see it, in person,' Sam insisted.

'Okay. It's upstairs, don't get lost. I'll find Ahmed and I'll meet you outside in one hour.'

Everywhere Sam looked there was history – ancient, ancient history – manifested in columns, statues, blocks of stone painted or carved with reliefs, mummified animals, even the capstone of a pyramid. Sam was beside herself, wanting to take in as much as possible. She passed diadems, pectorals and other jewellery made of gold, silver, and precious stones. She saw royal coffins and stone sarcophagi; canopic jars used for the storage of a mummy's vital organs; stelae inscribed with hieroglyphs; and weapons, chairs, beds and thrones.

She stopped to gaze on the 3,500-year-old stone face of Hatshepsut, the third queen to rule Egypt and, after declaring herself Pharaoh, the only woman ever to reign as King. Sam smiled because there was something about Hatshepsut's serene yet resolute expression that reminded her of Maggie.

Finally in a room on the first floor she found what she was looking for: the legendary funeral mask of Tutankhamun. It was the most exquisite hand-made thing she had ever seen. Framed by the royal headdress of gold and lapis lazuli, the boy Pharaoh's features were so finely wrought in beaten gold that Sam realised she was waiting for it to breathe.

# Chapter Sixteen

Cairo, September 21, 1998

'HAPPY?' MAGGIE ASKED, WHEN SAM EMERGED INTO THE BLINDING sunlight, squinting and grinning like an idiot.

'Oh yes!' Sam sat down next to Maggie on the steps and took the offered bottled water. 'That was, it was indescribable. Thank you.'

'There's no need to thank *me*,' Maggie said.

'I wouldn't be here if it wasn't for you,' Sam said. She cast her gaze around at the museum, its lawns and palm trees, and the crowds of tourists flanked by Egyptian touts and hawkers. 'I may *never* have got here at – all...' She frowned.

'If it wasn't for Lloyd's death and Noel's mysterious postcard,' Maggie reminded her.

'That's true,' Sam said, distractedly, turning back to her travel companion. 'Maggie.'

'Yes, Sam?'

'I think we're being followed. Here, take this.' She handed Maggie the water. 'And while you're casually taking a drink, look behind me.'

'Why on earth would anyone be following us?' Maggie laughed, but did as Sam requested. 'I can see a lot of tourists and a great many Egyptians, including Mohammed your friend from earlier, but no one I recognise and no one who is acting suspiciously.'

'I saw one of the men from the hotel lobby loitering under the palm tree just beyond were Mohammed was standing,' Sam stated.

'Loitering?' Maggie repeated. 'We're staying at a tourist hotel, within walking distance of one of the city's main tourist attractions, Sam, we're bound to see the same people more than once.'

'But he was *watching* us and he's a local, not a tourist.'

Maggie chuckled. 'And now you're going to tell me it was the man with the fez.'

'Yes,' Sam said indignantly. 'The man with the fez, the moustache and the bad skin, who was in the lobby and then followed us into the bar.'

'Are you sure it's not a case of 'all these Arabs looking the same' – to *you* at least? Perhaps it's the fez that looks suspicious.'

Sam scowled. 'Behind me is a middle-aged probably American couple dressed in safari suits, she's an *un*natural blonde, he's got no hair under his hat. There's two red-headed guys, probably brothers, sitting on the retaining wall, and next to them are two handsome young Egyptian men wearing black trousers and white shirts, who look like students rather than 'expert museum guides'. There's a small tour group, comprised of three inappropriately-dressed women and five just plain badly-dressed men. An elderly Egyptian man in a blue nightgown thing is offering a trinket to a snooty-faced woman in a red dress; and three Egyptian men are doing I don't know what, but the one with the beard is wearing a beige gown and turban and the other two, who are alike enough to be father and son, are wearing dark green gowns and brown turbans. Beyond them is the guy in the fez.'

Maggie's eyes grew wider as Sam correctly identified half the people who were loitering in front of the museum.

'The nightgown thing is called a *galibeya*,' she said seriously, before they both burst into laughter. 'There's no man in a fez,' Maggie managed to say, 'at least not anymore. If he *was* watching us then I'll wager he's going to pounce on us later and invite us to his cousin's very-best perfume shop. Don't worry about it, Sam.'

'Whatever you say,' Sam agreed reluctantly. 'Did you find out about Noel?'

'Yes, and no. He hasn't done any consultancy work here for nearly two years and Ahmed hasn't seen him since January. Noel had only just moved into a new apartment in Maadi, which is a district about 10 kilometres south of here, where most of the expats live. Ahmed said Noel had almost finished his ninth book and was heading off to Mexico in June to research to the next.'

'So he mightn't be here at all,' Sam said.

'Or he might be entrenched in his apartment tapping away at *Jake St James and the Curse of the Aztecs.*'

'Jake St James?'

Maggie shrugged. 'A hero has to have a memorable name.'

Half an hour later Sam leapt out of the taxi, in which she and Maggie had been crammed with three German businessmen because the driver had refused to go anywhere till his car was full, and stood on the footpath muttering 'ser-veece taxis, very bad drives'.

'Emil did warn you,' Maggie reminded her.

'Do they all have to pass a lunatic test to get their licences here or something?' Sam followed Maggie into the decrepit *Riverview* apartment building which, as old as it was, was quite modern by Cairo standards.

Maggie pushed the intercom button for apartment 20 and, hearing an unfamiliar voice, asked for Noel Winslow.

There was silence on the other end for quite a while before the man said, 'Who are you?'

'My name is Dr Tremaine, Maggie Tremaine. I'm a friend of Noel's from Australia.'

Another pause, then the interior door clicked open. 'Come on up. Top floor at the front.'

The lift wasn't working so about three centuries later Sam and Maggie stood panting on the 10th floor landing. The door opposite was opened by a middle-aged man with a somewhat boyish face, deep blue eyes, and greying hair brushed back into a short pony tail. He ushered them into a huge living room lined with bookshelves, crowded with an odd assortment of furniture, and cluttered with books, magazines, newspapers and half-packed boxes.

'Please come in. I've just made some fresh lemonade,' he offered, waving them to the wicker table and chairs on the balcony overlooking the river. 'I've heard a great deal about you Maggie Tremaine. I'm Patrick Denton.'

'Ah, Patrick,' Maggie said, pleased she could finally put a face to the name she'd heard many times over the years. 'This is my friend, Sam Diamond.'

Sam shook his offered hand and sat in the seat he indicated, but she got the impression that while Patrick Denton was being extremely hospitable it was obvious he was also stalling. She wondered whether they had intruded on Noel Winslow's most creative time of the day.

'Are you two moving again?' Maggie asked, nodding at the boxes as she accepted the glass of lemonade.

'I *was*,' Patrick said, shifting uncomfortably in his seat. 'Noel died four months ago, Maggie. He went out for coffee with an acquaintance, had a stroke in the cafe and never recovered.'

'Oh my god, Patrick, I am *so* sorry. I had no idea.' Maggie reached out and held his hand.

Four months ago? Sam felt like a pair of cold clammy hands had just given her a rub down.

'My first thought after his funeral was that I had to go home, but I didn't leave the apartment for a month; I sat here staring out at that timeless, never-ending damn river, till I nearly went mad. It's the lifeblood of this country you know, but I felt like it had bled me dry. I would have starved if not for friends who dropped in daily with food.

'When I did decide to go back to Canada they brought boxes and I started packing away 20 years of my life with Noel. Then one morning I just walked out, wandered down to the Nile, *didn't* throw myself in, and went for coffee where Noel and I used to lunch every day. I realised that with or without Noel, but mostly because of him, *this is* my home. So now I'm slowly unpacking again.'

'*When* did he die?' Sam asked softly.

'The same day, thankfully. The doctor said he wouldn't have known what hit him.'

'I mean exactly when, what day was it?'

'It was a Friday,' Patrick replied, puzzled by the question. 'May 29th. Why?'

Sam looked meaningfully at Maggie who looked questioningly back at her. 'That was the day after he sent the postcard to the Professor,' she said.

'What postcard?' Patrick asked.

'Noel, at least we're guessing it was Noel,' Maggie explained, 'sent Lloyd Marsden a postcard of the Nile Hilton with a very cryptic message. That's why we're here.'

'Lloyd sent you?' Patrick asked.

'In a manner of speaking,' Maggie replied. 'Lloyd was murdered in Melbourne last Tuesday.'

'Good god, how dreadful,' Patrick exclaimed. 'But what could that possibly have to do with Noel? I don't understand why you're here?'

'We think Lloyd's death is linked to whatever it was Noel was trying to tell him in the postcard.'

Patrick shook his head in amusement. 'It sounds like you've read one too many of Noel's books, Maggie. Although...'

He got up to rummage around in the antique desk by the window. 'It might explain this rather curious thing I found while going through Noel's effects. Where on earth? Ah, here it is.' He returned to his chair and handed Maggie a cigarette tin. 'Open it.'

Sam leaned over as Maggie removed the lid. Inside was a small green envelope labelled:

For Lloyd or Muu-Muu *only.*

'MM,' Sam said. 'His postcard said "inform MM". Who the bloody hell is Muu-Muu?'

'Um, that would be me, actually,' Maggie admitted sheepishly. 'Sam, I swear I had no idea that MM meant Muu-Muu. It was a pet name that Pavel gave me back in 1968 because of this, in retrospect, insanely awful caftan thing I used to wear. There were only three people in the world who called me that, Pavel, Noel and Lloyd, and none of *them* used it in the last 15 years because I would have throttled them.'

'Okay, *Muu-Muu*,' Sam teased, 'it seems you're licensed to open the envelope.'

Maggie did so and removed half a drink coaster, with a six-digit number and the words 'Americo Bank' scrawled under the beer logo.

'Does it help?' Patrick asked.

'Not really,' Maggie fibbed. 'But can we hang on to it?'

Patrick shrugged. 'You're the only Muu-Muu *I* know.'

# Chapter Seventeen

Cairo, September 21, 1998

'WHAT IF NOEL'S DEATH *WASN'T* NATURAL CAUSES?' SAM ASKED, AS they emerged from the Riverview apartments onto the street.

'Oh, Sam,' Maggie sighed, turning to head for the corner and the main road along the Nile. 'There are some coincidences which are just that. Not everything is connected. Besides, I'm sure a doctor knows a stroke victim when he sees one.'

'Yeah, sure, which means he wouldn't have thought to look for something else – like poison,' Sam stated. 'The forensic pathologist in Melbourne initially thought the Professor had had a stroke.'

'I didn't know that,' Maggie said, stopping in her tracks as the colour drained from her face. She reached for Sam's arm. 'That makes it more than a coincidence then.'

'You look like you've seen a ghost. Do you need to sit down?'

'No, I'm fine. But you know my friend Alistair Nash, the one who died in the car accident last October?'

'On the same day his museum was burgled,' Sam nodded.

'The accident happened when he lost control of his car – after suffering a stroke.'

'Oh boy, this is getting too weird. Oh shit, it just got weirder.'

'What, why?'

'It's the suspicious fez from the hotel. He's just up the road there, this side.'

'Are you sure?' Maggie glanced casually at the man leaning against a car about 30 metres away. She couldn't see his face clearly but he was indeed wearing a fez.

'*Yes* I'm sure. Come on, we'll cross the road, take a tourist stroll along the river in the opposite direction and get the first taxi that comes along.'

They were lucky. An empty taxi heading back towards Cairo did a u-turn and skidded to a stop in the gutter in front of them. Maggie babbled something to the driver as soon as they were in the back seat. He planted his foot with apparent glee and sped out into the traffic, barely missing the back bumper of the Mercedes in front.

'What's the fez doing?' Maggie asked Sam, who was looking out the back window.

'He's about five cars back and determined not to lose us,' Sam stated, turning to sit properly on the seat. 'His cousin's perfumes must *really* be something special.'

'Ha, ha.' Maggie leant forward to speak to the driver. 'Khan el Khalili,' she said. 'And we'll double your fare if you don't stop to pick up any other passengers.'

'We're going shopping *now*?' Sam asked in amazement.

'We're going to lose ourselves in the most labyrinthine market in the world,' Maggie smiled. 'He won't be able to keep track of us there.'

'*Insha-allah*,' Sam laughed. 'He'll probably just go back to the hotel and wait for us.'

'Then we'll walk right up to him, in public, and ask him what the hell he wants.'

Sam wondered if the speeding taxi driver had found an anomaly in the space time continuum when he deposited them, 35 minutes later and six centuries ago, at one of the medieval gates of the area known as Islamic Cairo. Towering minarets loomed over streets crowded with people and animals, and lined with rickety, balconied buildings that looked set to topple at any moment – although they'd probably been 'about to fall' since the 10th century.

Islamic Cairo, Maggie had explained, was no more Islamic than any other part of the city, it was just much older. The Khan el Khalili, through which they now walked, was a maze of stalls selling fruit and vegetables or displaying open barrels or trays of rice, beans, nuts, cheeses, aromatic spices, and a host of exotic and unrecognisable delicacies. There were shops where artisans toiled, as they had for centuries, on their woodwork, glassware or jewellery; and cafes, where the aroma of cooking food wafted around men who sat drinking coffee while they talked and puffed on a sheesha, or water pipe.

Maggie constantly waved off merchants who kept on extolling – even after they'd walked by – the excellence and best prices of the leather goods, fabrics, Pharaonic relics, perfumes, spices, clothing or souvenirs displayed in their open-fronted shops.

Sam felt like all her senses, plus a couple she didn't know she had, were being teased, assaulted and tantalised. If it wasn't for the smell of exhaust fumes and the occasional Coca Cola sign or shop selling runners and T-shirts, she would have been convinced she'd stepped back, way back, in time.

'Coffee,' Maggie announced, taking a seat at a table in an open-sided restaurant, next to group of lounging camels. 'How are you feeling?' she asked, realising Sam looked a little odd.

'Overwhelmed, awe-inspired, and starving,' Sam enthused.

Maggie beckoned a young boy to their table, held up two fingers and said, '*ahwa saada* and *kushari,* okay?'

'Okay,' he nodded.

'Coffee, no sugar, and a noodle dish,' Maggie translated for Sam. 'Very Egyptian.'

'This is great,' Sam grinned. 'But Maggie, you have to promise we won't get separated. I have absolutely no idea where I am and it will be getting dark sometime soon.'

'I promise, Sam,' Maggie said, crossing her heart. '*Insha-allah*,' she added quietly.

'Maggie,' Sam growled.

'I promise, I promise,' she grinned, and leant back so the boy could place the food on the table. 'Just eat, Sam, there's no need to dissect it.'

'I like to know *what* I'm eating,' Sam explained.

'Black lentils, fried onions, rice, noodles and a tomato sauce,' Maggie said, taking a mouthful.

'Mmm, oh yum,' Sam said, following suit. 'But I have to say, the coffee looks strong enough to stay in shape without the cup.'

'Hello, hello, you want perfume?'

'*La' shukran*,' Maggie snapped at the bearded man who had approached their table.

'They don't give up, do they,' Sam commented.

'Never,' Maggie laughed. 'You know the Khan started life as a caravanserai, built by Sultan Barquq's Master of Horses in the 1300s. It was a simple inn and way station for caravans, and I don't mean the sort that retired Australians drag around the country behind their cars. Merchants, travellers and their trains of camels used to rest here and do a little trading.

'When the Ottomans took over Egypt in the 16th century it grew into a fully-fledged Turkish bazaar attracting traders from all over the known world. It was–'

'Maggie, I thought you said the fez guy wouldn't find us here.'

'It was a hundred to one against that he wouldn't. Where is he?'

'Loitering by the spice stall behind you.'

'Well, we'll just let him loiter while we finish our food, and then we'll lose him again.'

'Is he still with us?' Sam asked 15 minutes later as she and Maggie stopped to investigate a stall of *authentic* relics from the Valley of the Kings.

'Yes,' Maggie replied, while ignoring the merchant who was explaining that the recently carved figurine she was holding was a centuries-old statuette unearthed near the tomb of Ramses III.

They continued walking, pretending to take interest in carvings, jewellery and a bizarre-looking vegetable floating in soup, until they turned another corner and stopped to buy a bottle of water.

'Perhaps we should split up,' Maggie suggested.

'No way, Maggie,' Sam stressed.

'Okay, but let's see what he does if he *thinks* we've separated. *I* won't get lost here, so how about we wander down to that perfumery on the next corner, have what looks like a serious arrangement-making conversation, then I'll tap my watch and walk off. You stay right there, don't move no matter what, and I'll come back in 10 minutes.'

'Okay,' Sam agreed reluctantly, 'in the absence of a sensible plan, that will have to do I guess.'

*Twenty* minutes after Maggie had pointed up the street, recited a bawdy limerick as if it was the most important information she'd ever imparted, tapped her watch and disappeared into the crowd, closely followed by the guy in the fez, Sam was still standing on her own – waiting. She had so far fended of marauding children wanting to sell trinkets by saying *imshi,* a lot; and had also deterred several grown-up shopkeepers and hawkers with her very firm '*la' shukran*', but now she was starting to get worried.

She checked her watch again. It was 5.45 and all was *not* well. When she looked up, the situation got suddenly worse as she noticed the guy in the fez was striding back up the street towards *her* with what could only be described as serious intent. There was still no sign of Maggie.

Sam had little choice but to stand her ground but just as Mr Fez reached out, apparently trying to grab her arm, another man barged between them. He shoved Mr Fez out of the way and sent Sam sprawling backwards over a box. She struggled to her feet and took off down the short alley next to the perfumery and rounded the next corner only to find herself in a cul de sac with a donkey.

'Shit,' she exclaimed, turning to go back the way she'd come only to find Mr Fez had already found her.

'Nowhere to go, Miss Detective,' he said.

'Yeah? What is it you want exactly?' Sam asked, moving so that she could see back down the alley, or rather *be* seen by anyone passing.

'The key,' he answered simply.

'What key?' Sam asked, backing up against the wall.

'Do not fool with me. Give me the key from the safety deposit box or I *will* take it from you.' He pulled out a decidedly nasty-looking knife as he moved closer. 'Is it worth dying for?'

'No, not all. You can have it, just don't hurt me, okay,' Sam pleaded, pulling a set of keys from her belt pouch and removing one from the ring. As he reached out for it, Sam swivelled on her left foot, raised her right one and slammed it into his knee. He went down in a screaming heap on the ground. The only problem was that he was still between her and the way out. As she kicked him again, she realised that someone was calling out as he ran down the alley towards her.

'Thank goodness,' Sam said. 'Oh shit,' she added. The help that was on the way had obviously come for Mr Fez. It was the *other* man from the hotel lobby, the swarthy-looking gent who had tried to hide his bad suit behind the newspaper.

Just make a run for it, Sam thought, but Mr Fez had other ideas.

His groan turned to a growl as he launched himself off the ground at Sam and slammed her head and body back into the wall. The whole world turned upside down, in a sickening swirl. Sam was vaguely aware that the other man was still shouting, then a fist connected with her jaw. She slid down the wall and into a very dark place.

# Chapter Eighteen

Cairo, September 22, 1998

SAM STROLLED, VAGUELY, ALONG THE CORNICHE EL NIL WONDERING HOW on earth she'd got from the cafe in the Khan with Maggie back to the Nile Hilton without her. But the hotel was there, up ahead on her left, its windows reflecting the last rays of sunset. She closed her eyes to enjoy the gentle breeze that brushed her face and when she opened them again she noticed a group of people, including the hotel concierge and the Miss Marple triplets, gathered around something on the ground near the gangplank of a multi-sailed white yacht moored to a pontoon.

It was none her business, but Sam was curious so she joined the circle to see what they were looking at. A man was lying face down on the ground, with an arrow in his back.

'It's definitely suspicious,' said one of the Miss Marples.

'Death on the Nile,' another nodded. 'Spooky.'

'Bizarre,' Sam commented.

'Are you all right?' asked the man next to Sam, placing his hand gently on her arm.

'*Very* bizarre,' Sam emphasised looking into the concerned face of Hercule Poirot. Don't be silly, she thought. It's not Hercule Poirot, it's Peter Ustinov. Wow!

Sam blinked and the great actor morphed into...into – *Moses*? She screwed her eyes shut and then heard a deep and gentle voice call out 'Gamal, *shy bi-nannah*'.

Sam opened her eyes again. Oh good, it wasn't Moses gazing down on her. But, the very old, red-turbaned and long-bearded man, wearing a green – what was is it? – ah, *galibeya*. and holding a wicker fan, did look remarkably like Charlton Heston.

'Can you sit up?' he asked.

'Yes, of course,' Sam replied, but found she only had enough strength to ease herself onto her elbows. She was lying on a divan in the corner of a shop jam-packed with Pharaonic antiquities.

'May I help?' Moses Heston offered, holding out his hands.

'Yes please,' she replied, allowing the big man to lift her up and back onto a pile of cushions. '*Shukran,*' Sam smiled.

He nodded and then beckoned to a skinny teenage boy with huge bright eyes who stepped forward and handed him a glass.

'*Shy bi-nannah,*' he said offering the drink to Sam. 'Mint tea.'

'*Shukran,*' Sam said again and took a sip. 'Am I still in the Khan?'

'Yes. I am Ahmed Omar, this my shop. And this my grandson, Gamal. He find you.'

'My name is Sam, Sam Diamond. *Shukran* Gamal.'

The boy grinned and sat crossed-legged at his grandfather's feet.

'Did he take anything, the Turkish who attacked you?'

Sam shook her head, she was still wearing her belt pouch and could feel the money belt still under her jeans. 'He was *Turkish*,' she said. 'But there were *two* men.'

Ahmed and Gamal had a long conversation during which Gamal gesticulated a great deal before finishing his story by punching his fist into his open palm.

'Gamal say the Turkish man pushed you into the wall, then he hit you in the face. He say the Mexican–'

'Mexican?' Sam interrupted.

'Yes, the Mexican tried to stop the Turkish from hurting you more. When the Turkish ran off, the Mexican went to see you are okay. He saw Gamal and sent him to get help for you. When I arrive there's no Turkish, no Mexican, just you. I carry you here.'

'I don't know how to thank you, Ahmed,' Sam smiled.

'No need. It is enough that you are not hurt too much. But why are you alone here?'

'I wasn't,' Sam explained. 'I was with another Australian woman, but we got separated.'

'Not good,' Ahmed shook his head. 'Where you staying?'

'Nile Hilton.'

'Long way. Maybe Gamal can take you to a taxi,' he suggested.

'If there was telephone anywhere around I could call someone,' Sam said hopefully.

'Yes, yes, good idea,' Ahmed pronounced. He reached over to the table behind Sam, and handed her a large mobile phone. 'I am businessman,' he laughed when he saw her surprised look.

Sam pulled Emil's business card from her pouch and punched in the number. 'Emil?'

'Yes, Emil,' he said.

'Emil, this is Sam. You know, Sam and Maggie.'

'Yes, Maggie.'

'No, it's Sam. I am in the Khan el Khalili, and I have *lost* Maggie. Could you come and get me, please?'

'How you get there, Sam?'

'Ser-veece taxi – very bad drive,' Sam said.

Emil cackled with laughter. '*Where* you are?'

Sam held the phone away from her mouth, 'Ahmed, could you tell Emil where we are, and ask the best place to meet him, please.'

When Ahmed finished talking he disconnected the call. 'He say 15 minutes. Stay here.'

Exactly 15 minutes later Emil walked jauntily into the shop of Ahmed Omar but stopped dead and did a double take when he saw Sam propped up on the divan.

'Did taxi crash?' he asked.

'No, why?'

'Very big hurt, Sam,' Emil stated, tapping his own chin then pointing at Sam's.

'A very big Turkish hit me,' Sam explained. 'I am okay though.' Although, as she got to her feet, she realised that her ribs hurt like hell.

'Come, bike not far. I take you back to hotel.'

'Bike?'

'Yes, bike. Limo too big for Khan. Not fit.'

Sam thanked Ahmed and Gamal again and started to follow Emil out of the shop. She stopped when she noticed something at the back of a counter near the door.

'Ahmed, could I buy this?' she asked, picking up a beautiful, hand-sized stone carving. It was Hatshepsut, a small replica of the head she'd seen in the Museum. She reached into her pouch, took out her wallet and removed 30 pounds. 'Is this enough?'

'It is *not* real, Sam Diamond,' Ahmed admitted.

'I know, Ahmed. But I like it very much.'

'It is my work.' He smiled graciously. 'But this is too much.'

Emil made a strange gurgling sound, as if he couldn't believe what he was hearing.

'Ten for Gamal,' Sam offered. 'Okay?'

Ahmed pressed his right palm to his chest and gave a slight bow.

'What you do, Sam? Promise to marry grandson?' Emil asked, as he led the way down the street towards an area crowded with small cars, wagons and livestock.

'*No* Emil, I did not.'

'Very strange. You offer 30 he should say 90. It only worth five,' Emil shrugged.

'Not to me, it's not,' Sam stated.

After a literally hair-raising ride through the streets and evening traffic of Cairo, Sam climbed off the back of Emil's motor cycle in front of the Nile Hilton. She glanced towards the river, relieved to see there was no crowd gathered around a dead body. There was no white boat either.

With Emil in tow, Sam decided to see if Maggie was in the bar before checking their room.

'Sam!' Maggie exclaimed with relief, waving her over to the table. 'I'm so glad you thought to come back here. I couldn't find you anywhere. Emil? What are you doing here?'

'I am rescuing,' Emil said proudly.

Sam sat in the chair opposite Maggie and glared at her. 'I need a beer,' she said. '*Now.*'

Maggie's eyes were now wide with horrified concern. She reached out and gently touched Sam's face. 'My god, what happened?'

'I was attacked by a knife-wielding suspicious *Turkish* fez who did *not* want to sell me perfume.'

'I thought I lost him,' Maggie said. 'It took ages to get him off my tail, and when I returned you were nowhere in sight.'

'That's because when he lost you, he came looking for me. And there I was – *waiting*,' Sam growled.

'I'm sorry, you were right; it was dumb idea,' Maggie acknowledged. 'Emil can you order us two Stellas and something for yourself, from the bar, please.'

'So what did he want?' Maggie asked when Emil was out of earshot.

'What did he want? He wanted the key, Maggie. And what's

more he knows I'm a cop. And the *other* man, the Mexican, he's following us too.'

'The Mexican,' Maggie repeated, in a tone that implied Sam had been hit a little too hard.

'Yes Maggie, the Mexican,' Sam said. She explained exactly what had happened.

'But Sam *I've* got the key,' Maggie said, when Sam had finished. 'What did you give him?'

'The key to my locker at work.'

'Why did you have that with you?'

'I've got *all* my keys,' Sam said.

'What on earth for?'

'I don't believe you, Maggie,' Sam was astounded. 'I was left alone, *by you*, in a foreign bazaar, where I was attacked by a Turk, rescued by a Mexican and helped by an old Egyptian who looked like Charlton Heston. This was followed by a warp-speed ride down Sharia Talaat Harb on the back of Emil's motor cycle, yet *you* want to know why I brought my house keys.'

'It's a reasonable question.' Maggie tried not to laugh.

'It's not funny,' Sam insisted. 'On the other hand, it's hysterical, or I am.' She broke into laughter herself. 'Do we have *any* idea what's going on yet?'

'Obviously the key we claimed here, goes with the number on the drink coaster and opens a safety deposit box at the Americo Bank,' Maggie stated.

'Obviously,' Sam agreed, as Emil returned to their table. 'But it's just another in an endless line of clues – to *what*? We haven't learnt anything at all, except that MM is Muu-Muu is you.'

'We've learnt enough to hypothesise that Alistair and Noel may have in fact been poisoned like Lloyd was. That is one coincidence that is too hard to swallow. And we know that there's a Turkish bloke out there who wants whatever it is we're looking for, and a

Mexican who is either your guardian angel or is simply waiting till we find whatever it is before pulling his own knife.'

'That's a lovely thought,' Sam said. 'But *what* could interest both a Turk and a Mexican?'

'And have been worth the lives of Lloyd, Alistair and Noel?' Maggie added and then frowned as she glanced around the bar.

'Not to mention *my* very close call,' Sam reminded her. 'I hope you've got some pain killers in your first aid kit because I'm developing a cracker of a headache.'

'Well don't drink any more beer Sam, you've probably got a concussion,' Maggie advised. 'But speaking of your close call, I rather think it's time we left this hotel. Once your assailant realises his key won't open anything this side of the equator, he's going to come looking for us.'

'Where do you suggest we go?' Sam asked. 'Somehow or other he knew to wait for us here. How many people knew that?'

'Quite a lot actually,' Maggie replied. 'Apart from the fact that I mentioned it at dinner in Melbourne the other night at a table full of *your* suspects, I also booked the room in advance which means that anyone who knew we were coming to Cairo could have found us quite easily.'

'Oh great'

'We need to split up,' Maggie began.

'Oh no, we are *not* doing that again,' Sam stressed.

Maggie leant forward. 'I will go to the phone in the lobby,' she whispered, 'ring my friend Michael at the Embassy and get him to book us a room, in his name, at the Hotel Mena House Oberoi. Emil can take you on his bike and I will take a taxi with our bags.'

Sam looked sceptical so Maggie added, 'You'll like it there, Sam. It's a grand and elegant old hotel about as close to the pyramids as you can get.'

Sam's eyes lit up. 'Okay. Although I believe a lifetime desire to see the Sphinx is clouding my better judgement. Explain why we have to go separately, though,' she requested.

'If we're still being watched by your Turkish friend he won't know which of us to follow.'

'Oh, like last time. Good plan.' Sam squinted at Maggie. 'Let's hope the Mexican isn't actually in cahoots with the Turk, and only helped out because he thought it premature to bump me off in the Khan.'

'This time you will be safe with Emil and we'll leave at the same time, after laying a false trail by telling the concierge we're checking out because we've decided to fly to Luxor tonight.'

'Maggie, the only good thing about this plan is that if Mr Fez-head turns up at our next hotel, we'll know your Embassy buddy is the mule who led him to us in the first place,' Sam stated.

'The mule?' Maggie queried.

'Mole, I meant mole,' Sam stammered. 'The informer, the rirty dat who squealed on us.'

'The rirty dat?' Maggie repeated. 'I think *you'd* better take the taxi, Sam.'

'I think we'd better get our stuff together and get out of here before I cark it completely. I do believe the day has caught up with and is about to overwhelm me.'

In the end Maggie took the taxi, or rather a series of taxis, while Sam clung on to Emil for dear life as he navigated a network of narrow backstreets before emerging onto to Sharia al Ahram, or Pyramids Road. By eight o'clock they were ensconced in their extravagantly luxurious suite at the Mena House Oberoi, where Sam was contemplating notions of untimely death versus immortality as she gazed in awe at one of the Seven Wonders of the Ancient World.

The largest and closest of the Great Pyramids, that of Pharaoh Cheops, rose shimmering with a supernatural glow from the dark desert of the surrounding Giza plateau. It was as if the ancient gods had left a light on to guide the Pharaoh's *ka,* or life force, home again after a spot of astral travelling.

Sam shook her head and moved the ice pack from her jaw to her temple. She knew the nightly Sound and Light Show was in progress and that, according to Maggie, even archaeologists and academics went a bit silly during their first pyramid experience, tending to pile adjectives and superlatives on top of wild theories, but Sam worried that she'd developed some kind of weird New Age side effect from having her head smashed into a wall.

Still she couldn't help but be completely awestruck. The pyramids, she knew, were not just monumental tombs to safeguard a dead king's desiccated, organless body and his household treasures, but were designed as indestructible sanctuaries to protect his life force and provide a place for his subjects to worship his immortal *ka.*

And in a sense Cheops and Chepren *had* achieved a kind of immortality whether their *ka* had survived four-and-half millennia or not. For even now, at the end of the 20th century *AD*, their names were still uttered with a kind of reverence because their beliefs had culminated in feats of engineering so incredible they had conquered history itself. The pyramids had outlived the pharaohs, outlasted invading Greeks, Romans and Arabs, survived Marmelukes, Ottomans and British occupation, and had withstood the ultimate test of time and the unforgiving desert.

How the hell did I get here? Sam wondered.

W*hy* did a stranger try to kill me? And why am I letting all this shit happen around me, without tying Maggie to the bed and dragging the truth out of her?

Because *Samantha*, you decided to make the most of a bizarre situation. Two days ago your being here was only a possibility in your wildest dreams, then Maggie says "we're going to Cairo" and your boss orders you to do just that, so you reply "oh okay, whatever you say". I mean who would turn down a free trip to Egypt?

'Who are you talking to?' Maggie asked, emerging from the bathroom dressed in a purple knee-length T-shirt.

'Cheops,' Sam replied. She was about to begin a serious interrogation of the woman before her when she noticed a strange mark on her throat. 'Maggie, I don't mean to get personal – well, yes I do – but is that a love bite on your neck?'

Maggie pursed her lips, waggled her head and said, 'What if it is?'

Sam opened her mouth, closed it, opened it again, then finally managed to say, 'Hercules?'

'Yes of course. Who else? I told you he got all my wires abuzzing. I'm sure you and Phineas–'

'We did *not*,' Sam protested.

'Why ever not?' Maggie asked.

'Apart from the fact that the opportunity did not present itself, *and* I was preoccupied with the wild idea that I had 20 hours to prepare for my first overseas trip, I have no interest in Mr Tall, Handsome and Arrogant. Besides, being with Marcus is kind of like having the flu, it affects your entire body but the moment you've recovered you can't even *imagine* feeling that bad.'

'Sam dear, I believe you have a problem if you equate good old-fashioned lust with the flu.'

'I wasn't. I was equating Marcus with the flu. When he's not in my space I don't give him a second thought, except as a suspect. Speaking of which I would like to know *exactly* what you told Jim Pilger to convince him that I should accompany you into this international bloody clichéd web-thing of murder and intrigue.'

Maggie's smiling face turned all serious and she sat down on the bed. 'I told him that I believed Lloyd's murder was connected to a missing and priceless artefact, that we were already on the trail of said artefact, and that it would reflect gloriously on him should we, on behalf of the Australian Government, recover whatever it is and return it to whoever owns it.'

Sam raised her eyebrows. 'Since when have we been on the trail of a priceless artefact?'

'Well we *must* be,' Maggie said. 'We've got Turks and Mexicans after us. What else could it be?'

'I have *no* idea Maggie,' Sam admitted. 'But none of that explains why *I'm* here.'

'Jim owed me a favour. I asked for you.'

Sam waited.

'It was a *very big* favour. Fifteen years ago Jim suffered a profound lack of judgement in his choice of bedmate during a week-long fact finding mission in Western Australia. I helped the potential problem go away by securing her a job she'd always wanted on a national magazine.'

'And?'

Maggie shrugged. 'I needed your help. That's how I got it, although Jim *could* see the potential PR value in my artefact story.'

'So you lied to him.'

'Not exactly. We *are* on the trail of something are we not? You wouldn't have agreed to come if you didn't think there was a good enough reason.'

'I don't know about that,' Sam said doubtfully. 'I was here before I had time to think about the logic of it.'

'*The Rites of Life and Death* show's visit to Cairo does coincide with Noel's so-called stroke, doesn't it?' Maggie said.

'Yes,' Sam confirmed. 'The exhibition was here from March 23 to the end of May, before going to Paris. Maggie, I think we need to talk to Patrick again. He said Noel went for coffee with an acquaintance, not a friend or a colleague, but an acquaintance. Maybe it was Barstoc.'

'Perhaps, assuming this has anything to do with you drug theory. But of all those involved with the show my money's on Enrico Vasquez. Why else would he be trying so hard to turn your attention towards everybody else?'

'Good point,' Sam noted a little vaguely because she'd just been struck with a "why didn't I think of it before" thought.

'What about your mate Pavel Mercier?'

'Pavel's not responsible for any of this,' Maggie said defensively. 'He's–'

'He's *dead*, I know Maggie. But it's the fact that he is dead *too* that makes him a potential piece in this puzzle. Where, when and how did he die?'

Maggie's face paled, for a moment. 'Peru, January last year, I think.'

'What do you mean, you *think*?'

'I mean I think it was January. In the last 25 years Pavel has been reported killed or rumoured to be dead at least 11 times, all in weird or sensational ways. You see he was so well known, throughout our little world, that an innocent story about Pavel coming down with glandular fever would sort of Chinese whisper its way along the archaeologist's/university/museum grapevine until it became a fact that he'd been killed in the jungle by a poison arrow.'

'He was poisoned?' Sam was incredulous.

'In 1973 he was poisoned, in 1978 he was killed in a landslide, in 1982 he had a heart attack while doing the deed with his non-existent Peruvian mistress, in 1990 he was shot by a jealous husband, in 1992 he died in a plane crash in the Andes.'

'And last year?'

'Last year he finally did it for real. He got knocked down by a car in Cuzco and died of his injuries in hospital three or four days later.'

'Are you sure?'

'Yes, I'm sure. After the poison arrow incident in 1973 I made Pavel promise to contact me every three months regardless of where he was or what he was doing. It became a sort of joke because although his work often kept him deep in the jungle for up to 10 months at a time he always managed to find someone to pass on his messages. I regularly got notes that simply said 'still ticking' or 'jumping for joy' or 'these old bones ain't what they used to be'.

'I received that last one in October '96, so when I heard about the car accident I ignored it until the start of February. When I didn't hear from Pavel, I contacted the manager of the hotel where he always stayed when in Cuzco. She sent me a newspaper clipping about the accident, dated December 29, and a box of his stuff.'

'Okay so it wasn't a stroke, but maybe he was run down on purpose,' Sam suggested. She got up to pace the room and work her idea.

'Pavel's death doesn't fit your Exhibition itinerary theory. Marcus's show did *not* go to Peru.'

'But maybe someone *from* the show did.'

Maggie laughed. 'I think you're starting a whole new puzzle here, with Pavel as the only piece.'

'No, no. His piece has to be connected somehow.' She stopped pacing and rested her forehead against the cold window as she stared blankly out at the Great Pyramids and sifted through the clutter in her memory.

Her eyes were shining when she turned to face Maggie. 'I think this whole thing has something to do with Manco City. That photograph is the only connection between all four men.'

'Forty years of friendship and parallel careers is a much stronger connection,' Maggie stated.

'But four out of the 16 people in that photograph have died in unusual circumstances in less than two years.'

Maggie shook her head doubtfully. 'You found that photo by

accident under a pile of magazines, Sam. There was no reference to it, direct or obscure, in the notes left by either Lloyd or Noel.'

'But the same photo was missing from its frame in Marsden's office.' Sam sat next to Maggie on the bed.

'And both Marsden and Winslow both referred to *the finder*; the Professor had a ticket to Lima, and Winslow's note said he was going to "seek the finder". I bet you Patrick will confirm that Noel Winslow had been struck with a sudden urge to visit Peru.'

# Chapter Nineteen

Cairo, Wednesday September 22, 1988

AFTER RUNNING A GAUNTLET OF HAWKERS AND MONEY CHANGERS ON their short walk down Talaat Harb, Sam and Maggie sat in the hushed atmosphere of the Americo Bank waiting for the manager; for it was only he, they had been informed, who could attend to the safety deposit box vault.

They'd already been waiting long enough for Emil, who had picked them up at 8 am in a nondescript vehicle, as per Maggie's request, to make his first drive-by. He had dropped them off around the corner from the bank, where Maggie had asked him to wait for 15 minutes, before cruising around the block to pass the bank – every 10 minutes until they emerged.

Sam had been tempted to comment that Maggie's precautions were taking the cloak and dagger routine a little too far, until she realised the normally cool, calm and extremely collected Maggie Tremaine was actually nervous.

'You realise this is not going to be as easy as getting the box at the hotel.' Maggie tapped her foot impatiently.

'It might be just as easy. If Noel left the key and the box number for Lloyd *or* you, then he probably left the box in your names as well.'

'Apologies Madame, for keeping you waiting,' said a tall, bony man with a face like a ferret. He was all nose, with beady eyes and a prune-like mouth overhung with a thick moustache.

Mr Halim introduced himself as the manager, escorted them through a security door, down a short hall and into a secure room where he offered them coffee.

'Thank you, but no,' Maggie stated. 'We would just like to check my box and be on our way.' Maggie placed the key and a page from a notebook, on which she'd transcribed the number from the drink coaster, on the table in front of her.

'I will also need your name and some identification,' Mr Halim pointed out.

'Of course' Maggie handed him her passport. 'My name is Maggie Tremaine.'

'This says Mar-ga-ret,' he enunciated.

'Yes, Margaret Selby Tremaine.'

'Very good. I will now check the number against the register and return here with the box if all is as it should be. You understand this is procedure for someone who has never been to our bank.'

'I understand,' Maggie nodded. 'This is nerve-wracking,' she said when Mr Halim had left the room. 'What do you suppose the 'procedure' is if I'm not authorised to claim the box?'

'A week of intense police interrogation which escalates into an international incident when the Australian Government has to negotiate your release from jail,' Sam said.

'You' haven't forgiven me for yesterday, have you?'

Before Sam could reply, Mr Halim re-entered the room, placed the safety deposit box on the table and left again, without saying a word.

'Boy are you lucky,' Sam said. 'I hear the Cairo cops are extra tough on fraud suspects.'

'Ha, ha,' Maggie said, before inserting the key to open the lid.

She removed a heavy tin, the size and shape of a school pencil box, bearing a label which said: *For LM or MT*.

There were also two manila envelopes – one addressed to Lloyd *or* Muu-Muu; and the other to Patrick Denton.

Maggie prised the lid off the tin and removed a great wad of bubble wrap, inside which was something wrapped in red cloth. She laid it on the table, glanced at Sam and unfolded the cloth.

'Good grief!' was all Sam could manage.

It was a finger.

A huge gold, she picked it up, *solid* gold finger; about 15 centimetres long by five thick.

Sam looked at Maggie whose expression registered something, puzzlement maybe, but *not* surprise. 'Maggie,' she snarled, 'you knew about this, didn't you?'

'Not – *really*,' Maggie replied.

'What is it?'

'It's a pinky finger, Sam. Apart from that I don't know, except–'

'Is this the missing and priceless artefact you told Pilger about?'

'Not precisely, no.' Maggie started to undo her shirt buttons.

'But it *is* a priceless artefact.'

'Undoubtedly, but I couldn't say whether it's missing or not, because I've no idea where it comes from.' Maggie pulled her shirt out from her trousers.

'Why are you getting undressed? And what on earth is that?'

*Under* her shirt, Maggie was wearing what looked like a soldier's utility vest, except this one was black, hugged her tightly around the stomach under her breasts, and featured a very large front pocket. She opened the pocket's velcroe flap, removed a cloth-wrapped object and placed it on the table.

'*That* is the artefact I showed Jim Pilger,' she said.

Sam removed the cloth and fixed her gaze on the artefact. She took a deep breath, to compose herself, because she had a feeling she knew *exactly* where it had come from, and wanted to ensure the urge to throttle Maggie Tremaine had passed – before she spoke.

She lifted and placed the enormous gold *thumb* next to the very gold pinky finger on the red cloth.

'Where did you find this?' she asked politely.

Maggie at least had the grace to look extremely guilty. 'Lloyd's cottage, in the box in the book,' she confessed. 'I'm sorry, Sam.'

'And you claim you don't know what it is, apart from the obvious?'

'I swear I don't, but I'm willing to bet there's at least three more pieces, fingers – somewhere.'

Sam paced the room, to the door and back. 'Honest to god, Maggie, if I were a six-year-old I'd thump you in the arm. *Very* hard. And if I was at home right now, I'd arrest you for obstructing a murder investigation.'

'I haven't obstructed anything at all, and you know it. We're here looking at this pinky finger because I did the only sensible thing and went right to the top of your bureaucratic tree and got permission for us to take this murder investigation in the appropriate direction.

'If I had shown this thumb to you at Lloyd's on Sunday, you would have felt compelled to admit it as evidence, and that unimaginative man-mountain Homicide detective would have ignored it or tried to shove it into his neat and cosy but completely inaccurate little theory about Lloyd's death being a one-off local murder.'

Maggie's voice, though still firm and righteous, had grown quieter in direct proportion to the anger expressed on Sam's face, which was now very dark indeed.

'Is there anything else you'd like to tell me?' Sam held her hands out and wiggled her fingers. 'Any other little secrets?'

'No. You know everything that I know. I promise.'

'Good,' Sam said, although her green eyes were narrow with

suspicion, 'because I do not appreciate being used. It is not nice finding out that you're not trusted by someone you trust and respect. Don't say a word,' Sam ordered, holding up her hand.

Maggie closed her mouth obediently.

'I especially don't like being kept in the dark. Had I known what we were looking for *and* that you already had part of it, I would not have stood around in the Khan el Khalili like a shag on a bloody rock waiting for a murderous Turk to beat the crap out of me.

'But, although I am sorely tempted, I am *not* going to handcuff you and drag you home because we *are* on to something here, and you're probably quite right about Jack's reaction, had I been in a position to turn this over to him.

'Besides, I can't pretend I've not made the most of this Egyptian expedition, nor can I ignore the fact – unfathomable as it is at the moment – that I like you, and despite everything I'm having fun.'

Sam frowned, as if she couldn't believe what she'd just said.

'Are you finished?' Maggie smiled.

'Yes. You can open the other thing now.'

'Thank you.' Maggie emptied the contents of the envelope onto the table.

'Oh good, another postcard,' Sam said cheerfully. 'What's it of this time?'

'La Compañía,' Maggie stated. 'It's a Jesuit-built church in the Plaza de Armas, in Cuzco. The card was posted from Peru on May 20th.'

'Peru no less,' Sam said, not in the least surprised. 'What does it say?'

Maggie turned the card over.

> Got your message. Come at once.
> Seek me on the board at Hostal Casona.
>
> Henri Schliemann.

'Ha! *What* did I say?'

'You said this had something to do with Manco City.'

'I did, didn't I. Who is Schliemann, do we know him?'

'Well, *Heinrich* Schliemann was the German-born archaeologist who discovered Troy. But I've no idea who Henri is.'

Sam raised an eyebrow. 'He *discovered* Troy. Maggie, he's probably *the finder*.'

'I don't think so dear, he's dead.'

'*Another* dead archaeologist?'

Maggie laughed. 'Heinrich Schliemann is *very* dead, Sam. He popped off round about 1890.'

'Oh,' Sam grunted. 'You know, there's something wrong with the progression of all these cards and notes. If Schliemann, whoever he is, posted this to Noel on May 20, and Noel posted his to Marsden on May 28, then why didn't the Professor do as Noel suggested and contact you, Muu-Muu?

'Even if we factor in a slow postal boat via China he would have got the postcard sometime in June, but he did nothing until he started going peculiar when Marcus's show arrived.'

'That's a very good point,' Maggie noted. 'No, I know. Lloyd spent a couple of months, on and off from early June, in the Northern Territory on a curatorial project for one of the Aboriginal centres. Also the postcard was sent to the cottage, which Lloyd only went to for the odd weekend away, and by the time he started to panic about all this, I was in Paris.'

Sam sighed deeply. 'I think it's time to talk to Patrick again.'


Patrick Denton had tears in his eyes as he slid the pages back into the envelope that bore his name.

'It's an official letter drawn up by a solicitor in London advising Noel's publishers that I have sole entitlement to all copyrights and royalties on his books.'

'That's wonderful Patrick.' Maggie squeezed his hand. She called out to Sam, who had excused herself from the room so she wouldn't intrude on Patrick's privacy.

Sam had to drag herself in from the balcony where she'd been standing, a glass of lemonade almost forgotten in her hand, as she drank in the view of the Nile instead. A huge white cruise ship, not unlike the one she'd seen while lying unconscious in Ahmed Omar's shop in the Khan, and 15 feluccas had passed by in the space of a few minutes.

Sam sat on the couch opposite Maggie and Patrick. As agreed she let Maggie begin.

'Patrick, was Noel agitated, excited or upset about anything in that week before he died?'

Patrick shrugged. 'Yes. All of the above, as well as vague as a violet and extremely jumpy. But that was situation normal in the final stages of writing every book.'

'I mean anything out of the ordinary,' Maggie said. 'As if he'd had strange or bad news; maybe just a few days before he died.'

Patrick thought for a few moments. 'Two days before, he spent ages on the phone, making international calls. He was annoyed because he couldn't get through to anyone he tried until he spoke to someone, um McBride I think, in Edinburgh.'

'Jean McBride?' Maggie asked.

'Maybe. Anyway, he was really upset after that. But all he would tell me, was that he'd lost an old friend. That she had died five months before and he hadn't known.'

'*She* had died,' Maggie repeated. 'You don't know who it was?'

'No. Noel said I didn't know her.'

'May I use your phone? To ring Scotland.' Maggie asked, already half way to the desk.

'Go ahead,' Patrick shrugged. 'What's this all about, Sam?'

'Probably nothing,' Sam lied, keeping her promise to Maggie

not to upset Patrick with any talk of foul play. 'You said Noel had coffee with an acquaintance the morning he died. Who was that?'

'Andy Baxter. He's an English mystery buff and aspiring crime writer who tracked Noel down through the museum just the week before. But Baxter wasn't there when Noel had his stroke.'

Baxter, my arse, Sam thought. She reached into her pouch and pulled out some snapshots of *The Rites of Life and Death* staff, courtesy of Ben Muldoon's surveillance team.

'Yeah, that's him,' Patrick said, pointing out Andrew Barstoc. 'Is he a criminal or something?'

'Or something, Patrick. He claims he's a businessman. *I* think he's a smuggler. And, before you ask, we don't know what he wanted from Noel, unless it was info about Lloyd Marsden,' Sam lied.

'I met Mark too, briefly,' Patrick said, tapping the photo of Bridger.

'Did Noel spend time with Marcus Bridger as well?' Sam asked, puzzled.

'Not really. Mark dropped Andy off at the cafe two days before Noel died. I didn't stay for lunch, so I don't know if they spent any time together. But Mark did come back to collect Andy.'

'I just spoke to Angie McBride in Edinburgh,' Maggie said, slumping down onto the couch next to Patrick. She was as white as a sheet and her hands were shaking. 'Her sister, my friend Jean, was killed in a hit and run accident two days before Christmas last year.'

'Oh shit,' Sam uttered.

'That is an understatement.' She took a breath and turned to Patrick. 'I don't suppose Noel had a sudden urge to go travelling anywhere just before he died.'

'Yes, he did. The day before he came home and announced we

were *both* going to Peru. Just like that. He'd booked tickets for the Saturday. We never made it, obviously.'

'Did he say why he wanted to go *there* in particular?' Sam asked.

'He'd changed his mind about Mexico and had decided to set the 10th Jake St James book in Peru, but he needed to track down a guy called Schliemann who was an expert in – something.'

Sam glanced at Maggie, as a shiver crawled its way up her spine. 'What now?' she asked.

Maggie's raised eyebrow and half smile spoke volumes.

'You're kidding?' Sam said. 'You're not kidding.'

# Chapter Twenty

Peru, Friday September 25, 1998

SAM STILL COULDN'T BELIEVE IT. ONE MOMENT SHE WAS TRYING TO GET her head around being in Africa, and the next she found herself on a whole other continent altogether. She couldn't believe that five days after unexpectedly leaving home for Egypt she was suddenly in South America. She couldn't believe she was travelling in a country she'd never considered visiting, and that she was within spitting distance of Maccu Picchu. But mostly she couldn't believe that she was going to die on her second day in Peru because *Maggie* had entrusted their lives to a questionably-qualified pilot who insisted on flying his antiquated cargo plane way too close to the ground. The *ground* in this case being the Andes, over which they were flying en route from Lima to Cuzco.

As the plane lurched through an air pocket caused, she had no doubt, by sucking up air currents from the sickeningly deep ravine below them, Sam tried to will her thoughts back to the spa bath at the luxury hotel in Lima where they'd spent the previous night. It didn't work. Nothing could take her mind off the truth she'd just discovered: Sam Diamond was scared of flying, at least in anything smaller than a 747. When she glanced at Maggie it dawned on her she was travelling with a lunatic. Good grief! Here they were flying towards certain death, in an aircraft held together by baling twine and wishful thinking, and Maggie was checking out the scenery and smiling.

Sam needed something to take her mind off the fear and nausea and as an in-flight movie was not an option she tapped her companion on the arm. 'Maggie, at what point does grave robbing become archaeology?' she shouted over the engine noise.

Maggie looked momentarily flumoxed by the question, but she recognised the white-knuckled, wide-eyed stare and rigid body of the classic *we're about to crash* passenger.

'I suppose it's a fine line when you think about it,' she replied obligingly. 'But archaeologists are scientists or, more poetically, we are historical detectives. We're looking for the truth in history, the facts about past civilisations and the connections between what was and what is. I suppose the main distinction between a grave robber and an archaeologist is motive. If you dig for personal profit you're the former; if you excavate to add to the body of human knowledge you're the latter.'

'Have you ever thought the person whose grave or tomb you're excavating might not recognise the difference.'

'I doubt they'd notice, Sam.'

'I guess so, but we don't know for sure, do we? What if Tutankhamun's *ka* was dragged into a void because all his stuff for the next life was ripped off by some archaeologist for our benefit?'

'I imagine he'd be quite upset,' Maggie acknowledged. 'Tell me about his mask again, Sam.'

'Oh, it was the most exquisite thing I've ever seen,' Sam raved, then grabbed Maggie's hand as the plane plummeted what seemed like a thousand miles in two seconds before levelling out again.

'We're gonna die,' Sam moaned.

'No we're not,' Maggie reassured her. 'So, Tutankhamun's mask; its *rightful* place is covering the mummified remains of a comparatively insigificant pharaoh. By rights it should still be in his sarcophagus, locked in his dark tomb in the Valley of the Kings. But if that were the case most of what we know about ancient Egypt would be unknown, because so much of it was recorded on the walls of tombs like his. A entire civilisation would be lost to us.'

'Well, is there a statute of limitations or something to guarantee a body has a bit of peace and quiet before some archaeologist digs it up again in the name of historical research? I mean how would you feel if one of your colleagues decided to have a close look at your mother?'

'I'd be upset, naturally,' Maggie smiled. 'But I think my mother would have a thing or two to say about it herself, seeing she's alive and well and living in Carlton.'

'Oh, sorry,' Sam said.

'Perhaps a cemetery becomes part of history when there are no descendants left to take out lawsuits or complain to the newspapers,' Maggie suggested. 'But unless civilisation as *we* know it takes a complete nosedive into obscurity and all the records we've been keeping for several hundred years get chucked into a giant shredder, I think we and our immediate ancestors are pretty safe.'

'Well I think we should conjure up a few curses, just in case,' Sam suggested. She knew she was babbling, but couldn't help it. The plane had jumped left for no apparent reason. 'I mean those old pharaohs laid curses against grave robbers didn't they, and just look what happened to Howard Carter and whats-his-name,' she said, stabbing the air with her finger.

'Ah, curses. Pavel could have told you all about curses. He was an expert on them.'

'Anthropo-things and the Supernat...*oh god*,' Sam clutched her stomach. 'Maggie are you sure the pilot's awake?'

'I'm sure. You know Pavel was a genius, unequalled in his field, but he was also something of a fruitcake; mostly due, I must admit, to an overindulgence of exotic plants. He not only studied and wrote about superstitions and the supernatural but he believed in all of it. Especially curses.'

'And you don't, I take it?' Sam asked.

'I do and I don't. I believe in the power that a curse can have on a gullible or paranoid individual. If you *believe* you're cursed then you will fall into the hole that everyone else has managed to avoid. But I doubt the curse on Tutankhamun's front door inspired the encephalitic mosquito that caused Lord Carnarvon's death; or that Carter – who lived another 17 years by the way – would still be around if he'd heeded the warning and not opened the tomb.'

Sam, who'd been concentrating on Maggie's face, screwed her eyes shut as the plane dropped, lurched, bounced and then screamed as if its wings had been ripped off.

'*We* are going to die. We're *going* to die. Yes. No question. We're dead.'

'We've landed, Sam.'

'We have? I knew that. Let me out of this thing.'


Cuzco, Peru, September 25, 1998


Sam paced the lobby of the quaint *Hostal La Casona* while Maggie conversed with the desk clerk in Spanish. The only words Sam understood were 'Schliemann' and 'archaeologist', both of which appeared to get a negative response. She wandered over to the front door and took another look at the amazingly baroque church of La Compañía and the Cathedral next to it on the other side of the huge Plaza de Armas. She was feeling almost human again after spending the entire taxi ride from the airport with her head between her knees trying not to throw up. Maggie kept pointing out interesting landmarks and Inca walls while Sam said she'd look at them later.

She stepped aside to let two bearded backpackers enter the hostel and spotted a noticeboard by the front door.

"Seek me on the board" Schliemann's note had said, so Sam went seeking. There were pamphlets about bus tours, business cards from trekking companies, a very old note from Sven telling Helga to meet him at Quillabamba, another from Helga telling Sven to get stuffed, and under a breakfast menu for the *El Ayllu Cafe* was a small blue card which read:

> *Noel, visit me at Mamakuna VII*
> *H. Schliemann esq.*

'Maggie, I've found him,' Sam called out.

'Oh, well that's useless,' Maggie complained, peering over Sam's shoulder. 'I've no idea what that means.

'Mamakuna is not a place, it's an Inca word for a class of chosen celibate women who served the Inca state. The Spanish called them Virgins of the Sun. They taught the women who were chosen to be wives of the Inca king or his nobles; they performed a host of religious functions related to sun worship; and, as spinners, weavers and brewers, they were very important to the Inca economy. But you can't *visit* them. Come on, let's go check into our hotel.'

'Aren't we staying here?' Sam grabbed her pack and followed Maggie across the plaza.

'Not unless you want basic accommodation, communal showers and only a slim chance of hot water. It's clean and cheap there, but I think the *Hotel Royal Inca* is more our style. After we've settled in, I'm going to call a friend at the Museum of Natural History in New York to see if she can identify this Henri Schliemann.'

'Why didn't you think to do that before we came all this way for nothing?' Sam asked.

'What? And miss that wonderful flight from Lima?'

'I am *walking* back to Lima, you know that don't you.' Sam was memorising landmarks in case Maggie decided to abandon her because she was complaining too much.

The *Hotel Royal Inca* was just what the doctor ordered and while Sam devoured her share of the lunch they'd requested from room service, Maggie put in a call to New York.

'I may have something,' she announced, hanging up the phone. 'My friend, Ruth, hasn't heard of Schliemann but she tells me that there are several internationally-funded excavations going on here at the moment. She thinks one or two of the sites are believed to have been special ceremonial centres for the mamakuna. It was originally thought that Maccu Picchu was such a city but that theory was discounted. Anyway Ruth is going to fax me a list of sites and anything else she can come up with that might help.'

Tweny minutes later, just as Maggie emerged from the shower, there was a knock at the door. Sam bounded off the bed to answer it and returned with a wad of fax paper.

'My god there's a lot of foreigners ferreting around down here,' she exclaimed, flicking through the pages. 'Names, maps, pictures, grid references; boy, your friend sure is thorough. *Whoa*, pictures.' Sam's mouth remained open in amazement.

'What? What have you found, Sam?'

'Huayna Picchu, North-East Seven!' Sam announced. She turned the picture around to show Maggie. 'Guess where we're going?'

'Where?' Maggie asked squinting at the bad fax copy of a photograph.

'Manco City,' Sam declared. 'Where else?'

# Chapter Twenty-One

Aguas Calientes, Peru, Sunday September 27, 1998

SAM SWATTED AT A BUZZING INSECT AND STRETCHED HER LEGS OUT IN THE hot springs that gave the village of Aguas Calientes its name. The presence of a group of rowdy trekkers had almost put her off this indulgence until she remembered this would be the last time she'd see hot water for a week. The trekkers, mostly American students, had been full of "amazing, incredible, next time I'm taking the train" stories of their four-day trek along the Inca Trail from Kilometre 88 to Machu Picchu.

'Just wait till you see it,' they'd all said and Sam had said 'yeah she couldn't wait', because she wasn't about to admit that she was within eight kilometres of Peru's most famous Inca ruins and was going to bypass them altogether.

While Sam had spent most of the previous day in Cuzco sleeping off the accumulative effects of a Turkish thrashing, jet lag and a marked increase in elevation, Maggie had gone on an equipment shopping spree and secured the services of a guide to take them to Manco City.

The guide was an old acquaintance, who had accompanied her

on previous treks to archaeological sites buried deep in the Andean wilderness; and the equipment included sleeping bags, mats, a tent, a stove, cooking pots, a compass, maps, torches and warm jackets. Sam didn't think they'd get further than the front door of the hotel with all that stuff but Maggie assured her that by the time they reached Richarte's home in Ollantaytambo, he would have organised the rest of their supplies and porters who would carry everything.

The first part of the trip from Cuzco had been uneventful, if travelling in the back of a truck through incredible mountain scenery can be labelled with such an understatement. Their journey had taken them north from Cuzco to the town of Pisac, where a bustling and colourful Sunday market had attracted crowds of locals and quite a few tourists. From there the truck headed north-west into the Sacred Valley, taking the only road that followed the course of the spectacular Urubamba River, and on to Ollantaytambo, a village built on Inca foundations.

Richarte, a jovial and friendly middle-aged man with a huge moustache, had greeted Maggie affectionately and conveyed them and their gear to his house where he provided a hearty late breakfast. Three hours later he bundled them, three of his sons, and what looked to Sam like enough supplies for a year, on to a local train bound for Machu Picchu. The railway was the only way to get to the ruins, apart from the four-day Inca pedestrian Trail, and the trip to Aguas Calientes had taken nearly two hours.

While Sam had enjoyed the scenery, Maggie and Richarte had pored over maps and charts trying to work out just where it was they were going and how best to get there.

The information provided by Maggie's friend, Ruth, indicated that archaeological teams had been investigating nine small ceremonial centres scattered around the area north of Huayna Picchu. Of these centres only two, Huayna Picchu North-West Three and North-East Seven, were currently funded and had teams carrying out excavation work. Site Number Seven – which they assumed was Manco City – lay about 17 km north-east of Huayna Picchu, the solitary peak that looked like it had sidestepped out of the mountains to act as sentinel over the ruins of Machu Picchu.

Richarte had finally determined that the best option was to strike out into the jungle from Aguas Calientes, rather than from Machu Picchu where the terrain for the first part of the trek would be too hard going; so they had disembarked from the train to set up camp for the night.

After the trekkers had left the hot springs, Sam gave herself 10 minutes alone before packing up and heading back to the campsite. Maggie was sitting cross-legged on the ground in front of their tent and Richarte and his sons were busy doing something with a large pot and a small stove.

'A good cup of coffee is the only thing in life worth dying for,' Maggie sighed.

Sam nodded at Maggie's mug. 'Does that mean that's good or bad coffee?'

'This one,' she declared, and then called out to Richarte in Quechuan before turning back to Sam, 'is worth killing for.'

Sam draped her towel over the tent and then ducked inside to get Lloyd's photo out of her pack. When she emerged, Richarte's eldest son, Victor, handed her a mug of coffee and announced that food would soon be ready.

'I've been thinking about Henri Schliemann,' Maggie said.

'So have I.' Sam sat next to Maggie and handed her the piture of *Manco City 1962*. 'Do you think it's possible he's in this picture? Tell me who you know.'

Maggie pointed to each figure as she named them. 'Pavel, Lloyd, Noel, Alistair and Jean. The woman next to Jean is Sarah Croydon, she's with the University in Wellington, and beside her is Louis Ducruet, who's a French Canadian anthropologist. That's it.'

'That leaves,' Sam counted the heads, 'five people who are

obviously guides or porters, one unknown woman and these three blokes.'

'There must have been at least one other person,' Maggie said, pointing to the shadow in the foreground. 'If he was there at all, Schliemann may have been the one who took the photo.'

'Oh, damn. Anyway, five out of the seven team members you can identify are dead. That leaves four, or five, members we don't know anything about, plus a Kiwi and a Canadian. Oh, no–'

'What?'

'Marcus's show goes to Wellington next, before finishing its world tour in Montreal.'

'I thought of that. And I tried to contact Sarah and Louis while we were still in Melbourne, to see if they knew anything.'

'I thought you said you'd told me everything,' Sam said.

'I did. I have. That slipped my mind because I didn't actually speak to either of them. Sarah was on a fishing trip with her husband, and Louis is somewhere in Turkey,' Maggie explained.

The sound of Richarte banging the side of the cooking pot with a spoon heralded dinner.

'It smells great,' Sam commented, as they lined up with their bowls to accept a giant ladle of noodle something from Richarte.

'Sopa a la criolla,' Richarte said. 'Spicy soup, with meat and vegetables. Would you like a Cuzquena?'

'Um, probably,' Sam said hesitantly.

'It's beer,' Maggie explained.

'In that case, definitely,' Sam said.

North-east of Huayna Picchu, Tuesday September 29, 1998

Nursing a mug of coffee, Sam leant back against the tree and closed her eyes. Her ribs ached, her shins and knees were bruised, her arms were scratched, she was filthy, exhausted and completely invigorated. It had taken nearly two days to travel only 15 km.

They had followed overgrown trails of Inca stone, slashed through vegetation so dense they could see nothing but the plants that brushed against them on all sides, and traversed rocky promontories where the view of the surrounding mountains was utterly breathtaking.

Richarte assured them they were following a trail the whole way, but half the time it was beyond Sam how he could tell the difference between path and jungle, or trail and rocky incline.

They had crossed two high passes on an Inca roadway barely two metres wide, climbing to well over 4000 metres before descending 1200 metres to traverse a valley floor or follow the trail over a lower pass.

The ruins of a roofless, round stone building which Maggie said would have been an Inca tambo, or roadside shelter for royal couriers to rest and corral their llamas, had been their camp site the previous night. And, two hours into their trek this morning, they had rounded a rocky outcrop to find themselves at the top of a flight of ancient agricultural terraces that swept around the hillside and disappeared down into the jungle which had overgrown the lower levels. The four upper terraces were about three metres high, five wide and a hundred long. The Inca had constructed them in the same type of cut stone blocks they used for their buildings and had filled them with rich valley soil fertilised with guano. The uppermost terrace had been reclaimed by a local Indian family who were tending their crops of potatoes and maize.

'Are you feeling okay, Sam?'

Sam opened her eyes. 'I don't think I've ever felt better in my life.'

Maggie laughed. 'Well, you look like hell.'

'Thank you very much.'

'I'd give anything for a comfortable motorised armchair myself. I think I'm getting too old for all this gadding about in the wilderness.'

'You love it, Maggie. You won't stop gadding until you're confined to an armchair.'

'Ha, you're probably right. Let's get going. Richarte says we're on the home stretch.'

Three hours later they were still walking. Sam brought up the rear on a precipitous section of trail that had been cut into the cliff face, leading down from a pass. Richarte halted the group as they reached the forest and pointed ahead to where the trail disappeared into a natural fissure in the rock.

'Is that wide enough?' Maggie asked. 'Have we come the right way?'

'Of course it is wide enough,' Richarte said, stamping his foot on the pathway of Inca-laid stones. 'Come, our destination must be very close.'

Richarte led the way, followed by Maggie and Sam, then Richarte's sons. The fissure was three metres across, wide enough, Richarte announced, for an Inca and his beasts. The ground underfoot began as smooth stone with a light downward slope but as they emerged from the fissure into dense forest the path became a narrow, winding and very steep stone staircase cut from the hillside.

Ten minutes and 129 steps later, Sam reached the bottom where Maggie and Richarte were paying close attention to a wall.

'Just look at this, Sam,' Maggie exclaimed. She ran her hand over the smooth stones. 'I still marvel at the artistry of the Inca builders. These polygonal blocks were cut with no regular pattern yet each fits perfectly with the stones around it. Not a scrap of mortar was used.'

'Is this the outside of a building?'

'I doubt it,' Maggie said. 'The Inca usually used ordinary rectangular blocks, still without mortar, to construct their buildings and palaces. Polygonal masonry, or multi-sided stone like this was considered to be stronger so it was more commonly used for agricultural terraces, like the one we saw this morning, or the walls of forts or cities.'

'So is this it then?' Sam asked. 'Have we found Manco City?'

'Richarte thinks this is North-East Seven. Whatever else it may be remains to be seen.'

'It's big, whatever it is,' Sam commented five minutes later as they continued to follow the trail beside the wall. Richarte disappeared around a corner as the wall and its path took a westerly turn. When Maggie and Sam caught up to him, he was standing, staring and shaking his head in disbelief.

'What is it? Oh. Wow,' Sam exclaimed.

Maggie, who had grabbed hold of Sam's arm, stared open-mouthed in awe and delight and–

'Bloody hell!' she said. 'And, and bloody hell!'

The view, through a trapezoid window in the wall, clearly qualified as an archaeologist's dream come true.

Below them were the ruins of a large multi-level ceremonial site. There was easily 40 buildings of different sizes and in various stages of reclamation, surrounding a central plaza. Some of the larger ruins on the far side were still overgrown with vines and other vegetation but those in the centre and to the left and right had been carefully cleared and maintained; and all were connected by pathways or staircases.

'*Intihuatana*,' Richarte said, pointing to the compound's highest point, a rock pillar standing atop a pyramidal stone platform.

'The hitching post of the sun,' Maggie translated. 'The Inca worshipped the sun god, Inti, and believed that the Sapa Inca, the king, was the son of Inti. The pillar worked like a sundial except the Inca astronomers used it to mark the time of year and predict the solstices. The Sapa Inca, as the son of god, had control of the seasons and the pillar was literally a hitching post that held the sun to the earth.

'In their quest to Christianise the Indians, the Spaniards destroyed the Intihuatana wherever they found them in order to crush the heathen religion. The post at Machu Picchu was the only one known to have survived, but only because the Spanish didn't know about Machu Picchu.'

'This one obviously eluded them too,' Sam noted. 'What are those buildings on the right?'

'The big one with the wide staircase would be the Temple of the Sun because it centres on the site's largest square or Sacred Plaza. The smaller building next to it was possibly the house of the high priest, and those empty terraces running down that slope over there are ceremonial baths,' Maggie explained. 'The ruins on the far side are typical canchas. The Inca built their residences in blocks facing a central courtyard. The cancha had only one entrance, like that archway on the left.'

'How do you suppose we get in?' Sam asked.

'The same way they did.' Maggie pointed to a group of tents on the east side of the plaza.

'The tail is descending again,' Richarte said. 'The entrance must be further on.'

# Chapter Twenty-Two

IT WAS ANOTHER FIVE MINUTES AND 53 STAIRS DOWN BEFORE THEY FOUND a wide gateway that led into a maze of high stone walls. They finally emerged on the third lowest of the compound's six levels, about 50 metres from the north-west corner of the Sacred Plaza.

'Where the bloody hell did you all come from?'

A young bearded Englishman, wearing boots, shorts and a singlet, emerged from a nearby building.

'Oh, we just wandered in from Aguas Calientes,' Maggie smiled. 'Do you have a gentleman by the name of Henri Schliemann working with you?'

'We've got a Henry Morgan,' he said ushering them across the plaza. 'But no Schliemann.'

'This *is* Site North-East Seven?' Sam asked.

'Yes, but you've come a long way for someone who ain't here.'

'How many people are on the team?' Maggie asked.

'Seven of us at the moment, plus a support staff of five or six,' he said leading them to the campsite. 'I'm Phil, by the way.'

'And who's in charge?'

'That would be Xavier. Dr Xavier Tremaine.'

Maggie stopped dead in her tracks.

'Do you know him, Maggie?' Sam asked. 'Is he a relative?'

'Xavier Tremaine...is my father,' Maggie said, as if she couldn't believe what she was saying.

'Your father? I didn't know archaeology was a family tradition,' Sam said, calculating he'd have to be in his late 70s. What on earth would he be doing way out here.

'It *isn't* a tradition,' Maggie snarled. 'My father was a pharmacist in St Kilda, until his death 15 years ago. Where is he? Where is this *Dr* Tremaine?'

'Um,' Phil hesitated, looking around, 'over there, on the log by the far tent with his back to us.'

Maggie grunted. 'Give me your gun please, Sam.'

'I didn't bring my gun, Maggie. What do you want a gun for?'

'There's a man I have to kill.' Maggie strode off across the plaza.

'What are you talking about?' Sam had to run to catch up to her.

'Him.' Maggie pointed to Xavier Tremaine. 'I have to kill *him*.'

Sam grabbed Maggie's arm but she shook herself free, stepped over the log and confronted the man with her father's name.

'You bastard!' Maggie pronounced, and then decked him with a swift right hook to the chin.

Sam raised an eyebrow and smiled down at the bear of a man lying sprawled, and laughing, at her feet.

'Pavel Mercier, I presume,' she said. 'There's a rumour going around that you're dead.'

'Oh no, not me,' he said, 'I am going to live forever.'

'You *are* not,' Maggie said through clenched teeth. 'Get up you old bastard, so I can knock you down again.'

'Maggie!' Pavel rolled over so he could stand up. 'My darling Maggie, let me explain.'

'Don't you dare *my darling* me. I've spent the last eight months believing you were dead.'

'I had a situation,' Pavel began, 'and the best way to handle it was simply, um, not to be. So after I got run down by a crazy in Cuzco, I chose to disappear.'

'*You* spread the rumour?' Maggie asked.

'What can I say, eh? I am sorry I worried you.'

'I wasn't worried,' Maggie declared. 'You were dead. What's to worry about?'

'And now I am not dead. So give me a hug.'

'No! And don't you dare.' Maggie tried to fend him off, but Pavel wrapped his arms around her and lifted her off the ground.

'Now, tell me who is your lovely young friend?' he asked, as he put Maggie down again.

'My friend is Sam Diamond. She's an Australian federal police officer. And the only reason you're not lying bleeding on the ground is that she didn't think to bring her gun with her.'

'She loves me really,' Pavel said to Sam.

'I can see that.' Sam shook his hand.

'Are you truly a police officer?'

Sam nodded. 'I am.'

Pavel shook his head as if life was strange indeed. 'Come sit down. You too, Maggie. Are you hungry?'

'No,' she said.

'I'm starving,' said Sam. 'And so is she.'

'Good, then we shall eat, drink and talk,' Pavel stated. 'Wait here, I'll talk to the cook.'

Sam glanced at Maggie, who was smiling despite herself, and then turned her attention back to Pavel who had finished with the cook and was now shaking Richarte's hand vigorously. She figured the no-longer-deceased Dr Mercier to be in his mid-60s, and he was obviously strong and fit. His blue eyes held a distinctly youthful glimmer, although his thick, shaggy grey hair, sideburns and droopy moustache made him look like he'd spent too much time in the '70s.

'What is his accent?' Sam asked. 'It's sort of multi-lingual.'

'You name it, Pavel has absorbed it,' Maggie snarled.

'Aren't you pleased that he's alive?' Sam teased.

'I will be, as soon as I get over being angry that he's not dead.'

'Have you forgiven me yet?' Pavel asked, returning with two folding chairs.

'Not this side of the millennium,' Maggie declared, but she gave him a hug before sitting down.

'So tell me how are things in the big wide world outside?'

'Aren't you in the least bit interested why we're here?' Maggie asked.

'You will no doubt tell me, when it suits you, my darling.'

'Maybe. But first you explain how you can be working here with all these people, yet rumours of you being alive did not circulate like the stories of your many deaths.'

'They all think I'm Xavier Tremaine,' Pavel shrugged.

'A pharmacist from Melbourne?'

'Tis a good strong name, your father's. And what would they know, eh?' he waved his hand around the compound. 'I've got nothing but young blood working here. None of these, these children know me from Adam, or from Pavel for that matter.'

'Or Schliemann?' Sam asked.

'Or him either,' Pavel laughed. 'And *now* I know why you have come. But where is Noel?'

Maggie took a deep breath. 'He's dead, Pavel. *Really* dead, unlike you.'

Pavel's good humour dissolved. 'Oh no, dear Noel. When was this that he died?'

'Nine days after you sent him the postcard from Cuzco,' Sam said. 'And a day after *he* sent a similar card to Lloyd Marsden.'

Pavel's eyes narrowed as he glanced from Sam to Maggie. 'I fear it is only bad news you bring. Something has happened to Lloyd too, no?'

'Yes,' Maggie confirmed, placing her hand on Pavel's arm. 'He was murdered in Melbourne two weeks ago.'

'*Merde!* He was murdered? By whom?'

'We don't know by whom, but we were hoping *you* might be able to tell us why?' Sam said.

'*Moi?* But why? Our business should not have come to this.'

'That's not all of it,' Maggie said, fishing around in the vest under her shirt. 'Alistair died in a car crash last year and Jean McBride was killed by a hit and run driver just before Christmas.'

'*Madre de dios,*' Pavel swore. 'Just like the crazy who tried to run me down.' He ran his hands through his hair. 'I thought Noel was just panicking. This is very bad.'

'We think all these deaths are connected; that they were *all* murdered,' Sam stated.

'Yes,' Pavel said, as if it was obvious. 'I can maybe explain, but it is a strange and long story.'

'You can start by explaining what these are,' Maggie demanded, handing Pavel the gold digits.

'Oh my god,' Pavel slapped his forehead. 'It all gets worse. When did you arrive in Peru?'

'On Friday,' Maggie said. 'Why?'

'This explains the earthquake,' Pavel moaned, holding up the gold thumb.

'What earthquake?' Sam asked.

'Five days ago you arrive in Tahuantinsuyu, and five days ago we have a very big tremor here in the city of the last Inca king.'

'Pavel this is *not* Vilcabamba,' Maggie stated.

'No, of course it isn't, Maggie. This is Inticancha, the last refuge of Tupac Amaru.'

'Inticancha,' Maggie repeated. 'The sun's courtyard?'

'Yes, or the enclosure of the sun god or, even more simply, Inti's House. But however you translate it, this *was* the home of

Tupac Amaru, and many of his followers continued to live here for 23 years after his death.' Pavel handed the fingers back to Maggie.

'I've never heard of Inticancha,' Maggie said shaking her head. 'And I don't recall any reference or even legend that suggested Tupac Amaru lived anywhere but Vilcabamba.'

'Vilcabamba was the front line, this was the fall-back position,' Pavel explained.

'How do you know?' Maggie asked excitedly. 'I mean how can you be sure?'

'I found a sort of diary in one of the tombs; and my team, this time, found documents sealed in a box under the Sun Temple. *Written* documents, Maggie, dated from 1544 to 1595.'

'Written? What do you mean, written?'

'Why is that odd?' Sam asked, noting that the archaeologist in Maggie had taken over and she seemed to have forgotten not only her anger at Pavel, but also *why* they had come all this way.

'The Inca had no written language, Sam,' Maggie explained. 'They had a very efficient system of counting and accounting, using coloured and knotted strings called *quipu*, but they had no written symbols to record their language.

'Nearly everything we know about the Inca prior to the conquest came from the writings of Spanish soldiers, priests or travellers who were recording a conquered people's oral history. This was a mix of fact, legend and pagan beliefs. And their writings, of course, were filtered through their own prejudices, motives or understanding.'

'The same can be said about many of the documents we found here,' Pavel noted. 'Those that recounted the stories of the Inca Empire are, as you say, a blend of historical truth and colourful mythology. But there are also observations of daily life and a journal which, though not regularly kept, recorded major events as they happened, including the death of Tupac Amaru and the last days of

Inticancha. The writer, Vasco Dias, was a Portuguese traveller who lived here, lived the Inca life, for nearly 50 years.'

'This is mind-blowing, Pavel,' Maggie exclaimed. 'Why are you keeping this discovery secret?'

'But I am not,' Pavel declared. 'We have been working here for two years now and keeping our sponsors well informed of our progress. While I admit we have not announced to the world that we have made this *great* discovery, our reports and research say as much – without actually saying it.'

'So you *are* keeping it a secret,' Maggie said, shaking her head. 'You announce the minor finds to keep the excavation funded but you neglect to give them the whole picture.'

'Naturally, Maggie. I want no interlopers here, trampling the place with their enthusiasm, until–'

'Until you have finished your work and published your own paper,' Maggie finished.

Pavel shrugged. 'What can I say? But my main concern, as always, is the sanctity of this place. The balance between the tangible and intangible here is very delicate. Until we reclaim Inticancha from the jungle and restore its connection to the Incas who lived here, we cannot understand the etiquette of the place. And I will not have ignorant foreigners traipsing irreverently around the ruins until we have secured the Courtyard of the Sun from all possible violations.'

Uh, oh, whacko alert, Sam thought.

Maggie, typically, was much more direct. 'For goodness sake Pavel, what *are* you talking about?'

Pavel gave Maggie a look that said she should know better. 'For nearly 400 years, the huacas hid and protected Inticancha from all those who would violate it. They have *allowed* us to work here, unharmed, because we mean no harm or disrespect.'

'What is a huacas?' Sam asked, wondering whether she really

wanted to know. The great Pavel Mercier was beginning to sound like a New Age guru.

'A *huaca* is a talisman in which the spirits of the gods reside,' he explained. 'The Inca ascribed supernatural power to a variety of objects, natural and handmade, to places they regarded as holy sites such as a caves, mountains or special rocks, and to natural phenomena like storms, eclipses, or even the birth of twins.

'Sickness or bad luck was thought to be punishment for neglecting the huacas. When cutting stone for building, the Inca would take great care not to disturb the spirits. The sculptor who carved the Intihuatana over there, for instance,' he waved at the hitching post, 'would have taken away from the original stone only those parts that were not occupied by huaca. Some huaca are even endowed with the power of commination.'

'The power of what?' Sam asked.

'The power to seek vengeance or exact punishment. Before Vasco Dias and the last few surviving Incas closed the gates behind them when they left in 1595, the high priest called on the huaca to curse any trespassers who walked with malice within the walls of Inticancha.'

Maggie groaned. 'Oh Pavel, not more curses.'

'Yes curses, Maggie. Do not laugh. The power of the huacas within these walls is palpable. Even these cynical young people who work with me have come to respect it. Every illness or accident amongst our team can be traced to an unintentional violation of the trust we have been given.

'In fact my very first visit here ended in disaster because one of our number maliciously breached that trust.'

'Was that in 1962?' Sam asked.

Pavel looked taken aback. 'Yes. How do you know this?'

'It was the Professor's photo of Manco City taken in 1962 that led us here,' Sam explained.

'No, my dear, it was this,' Pavel pointed to the gold digits in Maggie's hand, 'this huaca that guided you here.'

'Get a grip, Pavel,' Maggie snapped. 'Sam's quite right, it was the photograph. We had no idea what these fingers were or where they came from. I fear you've been indulging in too many mind-altering substances with all this talk of huacas. You're a scientist, man, or have you forgotten that?'

'No, my darling, I have not forgotten,' Pavel laughed. 'But I also recognise that there are some things in our world that science simply cannot explain. You hold in your hand part of Inticancha's most powerful huaca. It has brought you and Sam on a great journey to find the truth of it and you reached the city safely because it recognised that your intentions are honourable. But just look at the havoc it has caused; so many dead friends.'

Maggie shook her head. 'Pavel, our friends are dead because a living, breathing human being is prepared to kill to get his hands on this valuable golden artefact. Pure and simple. No curses, no magical mystery tours, just plain unadulterated greed.'

'But Maggie,' Pavel sighed, 'everything is connected. 'The tremor we felt here marked your arrival in this country. This was *not* a coincidence but a message from the huaca you carried to the spirits of the Incas who once lived here, that the Hand of God had come home to Tahuantinsuyu.'

'The Hand of God!' Sam declared. '*That's* what '*hanosgoo, hancsgoc*' means.'

'Hanosgoo, what is this word?' Pavel asked.

'Professor Marsden left a note, or he *tried* to. We couldn't decipher it because he was dying, and probably hallucinating, when he wrote it, so the message wasn't complete.'

'Hallucinating? Lloyd?' Pavel queried.

'The Professor was poisoned with a lethal cocktail of peyote and curare,' Sam explained.

'*Merde!*' Pavel was horrified. 'But who would be so cruel?

Maggie, Sam, please explain everything. Tell me about Lloyd and Noel and how the huaca led you here.'

Maggie rolled her eyes at Sam, but together they told Pavel about Lloyd's death, their reasons for believing that Noel and the others were also murdered, their suspicions about *The Rites of Life and Death* team, and all the clues that had brought them, finally, to Inticancha.

'This is too terrible,' Pavel pronounced, when they were finished. 'It is *all* tragic but poor Jean was not even involved. She was not one of the Guardians.'

'Guardians of what, Pavel?' Maggie asked cautiously.

'Of the huaca, of course. There were only six of us sworn to protect the Hand of God. Jean was not one of them.'

'It's time to come clean, Pavel,' Maggie stated. 'Will you *please* tell us what this is all about.'

Pavel stood when a banging on the other side of the campsite announced that dinner was ready.

'We must have food,' he said, when Maggie started to object. 'Come to the cafe, I will talk while we eat. This is a long story with two parts, although now we seem to have a third instalment.'

The 'cafe' was five tables set up under the huge trees on the corner of the plaza. While they waited for the cook to spoon out thick stew into their tin plates Pavel, claiming Maggie as his sister, introduced her and Sam to the four men and two women who made up his team.

'Do *not* drink the coffee. It is diabolical,' Pavel warned. 'There is water and juice in the jugs on the tables. Go, sit, I will bring the bread.' He pointed to a table set apart from the others.

As Maggie passed Richarte in the dinner queue she whispered in his ear. He gave a short laugh and nodded.

'What was that about?' Sam asked as they sat down at the table.

'I don't intend to go without coffee, so I asked Richarte to brew some for everyone.'

# Chapter Twenty-Three

Inticancha, Peru, September 29, 1998

WHEN PAVEL SAT DOWN WITH HIS STEW, HE STARTED TALKING ABOUT THE day's work until Maggie whacked her spoon on his plate.

'Pavel, please stop beating around the bush and get to the damn point.'

The big man shrugged apologetically. 'Sorry. It is habit. But, you're right, I will begin.

'This whole thing, this mystery that has brought you here, started during the height of Inca resistance against the Spanish. Remember the Indians had no frame of reference for *our* calendar so these events, as related to Vasco Dias, happened when they happened,' Pavel threw his palms up, 'sometime after Manco Capac's unsuccessful siege of Cuzco city. Sam, do you know about this?'

'I know the basics about Manco, Tupac Amaru and Vilcabamba,' Sam replied. 'If I get lost, I'll ask questions.'

'Okay, and I will put approximate dates on these events. After the siege, Manco, along with his 20 or 30,000 warriors – we cannot be sure of the number – retreated into the jungle where he began rebuilding his kingdom and the new city of Vilcabamba. In about

1538 one of Manco's soothsayers informed him that the huaca of the Silent Springs, a small waterfall in the hills beyond the city, wished to speak directly to the king. Now this was unusual because the invisible powers of the natural world could only communicate with the intermediaries, or soothsayers, who had the ability to understand the language of the huacas and interpret omens.

'Manco was escorted to the Silent Springs where he was given some *vilca*, an hallucinogenic plant that aided communication with the huaca, and left alone.

'On the second day of his quest he was visited not by the huaca of the springs but by the Sun God himself. Inti came to Manco in a vision, laid his right hand on the rock wall beside the Silent Springs and revealed a vein of gold, which he extracted and laid at the king's feet.

'Inti instructed Manco to get his finest goldsmith to fashion a powerful huaca that would protect the Sapa Inca and his people from further harm from the invaders. The huaca would reveal 'itself' as always, Inti said, and take the form of *his* fingers. The leftover gold was to be crafted into a wrist band.

'The six separate pieces, Inti commanded, were to be taken to the far reaches of Tahuantinsuyu to guard the 'four quarters'. Manco was told he could choose the sacred place for each of the pieces himself, but that the fingers of the Sun God's hand must always be kept in formation, with the thumb to the west and the little finger to the east. The wrist band would protect the southern frontier.

'Manco returned to Vilcabamba and followed Inti's instructions. When the Hand was complete, he selected six of his most trusted couriers, and a warrior to travel with each, and dispatched them in different directions along the Inca roadways. The task given these men was a lifetime one. They were required to stay with their sacred piece, to protect it, and were empowered to choose a successor to act as Guardian on their death, but they were *never* to return to Vilcabamba unless the safety of the huaca itself was threatened.'

'This is a lovely legend, Pavel,' Maggie noted sarcastically.

'Legend it may be, Maggie my dear; mystical, magical and unbelievable too. But you have been flying around the world with two of Inti's fingers in your pocket, so there is *some* truth in this legend.'

'Well, *I'm* intrigued,' Sam said, giving Maggie a don't-be-a-spoilsport look. 'What happened next?'

'The Sapa Inca and his warriors continued to harass the enemy but Manco began to worry that his kingdom was too vulnerable with only one city, which the Spanish knew existed, so in about 1542 he started building fortified towns deeper in the jungle. One of these, he decided, would be built as a royal city; a place waiting to receive him should the Spanish ever take Vilcabamba.

'Manco entrusted the construction of this city, Inticancha, to his son Tupac Amaru. Tupac was still quite young but Manco endowed him with a title akin to vice regent which gave him complete authority. The young prince decided that the second thing to be built, after the Sun Temple, would be the *Acllahuasi*, the House of the Chosen Women, so that most of the mamakuna could be relocated from Vilcabamba immediately.' Pavel pointed to the large roofless building bordering the Sacred Plaza opposite the Sun Temple.

'Manco Capac agreed this would be a good thing. Another thing the Sapa Inca and his son decided was that no raids were ever to be carried out from Inticancha. It *was* regarded as a sacred place, but the decision was one of strategy rather than reverence. By using Vilcabamba as the base for all their attacks on the Spanish, they reasoned the enemy would never know that Inticancha existed.'

The arrival of Richarte and his coffee pot interrupted the story. Pavel took a sip. 'Richarte, my friend, you realise I can never let you leave here.'

'My wife would track me down and drag me home.'

'Where were we?' Pavel asked, when they were alone again.

'Oh yes. It was about this time, in 1544, that Tupac Amaru first met Vasco Dias who was wandering on a trail near Vilcabamba. Tupac ordered his bodyguard to execute Dias on the spot but the foreigner, uncharacteristically, threw himself on the ground and *bowed* to the Inca. Dias was 27 years old, had been in the New World for three years and in Cuzco for one, but had learnt enough Quechuan to make Tupac understand that he was *not* the enemy.

'Tupac returned to Vilcabamba with his captive, where Manco too was impressed by the young man's efforts to communicate in the Inca's own language. Though not completely trusted at first, it soon became obvious that Dias was not interested in either gold or the actions of the raiding parties, and he and Tupac eventually became friends.

'A year later, five weeks after the death of Manco Capac, a badly injured Inca stumbled through the gates of Vilcabamba. This man was the warrior who had been sent with the Guardian of Inti's thumb. The very same one you have been carrying around the world, Maggie,' Pavel said.

'The man said he had returned with his piece of the huaca because it was safe no more. The Guardian had been killed by a Spanish soldier who had come across the sacred place and tried to steal the golden huaca. The warrior battled with the soldier and although badly wounded himself managed to slit his enemy's throat. It took him five weeks of walking, hiding and tending his wounds to make it back to Vilcabamba.

'A soothsayer, who two months before had warned Manco that his life was in danger, calculated that the Sapa Inca and the Guardian had died at the same time.'

'And you know all this from the documents your team found?' Maggie queried.

'No, all this was recorded in the journal of Vasco Dias,' Pavel stated.

Sam cocked her head. 'You said *you* found a sort of diary and your team *this time* found the documents. When did you actually discover his journal?'

'She's got a memory like an elephant,' Maggie explained when Pavel stared at Sam in amazement.

'She must be a good cop too to pick up on little clues like that,' he said admiringly. 'I found the journal during our first visit here. But that revelation is getting ahead of the story.'

'Please go on, Pavel,' Sam urged.

'Following the death of Manco Capac, his first son became king but decided to live with the Spanish in Cuzco. Titu Cusi, Tupac's older brother, then became Sapa Inca and, after a vision of his own, recalled the rest of the Guardians, entrusted his younger brother with the Hand of God and told him to keep it safe in the Sun Temple at Inticancha. This was 1547 and Vasco Dias accompanied Tupac Amaru on that journey. It was his first visit to the secret city.

'For the next 27 years life went along. Titu Cusi continued his guerrilla attacks on Spanish outposts and several times a year Tupac would make the journey from Inticancha to join his brother's raids.

'Vasco Dias sometimes stayed behind in the secret city but most often he made the trip to Vilcabamba with his friend and on occasion would slip into Cuzco to spy on the Spanish.

'On the death of Titu Cusi, Tupac Amaru, the last of Manco's sons, became Sapa Inca. A year later, in 1572, a runner brought word to Inticancha that a great many enemy soldiers were gathering in Cuzco. The Sapa Inca returned at once to Vilcabamba to prepare his warriors for battle.

'But when Dias, who had travelled on to Cuzco, returned with the news that the Spanish Viceroy was raising an army to destroy Vilcabamba, Tupac realised it was time to fall back.

'Viceroy Francisco de Toledo, the bastard,' Pavel snarled, 'had made it his personal mission to finish off the Inca once and for all.

'Tupac ordered Vilcabamba be burnt to the ground, so the Spanish would gain nothing from their efforts. His people set fire to their stores, their homes, the palaces and temples, then disappeared into the jungle. Tupac remained until the end, taking charge of the destruction of his father's great city. But in the end he stayed too long. He was supervising the removal of sacred items, including the punchao and the mummies of his father and brother, when the Spanish entered the smouldering city.'

'Mummies?' Sam queried. 'I didn't know the Incas were into mummification.'

'Oh, they were *into* it in a big way,' Maggie said. 'The process and their motivation for it was quite different from that of the Egyptians though. The Sapa Incas believed they would live forever in the form of mummies, so the bodies of kings, nobles and other important people were dried, dressed in finery and sat up on chairs in special niches or caves were they could continue to give advice and be fed and attended to by family members. The shrivelled corpses were carried out on litters for festivals or special ceremonies, given food and drink and generally treated as if they were alive.'

'And the punchao?' Sam asked.

'The punchao,' Pavel said, 'was a golden effigy that contained the dust of the hearts of past Inca kings. Tupac did not save his father but he fled into the jungle with the punchao; to no avail however. The Spanish troops hunted and captured him, dragged him back to Cuzco and publicly beheaded him.'

'Where was his *mate* Vasco Dias during all this?' Sam asked suspiciously.

'Tupac had sent him ahead with the high priest but when Dias heard the king had been taken prisoner he hurried back to Cuzco. He witnessed the execution of his friend, the last Sapa Inca, and was so appalled, and ashamed of his kind, that he returned here to Inticancha where he remained until the compound was abandoned in 1595. Only 32 of the city's population of nearly 2000 had survived an outbreak of the common cold. Dias himself was 78 when they closed the gates and left here forever.'

'And then?' Maggie prompted.

Pavel responded by tapping his mug on the table and winking at Sam.

'Richarte, could we have some more coffee please,' Maggie hollered.

'Thank you my dear,' Pavel said. 'Now to part two of this story. In 1962 my team set out from Machu Picchu in search of the lost city of the Incas. When we came across this place a month later we were convinced we had found Vilcabamba.'

'Hence the photograph being given the label Manco City,' Sam said.

'Yes and no,' Pavel said. 'By the time that picture was taken we knew this was not the fabled lost city but another built by Manco Capac. Proof of this we found in the only other of Dias's documents that we found on that visit.

'We'd been here three weeks before I found the journal hidden in a cavity under a niche occupied by a mummy. I called everyone together and we spent the night poring over the writings of Dias. Of course nearly everyone was then intent on turning the ruins upside down to search for the Hand of God. We all assumed it would still be here, as Dias had made no mention of it being taken from the city when they all left.

'Lloyd was quite beside himself with the prospect of finding such an incredible artefact, Noel was like a boy on a treasure hunt and that annoying William Sanchez actually got up before dawn the next morning to start digging in the Sun Temple. It was the violent earth tremor he caused that woke everyone else up.'

'He caused it?' Maggie said dubiously.

'Yes, Maggie. He was violating the most sacred building in Inticancha and the huaca got really pissed off.'

Sam laughed, she couldn't help herself.

'This was not funny, Sam,' Pavel insisted.

'I'm sorry. It was the image of inanimate objects getting pissed off that I found amusing.'

Pavel smiled. 'I admit, it *is* something you have to experience for yourself. Anyway I laid down the law, that we would only proceed in a methodical, professional and, above all, respectful manner. Anyone who did otherwise, either through greed or impatience, would be forcibly evicted from Inticancha and banned from working on the dig.'

'Did everyone follow the rules?' Sam asked.

'We had no more warnings from the huaca so I had to assume they did. I suspected that Sanchez had been digging around the Acllahuasi, but I never caught him at it.'

'I don't know Sanchez,' Maggie said. 'Was he with us at the other site the year before?

'Yes, he was the one with the tall tales about his exploits on other digs. Very irritating he was. He was always going on about his Inca ancestors even though he was more American than I ever was. His grandfather was a mestizo who married a Texan woman. Sanchez was born in Dallas and his own wife came from San Francisco where he lived when he wasn't boring us all to death.'

Maggie shook her head. 'He must have been boring because I still can't place him.'

'Well you *must* remember his idiot son Paolo the night we all tried the vilca.'

'You tried the hallucinogenic plant?' Sam asked in amazement.

'I did not,' Maggie said emphatically. 'And neither did Lloyd. Someone had to ensure they didn't all dance off into the jungle, never to be seen again. I remember Sanchez and his son now, though.'

Pavel turned to Sam. 'This boy, he must have been about 10 years old, went into a frenzy on the vilca. When he calmed down he just sat for hours repeating that he was the reincarnation of Tupac Amaru.'

Maggie snorted. 'I seem to remember you having an interesting conversation with a wall in the high priest's house that night.'

'This is true, but while the rest of us were nursing our hangovers the next day, young Paolo remained convinced he was Tupac.'

'You can talk, you silly old man. That little chat you had with the spirits changed forever the way you approached your work. To this day you believe the huaca have the ability to get pissed off.'

'Absolutely! And, as we discovered right here in this very city, they also have the power to direct malevolent emanations that literally shrivel the desecrators of their sanctuaries.'

Maggie raised an eyebrow, and Sam wondered just how much more woo-woo stuff she could take and still keep a straight face.

'We found the Hand of God on our 53rd day,' Pavel continued, ignoring their scepticism. 'It had been hidden inside the second, smaller altar in the Sun Temple. We celebrated long into the night, but were woken again the next morning by an earth tremor, which toppled most of what remained of the Acllahuasi's front wall.

'We discovered that Inti's Hand was missing, and so was William Sanchez and his idiot son. Half our porters then ran off and left us because they feared punishment from the ancient ones and, of the others, only two would join us to follow the thief.

'We didn't have to go far. We found Paolo cowering under a tree near the almost unrecognisable body of his father, which was floating in the pool of a hot spring. Paolo said 'a big wind' had knocked his father into the pool where the hot steam had fried and shrivelled his skin in a few seconds. The water when I, cautiously, dipped my finger in was lukewarm and there was no steam.

'We returned here with the Hand, after burying Sanchez in the jungle, and tried to figure out what we should do. During the night one of the remaining porters tried to take the Hand, perhaps to protect it from us but maybe he just wanted the gold. Once again we were woken by a tremor. We found the porter in the plaza, kneeling where he had stumbled and dropped the box in which the Hand was kept. The pieces lay jumbled on the ground.

'And we watched, helpless, as that man died in agony; of what we did not know. It may have been a heart attack or just plain fear.'

'Pavel, this is too unbelievable for words,' Maggie said.

'It is the truth, I swear. Half my team were scared witless and wanted to get out of there, as did the rest of the porters. They all swore they would never reveal the location of Inticancha or speak to anyone of the Hand of God and what it had done here.

'When they were gone, there were six of us left. We consulted the journal of Dias and I spent some time in the Sun Temple thinking about our plan. I placed my hand on a map of the world to explain it better. I got no bad vibes and there were no more earth tremors so we decided the huaca, and maybe even Inti himself, approved of my idea.'

'Which was *what* exactly? Though I'm afraid to ask,' Maggie said.

'We planned to take the six pieces of the huaca to the furthest reaches of *our* world, to protect Tahuantinsuyu forever.'

'You've got to be kidding, Pavel.'

'I kid you not at all, Maggie,' Pavel said. 'We had seen with our own eyes the vengeance of the Inca spirits, yet we did not want to leave the Hand of God in Inticancha for some other greedy or just unfortunate person to find.

'Three days later we left, with the Hand in its box, to walk back to Machu Picchu. We caught the train to Cuzco and then carefully planned our departures from that city so that each of the pieces we carried remained in formation.

'Lloyd took the thumb west to Melbourne, the index finger went north to San Francisco with Barbara, the middle finger to Montreal with Louis, the ring finger to London with Alistair, and the little one went with Noel to Cairo. I took the wrist band to Chile, where I hid it amongst some insignificant artefacts in a museum in Punta Arenas.'

'Oh, my, *god*,' Maggie exclaimed. 'The Tahuantinsuyu Bracelet!'

'Yes indeed, Maggie. I worried when the Chilean authorities made such a fuss over it, after customs luckily caught that thief 10 years ago. They had no idea what it was, of course, but I was relieved when they put it in the museum in Santiago, even though it *was* too far north, relative to the other pieces. I trekked here straight away but there were no bad omens so I knew the Hand was safe.'

'Not so safe, Pavel,' Maggie said. 'The bracelet was stolen in Paris nearly three weeks ago.'

'Oh *merde,* oh shit,' Pavel swore. 'What was it doing there?'

'It was on tour with an exhibition. I was actually in Paris, at the time, trying to mediate that never-ending dispute between the Chileans and Peruvians over the bracelet's rightful ownership.'

'Was it on tour with this *Life and Death* thing you were talking about?'

'No. But, coincidentally, Marcus's show *had* just left Paris.'

'Coincidences, pah! I don't believe in them,' Pavel pronounced.

'Me either,' Sam agreed. 'And it now seems pretty certain that the bracelet is in the hands of whoever is tracking down all the pieces and killing your so-called Guardians.'

'We must formulate a plan,' Pavel decided, drumming his fingers on the table. 'I have been thinking while I've been talking–'

'It's nice to see you can still do that, my dear,' Maggie commented.

'There is much I can still do, Maggie. I think it's time for Pavel Mercier to rejoin the living.'

'And do what?' Sam asked.

'Help you unmask the killer and, more importantly, restore the Hand of God to its people.'

'And just how do you propose we do that?' Maggie asked.

'With subterfuge, deceit and outright lies,' Pavel said. 'When does the ICOM conference start?'

'Saturday week, October 10th,' Maggie said hesitantly.

Sam raised an eyebrow of suspicion. 'Why?'

'Here is my plan,' Pavel offered.

'I hope it's not as ridiculous as the one that got us all into this in the first place,' Maggie said.

Pavel ignored the comment. 'Tomorrow, we shall set off for Cuzco, from where we will make contact with Louis and Barbara to make sure they attend the Conference. We will also seek out a craftsman to fashion a replica of the Hand Of God.'

Maggie and Sam exchanged worried looks but said nothing.

'We will then go to the conference in Melbourne where I will announce, to my assembled colleagues, details of the greatest archaeological find in the Americas since Machu Picchu. I will regale them with stories of Inticancha, the *true* lost city of the Incas.'

'Pavel this sounds like a lovely bit of grandstanding for your personal edification,' Maggie said.

'Yes! That is exactly how it should seem. And just in case the murderer is *not* one of this *Life and Death* team we will do a little pre-publicity, spreading vague rumours that, not only am I alive, but I have discovered an important Inca relic. Maybe we can use this internet thing my young friends here have been telling me about. That way we can be sure that *anyone* who has an interest in the huaca will be right where we want them.'

'And *then* what do we do with them?' Maggie asked, scratching her head in frustration.

'Then Sam can arrest them.'

'I don't understand why we need to have a replica of the hand made,' Sam said.

'If we do this right, Sam, *everyone* will be there. When Pavel Mercier comes back from the dead to announce the discovery of Inticancha and the Hand of God, I need something to 'unveil'. And what better way to flush out this murderer than to make him question the authenticity of the pieces he already has.'

A shiver rippled up and down Sam's spine as she recalled exactly why she was involved in this case, and the likelihood of how – in so many ways – Pavel's ridiculous plan could screw that up.

'Pavel, I was put on this case, in the beginning, to make sure that the Professor's murder had no adverse affect on this very important Conference,' she said.

'I don't think *using* ICOM '98 to flush out someone who has been travelling around the world killing people and stealing things that don't belong to him would be regarded, by my bosses, as damage control. Daley Prescott will have a pink fit for a start, and I'll probably be assigned desk duty for the rest of my life.'

Pavel looked from Sam to Maggie and back to Sam. 'Do you have a better idea?'

# Chapter Twenty-Four

Cuzco, Peru, Friday October 2, 1998

TWO HOURS AFTER THEY CHECKED BACK INTO THE *HOTEL ROYAL INCA* and washed away the dirt of the two-day trek and long train trip back from Inticancha, Sam and Maggie were sitting at an outdoor cafe table in a street off the Plaza de Armas enjoying icy cold beers. Pavel, registered as Henri Schliemann, had left them to go off on his mission to find an expert craftsman.

'There's nothing better than a cleansing ale.'

'You realise this is complete lunacy,' Maggie said.

Sam shrugged. 'I haven't been able to come up with a better plan, have you?'

'No, but that doesn't mean that Pavel's is worth pursuing.'

A crowd of people suddenly surged down the narrow street and in the ensuing tangle of tourists, table legs and one angry waiter who had just arrived with their meal, Sam knocked her beer over. When the waiter finally stopped apologising for the mess and left them in peace Sam realised that Maggie was staring down the street with a peculiar expression on her face.

'What's up? You look like you've just seen a pissed-off huaca.'

'I'm not sure, but I think I just saw Pablo Escobar spying on us from that doorway down there.'

'Oh no, not another dead man walking.'

'What? Pablo's not dead.'

'Oh, yes he is. The Colombian police killed him in a rooftop shootout five years ago, back in 1993.'

'What, who are you talking about, Sam?'

'Pablo Escobar, the Colombian drug lord; history's richest bad guy.'

Maggie laughed. 'My Pablo Escobar – not that I'm claiming the little weasel – is a curator from one of the museums in Cuzco. He's the bloke I had to deal with in Paris over the ownership of the Tahuantinsuyu Bracelet.'

'Well we *are* in Cuzco, Maggie, so it's not entirely unlikely that we'd run into him.'

'But he was *watching* us.'

'He probably couldn't believe it was you sitting here. Don't worry about it, unless you think *he's* behind all this stuff we're investigating.'

Maggie snorted. 'Not likely. The man's an imbecile who couldn't organise his sock drawer without help.'

After dinner Maggie suggested a stroll around the Plaza to stretch their legs. 'Otherwise we may find we can't walk at all tomorrow.'

As they passed the church of La Compañía, which was lit up like a Christmas tree, Sam caught a glimpse – before he stepped back into a large group of people behind them – of a man wearing a dark green shirt. It was the fourth time she'd noticed him in 10 minutes, although she still hadn't managed to see his face.

'What's wrong?' Maggie asked.

'What colour shirt was your Señor Escobar wearing?'

'Red, I think. Why?'

'I think we're being followed. I keep seeing the same green shirt.'

'Is it being worn by the same person, or is someone handing it around the Plaza to confuse you?'

Sam laughed. 'Okay. So now I'm getting paranoid. Maybe we both need some sleep.'

They crossed the Plaza and walked down the street that led to their hotel but as they entered the smaller Plaza Regocijo, Sam put her hand on Maggie's arm and guided her straight ahead.

'What? The hotel's over there.'

'I think Mr Green Shirt is behind us again,' Sam whispered.

They took the next street on the right, quickened their pace a little and then took the next left.

'Alley,' Sam urged, and they slipped into a dead-end lane and stood quietly in the semi-darkness.

Sam flattened herself against the wall near the corner and waited. A few moments later the only approaching footsteps she could hear stopped just short of the alley. Sam took a silent breath, reached out and grabbed the man by the front of his green shirt, dragged him around the corner and tripped him over her leg. She still had hold of him with her left hand as he stumbled backwards, into a pile of rubbish, babbling something unintelligible as he fell. Sam swung her right hand back ready to to punch him in the face if he moved.

'Good heavens!' Maggie exclaimed and grabbed Sam's arm. 'Don't hit him. At least not till we find out what the hell he's doing here.'

Sam stepped to one side and looked at the man properly for the first time.

Enrico Vasquez looked right back at her.

'What the bloody hell *are* you doing here?' Sam demanded.

'Would you believe I was sightseeing?'

# Chapter Twenty-Five

Cuzco, Peru, October 2, 1998

ENRICO VASQUEZ INSISTED ON PAYING FOR THE 'LONG COLD DRINKS IN A nearby cafe' he'd suggested as an alternative to Sam beating him up to find out why he was stalking them through the streets of Cuzco when he should have been looking after his exhibition in Melbourne. When the waiter left, Vasquez lit a cigarette and inhaled deeply.

'I realise this looks very suspicious–'

'That's an understatement,' said Sam.

'I know I was already on top of your suspect list,' Vasquez continued, 'but I can assure you my being here has nothing to do with the death of Professor Marsden, at least not directly.'

'What makes you think you're our prime suspect?'

'From our first meeting I knew I was *your* prime suspect, and not because the Professor and I were seen having a disagreement, but because of a certain bias on your part.'

'Bias? I don't understand,' Sam said.

'People too often forget that appearances can be deceptive,' Vasquez said. 'A pretty girl like you, Detective Diamond, takes one look at a man like me and sees a short, dark foreigner, so you think "he must be guilty". Yet you disregard the good-looking Andrew Barstoc even when you have information that suggests he may be up to no good.'

Pretty *girl*, Sam thought. 'You think Andrew Barstoc is good looking?' she asked, as if Vasquez must be the only person in the world who held that opinion. 'You do yourself a disservice, Señor,' she added with a smile. 'But I agree with you on the subject of appearances. I, for instance, am a much smarter woman than I am a pretty girl.'

Vasquez ducked his head apologetically while Maggie hid a smirk in her glass.

'I'll be honest with you, Señor Vasquez, I didn't take to you on our first meeting – but only because you were rude and sexist. And yes, you *are* a suspect, but that is mostly because you were so intent on directing attention away from yourself onto others.

'As for Andrew Barstoc he is, as far as I know, where he should be – in Melbourne with your travelling show. You on the other hand are sitting here, half a world away from where you're meant to be, and still casting aspersions.'

'I apologise for misjudging you,' he said. 'Perhaps as a foreigner, I am too quick to assume prejudice–'

'Señor, your exhibition team is comprised of two Englishmen, an American woman and you, a Colombian, so as far as I'm concerned you're *all* foreigners.'

'*He's* not Colombian,' Maggie declared. 'He was begging for his life in Quechuan in that alley.'

'He's not? You're not? But you told us–'

Sam shook her head. 'Oh, no you didn't, did you? What you said was, "I have come from Colombia".'

'I did not mean to mislead you Detective, but the fact that I am Peruvian was not relevant to your investigation. Keeping my nationality a secret *was,* however, important to my own work.'

Maggie laughed. 'Why? Don't tell us Marcus has something against Peruvian curators.'

'No, but he may not have hired me as his curator if he knew I was a Peruvian policeman.'

Maggie stared at Vasquez as if he'd admitted to being a Martian, while several pins could be heard dropping in the ensuing silence.

'Are you saying you're a cop, not a curator?' Sam finally asked.

'I am fully qualified in both fields, Detective. But I am more of a spy than a cop. My job is not dissimilar to yours with your Government's Cultural Affairs Department.'

'I am not a spy,' Sam pronounced.

'I'm aware of that. I merely meant that the department I work for is concerned with cultural affairs, specifically our stolen cultural heritage.'

'Enrico,' Maggie snapped. 'Stop talking in circles and tell us why you were tailing us, or Sam will take you back to that alley.'

Sam gave a look. *Oh sure, me and whose army?*

Vasquez smiled. 'I am an undercover operative for my government's Heritage Retrieval Department,' he said. 'It is my job to track down any Peruvian cultural property held by foreign institutions.

'As you well know, Maggie, this is no small task, as many museums do not know exactly what they have. I have found things, of historical significance to us, lying around in dusty storerooms or mislabelled in forgotten display cases. Even with modern technology it could take decades for them to catalogue their collections and, in the meantime, curators like your friend Lloyd Marsden and all those other dedicated collectors are retiring or dying off.

'No disrespect intended, but when these old experts are gone, so much more will be lost to us. These people have been accumulating–'

'Enrico, we don't need a lecture,' Maggie remarked.

'Forgive me, it is not often I get to speak of my real job.'

'What do you do with all this information you collect?' Sam asked.

'Add it to an inventory of the artefacts and few remaining treasures of my country held by foreign museums. I have been using exhibitions like Marcus's as a cover for nearly 15 years.'

'Why all the secrecy?' Sam asked. 'Why can't you just rock up to the Museum of Victoria, flash your credentials and say "show me what you've got"?'

'If it were only that easy,' Vasquez sighed, lighting another cigarette. 'But I have no more authority in your country than you do here, Detective.'

'I wasn't talking about your police badge,' Sam said. 'If you're respected enough in your other job to have been curating exhibitions all over the world then surely, just out of professional courtesy, the museums you've been visiting would provide you with the information you're seeking. It's my understanding that most institutions these days are in favour of the repatriation of cultural material. It's even on the agenda for ICOM '98.'

'The fact that it is on the agenda as an issue to be resolved indicates just how widely the concept of deaccessioning is actually accepted.'

'He's quite right, Sam,' Maggie said. 'It may be generally accepted as the right thing to do, but there are some things that some museums will never want to give back.'

'And, as I said before, Detective Diamond, many museums do not know what they have, and some of their curators would like to keep it that way. So my concern is with those items that are *not* on display or already part of a public claim or dispute.'

'Like the whats-a-name bracelet that Maggie was mediating in Paris,' Sam suggested, vaguely.

'Exactly,' Vasquez said, registering amusement rather than surprise at the suggestion. 'We knew where that artefact was and were already negotiating its return, so it was not part of my inventory or of concern to my department – until it was stolen, of course.'

'What do you do with this inventory?' Maggie asked.

'My colleagues in Heritage Retrieval use my information to begin negotiations with foreign museums for the return of items that belong to us. This approach is occasionally successful but not often enough, so we sometimes employ other tactics.'

'Like what?' Maggie asked carefully, as if she already had an inkling of his answer.

'My department sometimes sends in extraction agents.'

'Extraction agents?' Sam queried. 'What–'

'Burglars, ' Maggie explained. 'He means they send in burglars.'

Sam was incredulous. 'You make a list of things and then you steal them?'

'I only make the inventory, Detective. My colleagues retrieve that which was stolen from us.'

'Good grief!' Sam glanced at Maggie. 'You don't seem surprised.'

'Oh I am,' Maggie assured her. 'There have been rumours going around for years about the existence of so-called Relic Recovery Teams. They were blamed every time there was an otherwise unexplained break-in at a museum. It's also a standing joke when pens or staplers go missing from our desks that an RRT must be responsible.'

Vasquez laughed heartily. 'I would like to point out, Maggie, that we are not the only ones who do this. Most countries that have had their culture plundered by foreigners have a secret Retrieval Department of some kind, and employ agents to reacquire their property.'

'If it's secret, Señor Vasquez, *why* are you telling us? You must realise you have just put the kibosh on your career as a spy.'

Vasquez shrugged. 'A recent promotion means I am no longer a field agent. And my government will, naturally, deny all knowledge of what I have told you, so the information is useless.'

'That means,' Sam said, suddenly suspicious of Vasquez's whole story, 'that you can't prove anything that you've told us.'

'You are correct. The nature of my work would necessitate a denial of my existence as well.'

'Enrico, did you hijack the Tahuantinsuyu Bracelet?'

Vasquez laughed. 'No Maggie, I did not. I was in Melbourne at the time. And I swear that neither my department nor my government was responsible. But the theft of the Tahuantinsuyu Bracelet is the reason I am here – following you.'

Maggie looked meaningfully at Sam who obligingly turned to Vasquez with a puzzled frown. 'Does this bracelet have any special significance?'

Vasquez threw his hands out. 'It belongs to us,' he declared. 'The Chileans had it and refused to return it. Now some unknown person has it and I intend to get it back.'

'But what makes you think we know anything about it?' Maggie asked, trying to look perplexed.

'A curious set of circumstances led me to believe that you were on the trail of the hijackers.'

'What circumstances?' Maggie snorted.

'Firstly, the disagreement Professor Marsden and I had on the day of his death. As I explained to you Detective Diamond, that conversation *was* quite heated because he and I held completely opposite views regarding the return of cultural property. When I brought up the subject of the Tahuantinsuyu Bracelet, however, the Professor suddenly became agitated, even angry. He said he had no desire to continue the debate. Then he left the building.'

'Why did you mention the bracelet?' Sam asked.

'It was topical,' Vasquez shrugged. 'Everyone knew Maggie was in Paris mediating the dispute.'

'Lloyd often just walked away from things he could no longer be bothered with,' Maggie said.

Vasquez nodded. 'At the time, I thought that was the case. In retrospect I realised he had reacted specifically to my mention of the bracelet.'

Sam threw up her hands. 'So? Maybe the dedicated collector was sick of having the topic thrown at him.'

'Possibly,' Vaquez agreed. 'But the very next morning, I learned that the Tahuantinsuyu Bracelet had been stolen. Later that day I discovered, when you brought me in for questioning, that Marsden had been murdered. Two days later you, Maggie, arrived in Melbourne fresh from your mediation of the 'Inca trinket fiasco', and three days after that you both left the country.

'This to me is very odd when you at least, Detective Diamond, are supposed to be investigating a murder.'

'Señor Vasquez you cannot possibly have any idea what I am *supposed* to be doing.'

'Granted. Does that mean I am right then? You *are* on the trail of the hijackers.'

'We are not,' Maggie stated emphatically. 'And I really wish people would stop putting my name and that 'incident' in the same sentence, as if *I* am responsible for it.'

'And I *am* investigating Professor Marden's murder,' Sam said. 'So it's beyond me why you think these apparently unrelated events mean we are looking for a stolen bracelet; especially one that was hijacked in Paris.'

'I do not like coincidences,' Vasquez pronounced.

'I don't know anyone who does,' Sam laughed. 'But let me try and squeeze your logic into a possible scenario. After thinking about this curious set of circumstances you decide that Professor Marsden, in his desire to collect one last great *thing*, masterminded the hijacking in Paris. Then along comes Maggie who, somehow, discovers her friend's part in the theft and rushes back to Melbourne to tell him this is 'just not on, old boy', only to find she is too late because one of his co-conspirators has bumped him off before fleeing the country. Maggie then manages to convince *me,* who she doesn't know from Adam, or Eve, to go gallivanting around the world on a quest for a stolen artefact.

'Of course, another possibility is that Maggie was Marsden's accomplice in Paris, and I've been corrupted into her cunning plot.'

Vasquez's dark eyes were shining as if he was hearing exactly what he wanted to hear.

'Enrico, she is kidding,' Maggie said, as she and Sam collapsed in laughter.

'But why else would your investigation of a murder in Melbourne take you to Egypt and Peru?'

'Señor Vasquez, as you cannot prove to me that you are anything other than a Peruvian curator *and* a suspect in my murder investigation, I am not likely to divulge the reasons for our being here; or going there.

'And if the little story I just invented bears any resemblance to your reason for being here then I'd have to leap to the conclusion that *you* are the alleged co-conspirator in the hijacking and would therefore qualify as the prime suspect in the Professor's murder. So, should I arrest you now?'

Vasquez was horrified. 'I *swear* I had nothing to do with Marsden's death or the theft of the bracelet. I realise I am disadvantaged by the fact that, right now, I cannot prove I am who I say I am, but why would I make it up?'

'I don't have the faintest idea,' Sam said. 'But why would you expect me to believe you?'

'Why not? You expect me to believe you are *not* on the trail of the Tahuantinsuyu Bracelet just because you say so,' Vasquez said. 'But *if* you are not, then why would a known dealer in stolen antiquities attack you in Cairo?'

'I beg your pardon?' Sam asked.

'The Turkish gentleman that my cousin saved you from,' Vasquez said with a smile.

'The Mexican was your cousin?'

'Obviously he is not Mexican,' Vasquez pointed out. 'And it was he who discovered you had left Cairo for Peru, which is why I am here.'

'Well,' Sam said calmly, 'Would you pass on my thanks to your cousin for following me around. That Turkish bloke, however, was only after my money.'

'Of course he was,' Vasquez stated.

'Well,' Maggie pronounced, 'I don't know about you two but it seems we're sitting around here not believing each other. I suggest we give up and call it a night.'

Sam smiled. 'Good idea. We could meet back here in the morning with a whole new set of implausible stories for each other if you like, Señor Vasquez.'

'Very amusing, Detective Diamond.'

# Chapter Twenty-Six

Cuzco, Peru, October 2, 1998

SAM AND MAGGIE, HOPING VASQUEZ HAD COME ACROSS THEM IN THE street by accident, wandered back to the *Hotel Royal Inca* by a circuitous route to make sure he wasn't following them.

By the time Pavel returned two hours later, they still hadn't decided whether Vasquez had been telling the truth. If he had, it meant he'd betrayed half a dozen state secrets in his attempt to find out what *they* were doing in Peru. Alternatively, he had fed them an inspired collection of lies to cover the fact that he was the one they were after.

'I hope he does not know I am here with you,' Pavel said. 'That would ruin our plan.'

'Oh, and that would be terrible,' Maggie said.

'Maggie, darling, this will work.'

'Pavel, darling, it is a ridiculous plan.'

'Both of you darlings please stop arguing,' Sam begged.

'Did you get the impression that he knew about the Hand of God?' Pavel asked.

'No. But then, as we said, we've no idea whether to believe him or not. Personally I vote for 'not' but Sam thinks his story is silly enough to be true.'

'I don't know what I think any more,' Sam admitted, lying back on the bed. 'But I have been wondering whether the person behind all of this might be someone from the original dig in 1962.'

'No way,' said Pavel.

'How can you be sure? You said most of your porters ran off, and the others left with half your team who were desperate to get out of there.'

'Yes, they were desperate – with fear. But I trusted their word and, having worked with most of them over the years since then, I have no reason to doubt them. Besides apart from the Guardians everyone else left *before* we came up with our plan to protect the Hand. And–'

Maggie thumped the table. 'I *have* to get something off my chest, Pavel. I understand why it never occurred to *you* to consider just how preposterous your original idea was, but for the life of me I can't fathom why Lloyd or Noel, and especially Alistair, not only went along with it in the first place but never came to their senses. As a plan it ranks highly amongst the most idiotic ideas of all time.'

'Maggie, Maggie, if you had been there, you would have gone along with us.'

'I doubt it. But *if* I had, I would've realised sooner rather than later *sometime* in the last 36 years just how ridiculous the whole thing was.'

'Please credit us with some sense, my dear. We talked many times over the years about who we would turn the Hand over to when the time was right. The problem was, the time was never right. It seemed that each time we settled on a possible new Guardian he would die or transfer to India or be arrested on fraud charges. It was quite bizarre. The last time Alistair brought it up was the night before the Cuzco earthquake in 1986. He never mentioned it again.'

'Pavel, for goodness sake, you don't think the Hand was responsible for these things?'

'I couldn't say one way or the other, my dear. But as I said, you had–'

'I know, you had to be there to understand.'

'I accept that you don't believe in these things but let me give you an analogy that you might be able to understand. You are, are you not, a lapsed Catholic?'

'You know I am a devout atheist,' Maggie stated.

'But I guarantee you can't tell me, in all honesty, that you could stand in the Vatican and scream out 'this is all bullshit'.'

Maggie straightened her shoulders. 'That's not the same.'

'Why, because you think God *might* get you in then end?'

'All right, okay, I get your point.'

Sam, who had been pacing the room, stopped in front of Pavel. 'You say *you* trusted the team members who left ahead of you, Pavel. Have you considered that one or more of your Guardians also trusted them, perhaps enough to reveal what you all decided in 1962?'

Pavel sighed. 'I suppose it is possible.'

'Which means there might be as many as five other people who know about the Hand being spread around the world. And if just one of them told someone else then there's no way of knowing how many people know about it.'

'But why would they tell anyone?'

'Oh, Pavel don't be so naive,' Maggie said. 'Not everyone spends the rest of their life looking under the bed for monsters because they got spooked by a horror movie one night.'

'It could've been an accident,' Sam said. 'One of them, even one of your Guardians, could've got drunk at a party and started telling a tall tale about a golden relic, a wicked curse and a strange plan that was put in motion to protect the descendants of the last Inca king. It'd make a great bedtime story too.'

'It seems possible that half the world might know your little secret,' Maggie teased.

'Oh *merde,* but this cannot be so.'

'Let's consider the possibility for a moment.' Sam rummaged in her pack for a notebook and placed it on the table in front of Pavel. She opened it to the page marked by the photo of Manco City, on which she had listed the names Maggie had identified.

'Which one is William Sanchez?' she asked.

Pavel pointed to the man beside Noel Winslow in the back row. 'And that is Barbara Stone, the other Guardian,' he said tapping the woman sitting in the front next to one of the porters. 'She lives in San Francisco,' he added.

Sam closed her eyes for a moment. 'When was the last time you spoke to her?'

He shook his head. 'Maybe the end of 1996. Why?'

Sam took a breath. '*The Life and Death* show was in San Francisco in June last year.'

'Oh my god,' Pavel exclaimed. 'We must find out if she is all right. Oh no, but she was moving, I don't know where to. This is dreadful.'

'It's much too late to do anything tonight,' Maggie said, taking hold of his hand. 'Tell us who the other two men in the photograph are.'

Pavel glanced at the names and then back at the photo. 'The man next to Sanchez is Dwight Jones and the big fellow in the front is Elmer Rockly. I'm sure you've met him, Maggie.'

'Shit!' Sam bowed her head and shook it.

'Now what?' Maggie asked.

Sam sat up straight again. 'You remember how I asked Rivers to check the internet for any odd incidents that coincided with the exhibition tour dates?'

'Yes, and he had some information on a failed suicide and a fire or something,' Maggie said.

'An art broker by the name of Dwight Jones died in a gallery fire in New York on March 15, 1997,' Sam said quietly. 'And a man named Elmer Rockly was killed in a hit-and-run snowmobile accident in Anchorage on July 6 last year.'

'I am going to throw up.' Pavel made a dash for the bathroom.

Sam added Sanchez, Stone, Jones and Rockly to the list, while Maggie poured more scotch.

When Pavel returned he stared morosely at the names. 'I have brought this on us.' He ripped the page from the notebook, screwed it up and tossed it across the room.

'This is not your fault, Pavel,' Maggie insisted. 'And we're all tired. We should go to bed.'

'You know,' Sam said, ignoring the suggestion. 'What if whoever is doing this doesn't actually know who the Guardians are.'

'You mean they're just killing off *everyone* who was there,' Pavel said, horrified.

'Yeah, or everyone in this picture, which amounts to the same thing,' Sam said.

'Who took the photograph?' Maggie asked.

Pavel shook his head. 'Pah, I don't remember. Maybe one of the porters.'

'What was the situation you had that made you decide to fake your death?' Sam queried.

Pavel laced his fingers together and stared at the floor. 'I had been, um, having an affair with a woman, a married woman here in Cuzco,' he confessed.

'Oh Pavel, not again!' Maggie said.

'Her husband, when he found out, reacted very badly.'

'How strange of him.'

'He threatened to kill me, Maggie. And when I was hit by a jeep that swerved across the road to get me, I knew he was serious.'

'Are you sure it was the husband driving the jeep?' Sam asked.

'No, I just assumed it was he.'

Sam frowned. 'If everyone thought you were dead why was Noel Winslow coming here to find you? In fact, now that I think of it, your postcard to him said, 'got your message' so how–'

'Noel knew I was alive. He was the only person who did.'

'Oh that's bloody charming, that is,' Maggie declared, stomping over to the bar to pour herself a whisky. 'And you couldn't let your other friends know you'd just changed your name and gone bush?'

'I didn't plan to be in hiding so long, Maggie. But when I got Noel's telegram about the Hand I thought it best to remain dead, and incognito at Inticancha, until he arrived to explain.'

Sam ran her hands through her hair in frustration, then suddenly smiled. 'There is one person we haven't considered at all.'

'Who?' Maggie asked, returning to the table.

'William Sanchez's idiot son. Whatever happened to him, Pavel?' Sam asked.

'I have no idea. He returned to Cuzco with the others. I think Jean put him on a plane to his mother in San Francisco. But, I remember now, that it was him, Paolo, who took the photograph.'

'And he would be, what, about 46 or so now?'

'Ooh, what an intriguing idea,' Maggie remarked.

'Far-fetched if you ask me,' Pavel said.

Maggie laughed. 'Well you're an expert on all things far-fetched, so you would know.'

'Let's play with this,' Sam suggested. 'Paolo would be about the same age as, say, Enrico Vasquez.'

'*And* Pablo Escobar,' Maggie laughed.

Sam joined her. 'Ha. You may be right. It *is* more likely that an idiot grew up to be an imbecile who can't organise his own sock drawer–'

'Without help,' she and Maggie finished in unison.

'But why would Paolo Sanchez be doing this?'

'Greed or revenge, or both, Pavel. They're two of the oldest and poorest excuses for bad behaviour known to man,' Maggie said. 'He might hold you all responsible for his father's death.'

'Pah,' Pavel snorted. 'It was his father's own greed that unleashed the vengeance of the huacas. We had nothing to do with William Sanchez's punishment or death.'

'But a 10-year-old boy is more likely to blame you.'

Sam laughed. 'Or he might have grown up believing he really is the reincarnation of Tupac Amaru.'

'I think you two have lost your plots. I am going to bed,' Pavel said, bumping the table as he stood up.

'No I'm not. Who is this?' he asked, pointing to the surveillance photos that had slipped out of Sam's notebook. 'I think I know him.'

'Of course you do, that's Phineas,' Maggie said. 'Marcus Bridger,' she added, when Pavel didn't seem to recognise the nickname.

'No not him, *him*,' Pavel stressed. 'The one with the nose too big for his face.'

'That's Andrew Barstoc. He's Bridger's right-hand man and my prime suspect,' Sam stated.

'Barstoc?' Pavel closed his eyes. 'Oh, *Andy*. He was on a dig with us maybe five years ago.'

'But he's not an archaeologist or anything,' Sam noted. 'He's a businessman.'

'You get all types on an archaeological dig, Sam,' Maggie explained. 'It's not just dedicated or loopy scientists like me and Pavel who like spending weeks in the jungle or desert digging things up. Doing a dig is a popular semester break activity for students of everything from history, anthropology and engineering, to psychology or business studies. Then there are the holidaying amateur archaeologists who work the rest of the year as lawyers, teachers or bus drivers.'

'Was Barstoc part of your new dig at Inticancha?' Sam asked.

'No. We only started work there, this time around, at the end of 1995.'

'Well, was anyone from the original dig on the one with Barstoc?' Maggie asked.

'Yes, Elmer Rockly was there that summer,' Pavel replied. 'In fact he and Andy, who was a poncy sycophant by the way, spent a lot of time drinking together.'

'So,' said Sam, 'if we return to one of our earlier theories that one of your Guardians *may* have told some of the other members of the original team, then it's possible that Rockly passed the story on to Barstoc.

'I love it! It's a classic Six Degrees of Separation, with a straight line from my prime suspect to the Hand of God in four steps.'

'What?' Pavel asked, as if he thought he'd missed a very important clue.

Sam laughed. 'There's a play, and a movie, called *Six Degrees of Separation* in which a theory is proposed that *everyone* in the world is connected by no more than six associations.'

'There's also a silly game called the Six Degrees of Kevin Bacon that demonstrates the theory,' Maggie said. 'You play by using movies to link any actor in the world to the American actor Kevin Bacon. There's even a search engine on the internet called the Oracle of Bacon that uses a massive database to work it out for you. You key-in the name of an actor, no matter how obscure, and the oracle connects that person through other actors to Kevin Bacon in as few steps as possible.'

'I don't think this internet is going to help our plan after all,' Pavel moaned. 'We don't even have a computer here and already I'm confused.'

'I'll give you an example,' Sam said. 'Even though I've never met him, there are three degrees of separation between me and Professor Stephen Hawking.'

Pavel looked lost again. 'Who?'

'The world-famous English physcist. Anyway, we are *connected* because I know an actress in Melbourne who's a friend of the English actor, Patrick Stewart, who played Captain Picard in *Star Trek*. Professor Hawking guest starred in one episode of that series.'

Pavel narrowed his eyes and studied Sam. 'Do these degrees benefit you in any way?'

Sam shrugged. 'I suppose I could call him up, introduce myself as a friend of a friend, and ask him to explain the Big Bang Theory to me in words of less than three syllables.'

Pavel laughed. 'It would be a much better idea to invite him over to put his genius to work on solving our little mystery.'

'Speaking of our mystery, Pavel' Maggie said, 'I suggest, you do not leave the hotel again until we all leave on Wednesday. If we really are going ahead with this so-called plan, then we should take a few precautions, especially with Agent 00-Vasquez hanging around.

'Sam and I can go looking for an internet connection tomorrow, once we work out what rumours we want to start and in whose lap we want to drop them.'

# Chapter Twenty-Seven

SAM SHARED A CAFE TABLE WITH THREE ENGLISH BACKPACKERS AND an American couple who were videotaping their lunch. She sat drumming her fingers while she waited for Maggie to show her face in an upstairs window across the street.

Three and half days of dodging spies or henchmen, or whatever they were that followed them every time they left the hotel, was starting to take its toll on Sam's nerves. It had been quite a lark at first trying to lose the men that Enrico Vasquez had obviously put in place to tail them.

On one occasion they'd taken five buses and two hours to get just half way across town to visit Maggie's friend Jonathan, who had a computer and modem. And on Sunday they'd caught five separate taxis from the *Hotel Royal Inca* to the *Hotel Royal Inca* just for the fun of watching the guy behind them scrambling for the next available taxi each time.

Vasquez himself took up permanent residence in a restaurant on Plaza Recogijo from where he waved cheerily to them every time they entered or left the hotel, but made no attempt at contact.

Pavel meanwhile had been hiding out, in either his room or theirs, nutting out the finer details of his great plan. Or so he said.

Sam suspected it was because he was embarrassed to be seen in public after Maggie had decided on Saturday morning that making Pavel less recognisable, and more respectable, was a good excuse for getting rid of his woolly mammoth look. She'd insisted he shave off his sideburns and moustache, for the first time in 25 years, and had then attacked his hair with a pair of scissors. He was now almost unrecognisable as Dr Pavel Mercier but because *he* thought he looked strange, he had adopted a rather startled expression.

'Would you like another coffee?' the waiter asked, bringing Sam back to the here and now.

'Um, yes please,' she replied. The Americans had finished filming their luncheon epic and were getting up to leave, so Sam slid along the bench seat to use the backpackers as cover from the spying eyes in the street.

She wondered whether it was time to start worrying about why it was taking Maggie so long to pick up a parcel. Not that it was safe for her to come out yet. The one person they hadn't quite managed to shake off their tail was still pacing the crowded street outside looking for them.

When Sam had first spotted him in the Plaza de Armas five hours before, she had turned away in such surprise and haste that she'd walked straight into a parked car. After Maggie helped her up off the ground Sam had wanted to confront the 'known dealer in stolen antiquities' right there in public, but Maggie insisted it would be more sensible to lose Mr Fez as soon as possible.

Easier said than done, Sam thought as she watched him, now emerging from a small hotel up the street. The man was obviously more accomplished at tailing people than any of Vasquez's cronies were. She and Maggie thought they'd lost him long before they entered this street, but while they were still trying to figure out which house belonged to Pavel's expert craftsman, Sam had spotted Mr Fez mingling with a group of tourists. It took them another half hour of aimless walking before they cut through a small market and doubled back.

So had Mr Fez, eventually, but not until Maggie was inside the house of Miguel Schneider and Sam was staked out in the cafe.

Sam glanced up at the window opposite and was relieved to see Maggie looking down on her, but she shook her head, held up four fingers and pointed to the front door.

'Excuse me,' Sam said to backpackers. 'Do you think you could do me a favour?'

'Maybe,' said the woman, cautiously.

'See that guy, in the baggy beige suit, hanging around the front of the little hotel? Well he's been hassling my friend and me for two days. He bought us a couple of drinks on Sunday night and now he won't leave us alone. He followed us all the way from our hotel today.'

'Where's your friend?' asked the younger of the two men.

'She's in that house on the corner over there.'

'What's she doing in the house?' the woman asked.

'It belongs to a friend of a friend. She was collecting something.'

The woman eyed Sam as if she was a drug runner. 'I don't know,' she said.

'Oh come on, Sandra, be a sport,' the other guy said. 'What do you want us to do?' he asked.

'Well, he's going in and out of places up and down the street looking for us. If you could just make sure he stays inside somewhere long enough for us to take off, it would be great.'

Sam noticed that Miguel Schneider had cracked open his front door.

'Sure, we can do that, love,' the young guy said. 'Come on.'

'Thank you.' Sam called the waiter and paid for her drinks and their lunch. 'It's the least I can do,' she said when Sandra objected.

Sam watched them wander slowly up the street, waiting for Mr Fez to emerge from a cafe. When he entered the shop next door, the two guys pushed their way in after him and Sandra gave a short nod. Sam raised her hand to Miguel, waved a thank you to Sandra and dashed across the street to meet Maggie on the corner.

'Pavel, go pack your stuff. We are leaving,' Maggie ordered, as she and Sam barged into the hotel room.

'What? Why? Did you get the Hand?'

'Yes, and we are leaving, *now*.'

'But we're booked on a flight to Lima tomorrow, Maggie.'

'And Vasquez probably already knows that, so he won't expect us to leave tonight.'

Pavel sat down. 'My darling, please take a moment to calm yourself. What is the hurry?'

Sam placed the parcel she was carrying on the table in front of him. 'The Turkish bloke who attacked me in Cairo has been following us for the last five hours. It's time to go home.'

'But the flights out of Cuzco are always overbooked. We'll never get on a plane at such short notice,' Pavel said, removing the string from the parcel.

'Two phone calls and we are out of here,' said Maggie who was already dialling. 'Hello Randolph? This is Maggie Tremaine. Fuel up your kite, I'm calling in another debt. We'll be there in two hours.'

'Oh no,' Sam wailed. 'I'd rather take my chances with Mr Fez.'

'What is wrong, Sam?' Pavel asked.

'Randolph P. bloody Fitzwanker, or whatever his name is, was the crazy barnstormer who flew us from Lima last week. We nearly died 53 times on the way here.'

'It will be dark by the time we leave, Sam,' Maggie said, as she dialled another number. 'You won't see the mountains this time until we plough into them, and then you won't care.'

'Oh lovely,' Pavel sighed with admiration, as he lifted the lid of the wooden box he'd unwrapped. 'Miguel has done a fine, fine job. It's almost as if his work was touched by Inti himself.'

Sam peered at the replica of the Hand of God. It was indeed beautiful workmanship. Five large golden fingers, each in its own velvet-lined recess, lay in a semi-circle, as if the Sun God had rested his hand in the box.

'There's no bracelet,' she noted.

'The bracelet, though mostly gold, also contains pearls and torquoise,' Pavel said. 'It would have been impossible to make without the real one as a model, and it would've been too expensive to try. Besides, part of my plan is to express my belief that the missing Tahuantinsuyu Bracelet is part of the Hand of God.'

'This is not real gold is it?' Sam queried, as Maggie joined them at the table.

'Oh yes.' Pavel picked up the thumb. 'They have been dipped in real gold. The moulds underneath are of whatever Miguel decided was the most appropriate metal to achieve the correct weight. May I have the real thumb, please my sweet.'

Maggie undid her shirt and removed the digit from her vest pocket. Pavel laid the replica in her other palm.

'My goodness,' Maggie exclaimed. 'You can hardly tell the difference between them, in appearance or weight.'

'I don't suppose either of you have thought about how we are going to get this through customs?' Sam asked.

'Oh, good point,' Maggie said. 'I'll have to ring and reschedule with Peter.'

'Who is Peter?' Sam asked. 'No, wait, let me guess. He's probably a friend at the Australian Embassy in Lima.'

'Very good guess, Sam dear. Now start packing you two.'

Forty minutes later Pavel Mercier, dressed in shorts, a very loud floral shirt, a Panama hat, and with a camera around his neck, carried his bags out to the car that waited in front of the *Hotel Royal Inca*. Vasquez glanced at him with disinterest and then returned his attention to his magazine, so Pavel went back into the hotel. He exited again moments later with Sam and Maggie's packs, which he added to his gear in the boot of the car, before shutting it. He made one more trip inside and, this time carrying a small overnight bag, got into the front passenger seat of the car.

'Jonathan, nice to see you again,' he said to the driver.

'Good god, it *is* you,' Jonathan said. 'It's nice to see you're not dead, Pavel, but what on earth happened to your hair?'

'Maggie happened to my hair,' Pavel grunted. 'If you would like to pull slowly out from the curb, as if we're leaving, the ladies will know it's time to join us.'

Jonathan did as he was asked and Pavel reached over to open the back door. 'Okay, stop,' Pavel said, as he saw Sam and Maggie make their dash from the hotel.

'Go, go, go,' Maggie said, as she and Sam threw themselves laughing into the back seat and slammed the door. 'What's the super agent doing?' she asked, as the car lurched forward.

Sam watched Vasquez as he leapt to his feet and gesticulated wildly at his colleagues in a black car, and at his foyer spy who had emerged from the hotel with his hands out as if to say, 'How was I supposed to know?'

'Oh, he is *pissed* off,' Sam said gleefully. 'If he was a huaca this plaza would be in ruins now. But he's marshalling his troops. There's one car on our tail already, and Vasquez is joining the chase himself in a jeep.'

'Don't worry, we can lose them,' Jonathan said. 'I'll head in the opposite direction to the air field too so they won't have a clue where we're going.'

'A long as we get there in one piece.' Pavel grabbed the dashboard as Jonathan made a right turn into a very narrow street and then a left into a stream of traffic.

'Oh yes!' Sam exclaimed, as a screeching of tyres, a cacophony of car horns and the sound of metal being mangled, accompanied her view of the black pursuit car's collision with a stationary truck. 'One down, but Vasquez is still back there.'

'How far back?' Jonathan asked.

'About five cars, and taking every dangerous opportunity to close the gap.'

'Okay, I've got an idea,' he said. 'Hang on, everyone. And Sam, you tell me the moment he's out of sight.' Jonathan swung the car through an intersection, and took the first street on the right.

'Can't see him,' Sam said.

'Good.' Jonathan swerved into a narrow street on the left, then turned sharply through an open gate into a small vacant block where he spun the steering wheel and slammed on the brakes. The car came to a rest, facing the gateway, with Pavel still howling in fear.

'Quiet, Pavel,' Maggie ordered. 'You're perfectly all right.'

'My stomach is still out on the street,' he complained.

'There they go,' Jonathan said, as Vasquez's jeep sped past. He drove out the gate and headed back the way they'd come but had to wait at the corner for a car to pass before making a left turn to follow the very slow driver down the street.

'Bloody Volvo drivers, they're the same the world over,' he swore. 'Get out of the way!' He overtook the car and sped through the next intersection.

'We're nearly there,' Maggie said half an hour later, as they cruised along a bumpy dirt road. 'That's one of the walls I was telling you about the day we arrived, Sam.'

'That's nice,' Sam said, peering out at a large section of Inca stonework that had been reclaimed from the hillside. 'I'm glad I actually got to see it before my untimely death later tonight.'

She took a few deep breaths as they turned onto a winding rutted track through a small forest and into a large clearing which contained nothing but a hangar and the plane from hell on the far side. Sam slouched down into the seat.

Jonathan parked the car and Maggie leapt out, stuck her fingers in her mouth and gave a loud whistle. Randolph sauntered out of the hangar, wiping his hands on a rag.

'Crank her up, mate,' Maggie requested. 'We're on a tight schedule.'

'Are you coming, Sam?' Pavel asked, looking in the back window at her.

'I was thinking of taking up residency in Cuzco,' Sam said, getting out of the car. 'The thought of getting back into that, that *thing* is making me nauseous.'

She helped Jonathan and Pavel carry the bags to the plane, mostly because she figured it would be more difficult to run screaming off into the hills if she was laden down with stuff.

Randolph had already started the engines, which Sam thought was a good thing, because the deafening noise would cover the sound of all the important bits dropping off.

Although that thought didn't help the fact that bits *were* actually falling off.

Sam stared in puzzlement as a second tiny piece of the wing leapt onto the ground. She turned around to see if anyone else had noticed and then realised that the source of the problem was the car that had just emerged from the forest.

'Get on the plane,' she yelled. 'Everyone, get on the plane *now*. Someone is shooting at us.'

Pavel, who was already inside, hauled Maggie into the cabin. Sam leapt in after her and then held her hand out for Jonathan. 'You can*not* stay here, Jonathan,' she shouted.

Randolph aimed his plane at the runway while Sam and Jonathan fought with the door, finally getting it shut.

Mr Fez, who obviously realised he wasn't going to catch them, stopped his car and jumped out to take better aim.

'Bloody Volvo drivers, they're the same the world over,' Sam swore.

'Is it the same Volvo?' Jonathan asked.

Sam nodded. 'The very same.'

'The bastard,' Randolph yelled, 'he is trying to kill my baby.'

'He's going to kill all of us if you don't get this crate in the air,' Sam shouted – as the wheels left the ground.

Maggie breathed a sigh of relief. 'I give him this much, he *is* persistent.'

# Chapter Twenty-Eight

Melbourne, Friday October 9, 1998

SAM PUSHED THE RECALCITRANT TROLLEY LOADED WITH THEIR BAGS towards the Arrivals exit doors. She had always wondered what this moment of coming home from an overseas trip would feel like. She'd been on the other side often enough, waiting for her friends in a sea of strangers waiting for their friends or families. She kicked the trolley wheel again, thinking it was a pity that not a soul knew they were coming; there'd be no one jumping up and down outside to greet them.

'This airport has changed since I was last here,' Pavel noted, as he helped Sam by kicking the wheel on the other side.

'When were you last here?'

'Maybe 20 years.'

Sam laughed. 'If you think the airport has changed, just wait till you see the city.'

The doors opened and the sea of strangers, plus one familiar face, all leant forward to see if they should get excited yet.

'Rivers? What are you doing here?' Sam asked, as he ducked under the barrier and followed them.

'Maggie called me. Hi Maggie.'

'I'm so pleased you could make it,' Maggie smiled. 'Herc, this is my dear friend, Pavel Mercier. Pavel this is my new dear friend, Hercules Rivers.'

Sam lost control of the trolley as Pavel and Rivers shook hands, as men absolutely have to do right then and there on the spot, across her and the luggage.

'Can we do the male bonding thing outside, please?' she asked, picking up the bag that had fallen off.

'Pavel Mercier?' Rivers said belatedly, once they were outside and he'd stopped grinning like an idiot at Maggie. 'But I thought you were–'

'Dead? Not any more, my boy,' Pavel said. 'I got bored, so I decided to visit a few friends.'

'It's a long story,' Sam said. 'What's been happening here?'

'Not a lot,' Rivers said, opening the back of his hatchback car and packing the bags in.

'Prescott has been in a completely deranged state ever since you left. Rigby put me in charge – thank you very much – of keeping the assistant director informed so that he wouldn't go off the rails and call an international press conference to deny his own rumours of a sabotage plot.'

Rivers held the front passenger door open for Maggie, and let Sam and Pavel fend for themselves in the back.

'Rigby in the meantime, is gathering his evidence against Haddon Gould, who is still his number one suspect, and Peter Gilchrist who is running a close second, although the fact the Andrew Barstoc disappeared for three days, and Enrico Vasquez just up and left the country, threw a serious spanner in his works. He now thinks you might be right about one or both of them being up to something, but he's pressing on with Gould and Gilchrist anyway.

'That's all I know.' He pulled out of the parking spot and headed for the exit. 'I've been on sick leave for two days.' He lifted his fringe to show Maggie the wound on his head.

'Good heavens, what happened?'

'I had an altercation with a drunk who used my head to see how strong his pool cue was. My head was stronger,' Rivers laughed. 'But it bled a lot more than his broken stick.'

'If you're not on duty, Rivers, perhaps you could drop me off at Jack's office,' Sam said. 'And then take Maggie and Pavel, oh and my stuff I suppose, to their hotel.'

'Well, well, well, if it isn't the world traveller home again, home again,' Jack boomed as Sam entered his office 40 minutes later. 'So how was Egypt?'

'Egypt was just fine, Jack.' Sam dropped into the chair opposite his. 'Peru was pretty good too.'

'Peru. I see. No I don't. Let me guess, you found another cryptic note.'

'Not so cryptic.' She pulled out the photo of Manco City 1962 and placed it on the desk. 'We found out why Professor Marsden was murdered, and why nearly everyone else in this photograph has also met an unpleasant end in the last two years.'

Rigby glanced at the photo then eyed Sam warily. 'I suppose you're going to tell me a story that involves a mysterious relic and probably a curse of some kind,' he said.

Sam raised her eyebrows in surprise.

'Oh god, you are aren't you?'

'What on earth made you say that?' Sam asked.

'This photo. It looks like a still from an Indiana Jones movie.'

'Well, it's funny you should say that Jack, because–'

'Before you go telling me any bizarre fairytales, Sam, there's something you should know.'

'What?'

'I've arrested someone for the murder of Professor Marsden.'

'Who?'

'Haddon Gould. He confessed this morning. We've got him locked up downstairs.' Rigby leant back in his chair and smiled at Sam. 'Reality is *such* a bitch, isn't it?'

For a man who had confessed to and been arrested for murder, Haddon Gould didn't look in the least bit guilty, or self-righteous, or worried about the consequences. In fact, if anything, he looked like he'd just been paid a great compliment and was trying very hard not to show how pleased he was.

Sam couldn't work out whether Gould was a cold-hearted bastard, a sociopath or just plain mad. She watched him run his hand through his blonde hair and adjust the collar of his shirt. There was no nervous tension in either gesture; the man was simply making sure he was presentable.

In Sam's experience most people, even witnesses and certainly suspects – whether guilty or not – displayed a discernible and understandable amount of fear, trepidation or bravado when facing two Homicide detectives across an official interview table. But not Haddon Gould.

There is something seriously wrong with this picture, Sam thought. She rewound the interview tape. If Gould was a murderer, he was the strangest one Sam had ever come across. He hadn't given the slightest hint of an 'uh oh I've been sprung, I'd better come clean'. He had simply and calmly admitted to the murder of Professor Marsden.

'So, now what do you think?' Rigby asked from the doorway.

Sam pressed the pause button. 'I think you'll be laughed out of court; if it gets that far.'

'What's *with* you Sam? The man confessed.'

Sam shrugged. 'I think he was improvising.'

'What the hell does that mean?'

'He didn't *tell* you anything, Jack. He just agreed with you.' Sam pressed the play button. 'You watch his face.'

'You *really* think I murdered Lloyd, don't you?' Gould gave a fascinated smile, as if being a prime suspect was an idea that appealed to him. He shifted slightly in his seat and then lifted his shoulders. 'Okay, I admit I did strike Lloyd.'

'You hit him in the face?' Rigby asked, obviously taken aback by the sudden admission.

'Yes, I hit him in the face.'

'And in the throat?' Rigby prompted.

'Probably,' Gould said. 'Heat of the moment, you know, I don't remember the specifics.'

'But the poison wasn't heat of the moment, was it?'

'The poison,' Gould repeated. He blinked several times but otherwise did not move a muscle. 'The poison was poetic justice.'

He smiled. 'I think I would like a lawyer now please.'

'It sounds like a confession to me,' Rigby stated.

'Jack, prior to this bit of the interview you did not mention that Marsden had been struck or poisoned. Now, most people – not that I think Gould fits into that category at all – but most people would say, 'yes I hit him, or I slapped or punched him' but Gould used *my* words from our initial interview.

'I asked him, and I quote, 'did you *strike* the Professor?' Can you see what I'm getting at here?'

'No, I can't.'

'You fed him the lines, Jack. You said, 'you hit him in the face', he agreed; you said 'and in the throat', he agreed. But when you mentioned the poison, he repeated your words, as if it was a question, took a second to process the information and then called it poetic justice. What the hell does that mean?'

'I don't know,' Jack admitted. 'You expect a sensible answer? The guy's obviously a loon.'

'He is that,' Sam agreed. 'There was no fear, no remorse, no sense that he'd been caught out. The man was *flattered*, Jack. Flattered that you thought he might have done what he's probably always wanted to do. But I bet you a year's salary he didn't.'

'You're on,' Rigby said. 'We've got motive, a confession and the ring we found in his office.'

'Which anyone could have planted,' Sam said. 'When is his lawyer expected?'

'Not until tomorrow morning, unfortunately. He was in Adelaide.'

'May I sit in on the second interview?'

Rigby scowled at her. 'I suppose. Yeah, why not. It might be interesting.'

# Chapter Twenty-Nine

Melbourne, October 9, 1998

MAGGIE LAUGHED UNTIL SHE CRIED. 'YOU HAVE *GOT* TO BE KIDDING.'

Sam grinned. 'That's pretty much what I said. Realistically, however, Jack can't ignore the confession or the fact that the murder weapon was found in Gould's office.'

Maggie shook her head. 'Haddon is not a devious man, Sam. He's more your brawling, knock 'em down and sit on 'em sort of bloke. His imagination only works when it's in paranoid mode and I doubt it could have come up with the idea of using a poison ring to kill Lloyd. But *if* he killed him, he wouldn't have left the weapon in his own office. Haddon might be a nutter but he is not stupid.'

'He seemed taken by the idea that he was the prime suspect. But *why* would he confess?'

'Maybe he's scoring one last point against Lloyd by helping the real murderer escape justice.'

'By going to jail himself?'

Maggie shrugged. 'But he's not likely to is he? And he does so love to be the centre of attention. We should talk to his wife Anna to see if we can find out why he hated Lloyd so much.'

The door to Maggie's suite opened just enough to allow Pavel to slip inside. He still wore his Panama hat and a version of his happy tourist clothes but the man himself looked miserable.

'Terrible news. A whisky please, dear Maggie.' He slumped onto the couch. 'I have just spoken to a friend in San Francisco who told me Barbara Stone died from a stroke in June of last year.'

'Bloody hell,' said Sam.

Maggie downed Pavel's whisky herself and then poured three glasses and handed them out.

Pavel waved his glass under his nose and inhaled deeply. 'This is not fair. Poor Barbara, she never had much happiness in her life. But my friend said she'd just started a new business in Venice Beach, one of those New Age shops, and she had fallen in love. She was happy, and then this bastard that we are hunting kills her. And for what? For gold? I will make him pay when we catch him.'

Sam knew it was pointless to comment on Pavel's last statement so she decided to change the subject. 'I called into my office after I'd seen Jack and asked my partner Ben to do a background check on Enrico Vasquez who, by the way, allegedly returned to Peru to visit his poor sick mother.

'Ben has also been running the surveillance on Barstoc, and he said that during the three days that our friend Andy *disappeared* he was in Sydney doing business with a couple of antique dealers. These business associates apparently *just* scrape through on the right side of legitimate but only, Ben says, because nothing has ever been proven against them.'

'What sort of antiques?' Maggie asked.

'I don't know. I didn't think to ask.' Sam said. She checked her watch. It was 5.30 pm. 'I intend to interview Barstoc again tomorrow, however, so I'll add that question to my list, right under the one about why he was pretending to be a crime fiction buff in Cairo.'

'Phineas, ever the show pony, is throwing a pre-Conference party in the hotel from eight tonight,' Maggie said. 'Why not join me and get Barstoc in a corner somewhere?'

'Good idea,' Sam said. 'Speaking of the Conference, I spoke to Prescott and asked him to check for any late registrations. It seems news of the mysterious Henri Schliemann's *discovery* may have resulted in as many as 15 last-minute delegates – including one Pablo Escobar.'

'I knew he'd be here,' Maggie smiled. 'I think he lost his purpose in life when the Tahuantinsuyu Bracelet was stolen in Paris. When he sees the Hand he'll have a whole new cause.'

'If he doesn't already know *all* about it,' Sam reminded her. 'Your friend Louis Ducruet is also on the list.' She pulled a piece of paper from her jacket pocket and handed it to Maggie.

'Yes, I have spoken with Louis,' Pavel said. 'He went home to Montreal from Istanbul to collect the middle finger, and he arrives here tonight. He will come straight to my room where we will rehearse our little performance for the official welcoming reception tomorrow night.'

'Has he been approached by someone from the *Life and Death* show or by anyone else about the Hand?' Sam asked.

'He said not that he was aware of.'

'I've been thinking about the show's itinerary,' Sam said. 'It started in New York, then headed west to San Francisco, north to Anchorage and east to London, bypassing Montreal altogether. Wouldn't it have been economically sensible to do Montreal after New York, seeing it's just over the border, rather than after New Zealand at the very end of the tour?'

'Montreal may not have been able to host the exhibition at that time,' Maggie said.

'It is more likely that the tour date had to coincide with Louis being in Montreal,' Pavel said. 'He has been working in Turkey since mid 1996. But it was common knowledge, even then, that he was taking a permanent University post in Montreal when Dan Geiger retires at the end of this year.'

'Well,' Sam announced, getting to her feet. 'I'm going home to shower and change into something that hasn't been squashed into a backpack for two weeks. I will meet you here at 7.45.'

'Good idea,' Maggie said. 'But whatever you do, don't get tempted to have a quick nap to combat the jetlag. I did that once and didn't wake up for two days.'

Two hours later, semi-refreshed but fighting an overwhelming tiredness, Sam was taking the lift back up to Maggie's suite when her mobile rang.

'Hey, Sammy,' Ben Muldoon said.

'Hey yourself. By the way, I didn't want to mention this in the office earlier Ben, but you're looking positively radiant, which happens to be an adjective I never thought could be applied to a guy, especially you.'

'Please don't make fun of me, Sam.'

'I'm not, Ben. I'm very happy that you're happy. You are still happy, I gather.'

'Oh I am. I am,' he laughed. 'We'll all have dinner soon, okay? But I'm in a rush right now, so let me fill you in. First of all, if Enrico Vasquez is a spy, agent or cop then his cover is way deep. I couldn't find anything on him that's not relevant to his job as a curator. Mind you I couldn't get any info at all on what he was doing from 1980 to 1983. That could mean he was telling the truth, and he was at spy school or something, or he just dropped out of circulation to harass tourists like you.

'I have also got the Boss's okay and have organised the surveillance team, led by me of course, to be at your disposal for this welcoming bash at the Exhibition Building tomorrow night. The guys, except for Sandra who's got herself a nice frock, have all hired tuxedos so they can blend in.'

'You're my hero, Ben.' Sam emerged from the lift.

'Yeah, well that's all the good news. The bad news is that the Boss expects to be fully briefed by you tomorrow and he wants to meet your friends Maggie and Pavel so he knows what to expect.'

'Oh, joy,' Sam moaned. 'I'll call him in the morning. He's obviously working Saturday as usual.'

Ben laughed. 'What else would he do with his day off?'


Maggie opened the door to her suite just as Sam was about to knock, and ushered her out into the hall. 'I hate being late for parties,' she said. 'I spoke to Anna Gould, by the way.'

'Good. Did you find out why her husband hated the Professor enough to confess to a murder he didn't commit?'

'Anna was beside herself,' Maggie said. 'She swears if Haddon is not found guilty and hanged, she'll kill him herself.'

'Does she believe he did it?'

'No, not at all,' Maggie laughed, as they entered the lift. 'But she does think he's completely lost his mind and she's very annoyed with him. She adores Haddon, *god* only knows why; he's possessive, jealous, irrational and childish.

'According to her, the rivalry between him and Lloyd began in 1977 when Haddon spent most of the year away on field trips. Lloyd used to socialise with both of them and continued to do so with Anna while Lloyd was away. They were just friends who went out to dinner, or to the theatre or art gallery but Haddon decided they were having an affair and that Lloyd was trying to take Anna away from him. That's how it started, but at the same time it seemed to Haddon that he was always losing out to Lloyd at work as well, which wasn't true either.'

'So Marsden and Mrs Gould were not having an affair.'

'No, in fact Lloyd wasn't–' Maggie hesitated as the lift came to a stop and the doors opened.

'Maggie!' exclaimed a short, broad-chested American man who launched himself into the lift.

'Eugene, how are you?' Maggie asked, through a clenched smile.

'Terrific as always. Have you heard the news?'

'What news?'

'About the discovery of an Inca city bigger than Machu Picchu.'

'No, I haven't,' Maggie said, feigning excitement. 'Where did you hear this?'

'It's been all over the internet apparently. Someone told a collegue of Bob Esterhauser who told me all about it on the flight from New Zealand this morning.'

'Who discovered it?'

'Bob wasn't sure, but he heard from someone else that a very wealthy retired German professor named Schreiber has been funding a team of amateurs in the jungle south-west of Machu Picchu.'

'South-west?' Maggie repeated.

The lift stopped again and a well-dressed English couple joined them and the conversation.

'Hello Maggie. I say, what do you think of the rumours about Vilcabamba?' the man asked.

'I've only just heard, Hugh. But this German can't be claiming he's found Vilcabamba. It's not lost.'

'He's saying he's found the *real* Vilcabamba,' Hugh stated. 'But I heard he was American. Isn't that right, Sophie?'

'No Hugh, you've mixed your stories up again,' Sophie said patiently. 'And you wonder how that rumour started about you trying to sell a collection of skulls you never had.'

The lift stopped again but a family surrounded by luggage decided to wait for an empty lift.

'So what are the real stories, Sophie?' Maggie resisted the urge to glance at Sam who remained unnoticed in the corner.

'A rich English industrialist and amateur archaeologist named Henry Steedman organised an expedition, comprised of American students, to explore the area west of Machu Picchu. He found a small but significant ceremonial centre and some quite astounding artefacts.'

'That's... a lot of detail.' Maggie stifled a laugh. 'Where did you hear all that?'

'Jennifer Pertwee's brother has just come back from Peru. He actually met this Steedman fellow but was sworn to secrecy until the find is officially announced. Now I *heard* that Steedman might be coming here to the Conference to do just that. But that is a rumour.'

'But everything else is fact?' Maggie asked.

'Oh yes, I have it on the best authority,' Sophie pronounced.

Sam wondered whether the rumour of Hugh and his skull collection had been started by Sophie.

'No,' Eugene disagreed. 'The guy's a German named Schreiber, and he found a big city south-west of Machu Picchu. That's what Esterhauser told me, and he got it straight off the internet.'

Sam rolled her eyes. The two people who, not two minutes before, had been the source of Esterhauser's information were now forgotten links in this incredible chain of bullshit.

'You must have him mixed up with the American that Hugh mentioned,' Sophie stated, obviously delighted she could sort out this mess for everyone. '*His* name is Harry Steinberg and he found a priceless Inca statue in the basement of a house in Spain.'

'Spain?' Maggie laughed, as the doors opened on the third floor.

'No,' Eugene argued, 'You've got him confused with the guy who found the Aztec statue. He *is* at the conference, I've met him already. Aren't you coming to Marcus's party, Maggie?'

'Yes,' Maggie nodded. 'I have to go downstairs for a minute.'

A second after the doors had closed, leaving them alone, Sam and Maggie burst into laughter.

'Good grief!' Sam exclaimed.

'Now you see how Pavel was killed in the jungle by a poison arrow when in fact he'd caught glandular fever in New Orleans.'

Sam grinned. 'We needn't have bothered with the internet. We could have told Sophie the truth, that Pavel Mercier was alive, had discovered Inticancha and was in Melbourne with the Hand of God and I'm sure her 'best authority' would still have devised Harry, Henry and an imaginary basement in Spain.'

'Not to mention Eugene's imaginary encounter with the non-existent finder of an *Aztec* statue,' Maggie said. They had reached the foyer, so she stabbed the button for the third floor again.

'Shall we join the party now to see if *anyone* has actually heard that a Henri Schliemann has discovered Manco Capac's secret city *and* a legendary golden artefact?'

Marcus Bridger was holding court on the far side of the crowded function room. It did nothing for Sam's ego that he looked at her most curiously when she smiled, as if he didn't recognise her. His vague nod suggested he knew he *should* know who she was, but couldn't place her in this context.

About 50 people were making the most of the open bar, courtesy of *The Rites of Life and Death* and, judging by the conversations that Sam could actually understand, a great many of them were talking about an amazing archaeological find in Peru – or Mexico or Chile or Spain. One man, who kept switching rapidly between French, English and Russian, was trying to convince his little circle of listeners that a treasure-filled Mayan funerary temple had been discovered on the Yucatan Peninsula.

'I wish you-know-who was here to enjoy all this,' Maggie said. 'But there's Andrew, let's go interrogate the life out of him.'

'We need to be a bit more subtle than that,' Sam insisted, keeping pace with Maggie as she manoeuvred through the guests towards Barstoc who was standing alone near the bar.

'Don't worry, I'll leave to you. In this you are the expert.'

'Good evening, Mr Barstoc,' Sam said pleasantly, before asking the bartender for two beers.

'Detective Diamond, Dr Tremaine.' Barstoc seemed oddly taken aback. 'How was Egypt?'

'So-so,' Maggie shrugged.

'Could I ask you a couple of questions, Mr Barstoc?' Sam asked. 'Regarding my investigation.'

Barstoc straightened his shoulders. 'Now is hardly the time. This is a social occasion, Detective.'

'Yes of course, I'm sorry. I just thought it would easier to chat here, rather than ask you down to the station tomorrow' Sam started to turn away.

'In that case, I'd be happy to talk to you,' Barstoc said hurriedly. 'It will save us both time.'

'Thanks. Firstly, could you refresh my memory about the exact nature of your other business interests.'

'I run an import-export business. I deal mostly in rare precious stones,' Barstoc said, as if talking to a forgetful child. 'But what does this have to do with your case?'

'Maybe nothing, Mr Barstoc. You said mostly precious stones, what other things do you collect?'

'Anything that my clients, and I have many all over the world, express an interest in.'

'Ah, that would explain why you met with the antique dealers in Sydney.'

'I beg your pardon?' Barstoc barely managed to stay on the outraged side of angry. 'Have you been following me?'

'Me? No. I've been in Egypt,' Sam smiled. 'But you did leave town in the middle of a murder investigation, so my colleagues felt they had to, at least, find out where you went. Were you after anything in particular from these acquaintances in Sydney?'

'Not that it is any of your business, Detective Diamond, but yes I was trying to track down an antique necklace for a client in London.'

'Okay, fine,' Sam shrugged. 'That's all I needed.'

Barstoc frowned but visibly relaxed and took a sip of his drink. 'That was painless,' he joked.

Sam smiled. 'Oh, by the way, I believe we have something in common. I hear you're a bit of a crime fiction buff. You're even trying your hand at writing a mystery, I gather. How's it going?'

'What?' Barstoc snapped, exhibiting a telltale sign of the flight or fight response by squirming as if his clothes were suddenly very uncomfortable. 'I don't know what–'

'Oh Andy,' Maggie chimed in, 'there's no need to be shy. Every writer has to start somewhere.'

Sam tried to look genuinely sorry. 'I didn't mean to embarrass you, Mr Barstoc. It's just that we met an old friend of Maggie's in Cairo who said he met you briefly when you sought out his friend Noel Winslow to get some advice. Andy Baxter, is that your pen name?'

Barstoc was speechless although his mouth looked like it was *trying* to help him form an appropriate response. 'How did you–'

'Put it together?' Sam asked. 'I happened to have a copy of your Exhibition catalogue with me.'

Barstoc raised his eyebrows. 'Why?'

'Oh god, don't ask,' Maggie butted in, with a laugh. 'This was Sam's first overseas trip and you've no idea the junk she took with her. She purposefully took her car and office keys, would you believe, but we're still trying to work out how or why she packed a guide book to Japan.'

'Maggie! Do you have to tell *everyone* about the keys.'

Barstoc ran his hand through his hair. 'I can see I'd better come clean,' he said. 'I'm not a writer. I am a freelance investigator, of sorts. I contacted Noel Winslow because I'd been led to believe he knew the whereabouts of an antique necklace I am still seeking.'

'An investigator?' Sam asked. 'For whom?'

'As I said, for my clients. I sometimes use my own, quite legitimate business as a cover to try and reclaim stolen jewellery. The necklace I'm looking for was taken from a house in London a year ago. It's priceless, but only if it's intact. It can't be broken down and sold for parts, so to speak. A few dealers, not all legitimate, told me that Noel might know who was interested in buying it. I told him the truth about myself, when I realised his interest in jewellery of this kind was academic. He'd made the acquaintance of antique dealers all over the world while doing research for two of his books.

'Do you know Noel or just his friend, um,' Barstoc snapped his fingers to help his memory. 'Patrick?'

'I knew Noel very well, Andrew,' Maggie admitted. 'Do *you* know that he died the day you last saw him? He had a stroke.'

Barstoc pressed his fingers to his lips. 'Oh, how terrible. He was a such a generous man.'

'What do you do when you find these stolen goods?' Sam asked, wondering whether Barstoc and Vasquez had attended the same school of humbug.

'It depends who has the item and who my client is. Sometimes I offer to buy it back, sometimes I call in the local police. Detective Diamond, I do this work through word of mouth, and no one on the team knows about it. I would appreciate it you could keep it to yourself.'

'Of course. And *I* appreciate your candour.'

Sam and Maggie watched Barstoc slither away into the crowd before turning to each other.

'Sounds plausible,' Maggie noted.

'Explains absolutely everything quite nicely,' Sam agreed.

'I think Andy and Enrico went to the Fairytale Academy together,' Maggie observed.

'Yes. And I'll be taking bets later that Haddon Gould will claim it was stress from his alien abduction that forced him to commit murder.'

'Sam! You're back from Egypt.'

'Yes, we are. Hi, Adrienne.'

Maggie held up a finger. 'Would you two excuse me, I've just spotted someone I need to berate.'

'Speaking of berating, Daley Prescott has just spotted me,' Sam said . 'Would you care to take a stroll around the room?'

Adrienne smiled. 'Of course.'

'So, how's the show going?' Sam asked, when they'd relocated out of Prescott's line of sight, and behind Marcus Bridger and a silver-haired man with a very proper British accent.

'Splendid,' Adrienne replied, 'considering Enrico had to dash home because his mother took a bad turn. But the grand opening was a great success and we've had big crowds every day.'

She continued to talk about the show but when Sam noticed that Barstoc had joined Bridger she turned half her attention to their conversation.

'Andrew, dear boy,' said the silver-haired gent, 'I was just telling Marcus I played 18 at Sunningdale with your father last week.'

'Really?' Barstoc asked, as if it was the least interesting thing he'd heard all night.

'Yes. He was telling me all about this new venture of his in Barbados.'

'Really?' Barstoc said again. 'I don't know anything about it, Edward. If you'll excuse me.'

'I hope I didn't speak out of turn, Marcus,' Edward said as Barstoc walked off.

'No, not at all. Father still hasn't forgiven Andrew. I doubt he ever will.'

*Father?* 'Adrienne, would you excuse me a sec, I'll be right back.' Sam made a beeline for Maggie on the far side of the room.

'Sam, dear, I'd like you to meet Athol Porter,' Maggie began.

'Hi, Athol. I don't mean to be rude but I need to talk to Maggie, urgently.'

'What is it?' Maggie asked, after they retreated to a quieter spot.

'Marcus and Andrew are brothers.'

Maggie laughed. 'No, they're not.'

'*Yes*, they are.' Sam repeated the conversation she'd overheard.

Maggie frowned. 'How very odd. Who was Marcus talking to?'

When Sam pointed to the man, now talking to someone else, Maggie said, 'That's Edward Fisher. I'll have a word with him. You stay here.'

Maggie was gone for five minutes during which Sam managed to avoid Daley Prescott again by joining a nearby conversation about the discovery of an Inca crown in Cuzco. No one missed her from the debate when she moved away to rejoin Maggie.

'Edward says that Andrew and Marcus are *step*brothers, Sam.'

'Well, I'll be damned.'

'Apparently Andrew had a falling out with his stepfather, Daniel Bridger, about 20 years ago. He was disowned and disinherited. Edward said he'd heard they'd recently reconciled, otherwise he wouldn't have mentioned Daniel in front of Andrew.'

'What do you think this means?'

Maggie snorted. 'I've no idea, Sam. It might *mean* nothing at all. Obviously the brothers are still close, at least close enough to work together, despite the father's opinion of Andrew. There could be any number of reasons why they don't acknowledge their relationship, although the most logical might be they don't want to risk Marcus being disinherited as well.'

'I suppose,' Sam agreed. 'But if Andrew is "the one", do you think Marcus knows about it?'

Maggie shrugged. 'Andrew said no one on the team knows about his *alleged* investigative work, but we know from Patrick that Marcus also met Noel Winslow, however briefly, in Cairo.

'So we can only guess at what Marcus does and doesn't know. His mind is a bit of a vacuum when it comes to other people's business and affairs anyway. If it doesn't directly concern him or, more importantly, make him 'look good' he pays little attention. I could tell him right now that I'd been nominated for a Nobel Prize, but he'd be surprised all over again if someone else told him the same thing about me five minutes later.'

'That explains the odd, "who the hell are you and why are you looking at me" look I got earlier,' Sam said.

'Anyway, considering what we went through in Cairo and Cuzco, I'm convinced Vasquez is... *the one*.' Maggie's tone was emphatic but her expression said something else entirely.

Sam frowned at her. 'But he's not–'

'*Enrico* dear, what a pleasant surprise,' Maggie said.

# Chapter Thirty

Melbourne, October 9, 1998

SAM TURNED TO FIND VASQUEZ AND ADRIENNE APPROACHING. 'SEÑOR Vasquez,' she said.

'Enrico has just now returned from Peru,' Adrienne said.

'And how is your poor mother?' Maggie asked, all concern and no sincerity.

Vasquez smiled, like a man sharing a secret. 'My mother is recovering, thank you. But my time at home was plagued by disaster. My poor cousin broke his nose and collarbone when his car hit a stationary truck. We still can't imagine how he managed to have such a foolish accident in broad daylight.'

'He must have been looking at something other than where he was going,' Sam suggested.

'Perhaps,' Vasquez agreed amicably. 'Detective Diamond, might we have a word in private about that matter I raised the last time we spoke?'

'Of course,' Sam agreed. 'How about we adjourn to the bar downstairs?'

'Good idea. You're welcome to join us, Maggie,' he added, as if it was an afterthought. 'You may actually be able to help me out. Would you excuse us please, Adrienne?'

'Sure thing,' Adrienne said, looking like she'd rather tag along to find out what the mystery was.

'Was he really your cousin?' Sam asked, once they were settled in a booth downstairs, after ensuring none of the other nearby customers were Conference delegates.

Vasquez smiled. 'No. But you were right, he wasn't watching where he was going. But enough about your clever escape.'

He pulled a folded but crumpled piece of paper from his pocket, smoothed it out on the table and turned it around so that Sam's handwriting was facing them. 'I found this in your hotel room, *after* you had checked out.'

'So?' Maggie said, as if the list of names from the Manco City dig meant nothing.

'Maggie,' Vasquez sighed, 'I know you do not believe I work for my government but please do not treat me like a fool. I recognised some of these names so I made the assumption that the others had some kind of professional connection. Would you like me to tell you what I discovered?'

'If you wish, Enrico, but I don't see the point,' Maggie smiled.

'Then humour me. Of the familiar names, I knew that Pavel Mercier, Alistair Nash and, of course, Lloyd Marsden were all deceased.

'So, I began with Noel Winslow. Being a fan of his mystery novels, I tried his publishers first and discovered he too had died earlier this year. I looked into the other names and discovered that Jean McBride had been killed in a car accident.

He tapped the page. 'I must admit, I worried you had gone a little strange, Maggie, making this list of all your dead friends.'

Maggie sighed. 'You get to my age, Enrico, and it hits you one day that all your friends are dropping like flies. It gets a bit disconcerting.'

Vasquez shook his head. 'I am sure it does but when I found out that Louis Ducruet was alive and working in Turkey and Sarah Croydon had recently opened an exhibition in Wellington, I knew this was not a list of the dead.

'I admit I have found nothing about Jones, Sanchez or Rockly, yet, but I did discover a great deal about the late Barbara Stone, whom I actually met once. And that's when I knew what this list was about.'

'Because of Barbara Stone,' Sam said.

'Yes of course,' Vasquez said. 'When I discovered she and her ex-business partner had been investigated by the FBI for fencing stolen antiquities I knew, despite your denials that you were, *are*, in fact looking for the Paris hijackers.'

'Enrico, I *swear* we knew, know, nothing of Barbara and the FBI,' Maggie said impatiently. 'But even if we did, how could a dead person help us find the hijackers that we are *not*, in fact, looking for?'

Vasquez scowled at her. 'I was hoping you would tell me.'

'Did the FBI charge her with anything?' Sam asked.

'No,' Vasquez sighed. 'The partner was jailed but there was no real evidence against her, which doesn't mean she wasn't involved; but then you know that already.'

'No we don't,' Sam stated.

Vasquez looked deeply puzzled, as if he wanted to believe them but didn't want to relinquish his theory. 'But why else would her name be on this list, with all these people who have had access over the years to the types of artefacts she was suspected of fencing? You can't really expect me to believe you are not on the trail of the Tahuantinsuyu Bracelet.'

'Señor Vasquez, you have a fertile imagination. *You* are on the trail of the Tahuantinsuyu Bracelet; *we* are looking for a murderer,' Sam pronounced.

Vasquez shrugged as if he was giving up. 'Then I suppose you are not interested in Andrew Barstoc's connection to Ms Stone, and the affair she was having,' he said, offhandedly.

Sam laughed. 'What is this *thing* you have about Barstoc? You've been throwing him in my face since we first met.'

'We – my colleagues and I – have long suspected him to be a major player in the illegal trade of stolen cultural property.'

'Well, if you *really* are a cop, or whatever you are, why don't you talk to *him* instead of us?'

Vasquez threw up his palms. 'I thought we could help each other in this matter.'

'Honestly, Enrico,' Maggie snapped. 'How do you expect us to believe anything you say when you can't give us any proof. I believe you are using your Masters in Applied Obfuscation to find out what we might know in order to conceal your own involvement in the hijacking.'

'But–'

'No buts, Enrico. I will say this one last time.' Maggie tapped the table for emphasis. 'We are not looking for hijackers and we don't care about the Tahuantinsuyu Bracelet. If we were, given the appalling behaviour of you and your henchmen in Cuzco, we would be coming *after you*, not trying to avoid you.

'What's more, having your accomplices shoot at us and our aircraft is not a sensible way to go about earning our trust and securing our assistance.'

'Who shot at you?' Vasquez seemed genuinely appalled.

'The Turkish gentleman who *you* claim is a known dealer in stolen antiquities. It is obvious you're in cahoots with him.'

Vasquez slapped his forehead. 'Maggie, I am on *your* side. Mr Aydin is no accomplice of mine. He is probably, however, an acquaintance of Andrew Barstoc.'

'Of course he is,' Sam said. 'And what else were you trying to imply about him before?'

'Something about Barstoc having an affair with Barbara Stone,' Maggie said.

'No, that is not what I said. Ms Stone attended the opening of our exhibition in San Francisco. She knew the Director of the Museum and was introduced to the whole team. Andrew then visited her in her New Age shop on several occasions.'

'That's it? That's your connection?' Sam asked. '*You* met this nefarious FBI suspect too.'

'But I am not a suspected trader in stolen artefacts,' Vasquez pointed out.

'You are in *our* book,' Maggie reminded him. 'So who was Barbara having the affair with? I hope you're not going to tell us you saw Lloyd Marsden in San Francisco so you jumped to the most illogical conclusion yet.'

'Of course not. Please be sensible,' Vasquez pleaded. 'I *know* this, because I saw them together and it was common knowledge, that Barbara Stone was seeing our Ms Douglas.'

My god, Sam thought; throw the works another spanner.

'Well that's interesting, I'm sure,' she said calmly. 'But what it has to do with anything, I *don't* know.

'I have an idea, Señor. Instead of following us around, making wild connections between unrelated things, devising bizarre theories, and spreading unsubstantiated gossip about your colleagues, why don't you come up with some way of proving you are who you say are.

'If you can do that, I promise when I have solved *my* murder case, I will give your request for assistance in *your* hijacking case some serious consideration.'

# Chapter Thirty-One

SAM WATCHED HADDON GOULD THROUGH THE ONE-WAY MIRROR AS HE straightened his jacket. He looked refreshed despite his night in a cell and actually smiled as he whispered to his lawyer.

'So, what do you say Jack? Shall we give it a go?'

'I don't know,' Rigby said doubtfully. 'I'm positive he's right for this. I asked him about the threatening postcard last night, and he admitted to sending that too.'

'Well he would, wouldn't he,' Sam said.

'I gave him no extra information, Sam. He told *me* which typewriter he used.'

Sam shrugged. 'So, he writes bad poetry.'

'You're the one who said the postcard and murder were connected,' Rigby reminded her.

'I can't be right about everything.'

'But you are right about Gould not being the murderer.'

Sam shrugged. 'I'm trying to save you some embarrassment.'

'Okay, okay. Let's do it.'

Sam and Rigby entered the interview room in silence and took their seats opposite Gould and his lawyer. While Sam opened a file and studied the page on top, Rigby turned on the tape recorder, stated the date, time and who was present, and then sat back and crossed his arms.

'Do you remember me, Mr Gould? We met the day after your operation.'

'Yes, Detective Diamond, I remember.'

'You told me that day that you did *not* strike the Professor. You said, and I quote, "and I certainly didn't kill him, if that's what you're implying". Do you recall that?'

Gould looked boyishly guilty, as if he'd been caught telling a white lie. 'Yes, that is what I said.'

Sam tapped the page in front of her. 'But that's nothing like the statement you gave Detective Rigby yesterday. I'm puzzled. Why did you do it?'

'You don't have to answer that,' Gould's lawyer advised.

'It's okay, John, I want them to know. I'd simply had enough of Lloyd's manipulating, his double standards, his–'

'No, what I meant was, why did you confess?'

Gould frowned. 'Because Detective Rigby here had all the evidence and I knew I could no longer deny that I'd killed the man,' he said, as if it was obvious.

'So you killed Professor Lloyd Marsden?' Sam asked.

'Yes,' Gould stated categorically, then he jumped – along with everyone else in the room – as the door was flung open and Dr Maggie Tremaine barged in as if it was a hotel bar.

'*There* you are, Sam. I've been looking everywhere for you.'

'Maggie!' Sam snapped, as Rigby leapt to his feet. 'You can't come in here.'

'Why ever not? Hello, Haddon, what are you doing here?'

'I'm being interviewed, Maggie. Go away.'

'Interviewed? What for?'

'Dr Tremaine, you must leave,' Rigby insisted.

'I've confessed to murdering Lloyd,' Gould said, proudly. 'I'm just explaining why.'

'*Haddon*,' moaned his lawyer.

'You're explaining why you confessed?' Maggie asked, as Rigby tried to usher her out the door.

'This is ridiculous,' Sam said. 'We'll have to do this later.'

'No, Maggie, I'm explaining why I *killed* him,' Gould persisted.

Maggie started laughing and shook herself free of Rigby's grip. 'Don't be ridiculous Haddon. Are you mad?'

'Dr Tremaine! I insist you leave,' Rigby demanded.

'Oh hush, young man,' Maggie snapped. 'I can't believe you're taking Haddon seriously. This is why you can never find a cop when you need one; you're all sitting around interrogating lunatics.'

'I am not a lunatic, Margaret Tremaine,' Gould declared.

'*Yes* you are, Haddon. It's one thing to have hated Lloyd for 21 years because of an affair he never had with your wife, but to confess to his murder is completely absurd.'

Sam glared at Maggie but addressed the suspect. 'Mr Gould, we're stopping the interview now.'

'No,' Haddon declared. 'I won't have that woman call me a lunatic without a comeback. We'll do this now, with her here too, or I won't say another word.'

Sam threw up her hands, Rigby collapsed back in his chair and Gould's lawyer dropped his head in his hands. Maggie and Gould just stared at each other.

'What would you know about Lloyd and Anna anyway, Maggie? And how could you begin to know how their affair made me feel?'

'But Haddon, they didn't *have* an affair. Not only was Lloyd completely asexual – that means, dear – that he had no interest in sex, but he lacked the necessary equipment to do the deed,' Maggie said. 'Although I suspect the latter was the reason for the former.'

'What are you talking about?' Gould demanded, as if Maggie was the mad person in the room.

'Lloyd lost all his important bits in a motorcycle accident when he was 16, Haddon. He *couldn't* have sex.'

Haddon Gould looked like a man going through a crisis of faith. The rug on which two decades worth of resentment had been resting, had been pulled out from under him. He nonetheless took a deep breath into further denial and said, 'That doesn't mean he wasn't in love with Anna and wanted to take her away from me.'

Maggie closed her eyes and shook her head sadly.

Sam sat back down in her chair, removed an evidence bag and emptied the contents onto the table. 'Mr Gould, are you confessing that because you suspected Lloyd Marsden of having an affair with your wife, 21 years ago, you murdered him by injecting him with strychnine using *this* poison ring contraption?'

Gould was sucking in deep angry breaths through his nose as he stared at the ring in front of him.

'Yes, Detective. That is exactly what I'm saying.'

Sam scratched her chin and smiled. 'That's interesting. I bought this ring at a toy store an hour ago.'

Haddon Gould looked perplexed. 'Lloyd wasn't poisoned with this ring?'

'You tell us, Mr Gould. Did you murder Professor Lloyd Marsden?' Sam asked.

Gould sat turning the plastic ring over in his fingers. 'I wanted to. I *could* have killed him,' he finally said, as if he would have been up to the challenge.

Rigby sat forward. 'I think you'd better run along home now, sir. Thanks for your time.'

'Do we have your undivided attention now, Jack?' Sam asked, after Gould and his lawyer had left. 'Because we'll need your assistance this evening and we want you to know what's *really* going on.'

Melbourne, October 10, 1998

Sam looked around Maggie's hotel suite at the assembled players for the upcoming charade. She hoped to hell this plan was going to work, because if it didn't she'd have to resign and go into hiding.

Louis Ducruet, who Sam had met an hour before, was still in a huddle with Pavel. A tall finely-built and balding man with a snow-white moustache, Louis had impressed everyone with his charm and level-headedness. And Maggie had assured her that Louis would prevent Pavel from going completely overboard.

Ben Muldoon, Rigby and Rivers were working out the logistics of how their teams would operate together; and they were all waiting for the Boss to turn up for his briefing.

'This is nerve-wracking,' Maggie whispered.

'Tell me about it,' Sam said. 'Are you planning any expeditions I can join if this is a disaster?'

Maggie nodded vigorously. 'I have a well-prepared escape for both of us.'

'Sammy, can I have a word?'

'Of course, Ben.' Sam made room for him on the side of the bed.

'I checked out that stuff you wanted. First up, Adrienne Douglas is as clean as whistle, not even a speeding fine. Barstoc on the other hand is a piece of work. He was adopted by Daniel Bridger at the age of 14 when Bridger married his mother. Young Andrew was always a loose cannon but when his mother died three years later, he went right off the rails. He pulled crazy stunts and was always being picked up for assault and petty crimes. The stepfather kept taking him back until Barstoc was busted for selling, get this, cocaine from his father's limo to kids at a local school. That was it. End of story for one of the heirs to what I gather is quite a sizeable family fortune.'

'I assume Barstoc was his mother's maiden name,' Sam said.

'No, it was her previous husband's name. She'd been married to a John Barstoc for a couple of years before divorcing him to marry Bridger.'

'Who was she before that?' Sam asked, casting a meaningful look at Maggie.

'Don't know. I didn't realise you wanted me to check her too,' Ben said.

'You don't suppose?' Maggie asked.

Sam shrugged. 'He's the right age, same as Vasquez and Escobar.'

'That's not all, Sammy. Bridger, the other–'

Ben snapped his mouth shut as there was no point competing with Dan Bailey's noisy arrival.

The Boss entered a room in much the same way as Rigby did, loudly and as if he was always on a mission. It would be interesting, Sam thought, to see how the two men worked together.

'Okay folks, fill me in,' Bailey demanded. 'I want to know every little detail and just how pissed off this whole thing is going to make Daley Prescott, because I guarantee he'll be on the phone to the Minister before the night is out.'

# Chapter Thirty-Two

SAM CHECKED HER WATCH. IT WAS 9.30 PM; ONLY TWO MINUTES LATER than the last time she'd looked, although it seemed like Maggie had gone to get drinks about three days ago. Marcus Bridger hesitated in passing just long enough to ask how her trip to Egypt had been and then excused himself to attend to someone much more important who was inspecting the entrance to his show.

Sam realised he was revelling in the happy coincidence that the official ICOM '98 welcoming ceremony was being held in the same space as his exhibition, which meant there were close to 1500 of his peers in spitting distance of his *pièce de résistance.*

Sam glanced up at the vaulted ceiling of the Exhibition Building and wondered, fleetingly, about the acoustics of the place. What she really wondered was *where* the sound of so many people actually went because, despite the crowd, no one was shouting to be heard over everyone else.

'Excuse me, Detective Diamond.' It was Enrico Vasquez – again; this time accosting her in the company of a tall elegantly-dressed man. 'I would like to introduce you to Miguel Richer, the Peruvian

Ambassador here in Australia. He is prepared to vouch for me and all the things I have been telling you.'

Sam raised her eyebrows. 'Really? Do you happen to have your credentials on you, Señor Richer?'

The man laughed politely. 'No, Detective Diamond, this is a social function.'

'I thought as much,' Sam said. 'I don't mean to be rude sir, but I don't know you; and I have doubts about your friend here. So if you'll excuse me, I have lots of other places to be.'

'But–'

'Nice try, Vasquez,' she said, as she walked away.

'The next shout is on you,' Maggie declared, suddenly appearing at her side. 'I'm not going back for love or money.'

She handed Sam a glass of mineral water and took a swig of her beer. 'Louis just arrived by the way. The rest of the troupe should be along shortly.'

'I'm worried we're not going to be able to control this,' Sam said. 'There's too many people, too many variables.'

'Don't worry. A good 80 per cent of the people here won't give a damn about you-know-who and his tall tales but almost true.'

'How can we be sure our culprit will make his move tonight?'

'We can't be sure,' Maggie said. 'We're taking a gamble that he thinks this is the best or only chance to get his hands on the Hand. The hijacking in Paris happened when the security was good but less than usual. If our culprit thinks there is no security here, he will take a risk – hopefully.'

'Detective Diamond.'

Sam swallowed, rolled her eyes at Maggie, and turned to face Daley Prescott who stood as neat as pin in a perfectly tailored suit that was not complemented by the hysterical expression on his face.

'Good evening, Mr Prescott. The opening function is going very well, don't you think?'

'I don't know, Detective. You tell me. I just met your colleague Detective Rigby who informed he has officers posted everywhere, and that I was not to worry because everything was under control. I wasn't aware that things were out of control, until I found out there were policemen everywhere.'

'And women,' Maggie offered.

'What?' Prescott demanded.

'There are quite a few policewomen too.'

'I might have known you'd have a hand in this debacle, Maggie Tremaine,' Prescott snarled.

'What debacle would that be, Daley?'

Prescott glared at her and returned his attention to Sam. 'The saboteur is at large in the building isn't he? What are you expecting? A bomb? A hostage situation?'

'Nothing of the sort.' Sam fought an urge to find a broom closet to lock him in until the 'debacle' was over.

'There *is* no saboteur. We are hopeful, however, that we may be able to find and arrest the person who murdered Professor Marsden.'

'Here? Tonight? You have to do it here tonight? This is a disaster.'

'It will be if you don't stop carrying on like a complete fool, Daley,' Maggie snapped. 'For goodness sake, get a grip man, and be quiet. Why don't you get a stiff drink or three.'

'Mr Prescott,' Sam said soothingly. 'I assure you our presence and our work here will go unnoticed. But I have to ask you, please, not to tell *anyone* we are here.'

Prescott rubbed his forehead and eyed Sam and Maggie suspiciously. 'I hold you responsible.'

'And I accept the responsibility entirely,' Sam said.

'Now, do run along, Daley,' Maggie suggested sweetly. 'Or I shall be forced to create a scene, right here, just for the fun of it. And it won't be pretty.'

Daley Prescott turned on his heel and disappeared into the crowd quite possibly, Sam suspected, to find his own closet in which to hide from the formidable Maggie Tremaine.

Sam stuck her finger in her ear to adjust the tiny listening device she was wearing, so she could hear what Rigby was saying. 'He's on his way in,' Sam repeated to Maggie.

'Ooh, showtime,' Maggie enthused. 'I'm going to find a better spot. Are you coming?'

Sam followed Maggie past a group of people who were determined to stand their ground near the bar, towards an area that had been roped off around a large-topped, waist-high pedestal. They stopped by the third head of Cerberus, beside the entrance to the *Life and Death* show, and waited.

'*C'est très amusant,*' Louis commented as he ducked under the rope to wait for Pavel.

Sam bent her head slightly to speak into the microphone concealed by a brooch on her lapel. 'The show's about to start, don't lose sight of the targets and report any odd actions or even reactions.'

'Sam dear, I think–' Maggie began, but a cheer then the sound of applause changed the whole atmosphere in the room. The words 'Pavel Mercier' seemed to be rippling through the crowd and a wide path was forming down the middle of the room as everyone moved aside to let him pass.

'Oh, good heavens!' Maggie snorted. 'He's like Moses parting the Red Sea.'

Pavel, grinning like a Chesire Cat, was enjoying his resurrection immensely. He kept stopping to shake hands with people who were saying they were glad he wasn't really dead or they'd known all along he wasn't. No one was paying attention to Ben Muldoon who was right behind Pavel, carrying his 'treasure' in a plain wooden box.

Sam put her hand to her ear. 'Barstoc has just made a beeline for our end of the room,' she whispered to Maggie. 'Ditto, Vasquez and Escobar.'

'I can see Enrico. Oh, he seems to be annoyed with us,' Maggie said, nodding to the angry Colombian standing with his hands on his hips, glaring at them.

'Would you like to deal with him, Maggie dear?'

'Certainly,' Maggie replied, and made her way around to the other side of the barrier.

Sam smiled as Vasquez actually stamped his foot at Maggie in indignation.

'Did Maggie know Pavel was alive?' came a familiar voice beside her.

'Um, no Marcus, not until earlier this evening,' Sam fibbed. 'She was quite annoyed with him.'

'I'm not surprised,' Bridger said.

Louis unhooked the rope to let Pavel and Ben into the performance area. Ben placed the box on the pedestal but Pavel raised his hands in warning, reached into his pocket and pulled out a compass.

'This side must face west.' Pavel turned the box around.

'*What* is he doing, Sam?'

'Your guess is as good as mine, Marcus.'

'Ladies and gentlemen,' Pavel bellowed. 'I would like to announce the discovery of a major archaeological site in Peru, *north-east*,' he stressed for all those who had got it wrong, 'of Machu Picchu. My colleague Louis Ducruet and I would like to tell you the story of Inticancha, the secret city of Manco Capac and the last refuge of the last Inca king, Tupac Amaru.'

'The man's barely back from the dead, and he's grandstanding already,' Bridger whispered in Sam's ear.

'Those of you who know me,' Pavel smiled, 'will know that any story I tell must feature an ancient curse on a priceless relic, or it's not worth telling. I promise not to disappoint you.'

The audience laughed as if they did indeed expect nothing less from him.

'I need a drink,' Bridger muttered. 'Would you like one, Sam?'

'No, thank you, Marcus.'

As Sam watched Bridger disappear into the crowd she noted that Maggie was correct about the level of interest in Pavel's announcement. While quite a few people were still making their way across the room to see what was happening, the vast majority had returned to their own conversations. Sam estimated there were just over a hundred people hanging on to Pavel's every word.

Sam concentrated on the faces in the audience as Pavel and Louis recounted their revised story of the discovery in 1962 of a remarkable ceremonial site and a 'golden hand' that caused localised earthquakes every time they tried to move it.

Pavel explained how they had to leave the relic in its sacred hiding place and abandon the site when one of their crew was badly injured. When they returned the following month, he said, the hand was gone and, as the site was constantly being rocked by tremors, they left Inticancha in peace.

Sam spotted Barstoc and moved to stand behind him as Pavel described his return to the site the year before, his discovery of the journal of Vasco Dias, the story it told of the city and the curse and the realisation of what had been stolen from Inticancha all those years ago – the Hand of God.

'What do you think of this bizarre story, Mr Barstoc?' Sam asked quietly.

Barstoc flinched but turned to face Sam. 'It's nonsense, of course. Pavel Mercier loves putting on a show. He's nearly as bad as Marcus in that respect.'

'But as fate would have it,' Pavel waved his finger, 'two weeks ago, I was in Cuzco and happened to see an article and photo in the paper about the theft in Paris of the Tahuantinsuyu Bracelet. Now this was an artefact that I knew about, of course, but had never seen – until then. And what did I see? The wrist band of the Hand of God.' Pavel paused for effect.

'So I set out to look for the other pieces. Remembering the bracelet had been re-stolen from a small museum in Punta Arenas in 1978, I went to Chile and discovered the bracelet had been sold to that museum in 1970 by an old man who needed money.

'I tracked down his daughter, and in her attic – where the old man's belongings had been stored on his death – I found the Hand of God.'

With a great flourish, Pavel lifted the lid on the box.

The audience took a collective breath at the sight of the beautiful golden digits of Inti the Sun God.

'What are you going to do with it, Pavel?' someone asked.

'Tonight it goes back to the vault, where it stays until I decide.'

'But you must return it to Peru,' Escobar shouted.

Pavel shrugged. 'Perhaps.'

Barstoc, Sam noticed, cricked his neck twice and then walked away.

'Where's he going?' Sam muttered into her brooch. 'Heading straight for Bridger' came the response. 'No, he kept right on going. He's gone to the men's room.'

The audience crowded in to get a better view of the Hand and Pavel and Louis began fielding questions. Sam looked around for Maggie and Vasquez but both had disappeared from sight.

'That Pavel is certainly one out of the box,' the woman beside her commented.

'Yes,' agreed her companion. 'It's like he hits a hole in one every time he tees off. Imagine *re*-finding the find of the century.'

Sam closed her eyes as an uncomfortable tingling took over her body. A hole in one, she thought. Shit!

'Ben, can you hear me? Oh good. What was the other thing you were going to tell me about Barstoc's stepfather?'

She stuck her finger in her ear to hear properly.

'Bloody hell,' she exclaimed a little too loudly, for someone standing on her own. 'Where is he? And where's Maggie?'

Sam looked wildly around but still couldn't see Maggie, so she pushed her way back through the crowd to Pavel. She tugged him on the arm so she could whisper a question in his ear.

'Yes, I believe so, Sam,' Pavel replied.

A scream from somewhere in the hall, was followed by another and another until someone yelled 'fire'.

Sam saw smoke billowing from inside *The Rites of Life and Death* exhibit. It took three seconds for the chaos to set in and then there was panic, pandemonium and people running madly in all directions.

Sam caught sight of Marcus Bridger, with a fire extinguisher, running *towards* his exhibition. 'Stay alert everyone,' Sam said. 'This *has* to be a set up.'

The lights went out.

'Sam, where are you?' Maggie called out.

'Over here,' Sam said, realising it was a pretty stupid response to give in pitch darkness.

Maggie found her anyway. 'Just before the lights went out I saw Escobar and Vasquez hovering around Pavel,' she said.

The emergency generator kicked in and a few lights at the other end of the room came back on.

Sam and Maggie turned to find Pavel and Louis helping Ben up off the floor. The box and the Hand of God were gone.

'Ben, we have to go in there after Marcus,' Sam pointed at the Exhibition.

'I just saw Vasquez go in through the exit,' Pavel said. 'He was carrying something.'

'Ben, you take the exit, I'll take the entrance,' Sam said, already on the run.

'Have those fools gone in to put out the fire?' Maggie asked, keeping pace with Sam.

'I don't think so, Maggie.' Sam headed through the open door behind Charon and into the catacombs. 'Tell me, what does Marcus's father do for a crust?'

'He's a heart surgeon, why?' Maggie asked.

'Because I'm an idiot!' Sam exclaimed, crashing into a wall in the dark before finding the exit from the replica Egyptian tomb into the Voodoo exhibit.

Maggie was right behind her all the way. They emerged into the semi-darkness of the central exhibition area which was thick with smoke from a well-contained fire in a large bin.

'Over there.' Maggie pointed to a man yanking something out of the main phallus display.

'Barstoc, Marcus,' Sam yelled, trying both names, but the man made a dash for the nearest wall and dived behind it. 'Don't run, there's nowhere to go.' She drew her gun.

'We've got the place surrounded,' Maggie declared. 'Ha! I've always wanted to say that.'

Sam crossed the space, edged up to the wall and snapped her body around it, weapon in front. There was nothing but an open doorway and Pavel's now empty box lying on the ground.

'Stay here, Maggie.'

'No way. What if he doubles back? I'd rather be where your gun is.'

'Make sure you stay behind me then.' Sam moved through the doorway and down a short corridor.

'What is that dreadful noise? It sounds like a koala on heat.'

'Shh,' Sam said, peering around the corner into the almost complete darkness of the large Apache burial ground exhibit. She could just make out the figure of a man on the far side. He was down on all fours and writhing in agony, but appeared to be trying to gather something together.

'Get up,' Sam ordered, advancing into the exhibit.

Her quarry, who was still trying to move away from her, let out a guttural moan as he struggled to his feet.

'Stop,' Sam yelled. 'I am a police officer and I am armed. Do not try to leave.'

She spoke into the microphone. 'Could we have some lights in the exhibition area please.'

'Tupac,' Maggie called out.

The man stopped in his tracks and straightened his back.

Sam glanced quizzically at Maggie.

'Well,' Maggie shrugged. 'It was one of *your* theories, Sam.'

'Tupac Amaru,' Sam shouted. 'Please, don't move again or I *will* shoot you.'

'If you shoot the Sapa Inca, I will shoot your friend.'

Sam reeled around to find Andrew Barstoc holding a gun to Maggie's head.

'If you shoot anyone,' Ben said, stepping out of the shadows, 'you're a dead man.'

The exhibit's artificial torches flickered to life, casting an eerie glow over the Apache burial ground and it occupants. Barstoc hesitated for a moment then dropped his weapon and held up his hands.

A crashing sound heralded the arrival of Enrico Vasquez, armed with a fire extinguisher.

'Don't move,' ordered Rivers, who crashed in behind him.

'But what is going on?' Vasquez demanded.

'We'll explain later, Enrico,' Maggie said. 'Sam, he's still trying to get away.'

'Marcus,' Sam said, moving towards him. 'Give it up. The Hand is trying to tell you are *not* Tupac Amaru. It's killing you, you fool.'

The self-proclaimed reincarnation of the last Inca king collapsed to his knees. Seven golden digits spilled out of the cloth he no longer had the strength to hold and lay scattered on the ground in front of him.

Dr Marcus Bridger forced himself into a sitting position, clutching the Tahuantinsuyu Bracelet to his chest as he grimaced in pain. 'It is mine,' he growled.

'Maggie, have you got the thumb and the other fingers?' Sam asked urgently.

Maggie yanked her shirt out and pulled the three digits from her vest.

'Which way is west?' Sam asked. Everyone just stared her. 'Come on, damnit, which is west?'

'Um, that way,' Ben pointed.

Sam laid the thumb to the left of Bridger, put Louis' middle finger behind him, and the pinky finger to the right.

'Help me, please Maggie. Find the other two *real* ones. Put them in the correct places.'

Sam tried to remove the bracelet from Bridger's hand. His whole body was soaked in sweat, he was dying a slow painful death, but he would not relinquish his prize.

'It's done, Sam,' Maggie stated.

'Marcus, let go you stupid bastard.'

Sam slapped him in the face, caught the bracelet as it fell from his hand, and placed it in front, and to the south, of the rest of the Hand of God.

Marcus Bridger, the idiot son of William Sanchez, fell backwards and into unconciousness.

# Chapter Thirty-Three

SAM, MAGGIE, PAVEL, BEN AND VASQUEZ SAT STARING AT EACH OTHER over the box in which the real and now complete Hand of God lay, with the thumb facing west.

After Sam had been officially re-introduced to Miguel Richer, the Peruvian Ambassador, everyone had agreed that Vasquez deserved an explanation.

'Well, that is some story,' he exclaimed. 'And you said *my* imagination was fertile.'

'What I want to know,' Rigby demanded, as he and Rivers joined them at the table in the Regency bar, 'is how you worked out it was Bridger.'

'It occurred to me,' Sam explained, 'that a man who plays golf at Sunningdale, as Daniel Bridger does, would not be the sort of man who would organise a protest to stop a golf course being built, which is what Marcus boasted that his "archaeologist" father had done.

'I knew my hunch was right when Ben confirmed that Marcus had *also* been adopted. Pavel then verified that the golf course protest *was* one of the stories William Sanchez *often* told about his exploits on previous digs.'

'Very clever, Sam.'

'Thank you, Maggie. But even so, at the time, I still thought that Barstoc was the main culprit; that he was, I don't know, *using* Marcus.'

'But it was the other way around,' Rivers stated.

Sam nodded. 'It was. Marcus, or should I say Paolo Sanchez, is convinced he is Tupac Amaru. And Barstoc, for some unfathomable reason, honestly believes that Marcus *is* the Sapa Inca and that they are spiritual brothers. He's quite obsessed by the notion. He claimed last night he would do anything to serve and protect him and, in fact, has done everything that Marcus asked of him.'

'So Marcus was using his precious phallic collection to conceal the pieces of the Hand he'd already collected.' Vasquez said.

'Yeah,' Ben snarled. 'Which is why he was so insistent on unpacking them himself when we searched your stuff at the airport. And probably why he was so pissed off with Barstoc.'

'That, and Marcus returned from Paris to discover that Professor Marsden was dead,' Sam added. 'Barstoc claims it was an accident that he killed Lloyd *when* he did. It was 'premature' he said, because they hadn't yet found the golden thumb.'

'Why is Andrew admitting to so much?' Maggie asked.

'He's whacko if you ask me,' Rigby said. 'But he seems to be admitting to anything he thinks we can prove.'

'Including anything he thinks we can prove against Marcus,' Sam said. 'It's the Sapa Inca spiritual brotherhood thing. Andrew Barstoc is prepared to go down for everything, to keep Marcus out of prison.'

'By the way,' Ben said, 'our colleagues in Sydney had a little chat with those antique dealers that Barstoc visited. According to one of these gentleman, who is now negotiating a reduced sentence in exchange for his cooperation, Barstoc was holding an auction.'

'What for?' Pavel asked.

'An Aztec dagger, some little statues and a gold mask.'

'The other artefacts from the Paris hijacking,' Maggie exclaimed.

'Which also explains why Marcus organised for the second lot of exhibits to get here a day early,' Sam said. 'He had to get out of Paris straight after the hijacking.'

'Will Andrew and Marcus be brought to justice for Noel, Barbara and the others?' Pavel asked.

Sam shrugged. 'There's a lot they'll never be charged with, Pavel, because it would be too hard to prove. But no doubt a couple of unsolved hit and run cases can be re-opened, once the relevant authorities have been informed.'

'What about Lloyd?' Maggie asked.

'Barstoc *will* be charged with Marsden's murder,' Sam said. 'And if Marcus ever regains consciousness, he'll be charged as an accessory, and for the theft of the various pieces of the Hand of God, including the hijacking of the Tahuantinsuyu Bracelet.'

'Which is finally back where it belongs,' Vasquez stated, patting the box.

'Yes, Enrico,' Pavel said. 'And tomorrow I will formally hand it back to Peru. If you are agreeable and feel you are capable of such a responsibility, I will suggest you are appointed as the official Guardian of the Hand of the Sun God.'

'I would be honoured,' Vasquez asserted, hand to his heart.

'Well, I don't know about you lot, but I am exhausted,' Sam exclaimed.

'I need a holiday,' Pavel agreed.

'I think I'm going to retire to Queensland,' Maggie laughed. 'I don't care if I never see another museum, or archaeological site, or jungle, or precious artefact of any kind. And, Pavel, if you find any more cursed relics, do not tell me. I don't want to know.'

'Maggie, my love,' Pavel laughed. 'You will never retire. It's not in you to be idle.'

'I agree with Pavel,' Sam said. 'You've got more energy than I've ever had, Maggie. I doubt you'll stop until someone forces your dead body to lie down and be quiet.'

'That's charming,' Maggie chuckled.

'And even then,' Sam continued, 'I'm sure you'll arrange to be buried somewhere significant so archaeologists of the 24th century can dig you up and announce a remarkable find.'

'Ah, now there's a thought,' Maggie said. 'Perhaps I'll have my thigh bone inscribed with an enigmatic message, for just such an occasion.'

'What for?' Sam laughed.

'To confound them, my dear. To confound them.'

OTHER BOOKS BY LINDY CAMERON
FROM CLAN DESTINE PRESS:

THE O'MALLEY MYSTERIES:
*BLOOD GUILT,*
*BLEEDING HEARTS*
*& THICKER THAN WATER*

*REDBACK*

*FEEDBACK*

*THE AMSARA CHRONICLES*

In case you're wondering, the International Council of Museums is a real organisation. You can google it. Their triennial conference is a real thing too. You can google where it is next. I mention this, because when I wrote this book back in 1997 Google itself wasn't a thing.

*Golden Relic* was originally commissioned by Museum Victoria and written *for* ICOM '98, which really was held in Melbourne in October 1998.

ICOM is a Paris-based international organisation of museums and museum professionals, established in 1946, to promote museology and other disciplines related to the management of museums and their activities.

In 1998, the organisation had around 15,000 members in 147 countries. (Membership more than doubled to 35,000 in 2017).

But back in 1998 – in a time when the internet-for-everyone was a sparkling new idea and even mobile phone technology was a novelty, and not terribly smart – ICOM provided a communications network for the growing global museum community.

One of the organisation's key activities then and now is to fight against the illicit traffic of cultural property and to deal with issues concerning cultural repatriation of artefacts.

Melbourne – acknowledged as a prime model of a successful culturally diverse city, rich in museums and galleries, theatres, parks and heritage buildings – was selected as the host city for the 18th general assembly of ICOM in 1998. It was the first time the conference had been held in the Asia-Pacific region, only the second time in the Southern Hemisphere, and Melbourne got to showcase its cultural and heritage attractions to 1700 museum professionals from 70 member-countries.

So, how did I come to write a murder mystery to help promote such a significant and high-profile conference – to the whole world?

The year before, in May 1997, the ICOM '98 committee in Melbourne had the novel idea of promoting the conference and the host city, by commissioning a contemporary thriller set within an international museum context.

The committee asked the Melbourne-based crime writers and readers group, Sisters in Crime Australia, to suggest some local writers to develop proposals for the project. The successful author would have her thriller serialised on the ICOM '98 website on the internet in the months leading up to the conference.

Four crime writers attended a briefing session with Museum of Victoria staff, from various departments, who apparently had no idea why they'd been called together.

It wasn't surprising therefore, that they all began by thinking a "murder mystery" was a dubious and bizarre way to promote their professions, their institution, and their city; not to mention the prestigious conference they'd lobbied so tirelessly to secure.

It took but an hour for them to realise the creative potential in the idea and they were soon suggesting not only likely candidates for the central crime, but why – and how – they should be murdered.

The competing writers then had three weeks to prepare their submissions, including a synopsis of the proposed full-length novel. This was no easy task as, apart from devising a mystery plot, new characters and a cliff-hanging style to suit the monthly serialisation, the 'communication objectives' of the thriller were to: attract delegates to the conference; promote the city of Melbourne and its museums; raise the profile of ICOM '98; and market ICOM in a 'serious but fun way'.

My submission was selected in July 1997, and I was commissioned to write a 10-chapter murder mystery; and given three months to do it. Oh, the novel also had to incorporate the conference theme of *Museums and Cultural Diversity – Ancient Cultures, New Worlds*; and one of the conference agenda issues, 'the repatriation of cultural material'.

*Stolen Property*, as it was originally called, is believed to be the first novel specifically commissioned by any international organisation for publication on the internet.

Under that title, it was serialised on the ICOM '98 website, one chapter a month from February 1998. The final chapter was published during the conference in Melbourne.

As it happened, my then-publisher, HarperCollins Australia, published it in paperback to launch it on the Gala Opening Night of ICOM '98.

This edition of *Golden Relic* is the first paperback since that 1998 version. So much has happened in the not-quite two decades since, that I have to remind myself what things were like for writers late last century.

For, although *Stolen Property / Golden Relic* was 'serialised on the internet', there wasn't much *to* the internet itself in 1997 when I was writing the story. There was no Google, no Wikipedia, and no other online encyclopaedias. I did all my research using library books – which I borrowed in person, from an actual library. The internet was still accessed by dial-up modems; desktop computers were way more common than laptops; and I, at least, was still 18 months away from owning my first mobile flip phone.

My smart phone now has more computing power than my computer then; and with Google at my fingertips I can even google when Google became a thing.

The other challenging thing about writing the story in 1997 was setting it in 1998.

In 1997 the wonderful 'old' Museum of Victoria was still open; but wouldn't be when *Golden Relic* was set, in September and October the next year. In 1997, the ground had been broken for the new museum but was basically a great big hole in the ground. I had to imagine what it might look like 12 months later when Sam Diamond was standing in the gardens looking at a half-built building.

Finally, I had my own woo-woo experience, as Sam calls the curious things that happen around her. I received my advance copy of *Golden Relic* – my first-ever published book – in the mail on Wednesday September 16, 1998.

If you turn to page five of this *Golden Relic*, you will see September 16 was the day – a completely random date I chose a year before – that the mystery in the museum begins.

I suppose Museum Victoria should be pleased no real archaeologists were harmed during the writing of this book.

LINDY CAMERON

Printed in Australia
Ingram Content Group Australia Pty Ltd
AUHW021005120324
391614AU00003B/39

9 780995 439498